WISH HUNTER

Book One of The Savannah River Series

HERO BOWEN

JORDAN RILEY SWAN

Copyright © 2021 by Jordan Riley Swan. All rights reserved.
Published by Story Garden, Columbus. StoryGardenPublishing.com
ISBN: 9781735587523 (paperback)
ISBN: 9781735587523 (ebook)
ISBN: 9781735587530 (audiobook)

Cover design by James T. Egan, BookflyDesign.com
Managing editor: Diane Callahan, QuotidianWriter.com
Copy editor: Crystal Shelley, RabbitWithaRedPen.com
Sign up for notifications of upcoming releases by Jordan Riley Swan at
JordanRileySwan.com

To Dave—may all your wishes come true

Chapter One

Once she stole this jerk's third wish, Nadia swore she would never invite another surgeon into her counseling office. She'd heard they could be egotistical butchers, treating their patients as little more than pounds of flesh on a table, but she'd always dismissed that stereotype—until she'd met Dr. Fitzpatrick. Not that Nadia claimed to be a paragon of virtue herself, but at least when clients left *her* office, they had all the pieces they'd come in with. As far as they knew, anyway.

"Mm-hmm, and how has the advice from our last session been working for you?" Nadia cracked her knuckles under the mahogany desk, jonesing for another double espresso to knock back. Anything to stop Dr. Fitzpatrick's self-absorbed monotone from making her slide off her high-backed leather armchair in a comatose state.

The surgeon sprawled across the client armchair—no chaise lounges here—and seemed determined to possess it with every inch of his Tom Ford nouveau tweed number. "You should've just told me to stick a bomb under my marriage," he huffed, pushing designer specs back up his nose. "Tell her my 'true feelings'? Everyone knows that's marriage suicide." He waved a hand up at her framed accolades. "I'm starting to think you printed those degrees off the internet."

"Did you follow the steps we talked through?" Nadia kept her tone professionally even, fighting down a smirk. Divorce was the last thing a successful marriage counselor wanted her sessions to come to, but man did she pity the poor woman who'd ended up with this pompous, middle-aged brat.

Many people made the incorrect assumption that marriage counseling was done in pairs, not realizing that the early stages were most productive on an individual basis. That way, partners didn't have to worry about saying the wrong thing in front of their spouse and making matters worse while the situation was at its most fragile. However, the wife in question had yet to book her individual appointments. Maybe she already knew the marriage was over and had no intention of fighting for it.

Dr. Fitzpatrick folded his arms across his chest. "Oh, I did *everything* you suggested. Why else would I bother to pay you?"

"And?"

"And I told her what I really thought about her artwork."

"How did she respond?" The stock question rolled off Nadia's tongue effortlessly as she grazed her pen across her notebook.

"How do you think?" A pinkish hue painted the surgeon's cheeks. Since it was October in Savannah, Nadia had the AC cranked up, so his flush couldn't be due to the room's temperature. The color in his face came from the palette of embarrassment. "It got heated."

"In what way?" Nadia encouraged, tossing out another textbook response.

She glanced over at the collection of knickknacks she'd purchased from Picker Joe's to add to the vintage feel of her Tiedeman Park office, though the moody cherrywood paneling, oxblood leather armchairs, and green-hooded banker's lamps already accomplished that. Her gaze lingered on a still-ticking brass carriage clock for a few seconds. She needed to move this along.

Dr. Fitzpatrick cleared his throat, as if he had a frog of guilt lodged in there. "I might've said something along the lines of 'Are you sure you're not sniffing the paint stripper in that supposed studio of yours, because something's making you blind to the rip-off Andy Warhols you're calling art.' I can't remember verbatim. I wasn't wrong, though."

He adjusted his tie. "And you know what the truth got me? A jar of dirty, brush-cleaning water flung in my face. She said I knew nothing about art if I thought her work was anything like a Warhol, and she made a nasty suggestion of what I could do with a soup can."

"Why a soup can?" Nadia's eyes drifted back to the clock.

"You know—Andy Warhol? The painting of the Campbell's soup can." When Nadia shrugged, he frowned as if she were an uncultured philistine. "Actually, never mind," he mumbled. "Your art knowledge probably stops at Rorschach tests and so-called art therapy. The point is, I did what you said, and that made things worse."

"Honesty can be painful at first," she said, the steady tick of that carriage clock shifting her mental energies to the real task at hand.

"Honesty is *never* the best policy," Dr. Fitzpatrick replied. "In fact, why don't you go ahead and put that over your door so no other poor bastards make the same mistake I did."

Nadia curved her lips into a rehearsed smile of sympathy, preparing to crack out one of her fortune cookie truisms. "I understand where you're coming from, Dr. Fitzpatrick. But even though honesty hurts, acknowledging those wounds is often a necessary first step, rather than letting them fester. It invites you to heal *together* and stitch that wound without any lingering resentment."

"Sounds more like a guaranteed stab to my back and my assets," he said as he ran a hand through his carefully arranged salt-and-pepper hair.

"But you being here is the real first step," Nadia reminded him. "If you thought it was over between you and your wife, you'd be in a lawyer's office right now instead of with me."

Dr. Fitzpatrick blew out a breath through his nostrils and shook his head, his tone shifting to the kind he probably used with his residents. "I'm not a quitter. Besides, I only came back to you because I bought these sessions at the three-for-one discount you offer up at the hospital. And since this is appointment number three, we're running out of time to patch up my problems here." Then came his usual mumble again. "Honestly, I don't know why Dr. Pargeter sang your praises. Unless you save the good advice for women?"

Nadia thought of sweet, despairing Jenny Pargeter, an OB-GYN at

Memorial Health who specialized in high-risk pregnancies and births. Her marriage had been a common, painful tale of romantic drift, the plates of a once-happy union sliding continents apart. But after session upon session of hard, raw honesty and several tissue boxes' worth of tears, it had concluded in a loving reconciliation that Nadia counted among her best successes. She was fairly sure she owed Jenny a commission, thanks to all the marriage-weary clients the doctor had sent her way since then.

Dr. Fitzpatrick was right—they *were* running out of time, but for very different reasons. Nadia slipped a casual hand into her skirt pocket, turning the smooth, wooden compass coin that nestled there. It was warm to the touch, like her favorite coffee mug on a cold day.

She hid a smile, savoring that warm, pebble-like surface and the confirmation it radiated: Dr. Fitzpatrick had an unspent wish.

The surgeon resumed his body-melting sprawl across the armchair. "If I wanted to be ignored, I'd have stayed home and saved the money."

Nadia let him stew in his own juices a moment longer, finding comfort in every turn of the wooden coin between her fingertips. Her goal had never been to fix Dr. Fitzpatrick's obviously lopsided and doomed marriage, but to ensure that he kept coming back for at least three counseling sessions—hence the discount. She needed the full trio in order to steal all three of the wishes he'd earned by saving lives as a heart surgeon. Ironic, considering he lacked much of a heart himself.

Too bad there wasn't a three-for-one package deal with wishes too. The more sessions she had with people, the more her pesky conscience came knocking at the back of her skull, eager to gain entry. But only one wish could be stolen at a time.

It wasn't as if he would miss the wish once she stole it. Most people —Dr. Fitzpatrick included—didn't even know that wishes existed or how to use them. Without her intervention, the three he'd had, including this last one, would simply go to waste. If she really thought about it, she was doing a civic duty by unburdening her clients of a weight they didn't know they had and bandaging up a few nuptials as she went.

"Thanks to you, Jessica is extra pissed at me." It appeared Dr. Fitzpatrick was eager to clamber out of the stewpot. Nadia marveled at the human need to fill a silence. It worked every time. "And *then*, she got all smug about 'proving me wrong' by selling her latest monstrosity of a finger painting to Miles friggin' Hunter."

"Did you offer your wife any support when she told you about this painting she sold?" Nadia asked. She'd heard of Miles Hunter. Everyone in Savannah had. He was basically Johnny Mercer's successor in the Savannah music hall of fame, though she'd overheard a few old dames saying his music wasn't to their taste.

Dr. Fitzpatrick scoffed. "You think I'd offer a word of congratulation after seeing that hideous splotch of colored canvas plastered behind Miles Hunter's stage last night? I couldn't get away from it, since she insisted on having the replay livestream on every TV in the damned house! She just sat there, glass of wine in hand, gawking at him. Oh, she said she just wanted to see her painting onstage, but unless it was down the front of his pants, I'm sure she was looking at something else."

Nadia was about to respond when Dr. Fitzpatrick continued, gaining steam. "I even told her about the dangers of torsion and impotence from skintight leather pants."

"What did she say?"

"She said that I wear loose pants all the time, so tightness can't be the only cause."

Nadia's face strained like a pre-sneeze as she squashed a chuckle back down her throat, not wanting to antagonize him. She didn't want him getting defensive and clamming up, since she still had to pry the pearl of truth out of him that would release his wish. He was probably just bitter that his leather-pants days were far behind him.

She grabbed a tissue and pretended to blow her nose so she could pull herself together. Her gaze caught the carriage clock again. Fifteen minutes until his time was up. Fifteen minutes to secure the wish. She really had to get her ass in gear.

With that in mind, Nadia took an ornate wooden box from the top drawer of her desk. Rustic charm radiated from the cherry-toned wood of the Polish keepsake box. On the lid, a ridged border of blackened lines alternated in horizontal and vertical rectangles. Burned into the center were hearts with leaves sprouting from the curved tops, a feature that had always reminded Nadia more of apples than hearts. Their tapered ends met at a ringed circle in the middle, from which corn poppies blossomed—a nod to the national flower of Poland.

"Ah, an old friend," Dr. Fitzpatrick said.

"I thought it might be useful to do the box exercise again," Nadia replied as she smoothed her fingertips across the lid, feeling those familiar indents.

He smirked. "It didn't do much good the last two times. I thought it would be like one of those worry dolls where you write down your deepest, darkest secrets, and in the morning all your problems are gone."

"There's no quick cure." Nadia softened her tone. "But the box exercise is still valuable, and I can see the changes from the last two times you did this, even if you can't. As I've told you before, this is your chance to be honest with yourself, in private, and jot down the events and struggles in your life that you'd never say aloud to anyone else—me included." It wasn't entirely untrue.

"I don't know. Seems like a waste of paper," he said as she pushed a small blank slip toward him.

"Since this is your last booked session, why don't we try it, just in case?" She rested a pen on top of the piece of paper. "After all, they say the third time's the charm."

His eyes fixated on the paper, but he made no move to pick up the pen. An amused smirk lifted the corner of his lips, and he sank back into the armchair, as if he intended to wait out the last fifteen minutes in silence. For the first time with him, Nadia felt a wobble of worry. Sure, she'd stolen two of his wishes already, but she couldn't afford to let any wish slip past her. If he didn't write on that piece of paper and put it in the box, she'd have hell to pay. And, considering it was unlikely she'd ever see him again now that his discounted sessions were up, she had to act fast and smart to get him back under her thumb. If superstition and niceties didn't work, maybe his money-tight nature would.

"It's part and parcel of the sessions you *paid* for," she said. "It's helped so many of my clients, I assure you. But if you don't want to take full advantage of what you bought . . ." She pulled the paper back as if to throw it away.

He lurched forward. "Hold on, I didn't say I wasn't going to do it."

Nadia pushed the scrap of paper over to him once more and sat back like she didn't care what he wrote. The surgeon chuckled as he hunched over the paper and tapped the end of the pen against his teeth, the clacking sound an assault on Nadia's nerves. The crucial moment had arrived, and the rest was out of her hands.

"What to write today . . ." He grinned. "'My wife is an ungrateful cow who leaves paint on everything she touches'?" His amusement faded as he poised the nib over the piece of paper.

Nadia faked a laugh. "Remember, this is about *you*: your secrets, your fears, your demons. This isn't about her, unless it's related. This is your moment, your time, your release from any burdens you've been carrying." She figured he'd like that—that this was entirely about him.

Dr. Fitzpatrick's expression morphed into one of serious contemplation as his pen scratched across the slip of paper. For a fleeting moment, Nadia witnessed real humanity in the surgeon's eyes, his tongue wriggling at the corner of his mouth as though he'd regressed to the boy he'd once been. The lines between his tidy eyebrows deepened.

Even jerks were people, just as flawed and sometimes vulnerable as everyone else.

She turned the box to face him and lifted the lid, sensing he was ready to put a heart secret into the shadows. With a sad little sigh, he placed the paper inside and closed the box before turning it back around to face her, like a briefcase of money for the kingpin to observe. But she had no intention of looking. That wasn't the point.

"I miss who we were," Dr. Fitzpatrick said quietly.

This happened sometimes. Though there was magic in the box, it didn't have anything to do with fixing relationships. Still, every so often, the process of sharing something so deeply important to a person would open them up to introspection as they closed the lid. Sometimes the act of confession, however secret, actually helped marriages heal.

"Who do you miss?" Nadia asked.

"Jessica and me." His head sagged like it was heavy with thoughts. "I miss who we were in college—before life and careers and all that other stuff got in the way. I trained to be a heart surgeon so I could help people, and that's something she loved about me. But the expectations and pressures changed me in a way I didn't expect. It deadened me."

Nadia smiled a genuine smile. "You know better than anyone that a heart can be made to beat again."

"How long have you been saving that one?" He mustered the ghost of a smirk.

"A while." She chuckled. "But the point stands."

He nodded slowly, as if contemplating his options, before lifting his gaze and blindsiding Nadia in a way she hadn't braced for. "Have you ever been married? I looked for a ring, and you don't have one, but I know that doesn't mean much."

Her insides wrenched. "I was, but . . . it ended."

That was all he'd get out of her. The rest belonged in a keepsake box inside her chest, the lid lifted only when she could bear to look inside. She rallied quickly. "Well, Dr. Fitzpatrick, that brings us to the end of our hour."

He unleashed a sigh, stretching out his arms. "Time flies, eh?"

"Nevertheless, I hope it helped."

He stood to leave, but when he was almost at the door, Nadia called him back with one final piece of advice: "Life goes on after divorce. Remember that."

He gave a silent nod and exited the office. With any luck, he wouldn't be back. She'd attained all three of his wishes, her first trifecta in years. It didn't really matter to her that they were the only three he'd ever get in his lifetime. But despite everything, she had wanted him to leave with a grain of advice that would actually help him, or at least inspire him to have another honest conversation with his wife.

Nadia sat back with a relieved sigh and toyed with the silver chain around her neck, coaxing the rings out from the neckline of her blouse, the gold stark against the silver. Wedding bands—hers and Nick's—side by side, warmed by her skin, always lying as close to her heart as possible. Even now, she regretted not taking his last name of Landa, although she'd wanted to. As always, her family had successfully pressured her into doing what *they* wanted her to do.

Shaking her head to dispel the creeping sadness, she picked up the wishing box. The rusty red heartwood was almost uncomfortably hot to the touch, signaling that the trapped wish was stowed safely inside. As for the slip of paper, that would remain a secret. She made it a point to never read a word; it was the least she owed her clients for their unintentional sacrifices.

If the unusual glimmer coming off the box was any indication, it was a reasonably potent wish. But who was she kidding? No matter what she brought home, it was never enough.

Chapter Two

Nadia steered her beloved, burnt-orange Chevy Nova toward home. Regardless of how the day's marriage wrangling or wish hunting went, the scenic route past Forsyth Park always blanketed her with a temporary serenity like no other. Spanish moss draped over the scarecrow limbs of live oaks that never lost their air of magic, with clusters of magnolias and dogwoods completing the canopy over the walkways that spilled toward the crystalline central fountain. Imposing houses lined the boulevard: a blend of Italianate beauties of red brick, Colonial mansions with gleaming white colonnades, and mystical Victorian-style buildings that looked as though they'd been plucked from England.

"Next up we have 'Rest Awhile' by Savannah's own Miles Hunter," the radio DJ crooned through the tinny speakers. Nadia switched it off, not wanting to be reminded of Dr. Fitzpatrick and his wife's divisive artwork.

But Dr. Fitzpatrick's question about Nadia's naked wedding finger had reawakened the stab of loss it represented. She had the ring still, but no husband. The house they'd lived in was long sold. Even though Nadia knew all of this, every day for the past year she tricked herself into believing that she was going home to him, and that he *would* be there, instead of under a tombstone at Laurel Grove.

Her hand fell onto the warm wishing box on the passenger seat next to her. Theft number fifty, basically halfway to the end of their debt. Maybe that significant milestone meant Nadia could ask to spend one wish of her own, especially considering what day it was—the one-year anniversary of the worst day of her life. A day that would be forever burned into her memory. She hadn't even taken off work today in hopes that the hours would fly past and she wouldn't have time to think about what had happened.

Her fingers absently trailed the line where the box lid sealed. It taunted her just how easy it would be to open. To take that wish for herself. *Ask for forgiveness, not permission, right?* All she'd have to do was put her hand in the box, feel the wish settle in the middle of her palm, and then press her hand to her heart. After that, she'd only need to find a candle and blow out the flame as she thought of her wish. But if the Wishmaster ever found out that Nadia had spent a wish meant to go toward the family debt . . .

Best not to chance it. Her grandmother would never approve of the wish she wanted to make, debt or no debt. In the months after the funeral, Nadia had begged and begged her grandmother, then her mother, to make this one exception, to help make her heart whole again. But the Wishmaster tracked every single wish that came through Nadia's counseling office, and her grandmother had once ranted, "You ever take such risk in using wish without permission, Wishmaster will know and then we lose all. You want your babcia and mama to be left powerless? Homeless? I cannot have you in my house if you do such thing."

With a conscious effort, Nadia pulled her hand back from the box and squeezed the sun-warm steering wheel. After a couple more turns, she reached the home straight, her car rattling up to the curb a few minutes later. With the box in hand, she got out and put the sound of the still-ticking engine behind her.

She wedged the wish trap under her arm as the shadow of the tall iron gates fell across her. Gold adornments twisted into the black, echoing the design that patterned the box in her possession.

Beyond the gates lay the Kaminski Mansion, a jaw-dropping Georgian Revival, with Ionic columns and a swan's neck pediment bordering the front door like a picture frame. Twin colonnades acted as proud wings on either side of the gray-painted brickwork of the main body, while ominous black shutters butterflied at every long window. A slate roof stood proudly above it all, having sheltered generations during notoriously fickle Georgia rainstorms.

The suffocating humidity painted Nadia in an unwelcome sheen as she pushed through the gate and along the garden path to the front door. The fountain of a winged messenger, which hadn't spewed anything in her lifetime, silently judged her as she passed, its chipped right wing a testament to her reckless childhood. She doubted it would ever fan its water into the sky again. Hell, it probably wasn't even plugged into anything. Now, it was just a place for pigeons to roost and get shooed away, sometimes with her grandma's potato artillery.

As she stepped through the front door, a familiar, gentle pull tugged at the elastic band of her nerves. It didn't concern her. The house was only making sure she was a permitted occupant.

"Mom!" Nadia called out. "You home?"

Newcomers usually needed a minute or two in the foyer to absorb the opulent interior, where a massive, gilt-framed oil painting of an ancient tree took pride of place in the center of the wall dead ahead. Nadia figured it was the closest she'd ever come to seeing the real Wishing Tree it represented. The Polish-made cabinets were inundated with plates of blue and white with miniature blue flowers in the middle. For Nadia, however, this was just home. She'd seen every ceramic, every painting, every silkscreen sheet of embossed wallpaper a million times.

A stifled giggle chirped through the labyrinth of corridors. Ears primed, Nadia followed the sound to the kitchen at the back of the house, which looked out over the terra-cotta patio and wildflower gardens beyond.

She stalled to a disgusted but unsurprised halt on the kitchen threshold. Pressed nearly diagonal against the central island, her mother was making out with some muscled slab of prime Georgia beefcake. And the poor soul looked hungry, judging by the way he was devouring her mom's lips. He stood a good foot taller than Nadia's mother, with floppy, sand-colored hair and busted Levi's. The cliché leather jacket was on the back of a kitchen stool, rounding out the sordid visual.

"Mom," Nadia said with a resigned air. If her mother wasn't careful, Nadia was going to start demanding a ribbon on the front door or something so she wouldn't have to walk in on these gross playdates.

Grace squealed and planted one last kiss on the guy's lips before playfully smacking him assward to the door. "I'll see you later."

"You bet you will," the guy replied as he grabbed his jacket off the stool's back. He slung it over his shoulder with a hooked finger and gave Nadia a maybe-I'll-see-you-too look as he sauntered out.

He wasn't even out the door before Nadia started in on her mom. She didn't care if he overheard. Maybe she even wanted him to. "Do you have to let *all* your boy toys inside the house? You realize there are perfectly good hotels all over Savannah, right?" Nadia crossed to the island and hopped up on a barstool, intentionally choosing one that hadn't been used as a coatrack. "What if one of these guys turns out to be something other than a cure for your boredom? I'm guessing you don't do background checks first."

Grace Kaminski brushed her daughter off with an irreverent wink. "Love is a game, honey, and I'll never stop playing it—because I'm a winner."

"Stretching it a bit, aren't you, Mom?" Nadia took a clean glass from beside the sink in the middle of the kitchen island and filled it to the brim.

Her mom's first wish to "play any game and win" was exactly why Nadia hated playing video games, card games—hell, even "I spy" as a toddler—with her mother growing up, because her mom did always win. Without fail. Although Grace had never specified, Nadia assumed her mom had spent her second wish on eternally youthful hair, since she didn't have a single gray strand on her head. All the better to entice her boy toys.

Grace smirked. "Some wishes are like taffy—you can stretch them pretty far." She glanced down the hall toward the now closed front door.

"Still, you don't have to up the ante every time a guy offers to show you his cards." Nadia could sling around figures of speech with the best of them. She took a gulp of cool water to slough away the sticky feeling of the relentless humidity.

Grace scooped her hand through her loose brunette hair: a carbon copy of Nadia's, though Nadia rarely wore hers down. "How else am I going to take a peek at their stack of chips, to see if they're worth a stake?"

Nadia suppressed the urge to make a comment about her mother getting a different kind of stake. It was too weird. Making jokes about her mom's famed appetite was another therapy session entirely.

With a sudden gasp, Grace pointed at the box that Nadia had placed on the granite island. "Is that what I think it is?" She leaned over and swiped it from under her daughter's nose, dancing a little jig.

"Ta-da." Nadia finished the rest of her water, her fingers itching to take the box back. But she was merely a cog in her family's big machine. At least, that was how it felt sometimes.

Her mother darted across to the den, just off from the kitchen. Humming to herself, Grace snatched up a stick of chalk and added a scratch to the big blackboard that hung from the wall, concealed from any part-time lovers who might smooch their way through the kitchen. The tally marks looked like a prisoner counting off their days to parole. In a way, that's exactly what it was. Not from jail, of course, but from a punishment just as stifling.

If they didn't pay off their debt to the Wishmaster, Basha and Grace would have their used wishes taken from them, along with their wishing box and the house. Worse yet, since Nadia had never used a wish for herself, she'd be forced to absorb three wishes from the Wishmaster's cellar of wish traps—and then give them all back for someone else to spend, effectively killing any chance she'd have of reviving Nick. It seemed deeply unfair that even the act of absorbing a wish into her body without spending it would count toward her lifetime total of three. But the Wishing Tree wasn't known for being fair.

"Lucky number fifty!" Grace cheered, setting the chalk back on its ridged, wooden plinth. At the top of the board, written in her elegant cursive and age-smudged by the last three years, were the words *101*

Not Dalmatians. It was punctuated with a winky face, as if it were schoolwork and not something Nadia's future happiness relied on.

"Are you counting wishes or men?" Nadia asked.

Speaking of men, her mother still hadn't mentioned Nick's "anniversary" once, not even over that morning's hurried breakfast. Had she forgotten, or was she just avoiding the subject entirely?

Grace fluttered her eyelashes. "If this was for guys, you wouldn't be able to see the board for all the chalk."

Despite herself, Nadia snorted down at her empty glass. Now was her chance to ask for the wish, especially with Basha still upstairs. For all her flaws, Grace was at least more lenient.

Nadia toyed with how to phrase the request. Guilt-tripping might work, since her blood, sweat, and tears had gone into the majority of those tallies, and today was the hardest she'd slogged through in the last 365—not including Nick's funeral, since that had been a nightmarish blur. If today didn't give her some leverage, she didn't know what would, as cold as it sounded.

Above all, she was tired of waiting. At their current pace, it'd take at least three more years to pay off their debt. If only she could leave Savannah, buy a wish somewhere else. But how could she abandon her mom and grandma to fulfill a debt that *she'd* indirectly caused? She wouldn't be able to live with herself if she took such an unforgivably selfish route.

Grace gave the board two gleeful middle fingers. "How's that for winning?"

Nadia had to laugh. "I wish I had half your energy. Might've come in handy, considering what today is."

"Nadia!" Grace hissed, her eyes flying wide. "Don't bandy the 'wish' word around like that. You should know better!"

Her mom refused to pick up on the second half of what Nadia had said, giving her the answer to her question: Grace was avoiding the memory of today. She hadn't forgotten a damn thing. Worst of all, Nadia wasn't surprised. Her family was good at pretending that people had never existed. She'd have to find another heartstring in her mother that could be tugged.

"What, I can't even say the word 'wish'?" Nadia asked. "Last I checked, I haven't saved any lives or stolen any wishes for myself." She nodded to the box in the crook of her mom's arm, biting down the bitterness in her voice. "And you've got the box. No candles around either. I think I'm good saying the *W* word."

Grace's expression relaxed, but not by much. "Still, best not to tempt fate. Don't want to accidentally waste this beauty." She kissed the box. "Think of how much trouble that'd cause."

"You know I wouldn't waste it if I ever got the chance to keep one."

Grace shot her a chiding look. "This one's not for you."

"Noted." Nadia mock-saluted, but her stomach sank at how quickly her mom had dismissed the slightest notion of giving her a wish. "But I'll need the box back so I can get rid of that surgeon's heart secret."

Grace waggled her eyebrows. "Should we have a little look? I've always wondered what goes on in a surgeon's mind."

"Andy Warhol," Nadia replied, beckoning for the box.

"Huh?"

Nadia shook her head. "Nothing. Inside joke. And don't pretend it's the surgeon's *mind* you're interested in." Grace handed her the box, and Nadia wiped the kissed spot with her sleeve. "He might be divorced soon, if you want his details."

Grace wrinkled her nose. "Too much baggage for me, I'm afraid. I like 'em free and young, no strings attached."

"All right, Geppetto."

Nadia lifted the lid to remove the slip of paper, careful not to touch the bottom of the box and accidentally scoop out the invisible wish inside. She tore up the note and let the pieces flutter down into the garbage disposal.

"I can't believe you still use that silly paper trick," Grace said with a customary *tsk* as she sat on the barstool opposite, but Nadia had flipped the switch to grind up the paper while Grace was mid-sentence.

"What did you say?" Nadia shouted above the mangling trash, pretending not to hear her.

"I said, you don't need to have them write down their secret. Just open the box and close it once they've spilled their guts!" Grace yelled back.

Nadia shook her head. "Can't hear you!"

"I said, you're wasting your ti—" The crunching din cut off, leaving Grace bellowing at the top of her lungs. She cut herself short, flashing Nadia a look that said *very funny*.

Nadia forced a chuckle. Maybe she should've been humoring her mother more to butter her up before asking for a wish, but she had always struggled to play nice.

"I do things my way, and it's working pretty well so far." Nadia thumbed at the blackboard hidden by the kitchen wall. "Paying the debt is all that matters. Not technique. Speaking of the debt, though . . . I've been thinking, and I had something I wanted to—" Nadia found herself cut off this time, by the creak of the serpentine staircase.

A moment later, Basha hobbled into the kitchen with her ruby-topped cane. Well, ruby-colored glass, anyway.

Nadia's grandmother looked frail, her face etched with a vast map of runnels that collected in a web at the corner of each hazel eye, as though she was straining to see in harsh sunlight. Her ashy white-and-gray hair was scraped back into a plump, netted bun, and giant amber earrings dangled from her ears, adding about ten pounds to her fifty-pound frame.

She coughed, phlegm rattling in her throat. "Leave our dziew-czynka alone. She and I are not so different," she rasped, her accent tinged with the motherland. "Back when I read tarot cards, I ask customers to write secrets on dollar bill and put it into box so I could 'see their futures.' Bit of money and a wish in my pocket. Never fail. The gullible are low-hanging fruit of wish-hunting world."

"In any world," Grace added.

Nadia had heard the story a dozen times, to the point where she could basically predict every phrase her grandmother would use, but she knew better than to interrupt the older woman mid-tale. Not if she wanted her knuckles un-rapped by that cane.

Grace, on the other hand, didn't seem to have any qualms. "It's just theatrics. It's not necessary."

"People are much more honest when they don't have to voice their thoughts aloud," Nadia countered. "How many of those tally marks up on that chalkboard are mine, and how many are yours and Babcia's?" She'd always used the Polish term of endearment for "grandmother" out of habit, but the American "Mom" had stuck.

Basha harrumphed. Grace harrumphed. The house probably harrumphed.

"I'm still putting scores on the board," Grace insisted, with a satisfied upturn of her red-painted lips. "I just don't get them there as fast as you."

Nadia held up her hands in surrender. "I brought wish hunting into the twenty-first century, that's all I'm saying."

From childhood, she and her older sister had been trained in how to steal wishes. That line of education hadn't been negotiable, but the way they went about it was. Nadia had decided to update the profession a touch by getting her master's in marriage and family therapy, precisely because that line of work would give her greater access to people's secrets. Sneaky? Probably. Helpful? Definitely—for her and her clients. Plus, she got a vague sense of normalcy from having a "real" career rather than pandering to tourists with a fortune-teller ruse. Crystal balls and tea leaves had never been her jam. Plus, with a judicious choice of office locations, she put herself in a prime place to capture wishes from people who had them in abundancy: hospital workers.

With everyone satisfied that they'd won the argument, Grace flapped her fingers into her palm. "Hand over the compass coin, daughter of mine."

"Are you hunting tonight?"

"Not tonight, but I plan to head out to Tybee Island tomorrow morning to scope out the lifeguards. For wishes, of course," Grace replied with a sly smile.

Nadia plucked the coin out of her pocket and gave it to her mom with a sigh. "TGIF," she said. Her workweek was over, at least for her day job. But she still needed to gather up the courage to make her request.

"Cocktails?" Grace asked, face brightening as she breezed toward the freezer where she kept her margarita mix.

Nadia fiddled with the chain around her neck. "Actually, there's something I need to ask you both."

Grace circled back to the island, where Basha now leaned. "What's up?"

Part of Nadia feared to speak the words aloud in case that somehow jinxed her, but she wanted this more than anything. Needed it, really. She could never forgive herself if she kept chickening out and let years and years blur past without ever truly *trying* to change the course of her life.

"I know we're halfway to repaying our debt to the Wishmaster, but it could take another three years to get to the end." Nadia gulped, steeling her resolve. "And what I need is urgent."

"Well?" Grace said.

Nadia took a deep breath. "I want to use the next wish we steal for myself."

Chapter Three

A morgue-like silence closed around the three Kaminski women. Unblinking, Nadia waited for some kind of reply from her mother or grandmother. Anything. Her muscles tightened like someone had turned a crank inside her.

Finally, Basha spoke. "Wishmaster would never allow it."

"But it wouldn't hurt to ask—" Nadia began.

Grace made a strangled noise. "Yes, it would, Nadia! If you ask to use a wish for yourself, the Wishmaster will increase our debt. We already owe too much. Think about how long it's taken us to get to fifty."

"I don't care if I double the debt, if I can get the Wishmaster to agree," Nadia shot back.

"But what would you even use it for?" Grace asked, her tone part accusatory, part panicked.

Nadia let the torrent of pent-up struggles tumble off her tongue, though she tried to maintain some counselor eloquence. "It's been a year since Nick died—and it's been unlivable. Not just today. Him not being here. I just can't . . . I'm not . . . I'm just not *me*. I feel like I'm a ghost. A shell of a person."

"Nadia, you're not . . ." Grace started, but the words slowed as she looked at Nadia's face.

"I can't *live* without him," Nadia continued tightly. "And frankly, I don't want to. I need him back, no matter what it takes. I want him here with me so we can have what we should've had. It's not getting easier—it's just getting harder."

She didn't have to tell them about the rift in her heart or the constant insomnia; her shuffling steps around her room every night and teary eyes every morning surely did that for her. Mornings were torture, especially when the days were sunny and mocking in their beauty. How could the world be so bright and happy while she was shrouded in the black, impenetrable grief of her husband's murder and his shredded reputation?

Grace walked to her daughter and gave her arm a squeeze. "Oh, honey . . ."

Nadia's head swam, her throat dry. She fought against the void that threatened to pull her in again. She needed this wish. Just one wish.

"We all miss him, sweetheart." Grace offered up a pitying look. "He was the best of men, certainly better than your coward of a father." Even now, her mom couldn't resist an opportunity to get a jab in.

"I just want him back," Nadia whispered.

Grace nodded sympathetically. "I know, honey. He didn't deserve what happened to him, but there are occupational hazards. People in that line of work—"

Nadia couldn't believe there was a "but" after her saying he hadn't deserved what had happened to him. Her mom had always lacked tact.

"That line of work?" Nadia repeated. "If he'd burned in a fire saving someone, maybe I could stomach it. Maybe. I mean, I knew that was a possibility every time he put on his helmet. But he was *shot*, Mom. It had nothing to do with his line of work, damn it!"

Basha leaned heavily on her cane and looked hard into her eyes. "I loved that boy down to his bones, but he was not . . . how you say? Entirely innocent, now was he? Who knows if his deeds before—"

"Don't! *Ever*," Nadia snapped before Basha could go down that road. "I want my wish. That's all I'm asking you. I don't want your opinions on my *dead* husband."

"Nick was good husband, good son-in-law, good man. But he is gone, and rodzina—family—remains. You do what is right for us all." Basha banged her cane on the floor. "Don't forget why we are in this debt in first place, wnuczka."

Nadia flinched, half remembering the hazy scene from three years before. She'd driven to a family gathering after being awake for thirty-six hours straight, courtesy of the final year of her master's program. She might as well have driven drunk. She was glad no one else had been hurt when she flew off the road and plowed into a tree, her liver battered to mush by the perfect storm of a defunct airbag and the steering wheel's attempt to push all the way through her abdomen.

Her mother put the family in 101 degrees of debt to secure an eleventh-hour wish before it was too late to save Nadia. The curved scar on Nadia's stomach from the underground surgery served as a constant reminder of that fact. That wish, and the consequent debt, had allowed Grace to grow her a new liver. Nick had convinced Nadia to take a medical leave of absence from her program for a short time afterward, but it'd taken her a full year after the accident to get over her fear of driving.

It didn't matter that she'd been unconscious when they'd asked for the wish. They were still paying off the debt because they hadn't taken the precaution of keeping a wish on hand for emergencies. Wishes used to be easy to buy in Savannah; they thought they'd always have access to them. Until the day they didn't. The day they needed it most. Grace had used her third and final wish after begging the newly "appointed" Wishmaster to give her one potent enough. Grace had spent it to save Nadia, and for that, Nadia would be forever grateful.

"I didn't ask you to pay such a steep price," Nadia replied weakly. "I can go to the Wishmaster myself and strike a deal that won't be your responsibility."

"I disown you if you seek Wishmaster alone!" Basha spat, her earrings swaying. "Debt of one is debt of all. Do not ask this. Is too much, dziecko."

Basha's retort lit an unexpected fuse inside Nadia. "And when the debt is paid? Then will you *allow* me to spend my own wishes?"

"Of course we would, Nadia." Grace clasped her hands together.

"We just have to pay off the debt first—and not give the Wishmaster more reasons to punish us."

Basha waved a hand. "Your mother try to protect your hopes, and I tell you again and again, but you never listen. Reviving dead is impossible. Is against rules! You think no one notice if dead man comes back to life? It must stay within boundaries of explanation." She wagged a finger at her granddaughter. "I am not who is saying no. Wishing Tree is saying no. Accept that, or you drive yourself mad."

Nadia didn't need reminding of the rules. She'd had them bored into her since she could toddle around.

"All wishes are technically against the laws of nature," she responded dryly. "And, sure, necromancy is *technically* impossible, but there are stories of people making it happen."

Basha snorted. "Pfft. Nonsense. Just like I tell you before."

"They're not," Nadia insisted. "People always say that wishes used to be more powerful and that resurrection was possible. Look at any old myth or legend with magic in it, and I'll bet your amber earrings that it was a potent wish."

Grace sighed. "Your grandmother's right. Maybe after the debt is paid, you'll think it over and find other things you could—"

Nadia stood and braced her palms against the countertop, meeting her grandmother's stubborn gaze. "It happened in our family, didn't it? An old story you used to tell us about a daughter being brought back from the dead—by my own great-great uncle. Are you going to tell me you pulled that out of your ass for the sake of some fireside storytelling?"

Basha's hazel eyes flickered, her web of wrinkles deepening. "I don't pull anything out of ass. I am not sideshow magician. But I do tell tales to entertain." She puffed out her chest, her ruffled blouse filling with indignation. Her cane protested against the tile floor as her grip shifted to one hand. "You are clearly passionate about this matter. But if you dare use wish for yourself, I will know, and I disown you for going against needs of rodzina. You won't see penny of inheritance, and that includes wishing box." She tapped the side of her temple. "Basha knows what you're thinking, Nadia."

It was never a good sign when her grandmother started talking in third person. Nadia cast imploring eyes at her mother, but as always, Grace said nothing. She never dared contradict Basha, never even hinted she might have a backbone *somewhere*.

"Besides, there is time limit to these things," Basha added dismissively, dropping an atom bomb on Nadia's realm of possibility.

"What?" The word came out of Nadia's mouth as a strange hiss.

Basha shrugged. "Is time limit. You think bodies stay fresh?" She gave a condescending sniff. "Is impossible to knit with rotten wool. Is same with fabric of person."

Nadia balled her hands into trembling fists. "How long?"

"Does not matter. We cannot fulfill debt before time is up," Basha replied matter-of-factly.

Nadia's guts morphed into a mass of writhing snakes, their nipping fangs dripping venom into her veins. How long did she have, exactly? The terror that she might miss the deadline made her want to grab back that wish trap and dip her hand right in, to seize the wish then and there.

"Why didn't you tell me earlier?" she snapped.

Basha mustered a gruff sigh. "I no keep from you. No wish is potent enough. Is no one living who has done this . . . even though is fairy story, so is not possible anyway."

The fact that Basha had first said no one *living* had done it, then tried to cover it up by saying it was a "fairy story" wasn't lost on Nadia, but she knew better than to press right now. Basha was in one of her moods.

"Fine," Nadia muttered.

"Fine? What is fine? What does that mean?" Basha prompted, making Nadia feel as though she were one of her counseling clients.

Nadia turned and left the kitchen rather than reply with something that would only make things worse. As she stepped onto the sweeping curve of the staircase, she could've sworn that Basha grunted in satisfaction.

Mounting the stairs, Nadia stomped past portraits of the Kaminskis, their oil-painted eyes homing in on her with silent judgment. She continued along to her childhood bedroom and entered, spinning on her heel to give the door a satisfying slam. But rather than closing with a resounding bang, the door bounced back and smacked into her face. She staggered away from it, her hands flying to her forehead.

"The house does not like to be treated so!" Basha shouted up. "Behave yourself, or I make you pick a switch from yard."

"I'm too old for this shit," Nadia muttered.

After living with Nick for so long—but not long enough—she'd almost forgotten that the old mansion had a mind of its own. Technically, it was a mind of *Basha's* own. When Grace was a toddler, Basha had used a wish to make sure the family home would always be protected, and it was still as strong as the day she'd uttered it. Though it didn't stretch to the gardens, which was unfortunate for the fountain with the cracked wing outside.

"What am I doing?" Nadia whispered.

It seemed that the grown woman she'd once been had disappeared the moment she'd moved back into her childhood bedroom. Being under the same roof as her family morphed her into a teenager again. She'd read enough articles to know this regression thing was a psychological phenomenon among "boomerang kids," but she'd never intended to come spinning back into this place. It was supposed to be temporary, after Nick died, but the anxiety-inducing thought of living alone had made it a more permanent deal, at least until the debt was paid off.

"It wasn't meant to be like this," she murmured. "You weren't supposed to leave me."

Nadia slipped off her olive-green pencil skirt and the breezy white blouse that hid her beloved rings. From her closet, she grabbed a pair of faded black jeans and one of Nick's old hoodies, putting them on and burying her nose in the fabric. She'd tried to preserve his smell, but time had wicked it away.

In the bathroom, she washed her face and wiped off a layer of concealer, which put her smattering of moles and freckles in harsh relief against her pale skin. Nick used to joke that her whole body looked like a dot-to-dot puzzle, and that fact still made her feel self-conscious on a beach. A few moles had made their way onto her face, including a noticeable one above her eyebrow and a smaller one above her top lip, but she didn't pay much attention to them anymore.

Maybe she should run away to Tokyo and try her luck there. Or London could be nice. Baghdad might be a stretch, but apparently the safety was improving. Those cities were some of the world's most plentiful wishing hotspots. But those dreams were as empty as her wishless chest. No matter how much she wanted to, or how quickly her window to save Nick was closing, she couldn't abandon her mom and grandma to the Wishmaster's debt.

Right before they'd gotten married four years ago, Nadia had told Nick almost everything about the wishing world—and when the debt landed on her lap a year later, he'd hugged her close, saying he would've paid any price to have her in his arms again. Those 101 wishes were *her* price to pay.

She wondered, not for the first time, what it felt like to absorb a wish. She'd never experienced it, but she'd heard about it plenty from her family. Like the taste of fine cuisine or a work of art, everyone had a different way of describing it.

Her grandmother once told her, "It feels like smooth caramel, with those—how you say? Poppet rocks inside. All fizzing and warm and molten, dripping over heart."

And her sister had countered, "No, it's more like cotton candy melting on the tongue, kind of fuzzy and a bit scratchy, but then it turns all syrupy and gives you that kick of giddiness you get when you're a kid, hyper on sugar. Only it's melting on your heart and not your tongue."

"No, no, no," her mother had said as she shook her head. "That's not it. Ever sat in a jacuzzi, in just the right spot? That's what it's like. Same kind of bubbly goodness, only in your chest." She'd sighed wistfully. "There's nothing in the world like it, unless you find a guy who's really good with his t—"

"Grace Kaminski!" her grandmother had scolded, though not nearly soon enough to prevent Nadia from being scarred for life. "You sit there while I fetch soap for filthy mouth. Basha didn't raise you to talk like that."

Those had been happier days, before the family had fractured beyond repair. With a sigh, Nadia left the bathroom and headed back into her bedroom. Grace was waiting for her on the edge of the bed.

"Mom," Nadia said curtly.

Grace bit her lip. "I know you're mad at me, but I wanted to talk to you privately."

"No such thing in this house." Nadia pushed her hands into the pouch of the red-and-black Falcons hoodie.

"Your babcia is just worried about the decisions you want to make," Grace said. "She's trying to protect you, honey, so you don't end up like your sister."

Nadia stiffened at the mention of her sister. Speaking directly about Kaleena in this house was tantamount to blasphemy. But Grace knew better than to say her name out loud, in case the house—or, rather, Basha—hit back in anger. At times like these, Nadia regretted that she hadn't adopted Kaleena's ballbreaker attitude. Her sister wouldn't have given a rat's ass what anyone thought. Kaleena had once told a new neighbor that their "minimalist" remodeling looked like a dentist's waiting room. She had been the kind of girl who spent her free time marching in the streets with signs that screamed "FUR IS NOT FAIR" and "DON'T BUY WHILE THEY DIE." But that was years ago, and so much had changed.

Nadia swallowed her irritation and shook her head. "Don't we all need a light at the end of the tunnel? It can't be all about the debt, Mom. What comes after? That's what I'm planning for—so we can all get back to our lives. You'll be able to roam for boy toys wherever you like, and Babcia might actually leave the house again, but I need something too. And that's *him*."

Grace fidgeted. She'd never been good at the serious mother-daughter talks. "Maybe if you'd taken that teacher's wish instead of letting her waste it, we'd be closer to letting that happen."

All of Nadia's good will toward her mom evaporated with that one sentence. Was it always going to be her fault, no matter what she did? Most people would've praised that act of kindness, but not her family.

Nadia burrowed deeper into the neckline of her hoodie, recalling

Angela Rhodes, a ninth-grade English teacher who'd saved one of her students from suicide and earned a wish in return.

She'd come to Nadia to discuss how the near tragedy had made her question everything, including the future of her marriage. It wasn't that she didn't love her husband anymore—it was more that her life felt awfully small and short after what she'd prevented. She'd wanted to do more with it: travel, meet new people, make a difference. Like most of Nadia's clients, Angela hoped to meet the end of her days feeling as though her proverbial cup was overflowing with memories and tales to tell.

"I don't regret it," Nadia said. "If anybody ever deserved a wish, it was that poor woman."

How could Nadia regret what she gave to Angela, who had been so sweet and almost apologetic about her wants, and had shown so much compassion for that student? To give the older woman a fighting chance, Nadia had subtly coached Angela into using the wish by asking guiding questions, like "If you could change one thing about your life, what would you wish for on your birthday candles?" Even if that decision had put her further away from her goal of escaping the wish-hunter life with Nick, she'd do it again. Wishes didn't exist just to be stolen or hoarded; they were meant to be used to better the world.

"I'm tired." Nadia didn't have any strength left for another twelve rounds with her mom. "But sure, maybe you've got a point." She didn't mean it; she just wanted Grace to leave so she could curl up in a ball and sleep.

Her mother made an awkward grunt of agreement. "You *look* tired."

"Thanks," Nadia muttered. She hadn't been asking for another insecurity.

"But then, why wouldn't you—" Grace stopped and stared off toward the small wedding photo that Nadia had half turned on the writing desk by the window so she could see it from her bed. It was the only one Nadia had put out to "redecorate" her childhood bedroom, and the only one she could bear looking at without dissolving into a puddle: her and Nick standing with their backs to the photographer, bathed in the burning sunset that glowed over the winery where they'd said their vows.

"You should've taken the day off work for the anniversary," Grace said. "We could've gone to Leopold's or something."

Nadia would've laughed if she had more energy. "I'm not twelve, Mom. And it's not exactly an ice cream occasion."

"No, no, right. Stupid idea." Grace seemed to be trying, but Nadia wasn't entirely sure *what* she was trying to do. Comfort her? Show she hadn't forgotten? It might've been a clunky attempt at motherly concern, but Nadia still appreciated the effort.

"To be honest, I've been thinking of going to the place where he died, for some sort of closure. If closure is even possible." Nadia wrung her hands inside her hoodie pouch. "But the thought of being there by myself freaks me out."

Grace's eyes lit up. "Why don't I come with you? We could go now, while it's still his anniversary. It might be good for you." She was clearly rolling with it now. "We could just drive by, if you're not feeling up to getting out, or we can buy some flowers on the way and leave them outside."

"Yellow pansies. And daisies." Nadia smiled sadly.

She remembered the faded vintage poster in her old kitchen, in the house she'd shared with Nick: "The Language of Flowers." Yellow pansies meant "I'm thinking of you," and daisies meant "I love you truly." Nick used to bring her flowers sometimes and tell her to check the poster, wearing a proud, goofy grin.

Grace tilted her head. "It's your bouquet, but I don't know if the store will have those."

"They're growing in the garden," Nadia pointed out, then hesitated. "But Babcia will probably tell me I'm plucking out a part of her if we take them. Or she'll make some other snide comment about us going out to visit a haunted house. Maybe we shouldn't bother."

Grace took hold of Nadia's hand and pulled her toward the bedroom door. "You get the pansies or whatever, and I'll distract your babcia. Meet me around the front in . . . how long do you need?"

"Ten minutes."

"Ten minutes," Grace confirmed. "I'll tell her I ate the last of the makowiec, and that'll put the heat on me. When she simmers down,

I'll say I'm heading out to get another from the bakery in town. Sound like a plan?"

A grateful smile tugged at the corners of Nadia's lips. "It does."

She watched her mom leave the room, then picked up the photo from her bedside table, tracing Nick's back with her thumb. Although Grace predictably hadn't stood up to Basha downstairs earlier, Nadia appreciated this one small act of rebellion.

Chapter Four

As Nadia pulled up to the curb opposite the building that loomed so large in her nightmares, she took her first look at the place she hadn't dared to visit. Until now.

Even in the darkening evening light, the blackened walls and gaping, windowless eyes of the house stared back at her through a cage of scaffolding. A billboard on the grass outside revealed a glossy advertisement for a new project coming in the spring of next year.

Nadia stiffened. If she'd delayed this visit any longer, she might've been staring at a pile of rubble instead. Would that have been better? Cathartic somehow? Unlikely. In fact, she had a sudden urge to chain herself to the scaffolding so they couldn't bring the place tumbling down.

Beside her, Grace fidgeted. Just then, the gut-wrenching lyrics to "Hope There's Someone" by Antony and the Johnsons haunted Nadia through the car speakers like some ghostly soundtrack. She changed the station with a sharp twist of the knob.

"Aww, I like that one," Grace complained.

The next radio station managed to find an even more melancholy song. Nadia snapped off the music and gripped the steering wheel. She laughed, but it was hollow and incomplete in the front seat of the car that used to be his.

Her mother eyed her warily. "Are you okay? Was this a bad idea?"

Nadia squeezed the steering wheel tighter. "I just need a minute."

He should be there beside her, blending his laughter with hers, before rolling his eyes and changing the station until he found a song that would make her smile.

"Nope, we can't have that sad stuff," he'd say. "I recommend a hundred milligrams of tasty riffs and a dose of killer saxophone solo for optimum mood change." He'd wax lyrical as he twiddled the knobs, knowing just how to land on the right station. "Back in the day, you couldn't get away from a saxophone, but you don't hear them anymore. It's a tragedy, if you ask me."

She'd grin at him through her tears. "Did your soul catapult forward from the 1950s or something?"

"You whippersnappers today with your rock and roll. You don't know the real stuff!"

"Did I say the fifties? I should've said the twenties."

"Must be why your babcia likes me so much," he'd throw back with a wink.

Grace cleared her throat, bringing Nadia back to the present. "Take all the time you need. But we shouldn't stay *too* long—I have to pick up that poppy seed cake before the bakery closes, or your babcia will smell a rat."

Nadia forced herself to take another look at the house. Even with the scaffolding and blackened marks where the fire had started to burn through, she could see the remnants of tangled vines knotting across the parts of the exterior that the firefighters had managed to get to in time. They sprawled out into the front yard like a flood of leafy serpents, twisting up the grayed pillar of a dried-up birdbath before continuing their journey across the fencing that acted as a boundary line.

"I thought it would look creepy, but it's not," Nadia whispered.

Grace arched an eyebrow. "Are we looking at the same thing?"

An old, ruined house that would soon be gone—that's all it was. There wasn't anything to fear here. At least, not on the outside. The inside was where it had happened. And Nadia had to decide just how brave she was feeling, with the freshly picked flowers resting on her lap. Would she leave them at the door, or would she break into the place she'd pictured a thousand times in her nightmares?

"I want to go inside," Nadia said, feeling a peculiar rush of adrenaline. But what she'd really meant to say was "I want to feel closer to him. I want to be closer to where he was when the lights went out."

Maybe there was some part of him left. An essence. A feeling.

Grace put a hand on Nadia's knee. "I don't think that's smart, honey. This house was condemned for a reason, and I can only imagine how many laws that would be breaking."

Nadia unclipped her seatbelt and got out of the car, taking the flowers with her. If Grace really wanted to stop her, she'd have to follow. Now that Nadia was here, there was no way she wouldn't venture inside.

She ducked under the bars of scaffolding, clambered over the sagging Do Not Enter tape that had already been torn away in places, and stepped into the building. Even a year after the incident, the smell of cinders and damp wood remained, although the unsavory undernote of urine and beer also permeated the air.

Anger prickled through her as she noted the empty glass bottles and wrappers scattered across the warped, blackened floorboards, as well as the graffiti that had been sprayed on the walls. Most locals knew that a murder had happened here. Clearly, this spot had drawn a few unwanted visitors who'd come to be voyeurs of her husband's place of death.

"Don't you have any respect?" she hissed to no one at all.

"Honey?" Grace called from behind as she pushed through the feeble tape.

Nadia said nothing and headed for the rickety staircase that led up to the second floor. Only a portion of the downstairs had been damaged during the fire. Though she had never been here before, the police reports had described the room where he'd been found.

"Nadia, stop!" Grace urged.

The wooden planks creaked and groaned underneath Nadia's feet, but she kept going until she reached the second-floor landing.

Ahead stood the empty doorway to the front-facing bedroom. She didn't know if the police had taken the door away after the murder, or if it had already been gone when Nick had come here to answer a reported fire. He'd just been doing his job on what should've been another average day.

"For Pete's sake, Nadia!" Grace appeared at the top of the stairs, looking pale and shaky. "These floors are unstable. You're going to get us both killed."

Nadia shook her head. "A few more minutes, then we can go."

She proceeded along the groaning floor until she reached the bedroom. There, she paused on the threshold and looked inside. The floorboards weren't scorched here, and the air smelled faintly chemical for some reason. She searched for some overlooked sign of the crime—a hidden bloodstain or shell casing—but of course the police would've already taken those in as evidence.

Her fingers went to the chain around her neck, where the wedding rings dangled. She closed her hand around them, as if they might open up a channel to her dead husband.

What really happened that night, Nick?

She tried to envision the scene and where he would have been standing. Likely with his back to the door. Otherwise, he would've heard his coworker and best friend, Chris, sneaking in with the gun raised. According to the fire department, Nick and Chris had arrived on the scene together after the arson call. Maybe Chris had planned the whole thing.

GSW to the back of the skull—that's what the autopsy report said. Would it have been instantaneous? Would Nick have felt pain first? Did he say anything?

More importantly, would that injury change who he was, if she could bring him back?

The fact that Nick's body was here in Savannah was another reason she hadn't upped and left. If she was put on the Wishmaster's permanent shit list for absconding while indebted, she might not be able to safely return to resurrect him.

"How would I word it, to make sure you came back right?" she whispered, hoping he could somehow answer her.

Grace tutted from behind her. "There's no use thinking about that, honey. I thought we were here for closure, not to give you ideas. But this whole business would be easier if we could wish away our problems, now wouldn't it?"

Nadia gripped her rings tighter as a flicker of inspiration came. If she could wish away the debt, she'd have free rein to use a second wish and maybe even a third to bring Nick back.

"You never know until you try," Nadia said, deadly serious. "*Could* I wish the debt away, if I had a wish to use?"

Grace gasped as if she'd been personally offended. "Honey, I was only messing around. Don't even think of trying something like that. No matter what wish you make, the Wishing Tree will only twist the outcome. It likes screwing with us. Even when I tried to turn stealing wishes into a game, it wouldn't let me win. Probably some arbitrary rule about how we're not allowed to do anything that lets us get more wishes than we'd normally find."

"But what if it worked? What if we could end the debt for good with one wish?" The more Nadia thought about the prospect, the more that hope bloomed in her chest.

"Well, the Wishing Tree might see that as wishing for more wishes too, so I doubt it'd work. It's not like your babcia and I haven't thought of it before—it's just too risky. Someone could die."

The unspoken words rang clear: *someone could die . . . like the creator of the debt*. After all, the Wishing Tree could interpret the debt creator as being Nadia herself, depending on how she worded the wish.

Grace glanced back over her shoulder, obviously wanting to leave. "Plus, the only way we could pull off something like that is if we got a wish that the Wishmaster doesn't have tabs on, and that'd be like winning the lottery."

Nadia shrugged. "People *do* win the lottery."

Her mind whirred with possibilities and a nice, neat checklist that was much easier to picture than to actually execute: find an unmonitored wish, use it to wish away the debt, find two more wishes, resurrect Nick, run away to some new place to start life afresh with him. Simple, right?

Grace looked like she was about to say something else when her phone rang in her pocket. She took it out and eyed the screen before swiping to answer, then stepped back out into the hall, leaving Nadia alone with her thoughts. Her mom was always taking calls at all hours so it wasn't too much of a surprise, but Nadia needed a pillar of moral support right now.

"Fine. Don't mind me," Nadia grumbled, letting her mind wander again.

Wishing lore was both incomplete and contradictory on the matter of resurrection. Saying "I wish to be a necromancer" or "I wish I could bring people back from the dead" wouldn't cut it. That was the quickest route to a flat rejection from the Wishing Tree. Not only that, but as her mother had pointed out, it was easy for the Tree to twist a wish's wording. Nadia wasn't sure how she'd feel about having a zombie husband with parts peeling off. Then again, as long as he didn't try to bite her, she could probably get used to it. She wanted to laugh, but it came out between her tears as more of a strangled wheeze.

The ache in her chest made it hard to breathe. She had her memories of Nick, but what about the memories they'd lost the chance to make? The ones they'd envisioned while walking past playgrounds and poring over the gift lists for other people's baby showers? The guest room that had been earmarked for a nursery? Hallways that were supposed to be filled with shrieks and laughs and hurried footfalls of little feet?

Their story couldn't end here. Anyway, what if Basha was wrong about the timeline, or lying? It was another futile hope, since the more Nadia thought about, the more she realized it was truly an unfeasible task, but she was trying not to dwell on the hopelessness right now.

But their debt to the Wishmaster. Maybe she *could* do something about that and stay well within the rules.

She turned at the sound of Grace's raised voice. "It would have to be soon," her mother said to whomever she was talking with on the phone.

Nadia stepped out into the hall. She had expected Grace to have finished up her booty call by now, or whatever it was. Instead, her mother was pacing back and forth at the bottom end of the hallway, closest to the stairs, with the phone pressed to her ear and a worried frown denting her forehead.

"We can't keep holding off," Grace continued, visibly agitated. "Right, that's exactly what I was thinking. Can you get boots on the ground by then? Mm-hmm. I know, but this is our only shot." She paused. "Fine, but get back to me as soon as you hear from them so I know what to expect. Thank you."

Nadia leaned against the doorway. "Who was that?"

Grace's head snapped up as though she'd been jolted in the spine with a cattle prod. "Nadia! Don't you know it's rude to listen in on other people's private conversations?"

"It's rude to take a call when you're supposed to be helping your daughter out on the anniversary of the day that made her a widow," Nadia retorted.

A ball of sudden dread rolled in her stomach. It took a lot to rattle her mother, and her mother definitely looked rattled.

Grace walked back up the landing. "What did you hear?"

"I'm not sure. You'll have to enlighten me." Nadia held her mom's gaze. "But it sure sounded like you were up to no good, and not in your usual way."

Grace hissed a breath between clenched teeth. "This is why there's no point in you thinking about wishing the debt away." She waved her now-blank phone at Nadia. "I'm taking care of it."

"What's that supposed to mean?" A rush of hope bubbled in Nadia's chest. If her mom had found a way to get rid of the debt, she'd have an express pass to Resurrection Town. And three whole wishing slots available to use for Nick.

"I've been talking to Mr. Caldwell," Grace said. "He's helping me find a way out of this debt. Three years doesn't sound like a long time, granted, but that light at the end of the tunnel that you were talking about might never happen." Her shoulders sagged, and she mumbled, "Especially considering who holds the lamp at the end of that tunnel."

Nadia's rush of optimism morphed into abject horror. Mr. Caldwell, the Atlanta Wishmaster? Had her mom lost her mind? She was talking about treason here, if she wanted to cross the Savannah Wishmaster like this.

"Are you hearing yourself right now?" she said. "If anything traces back to you, do you—"

"Your babcia is worried that our Wishmaster won't release us from our debt, even after the debt is paid," Grace replied in a hurry. "You know how she feels about Babcia. She'll keep us indebted just to spite your grandmother."

Nadia swallowed thickly. "So, you're just going to get into debt with some other Wishmaster instead? I doubt Mr. Caldwell is doing this out of the goodness of his heart." She ran a hand over her hair. "Actually, what *is* he doing?"

"Nothing is set in stone."

The vague reply made Nadia cross her arms. Grace and Basha never told her anything, always treating her like she was still a little kid. This was the ice cream situation all over again. But she wasn't about to let this slide.

"Are you staging a coup?" Nadia asked.

Grace checked the clock on her phone. "It's all in the negotiation stages. Nothing for you to worry about, but we should really be going. The bakery closes in half an hour."

Nadia's mother disappeared down the unstable stairwell. What Grace had done was downright dangerous—this type of treachery could get their wishes taken away in retaliation, and they'd have no chance of pleading their case. More than that, though, striking a deal with the Atlanta Wishmaster could trap them in another debt to yet another power-hungry dictator, just one with a different name. Though she had never met Mr. Caldwell, she'd heard the rumors about his particular skills.

Nadia stared down at the floorboards. She didn't want to stay any longer, surrounded by so many terrible memories.

"I'll bring you back, Nick," she whispered to the empty room, "before our time runs out."

Leaving the flowers on the floor, she hurried after her mother.

~

"Let's play the silent game," Grace said when they'd gotten back into the car. "Whoever can be quiet the longest wins the game."

So, as they drove back to the Kaminski Mansion, Grace remained tight-lipped, and there was nothing Nadia could do about it now that her mom had implemented her win-any-game wish. It felt more for theatrics, anyway, given that her mother probably planned on being quiet until Nadia stopped asking about her plans for treason.

Once she pulled into the driveway, Nadia killed the engine. "You'll have to tell me eventually. Or am I supposed to wait around until Rome starts burning, huh?"

"You make it too easy for me to win the silent game," Grace said. She got out of the passenger side, slamming the door a little too hard.

As Nadia left the car and walked toward the house, she was startled to find her mom standing still and quiet, staring down at the ground in front of the garden gate.

When she saw what her mom was looking at, she froze too. A spray-painted symbol glared up at her from the flagstone: a long red feather with a rippling tip that made it look like it was ablaze. The feather of the Zhar-Ptitsa, a phoenix-like bird from Slavic folklore known for fulfilling wishes. But the message was instantly recognizable to all wishmongers in Savannah—it meant "strike one."

"No, this can't be right," Grace rasped. "The Wishmaster doesn't have a reason to do this. Unless . . ."

At that moment, Nadia spied a strange shimmer, like a mirage, moving just beyond the garden gate. Her heart pounded as the flicker took shape as a man. If he'd just wandered a short way onto the porch, the house would've dealt with him, but the Wishmaster had evidently warned her lackeys against doing that. The good-looking Korean man was taller than Nadia, with dark hair, angry eyes, and a wishbone flower tattoo that seemed to sprout from beneath the neckline of a Gucci T-shirt. She vaguely knew him, though he was higher up in the Wishmaster's rankings than the usual intermediaries Nadia dealt with.

"You shouldn't be creeping around in people's gardens, Croak," Nadia said as bravely as she could manage. "Folks might get the wrong idea."

"I just wanted to make sure someone appreciated my artwork." He swept a multi-ringed hand down at the spray-painted feather. "A masterpiece, if I do say so myself."

She nodded and said through gritted teeth, "We see it. Now get lost."

"You want a second feather already? Wishmaster's not keen on disrespect to her people," he shot back.

Grace fidgeted. "She didn't mean anything by it, Croak."

"Let's hope not." He puffed out his chest, stretching the letters on his shirt. "What are the two of you doing out so late, anyway? Kinda suspicious, don't you think, after you pocketed that wish from the heart surgeon today? I hope you weren't trying to use it."

"No!" Grace replied, a note too fast. "I'm going to deliver it tomorrow, as promised. We don't even have the box with us. It's in the house."

Nadia scowled. "What, are we not allowed to leave the house now? Is that some new rule? How would I get the Wishmaster her precious wishes?"

She didn't even understand why they were getting a feather in the first place—unless it had something to do with Grace's phone call to Mr. Caldwell. Everyone double-crossed everyone in the wishing world, and if Atlanta's Wishmaster thought he could get a better deal by ratting out a potential betrayal to Savannah's, he no doubt would.

Croak's eyes gleamed. "Nah. Just know I'm around. I'm always watching." His expression hardened. "Especially you, Clover Eyes."

Nadia snorted at his use of her code name. "Especially me? What did I do?" She scuffed the toe of her shoe against the spray paint and felt a slight tingle. "Don't tell me this warning is for me. Are you afraid that the littlest Kaminski is going to stage a coup or something?"

She chose her words carefully, trying to feel out what Croak knew about her mother's conversation.

"Not too far off the mark, is it?" Croak hissed, turning to Grace. "You have your warning. I'm sure you can figure out why."

Grace blanched, and her hand went subconsciously to her back pocket where she kept her phone. Nadia's stomach sank. Had the phone been tapped? Had Croak followed them to the condemned house and eavesdropped on the conversation? Or was there a different reason altogether for the warning?

Nadia forced a tight laugh to try to ease the tension. "Can't you take a joke?"

"Sure. Let me know when you tell one." Croak sneered at her. "Now, stay on the up-and-up, or else I'll be back. This feather has already added ten more wishes to your debt. And you really don't need a second one, do you? After all, the third might cost you all of your wishes—spent and unspent."

Basha had been right. Maybe the Wishmaster didn't intend to let them off the hook after the debt was paid. Maybe the tally would simply continue to increase. It wouldn't be hard for the Wishmaster to keep making up allegations and transgressions—even if this one wasn't all that fake. Nadia looked to her mother and saw her suspicions reflected back.

"No problem," Nadia said bitterly to Croak. "Thanks for making a shitty day that much shittier."

He smirked. "Any time."

He started to walk away, but Nadia wasn't about to let him have the last word.

"And tell my sister to fuck off," she shouted at his wide, retreating shoulders.

Croak laughed but didn't turn around as he spoke. "Keep it up, and maybe you'll get the chance to tell her yourself. I hope I'm there to see it. I've always wanted to hear somebody's last words."

Nadia wisely bit back a reply about what happened to tyrannical Wishmasters like Kaleena. It had happened to the old Wishmaster, after all. And history had a habit of repeating itself.

Chapter Five

The next evening, Nadia found herself summoned to a family war council around the breakfast island in the kitchen. The meeting had come a lot later than she'd expected, in truth, but her mom and grandmother tended to make big decisions without her input.

Nadia poured herself a cup of coffee and settled down on one of the stools. "I take it you've discussed Mom's scheming, then? Makes a change from me being the one in your bad books, Babcia."

Basha shot her granddaughter a warning look. "Is no victory, dziecko. We are in bad books because of debt. I pay because Wishmaster knows wording of my wishes. Of my Grace's wishes. Wishmaster would find way to destroy house—everything we own—if we disobey. And she will take all hope of wish from you too. Don't forget this."

"As if I could," Nadia muttered.

"Your mama's idea was good. Execution was bad," Basha said. Grace had evidently won her over already. "But we do as we always do —we keep heads down, we play nice, and we soon be back on Wishmaster's good side."

Nadia snorted into her cup. "When have we ever been there?"

"You make good point." Basha raised a finger. "But this is plan. Is better to have devil you know in power than devil you don't. Though your sister is worst of devils—but no matter."

The river of hatred between Basha and Kaleena flowed upstream and downstream. While Nadia knew that Basha's anger came from Kaleena abandoning the family and saddling them with the debt, she'd never fully understood why her sister hated their grandmother so much. Judging by the timing of the fallout, it had something to do with the events of three years ago, when Kaleena had first seized power, but Basha kept her secrets locked up like the crown jewels.

"If is not Kaminski in Wishmaster seat, more danger for us," Basha continued. "That pest, Adrian, found out what Kaminskis can do if threatened. He try to hurt us, we hurt him. I have enough of Wishmasters hurting my family—they hurt my parents, they hurt me, they do it no more. But is different with this Wishmaster. We keep sweet, we will survive." She wagged her finger at Grace. "No Atlanta. Is recipe for disaster. Has gained us one feather already—I say no for us getting another."

Nadia wasn't sure if this was all for show. Unable to eavesdrop as her mother and grandmother plotted and planned through the course of the day, she had no idea if they'd secretly been discussing how to proceed with Mr. Caldwell. But she had to hope they weren't stupid enough to carry on down that path. Her grandmother was right—it *was* a recipe for disaster, and a huge turf war. If they unseated Kaleena, it would create a power vacuum that people would gladly kill to fill.

Grace interrupted Nadia's thoughts with a tap to her wrist, as if tapping the face of a watch. "You need to get going."

"I do?" Nadia frowned. "There's nothing on my calendar but a date with my TV."

"Will rot brain, these shows," Basha tutted. "You go to drop-off, silly dziecko. Wish needs delivery."

Nadia eyed her mom. "You told Croak that *you* were going to make the exchange."

"We need someone who's good at schmoozing to get Black Hat on our side," Grace replied. "If you're nice to him, hopefully he'll pass the word on to the Wishmaster that we're remorseful."

Nadia groaned. "You mean you need someone he has a crush on."

"Kind of, yeah." Grace shrugged. "So, get your sweet cheeks moving. I just texted you the meeting spot."

Nadia wasn't looking forward to the prospect of kissing up to Black Hat. He was one of the easier intermediaries to deal with, but only after she let him flirt with her without giving him the stink eye. She always felt the need to take a long shower after talking to him. Somehow, her lack of interest in no way deterred Black Hat from continually attempting to get in her pants, one bad pickup line at a time.

Reluctantly, she got down off the stool and picked up the wishing box, which sat pointedly at the end of the breakfast island. There was no use arguing with her mom and grandmother, but it felt a bit rich that she had to do this, when her mom had barely gotten a slap on the wrist for gaining them a feather—and ten more wishes on their debt.

Nadia pulled her hood over her head and trudged out of the house. As she walked down the garden path and out the gate to the Chevy, she caught sight of the faded glint of the spray paint on the walkway. She swallowed thickly and skirted around it, as if stepping on it might add another fifty wishes to the tally.

The debt was beginning to feel even more insurmountable. If her sister really didn't intend to let them all off the hook when it was paid, then she'd never be able to revive Nick. It would all be for nothing, giving way to a life of eternal servitude: no husband, no new start, no chance to get away from this wish-hunting life. The debt would *become* her life. It already felt like it had.

Impossible as it might be, the only way she could ever find freedom was to wish away this debt before Nick's deadline came around. And she still didn't know exactly how long she had. Her arm tightened around the wishing box, but there was no point in daydreaming—this wish was already documented. Maybe after this one had been delivered, she could begin to think about ways of tracking down a wish outside of the Wishmaster's all-seeing gaze.

～

At the imposing gates of Bonaventure Cemetery, two statues stood sentinel—one clutching a vase, the other leaning into a cross. After locking up the Chevy, Nadia had stuffed the wishing box inside her battered maroon leather satchel, which she slung across her body. She breezed past a tourist group waiting for a good spooking, courtesy of the evening tour guides.

The honeyed light of early evening spread across the sprawling expanse of Bonaventure and the Wilmington River beyond it. Even in the daytime, the cemetery oozed eeriness. Lifelike statues waited around every corner to startle the heart, and they took on a whole different level of sentience when evening crept in. Over the years, Nadia could've sworn she'd seen a few of them move out of the corner of her eye, especially Little Gracie, Bonaventure's famous sitting figure of a small girl taken by pneumonia long before her time.

Nadia wasn't usually a superstitious person, but cemeteries had the same palpable yet inexplicable sensation that made people speak in hushed tones when they stepped into libraries and places of worship: the epicenters of countless stories that inspired and enthralled. Cemeteries were no different, for what were lives but collections of stories, relayed through those left behind? And Nadia was the keeper of Nick's stories, though they might never be finished.

Striding along the open gravel pathways that crisscrossed between plots, she double-checked the name her mother had texted her: Marie Corbin. A grave she knew from the last time she was coerced into doing a drop-off. Because of the throngs of tourists, the wishing world contacts rarely chose a famous grave like Johnny Mercer's, or Conrad Aiken's well-known bench with the thought-provoking inscription *Cosmos Mariner—Destination Unknown*, though sometimes Nadia liked to walk past them anyway.

Her favorite, if a person could have a favorite gravestone, was Corinne Elliott Lawton's. A young woman, now immortalized in stone, perched beside a large white cross, as though she were just resting her legs after a trek around the cemetery. She'd died the year she was meant to turn thirty-one, the age Nadia was now. Perhaps that was why Nadia liked it—as a reminder of where she very well might've been if not for her mother and grandmother hovering around her after Nick's death.

Nadia kept walking, mulling over the feather warning and her upcoming schmooze with Black Hat. She wasn't even sure she knew *how* to schmooze anymore. But the threat of turning that feather into two made her determined to try. Still, she checked the back pocket of her jeans, where she felt the comforting outline of her folding knife—just in case Black Hat or another of her sister's cronies decided a feather wasn't punishment enough.

She cut through a border of shrubs and slinked past a live oak to reach the Corbin family plot, marked by a tall Celtic cross. Black Hat waited, wearing his signature black top hat. He was in his mid-twenties and pale in an I-might-be-a-vampire-or-at-least-severely-anemic kind of way. She couldn't decide if the combination made him look like a confused goth, a failed magician, or a cemetery tour guide—and in Savannah, those three weren't mutually exclusive. Whichever it was, the ensemble served its purpose, since when he wasn't picking up wishes, he actually *was* a tour guide. It was all part of the Wishmaster's strategy of finding ways to hide in plain sight.

Black Hat usually went solo, but another guy stood nearby, sunglasses on, hood up. Not exactly incognito, if that was what he was going for. Sunglasses, in the evening, in a graveyard . . . He might as well have been wearing a neon sign that said *Hey, you, don't look at me!*

He was probably the buyer. Sometimes they tagged along with the intermediary if they were in a rush to get their wish. But there was something oddly familiar about the hooded figure.

"The only song of his that most people can name is 'Moon River,' which is a damn shame. I'm a 'Fools Rush In' man myself," Sunglasses said to Black Hat. He hummed a line as he shoved his hands into his pockets.

"Ah, of course," Black Hat replied, looking entirely lost for words.

"Not the version you're probably thinking of," Sunglasses went on. "Everyone thinks about Elvis first, but that ain't the one. Nah. Johnny Mercer's lyrics were killer. Man, he—"

Nadia decided to relieve Black Hat from the impromptu Johnny

Mercer lecture and stepped out onto the open plot, ready to schmooze.

"Evenin', Clover Eyes." Black Hat tipped his hat to her as she approached. Using real names was thought to bring bad luck in the wishing world, but she still berated herself for choosing such a cliché code name way back when.

She mimicked a return tip of a nonexistent hat. "And to you."

"Aren't you hot in that?" He eyed her up and down. It seemed like a silly question, given that his companion, Sunglasses, was wearing a wool hoodie, but the innuendo didn't escape her notice.

"Nope. I'm just right." Nadia patted her satchel. "Number fifty."

"Halfway there!" he replied, a little too cheerfully. "Well, plus ten more."

She forced a tight smile. "You heard, then?"

Black Hat nodded, then shuffled closer and nudged her arm. "Can't say it bothers me too much, to be honest. Means we get to spend a few more evenings like this."

"My favorite dates in the calendar." She hoped she didn't sound *too* sarcastic. "Anyway, seeing how wish hunting is starting to slow down, we'll probably be having these meetings until I'm dead."

He grinned, seeming to take her words at face value. "I won't let 'em forget you, Clover Eyes. I'll probably be prowlin' around here, tellin' folks to watch out for your ghost."

"If I'm going to haunt someone, you think it should be you?" Nadia said with a smirk.

"Why not? I'd be good company."

"I wouldn't want you selling tickets. You'd rip people off." She tested the waters of how much she could tease him, since that was their usual schtick. He'd be wary if she acted too differently.

Black Hat's eyes widened in mock outrage. "Me? I'm a Boy Scout, man!" He chuckled. "But fine, I admit it—I'd totally charge for them tourists to come watch me and the ghost of Clover Eyes. I'd tell 'em you was my jilted lover who died of a broken heart. Everyone goes wild for a ghost-slash-love story."

"I'm more a revenge story kind of gal, really." Nadia gave him a pleading look that said, *Let's get on with this.*

"Hey, I didn't tell you the good news, did I? I'm movin' up. The Wishmaster's got an important mission for me," Black Hat bragged, leaning closer to her. "Can't say much more, of course."

"Wow, it's a shame you can't tell me what it is," Nadia deadpanned. It was getting harder to keep up the schmoozing attempt.

His sarcasm radar seemed to be on the blink. "I mean, I'm not supposed to, but . . . you're cool. I'll be chasin' down a target that recently got themselves a big wish. I'm talking top-shelf here."

Contrary to what Nadia had expected, that little bit of information actually piqued her interest. A wish that potent could earn Kaleena a pretty penny, but she was known for hoarding top-shelf wishes rather than auctioning them off as Adrian had. Perhaps the Wishmaster had a particular endgame in mind.

"Everyone's jealous," Black Hat continued. "It'll probably be super under the radar, dangerous business, but I'm up for it."

"Who's the target? Anyone worth mentioning?" Nadia pretended to pick fluff off her hoodie, praying that if she acted nonchalant, he might be nonchalant with his answer.

Black Hat faltered, seeming to choke on his words to stop them from coming out. "Uh, you know, it's all top-secret intel, so I can't really talk about it."

"Too late," Nadia shot back. "You already told me about it."

Sunglasses burst out laughing, flashing pearly whites. "She got you good, man!"

"She did *not*," Black Hat insisted, but his shifty eyes and beet-red cheeks suggested otherwise.

Where had she heard the stranger's voice before? There was something about the way Sunglasses had said "she got you good" that sounded maddeningly familiar.

"Well, good luck, then." Nadia opened the flap of her satchel. "I was just trying to be a Good Samaritan and offer some help, but I should've remembered that 'the Black Hat' stalks alone. Now, let's get this over with, preferably before the tourists come around and think they've seen the ghost of a Victorian sideshow act."

Black Hat gave her a wounded look. "You don't like the hat?"

"Sure I do. *Mary Poppins* was my favorite movie as a kid."

She was about to grab the box when footsteps crunched on the dirt path behind her. Her blood ran cold, and she spun around. Three shadows slithered out of the dogwoods.

The figures were dressed in black jeans and black T-shirts, with black Falcons ballcaps obscuring their faces, so it was only when they got within spitting distance that she recognized them. Dominic, Tony, and Lemmy: three of Adrian's pet thugs who hadn't quite gotten the message that their old Wishmaster didn't run things anymore.

"You owe us a better wish than what you gave Mike yesterday, so cough it up." Dominic, the leader of this hulking trio, pointed a sausage finger at Black Hat.

Nadia's heart pounded as she edged away from them. She didn't want to be guilty by proximity and *definitely* didn't want to get caught in a cross fire. Sunglasses ducked behind the stone cross that headed the Corbin family plot, clearly looking to create a barrier between him and any bullets that might fly by if the situation went south.

Black Hat shrugged, as if he wasn't worried at all. "Ah, so that guy was one of yours, huh? Well, I wouldn't have sold it to your friend if I'd known *you* were the one tryin' to use it. The Wishmaster has you on the no-sell list."

Dominic stepped closer, his expression stoic.

Black Hat put his hands up—not in surrender, but more as a warning. "Don't do anythin' stupid now. Besides, the one I sold your friend came from a guy who pulled three babies from a car crash. No way it wasn't potent enough, unless . . . What'd you wish for?"

"None of your damn business," Dominic snapped.

"Then I guess it was out of bounds for the Wishing Tree. But the wish was solid. Pure gold."

Black Hat's voice was steadier than it had the right to be. He seemed confident—maybe too confident—that the Wishmaster's power and reputation would save him from the trio, but Nadia wasn't so sure. This was exactly why she had refused to serve her debt by being an intermediary. When wishing customers made complaints, they tended to prefer bullets and blades to phone calls and emails.

Dominic's piercing eyes settled on Nadia. "Who made the wish you're selling?"

She hesitated a moment, weighing her options. If Dominic took the wish, Kaleena would blame him, not her. If she tried to deny Dominic, she had no idea what he might do.

"Heart surgeon," she replied, "though when you weigh it up against a triple baby saver, I doubt it tips the scales." She mimed holding two bowls in each hand, like Bonaventure's own Bird Girl statue.

Dominic extended his palm. "Hand it over."

Sunglasses suddenly seemed to find his voice again and stepped out from behind the stone cross. "Uh, I don't think so, man. I paid a *lot* of money for that wish, and I'm not letting anybody swipe it out from under me."

Nadia stared at him, wondering if he was a sandwich short of a picnic for being so brazen with Dominic. Did he want his trip to the cemetery to be a permanent one? Maybe he couldn't see them properly because of those stupid shades.

"There are rules to the game, Dominic," Black Hat barked. "And I know you know 'em, so back off."

Dominic sneered. "Try me."

"When the Wishmaster finds out you—"

Black Hat didn't get to finish what was sure to be a rousing speech. Dominic lunged at him and landed a nasty left hook to his jaw. The crunch of teeth made Nadia flinch. Black Hat staggered backward and dropped to the ground, dazed—but not so out of it that he couldn't find the gun in his belt. It was in his hand even as he struggled onto one knee, the silenced muzzle coming up to meet Dominic between the eyes.

Black Hat fired.

The muffled pop of the small gun startled her, but Nadia wasn't surprised to see the spark of the bullet as it ricocheted off Dominic and pinged away, embedding itself in the Corbin family's cross.

Bulletproof. Not an uncommon wish, especially in the black market.

Nadia fumbled out her knife, ready to put her Krav Maga classes to good use if she had to. Her thumb searched for the little metal button that flicked out the blade.

"Get down!" Sunglasses roared in Nadia's ear, slamming into her, pushing them both to the ground. He landed on top of her with a thud that knocked the breath out of her and sent the wishing box flying out of her satchel.

A second bullet ricocheted off Dominic and snapped over their heads—right where Nadia would've been.

Chapter Six

Heart tap-dancing against her rib cage, Nadia stayed flat on the grass, panting through the weight of the man-shaped lump on top of her. Time had taken on a mind of its own, slowing as if everyone were wading through molasses, while her thoughts felt like they were running on fast-forward.

She assessed the situation. Dominic's lackeys—Lemmy and Tony—had Black Hat's head smashed into the dirt. It seemed a little counter-productive if they were trying to get him to talk, but maybe that wasn't the point anymore.

Her heart dropped when she saw the wishing box several feet away. It had taken a fatal hit. A jagged crack splintered down the middle of the rust-toned heartwood, where it had collided with the edge of a nearby headstone. Unfortunately, she wasn't the only one who had noticed the damage.

"Get up!" Dominic shouted, seizing her by the arm and dragging her out from underneath Sunglasses.

Nadia shook off his grasp and dusted the dirt from the front of her jeans. She winced at the headache that was just beginning. She must've been pushed down harder than she'd thought.

Beside her, Sunglasses got back on his feet, then patted frantically at his hoodie pouch. She caught a glimpse of something round and wooden in his hand before he turned and hid it from view.

Nadia didn't have time to worry about his problems, though. She stumbled over to the splintered remains of her wishing box and gingerly reached into its depths. No telltale thrum vibrated back. No warmth radiated up to tempt her fingertips.

"You cost me the Wishmaster's payment," she snarled at Dominic.

He snorted. "Like I'm going to just take your word for it that it's gone."

"Go ahead, then." She held out the broken box.

Dominic snatched it from her. He swirled his hand inside the wood, then pressed his palm to his heart. A grunt of annoyance followed. Obviously, he hadn't felt the mystical spark that ignited in people when they absorbed a wish. Just as she'd said, the wish was gone. It had slipped through the literal cracks and disappeared into the ether. No one could ever use it now.

Dominic shoved the box back into her hands with a scowl and muttered a long string of profanity. He stood over Black Hat's moaning form.

"The Wishmaster will hear about this," Black Hat rasped through bloody lips.

"Good," Dominic replied. He nodded to his companions.

Lemmy gave Black Hat one last kick in the face for good measure, and the downed man whimpered. Tony delivered the final insult by stomping on the intermediary's titular accessory, leaving both man and hat crushed on the ground.

Once the trio of thugs had stalked off through the shrubs, it took Nadia a minute to fully grasp the intensity of what had just happened. The flying bullets. Her broken wish trap. Adrian's men sniffing around for a potent wish. And her too-close-for-comfort brush with death. Her arms felt heavy as she stared down at the splintered remains of the heartwood in her hands. Grace and Basha would murder her in a thousand creative and abstract ways when they found out she'd lost the wish she was supposed to sell. She could only hope that the Wishmaster would blame Dominic for the incident and that this wouldn't somehow earn her another feather.

When she looked up again, Sunglasses had rushed over to help Black Hat to his feet.

"You okay?" Sunglasses asked the other man.

Black Hat pinched his nose and slurred through cracked teeth. "I look okay to you?"

"Yeah, guess not." The buyer folded his arms across his chest. "You said this'd be a simple, smooth transaction. I'm not game for all this mafia-style shit."

Nadia clutched the cracked wishing box under her arm and ducked down to retrieve her satchel. Walking over to the two men, she buried a hand in her bag and fished around for a packet of tissues. It was the least she could do, since Black Hat had gotten his ass beaten because of her lost wish.

She handed Black Hat the tissues. "Here. These will help. You probably want to get yourself to the ER."

Black Hat's face was already bruising purple. "My nose is broke," he said. "Is it true girls like a guy with a broken nose? Means I'm tough, right?"

Nadia couldn't decide whether to laugh or cry. Losing a wish was irritating, sure, but it wasn't the worst thing in the world. Breaking the wishing box, however . . . *She* would find herself bleeding when she told her grandmother what had happened, only her blood would be coming out of her ears. Given the rarity of wish traps, the only way to get another would be to borrow one from Kaleena, and that loan would cost them another batch of wishes.

"I want a full refund from the Wishmaster for this, you hear? Plus the wish I came here for," Sunglasses said, even as he handed Black Hat the crushed remains of the stovepipe hat. "If I wanted to get shot at, I'd play 'Welcome to Atlanta' at the Superdome."

Black Hat nodded effusively. "Of course. Absolutely. The Wishmaster will make it right. I promise."

"Glad to hear it." Sunglasses pulled his hood farther down his forehead.

"Of course, I don't make the schedule, so I can't guarantee when you'll get your wish. And I don't suppose, after all this, you'd still want to sell your wishin' jar we talked about, would you?" Black Hat asked hesitantly.

Sunglasses sniffed. "First, I want my money back—*and* my wish. Then we'll talk about the wishing jar."

So that was what she'd seen him take out of his pouch. Looking closer at his hoodie, she could make out the slight rounding of the jar's outline.

Black Hat held his flattened hat to his chest, like he was standing graveside at a funeral, and gave a defeated sigh. "I really do apologize for all this, sir."

Nadia's eyebrows shot up. *Sir?* Black Hat was laying it on thick. He was probably trying to keep the wheels greased for their coming negotiations.

"It was my fault for bringin' you," Black Hat continued. "I should've arranged a pickup instead, but I couldn't help myself. I mean, it's *you*. How could I resist?" He turned to Nadia. "Sorry to you too, Clover Eyes, but you know how these things can go sometimes. I'll catch you later, no doubt."

"ER. Go. Now," Nadia urged, her curiosity about the buyer's identity returning. For Black Hat to turn on what passed for charm, Sunglasses *had* to be a big deal.

Black Hat nodded, pushed himself up with a groan, and limped off to the bluff opposite the entrance.

Left alone with Sunglasses, Nadia turned to him with a bashful smile. "Hey, uh . . . thanks for saving my life back there."

His eyes widened, and Nadia inhaled sharply, realization hitting them both at the same time.

"I saved your life," Sunglasses parroted, a grin spreading across his face. "*I saved your life!* This is better than winning a Grammy!" He flung himself into a victory dance, his arms flailing and his hips gyrating as he jigged around the Corbin family plot. Any onlookers might've thought some kind of ritual was going down, while Nadia just stared in disbelief.

"I can feel the tickle!" He whooped, pausing in his dance to punch the air. "Ooh, that feels *good*! That's like standing next to a subwoofer and getting some nice, heavy bass in your lungs."

Instead of that syrupy, cotton candy, fizzy jacuzzi, bass-thumping goodness that everyone else got, irritation bristled through Nadia's chest. This clown—whoever he was and whatever his story—had knocked her flat and sent her wishing box flying, and yet he'd been rewarded with a wish, while she had her shrieking grandmother to look forward to. She immediately wanted to rescind her thanks.

"This is serendipity right here!" he said. "I mean, I almost died for it, but it was worth it in the end."

Her gloating savior took off his sunglasses and rubbed happy tears from a set of umber-toned eyes. Recognition hit Nadia, flaring up visions of abstract finger paintings and tight leather pants.

Miles Hunter, local guitarist and singer turned internationally famous rock star.

No wonder this drop-off had been set up in a public area, rather than one of the Wishmaster's private safehouses, where Dominic and his goons wouldn't have stood a chance of getting so close. Miles was a major celebrity, and Kaleena had probably decided not to risk revealing said safehouses to the tabloids, in case the general public caught wind of the wish-making world's existence. Secrets held power, after all.

"This is *perfect*. It couldn't have worked out better if I'd planned it." Miles cast those brown eyes in her direction, evidently expecting further appreciation for his heroic moment. Being a megastar and all, he was probably used to a standing ovation, fanatical screams, and thunderous applause. He wasn't about to get any of that from her.

She started to walk away, tossing a comment back over her shoulder. "You wouldn't have a wish if you'd planned it."

"Huh?" He caught up to her in a few long strides, slipping his shades back onto the bridge of his nose and peering at her over the rims.

"Wishing rules," she replied, sounding a little too much like her grandmother.

He shrugged. "I don't get what you mean. I'm not 'into' this thing." He made air quotes as he said *into*. "It's like prog-rock to me; I just dip my toe in every now and again, then remember why I stayed away."

"I'd say you jumped in pretty deep this evening, but what do I know?" She forced herself to sound cheerier as they moved toward the cemetery entrance. "Basically, you can't put someone's life at risk in order to earn a wish by saving them. Big no-no, and you don't get anything for it—other than a dead person if you screw it up. You could arrange it so that some unknowing bystander saves the person and earns a wish you can then steal, but that's just as terrible and risky."

"Ah, got you." He nodded sagely. "But I'm not gonna complain about a free wish when I was about to pay megabucks for one. It doesn't matter how much money you got—there's nothing quite like a freebie."

She should've figured out who that rich voice belonged to long before he took off his sunglasses. He had a unique, gravelly tone that filtered into his music. At least, that seemed the case for the songs she'd absently listened to on the radio. His voice matched his tall, broad stature, though his face was prettier than she'd expect from someone with such a husky, almost weathered tone. She'd assumed it was all makeup and Photoshop, but he really did look like his magazine covers, with flawless, dark skin and cheekbones so high she could imagine tiny skiers slaloming down to his defined jaw. His plump lips had a natural sheen, and his eyebrows didn't have a single strand out of place. Based on the photos she'd seen in Grace's magazines, he had close-cropped hair underneath his hood, and the kind of forehead used in Botox promos, but he was keeping all of that under wraps for now.

"You definitely got lucky." Her eyes turned up as a warm raindrop landed on her nose.

He smiled proudly. "So did you, by meeting me. You'd have a bullet through you if you hadn't."

"Good point." Really, the near-death experience should've turned her into a crying mess, but she felt restless instead, life buzzing through her veins.

"Hey, that reminds me," he continued. "I swear I saw at least two bullets ping off that big dude who did all the talking. What's the deal there, huh? He bulletproof or something?"

Nadia kept walking, head down. "Yep, a lot of guys like that are. I'd say it's the most common wish for people who make their living like that." She pretended to pull a trigger. She'd heard incredible tales of comical shootouts, where the bullets bounced off everybody and transformed wherever they were fighting into a cheese grater.

"We should get out of the rain," she muttered as a few more splashes spat down from the swollen clouds that had charged in overhead.

Those few splashes turned into a deluge. Throwing her satchel over her head in a makeshift umbrella, she took off at a faster clip and jogged along the sandy network of paths to the cemetery exit, putting Miles in soggy pursuit.

At the gates, Nadia slowed to a walk and dropped the satchel to her shoulder. She closed her eyes for a moment, letting the downpour slough away the stress and fear. The air carried that blood-metallic tang of ozone, and a growl of thunder bellyached in the distance. Without warning, her memory hit her with a gut punch: those lost days where she'd run around the garden when a summer storm came, Nick throwing an arm over her shoulder until they were soaked to the skin and her ribs ached from laughing. Returning to that life felt like an unattainable dream, given the omnipresent weight of the debt.

Her eyes snapped open. *Wait* . . . Her chance at freedom was right behind her, inside of Miles. What if this was the untracked, born-in-the-wild wish she'd been waiting for? If she could use it to clear the debt, there was no way Basha or Grace could argue. This would, in essence, be the very last wish on their tally—that is, if the wish was potent enough. And it was a wish he'd earned by saving *her* life, but she tried not to think too hard about that fact.

Miles came to a stop next to her, bending at the waist to catch his breath.

Sorry, Miles, but I need that wish. Her mind whirred as she scrambled for a way to delay his coming goodbye. Without a functional wishing box, stealing a wish would be nigh on impossible. But Miles had a wishing jar on him, though why anyone would want to sell their wish trap, she had no clue.

Like he had said, it was serendipity. All she needed to do was take his jar, coax a secret out of him, run off with the jar and the wish, and then this gigantic mess of a day would have a pleasant ending.

"You're fast," Miles said, panting.

She slipped on a nervous expression. "I think my adrenaline is still spiked. Didn't mean to run that fast."

"I wasn't *that* far behind," he protested. "I don't know about you, but once I get home, I need a drink and twelve hours of shut-eye to forget about all this. Are you going to be okay out h—"

She hugged herself around her middle and forced a shake into her body. It was only half an act. She *had* nearly died.

"Not to sound needy," Nadia said, "but I think I'm still feeling a little unsteady. Do you mind keeping me company for a few minutes until I can settle down?"

She didn't know if he was the type to abandon a woman in a rain-spattered cemetery entrance after they'd been shot at, but she figured she was putting on a decent damsel-in-distress display.

"Any other day, sure, but I should get going before somebody recognizes me," Miles replied, casting a wary look around. "You should get home and rest." His sunglasses came back up to his cheeks, rain tracing down the front of them in beads.

"Did you bring your own car?" Nadia asked, hoping for at least a little luck.

He snapped his fingers. "Damn it." A headshake accented his sudden frustration. "That Black Hat guy drove me down here. My fans know my ride, so there was less chance of being spotted if he took the wheel. Now he's gone. I didn't even think about that, to be honest."

"Then we can help each other. I'll trade you a ride for a little company." Nadia shuddered at the unintentional innuendo. "I mean, can I drop you off somewhere?"

Miles answered with a wave toward the parking lot. She led him to her Chevy, jittering with anticipation as he walked around to the passenger side.

He prodded up his sunglasses—which were probably too smeared with rain to see anything other than vague shapes—as he eyed the car. "Nice. Not my usual style, but it's cool." He opened the door and got in as Nadia slid into the driver's seat.

"Can I ask you something?" she said, twisting around and putting her broken wishing box onto the backseat.

He leaned casually on the narrow doorsill. "Sure you can."

"Are you Miles Hunter? I wasn't sure, with the shades and the hoodie, but you look a lot like him."

His body language contracted like a tortoise, his head sinking farther into his hood. "I've just got one of those faces. Everybody thinks I look like somebody they know."

"Perhaps. But you mentioned having fans, which kind of gave it away." Nadia tried to make herself look as nonthreatening as possible by shuffling as far back against her door as the vinyl and metal would let her. "I'm a big fan, but I'm not one of those unhinged ones who's going to keep you in my basement or anything. Your Achilles tendons are safe!" She laughed, but it came off way creepier than intended.

He slowly reached for the door handle. "Maybe I'll just take a cab. No need for you to go out of your way."

"Sorry, I'm a bit nervous," she blurted out. The counselor in her recognized it as a Freudian truth. "This might come as a surprise, but I don't play chauffeur to too many famous musicians, so that all came out wrong."

He gave a half-hearted hum.

She switched tactics, realizing she'd put him on edge. "To tell you the truth, I'm not that big of a fan. I don't know why I said that. It's just that I know the artist who made the painting for your last show. She's the die-hard groupie, and she was horrified that I'd never heard any of your music. She introduced me to it recently, but . . . Well, you're not how I expected you'd be."

He moved his hand away from the handle. "How do you mean?"

"I didn't think someone like you would put their life on the line to save someone like me," she replied quietly. "I guess you can't judge a rock star by their album sleeve, right?"

"I like that one. Though I prefer to be called a musician, to be honest." The ghost of a smile crept onto his lips. "You're pretty sharp, Clover Eyes."

"Oh, it's Rebecca. Clover Eyes is just a nickname. Obviously." Maybe a real name would soften him up, even if it wasn't actually *her* real name. "Listen, if you don't have a ridiculously packed schedule, would you let me buy you dinner? A thank-you for saving my life, and to congratulate you on your new wish. It's not often you get one after you've lost one, so we should give it due respect."

He perked up at the mention of food. "I could do dinner." He paused, one perfect eyebrow boomeranging upward. "But I'm not sure it's cool to grab a bite with a wish hunter, in my condition. Who's to say you won't try to take this wish, huh?"

She put up her palms. "I couldn't, even if I wanted to. My wishing box is cracked in half. I'm decommissioned. Powered down. Hands tied. A kitty with no claws." She dropped her chin to her chest in case her eyes gave her away, trying not to cringe at how much she was over-selling it.

She peeked up through her eyelashes to find Miles's body language relaxing.

He settled back into his seat. "I'm already in your car, and I'm hungry as hell." He tapped his fingers on the slim sill, apparently content again. "Might as well take the edge off this evening. I'm thinking spicy food. What about you? It totally chills me out. Something to do with Scoville scales and endorphins."

"I can't promise endorphins, but how about Mexican?" Nadia resisted the urge to grin.

He tipped his head in a half nod. "Sure, that works, as long as it's legit. I can't stand these places that claim to be the real deal, then all their food is about as spicy as mayonnaise."

"I know the perfect place," Nadia assured him. "And the lighting's pretty dark, so you won't have to worry about being seen." Though she hoped he'd take off his stupid sunglasses.

He shrugged. "I'll save my review for after we've eaten."

She pulled out of the parking lot. Glancing at the dashboard clock, she figured she had about an hour to take his jar and come up with a way of prizing out his most precious secret. Difficult? For sure. Impossible? Not with so much hanging in the balance.

Chapter Seven

Spanish guitar floated through the crowded hole-in-the-wall Mexican restaurant not far from Bonaventure Cemetery. Miles had his eyes closed, his fingers drumming against the slightly sticky table to the rhythm of the mesmerizing tremolo. Nadia watched him intently, though she didn't have music on her mind. He had that wishing jar on him—and a wish inside him that had the power to change her life.

"That's a guitarist's Everest right there," Miles said. "And 'Memories of the Alhambra' is the summit. You play that, you can play anything. It sounds like two guitars, right? But it's just the one. You have to almost . . . ripple your fingers to get that trembling effect." He tried to demonstrate, but he just looked like he was scratching the chin of a particularly small kitten.

"Have you managed to peak that figurative mountain?" Nadia asked.

His eyes opened. "I wish."

"Do you?" She nodded toward his chest.

"Oh, man, I'd love to spend a wish to bag that skill, but this puppy feels like it's for something else. Something bigger. This is a full-orchestra wish, not a jazz-quartet-in-a-smoky-dive-bar kind of wish."

He patted his damp T-shirt. His soaked hoodie was drying on the radiator beside the nook table they'd managed to snag. As for Nadia, she was enduring the chilly, wholly unpleasant feeling of wet fabric on skin, since she had only a camisole underneath. She kept her arms crossed.

"Is that Miles Hunter?"

Nadia heard the not-so-discreet whisper from somewhere across the throng of diners. He'd already signed three autographs and posed for even more selfies since they'd sat down.

"What are you thinking of spending it on?" she pried. "If it's not to get rolling fingers, or whatever you just said."

She wanted to make sure his idea wasn't something altruistic. If he said anything in the ballpark of what Angela Rhodes had shared she'd do with a hypothetical wish, then Nadia might have to let him off the hook. As much as she wanted the wish to get rid of the debt, she was already feeling a little guilty about preparing to steal it. Especially considering that the life he'd saved to earn it was her own, as her conscience unhelpfully kept reminding her.

Miles hummed a tune that clashed with the restaurant's playlist —"Jukebox Hero," if she wasn't mistaken, though music wasn't really her forte. That had been Nick's domain.

"I'm still deciding," Miles said at last as the server came up, likely to ask if they were ready to order. She walked away again before Nadia could stop her. Had his response been for the waitress's benefit, or was it an answer to Nadia's question?

"I'll probably settle on how to word my wish later," he said, looking at her. "I need to get all mellowed out, maybe in the tub, with a Jo Malone candle to blow out when I say those magic words and make great things happen." Miles did a little shuffle dance in his chair. "Ooh, that made me feel all tingly just thinking about it!"

As soon as he puffed out the flame of his fancy candle, the wish would be gone forever in its pliable, unused form. Nadia couldn't let him get that far. She had to take the wish right now while she had him in front of her. And that meant turning this dinner conversation into a subtle interrogation.

"So, this must be your second wish?" Nadia asked, sipping her tamarind-flavored bottle of Jarritos.

"Nah, this is lucky number three," he said. "What'd you spend *your* wishes on?"

The question threw her a little. "Oh, I actually haven't used any wishes. Yet, anyway. I'm waiting for the right opportunity to come along."

He leaned forward, chuckling. "It's wild that I can finally talk to somebody about this other than my parents. Anybody else would think I was into some Keith Richards shit and needed to lay off." There was a momentary pause as he seemed to realize how that could sound to a stranger. "Just so you know," he added, "not all musicians are into that. I prefer to treat my body like a temple these days."

"Hence the bubble baths, right?" Nadia flashed him a grin to let him know she was only teasing.

"They're good for circulation. Dry brushing too. It'll change your life." He craned his neck to scan the restaurant. "Where's the server when you need them? I'm starving. They're losing a star for this."

"Actually, she came over, but I think she was a bit nervous because you're . . . you. She probably didn't want to interrupt while you were in your Spanish guitar zone," Nadia told him, before he got trigger-happy with his Yelp account. "You're like the next Johnny Mercer, maybe better. People can get intimidated. I'm sure she'll be back in a minute."

The flattery seemed to please him. He sat up straighter in his seat. "I'd rather be compared to Hendrix or B. B. King, but everyone jumps to Mercer when I'm home. But I'll never beat him in the Savannah hall of fame, that's for sure, considering the obvious." He pointed to himself. "I'll have to wait until all the old money and their offspring die out before they put a Black man above a white guy."

It was the first time she'd seen a crack in his bravado. He had a smile on his face, but it was a bitter one. Savannah had its muddied history, same as all places, but in a city that celebrated being Georgia's oldest and still breathed bygone days with its horse-drawn carriages, it wasn't a surprise that some people refused to budge into the modern day.

"Change is coming, and the old money is hanging on by a thread," Nadia replied, fully realizing the irony of her statement.

Her family's hardships were nowhere near comparable to what Miles's family must've experienced, but she didn't count herself among the Savannah elite. She'd never been to a cotillion or been a member of a country club, and the Kaminskis rarely found themselves on any gilded guest lists. As far as high society was concerned, they were still the Poles who'd moved in next door, fresh off the boat, despite being here for three generations.

"I'm writing that down." Miles took out his phone and tapped rapidly. "Don't sue me if you hear it in a song."

She smiled. No, she had a different repayment in mind.

The food came twenty minutes of music talk later. Nadia figured that an appetizer of letting him ramble about his passions was the best way to dive into the entrée of his personal life and, hopefully, his most guarded secret. Food was supposed to be the way to a man's heart, after all.

"It's kind of odd that your parents know all this wishing stuff." Nadia tried to elegantly eat her taco, but there was no such method. "Are they 'in the biz,' as you musicians would say?"

"We never say that," Miles said, and her ego soundly deflated. He dabbed the corner of his mouth with a napkin, then continued. "It's more of, like, a family tradition. Each descendant gets a wish when they turn eighteen, and it's gifted in a wishing jar." He bit into a tamale and huffed through the heat.

Nadia's jaw dropped. "*Everyone* gets one?" The Hunter family must've had an incredible cache of wishes stowed away somewhere.

He nodded. "Man, it seems like forever ago since I got mine. I swear time speeds up in your twenties. One minute, you're flashing your ID around because you can legally drink, and the next minute, the big three-oh is slapping you in the face."

Nadia had assumed Miles was still in his twenties. Had one of his wishes been to keep his youthful, rock star good looks? She hoped not.

"Beauty" wishes had a nasty habit of going awry. Some serious *Death Becomes Her* consequences.

"Are the wishing jars unique to everyone in your family, or are they all the same?" She needed him to bring out that jar while thinking it was his idea. "You know, heirloom-type thingies."

He gulped down ice water. "You know what? I don't know. I never thought to ask. Only child over here, so I didn't have anyone to compare jars with." He resumed his tentative nibbling of his tamale. "How about you? You got any siblings?"

Nadia shifted in her chair. "I've got an older sister, but my mom is more like a sibling, or the troublemaking aunt who swings by every Christmas to wreak havoc after a few drinks."

"You don't get along with your mom? Or is it that you don't see her often?" He seemed genuinely interested, and she figured a little give-and-take, emotionally speaking, might make him more inclined to spill secrets.

"Neither. I see her every day, and we're . . . mostly close, but my grandma is more like the mom figure," Nadia explained. "It suits them —both of them—better that way."

Miles nodded. "Are all your family wish hunters too? Like the Osmonds or the Jacksons of the wishing world?"

"My grandma is pretty much retired, my mom takes a casual approach to it, and my sister . . . Well, she's doing her own thing these days." Nadia drew a sad face into the condensation on the Jarritos bottle as she spoke. If she told him that her sister was Savannah's Wishmaster, it would only invite unwelcome questions. "But we've been wish hunters for generations, all the way back to the motherland."

He canted his head. "And that's where?"

"Poland."

He gave a low whistle. "Czesław Niemen! One of the best rock balladeers to come out of the twentieth century. He made singing in your own language cool, long before K-pop came along. Hell of a voice. Smooth as butter."

"I can't say I've heard of him," Nadia admitted, suddenly feeling unpatriotic.

"You should check him out. He's dead now, but like so many greats, his legacy lives on." Miles turned wistful, as though imagining what his own legacy might be. "Do you like the family line of work, then? Or are you like a third-generation kid who just has to take up the business?"

Nadia chuckled tightly. "The latter." It was the first time she'd openly admitted to someone other than Nick that she didn't like her family's vocation.

"Why keep doing it? If your big sis is doing her own thing, like you said, then why don't you?" Miles said it so casually that she envied his naïveté. "I mean, wish hunting must be the equivalent of busking when you can't sing. It doesn't pay well, and it scoops out another piece of your dignity every time you do it."

Nadia eyed him. "It's more of a debt I have to pay."

"Lemme guess, you screwed up something massive with the Wishmaster?" Miles finished the last of his now-cooled tamales. Maybe he knew a few things about the wishing world after all.

"Not exactly. I nearly died in a car accident, and my family used a super potent wish to save my life. One that cost them a hefty amount," Nadia said. "Plus, my family would disown me if I abandoned the business. And Polish grandmas can be terrifying when you go against the status quo. I'd rather face a flesh-eating, gut-liquefying, fire-breathing demon than get on the wrong side of my grandma."

"That's rough," he replied. "Makes me feel pretty happy to have been born to my parents."

Trying to shake off the fresh flush of annoyance, she focused on the job at hand. "Did they ever teach you how to steal wishes? Your folks, I mean. It must be in your history somewhere, if you all get wishes when you turn eighteen."

"I'm sure I've got some wish-hunting ancestors, but the knowledge got lost at some point down the line. We were left with the instruments, but they had the sheet music." He hesitated, fingers poised over his taquitos. "Would you be up for sharing trade secrets?"

She narrowed her eyes, catching a subtle, darker shift in his expression. "How do you think it works?"

"Maybe I've had one too many brain cells jiggled out of place by not wearing in-ears, but I always figured it'd be some type of blood ritual. Like, you prick the victim's finger or something, put their blood inside a wishing jar, and—*bam!*—you get their wish."

She feigned shock and nodded eagerly. He was all the way on the wrong side of the fence with his guess, but Nadia got the feeling he hated being wrong, and that was about to work perfectly to her advantage.

"If that was a guess," she said, "then you need to go put numbers on the lottery right now because you got it in one. Why else do you think people get so weirded out about wish hunting? Blood freaks folks out, but you get used to it once you've done it a few times. And it's only a bead or two at most, unless you're slippery with the needle."

Miles puffed out his chest, visibly thrilled he'd guessed "correctly." "Mom and I figured it out years ago, after I showed her my wishing jar. We saw this little dark stain at the bottom. I mean, I'm no forensic genius, but blood's pretty obvious, even when it's hella crusty and old. We agreed that wishes were probably collected by taking a bit of the life juice. A Sleeping Beauty deal, without the thorns and the coma."

"Maybe your mom somehow remembered it subconsciously," Nadia said.

His brow furrowed. "I dunno. She definitely didn't know for sure that was how it was done because her mom and grandma never said, but it seemed believable enough." His shoulders slumped. "Wish I could tell her we had it right."

"Is she not around anymore?"

Nadia had assumed his parents would still be living in Savannah, since this was his hometown. But maybe she was just projecting her own family's stubbornness onto his.

Miles smiled sadly and pointed a finger upward.

"Ah . . . I'm so sorry," she said, looking down at her hands.

He shrugged. "She passed a couple years back. Cancer. It's why I quit touring for a while. Kinda dropped out, you know? My world lost its rhythm when I lost my mom. Let me tell you, 'comebacks' suck at the best of times, but after that? Shit, I'm surprised *anybody* bought the last album. *Rolling Stone* called it 'twelve tracks of unrelenting misery, appropriate only for listeners with a residual emo allegiance.' That's why they tell you to never read the reviews." He scratched his sharp jaw. "I would've wished the cancer away if I could've, but I couldn't get my hands on a wish in time. Seemed to be some kind of chaos with your people back then."

If it was when Nadia suspected, she could guess the date his mom got sick. After Adrian had fallen—and ran off to who knew where—there'd been a brief power vacuum. It hadn't quite been a one-horse race, despite Kaleena being the one to overthrow Adrian. Other groups had muscled in from all over the region, gunning to take the top spot in Savannah for themselves. But in the end, there was no doubt who'd come out on top. The lucky would-be Wishmasters scurried away with their tails between their legs back to wherever they came from—and the unlucky ones wound up feeding the fish in the Savannah River. With all the turmoil at the top, it had been nearly impossible to buy a wish then, since they were getting used up in the turf war faster than they could be stolen.

"I'm not sure it would've helped, even if you had," Nadia replied awkwardly. "Healing wishes often don't play out the way you want, since wishes can't affect other people directly. With my accident, my grandma and mom couldn't wish for me to be healed, so they had to wish for an organ replacement. That's the only reason I survived."

He smiled stiffly. "I figured as much. Everything has to be in sync, right? If I'd wished for a way to save her, it would've come out all jumbled and wrong. All Monkey's Paw–like, right?"

She nodded. "Speaking of moms . . ." Nadia wanted to push the conversation away from thoughts of lost loved ones. "Mine is going to murder me for breaking the wishing box. It was an heirloom, which is why I asked if all your family jars are the same." She almost cringed at the clunky segue. "Honestly, even though I've been in this business my whole life, I never knew they came in forms other than boxes." It was a lie, but one she hoped he'd buy.

He put his hands into his kangaroo pouch. "Do you want to see it? Since we're trading knowledge and all." He leaned forward, as if to hide what he was carrying. "I only brought it along because that Black Hat kid said it might get me some money back. Wish traps don't come cheap, seems like."

Nadia had to resist bouncing in her seat. All this tit-for-tat talk was about to gain her a bunch of tat, if that was polite to say.

"I told him yeah because it's not like I've got any use for the thing anymore," Miles continued. "I don't capture wishes, and I've got zero interest in being a thief like you and Black Hat. I prefer to steal hearts onstage."

Don't roll your eyes, don't roll your eyes, don't roll your eyes. She couldn't believe anyone would actually say that out loud and not want the ground to swallow them up in embarrassment.

He produced the object she'd been seeking for the entire conversation. It looked like the love child of a small urn and a whimsical gift shop honeypot. The wooden jar was pale and glossy, with vines coiling across the curvaceous shape where they'd been burned into the wood. Like all wish traps, it was certainly made from the Wishing Tree itself, although Nadia wondered how the Tree yielded so many wooden contraptions without ending up in bits. Their ancestors must've known, but the Wishing Tree was said to have hidden itself away centuries ago, and thus no more wish traps could be created. She really wasn't looking forward to telling Basha what had happened to their priceless wishing box.

"Can I take a closer look?" Nadia asked, swallowing her eagerness. "I know a thing or two about wish trap value. I also know Black Hat. He probably tried to rip you off."

Miles sniffed. "I knew he was shady as soon as I saw him. Although, in fairness, when I bought my second wish, that went off without a hitch."

He handed the jar to her as if it were a tourist knickknack and not an irreplicable museum-quality object.

Nadia opened the hinged lid and felt the slight suck of a rubberlike seal around the rim. She peered inside. "I see what you mean about the little stain."

It had smudged against the bottom of the vessel, but she knew it wasn't blood—it was the burn mark of a death wish. Usually, they appeared when someone tried to take the wish of a dead person, in that strange limbo before all the lights went out in the brain. When someone died, their wishes evaporated—both used and unused—but she'd heard a myth that there was a specific second when a wish could be taken with the deceased's last breath, no heart secret or exact wish wording required. The trouble was that those wishes apparently went bad 99 percent of the time, since they hadn't been timed right. As for the 1 percent, the secretive art of attaining the death wish had long been forgotten.

"Have you ever told anyone about your wishes? Not just that you have them, but what wish you actually made when you blew out those candles?" she asked, still examining the jar. It had a good energy about it, though it lacked some of the life experience of her broken wishing box.

Miles looked uncomfortable. "Can't say I've ever mentioned either."

Most wishers knew to *never* tell someone what wishes they'd made —particularly not with the exact wording—in case hope stealers decided they wanted to destroy that used wish or take it for themselves. That superstition had leaked into the wider world, as many wishing things did, with the idea that a wish wouldn't come true if you told it to anyone. Nadia had no interest in stealing used wishes, but she understood the appeal; some wishes were more potent than others, and stealing the exact wish meant you'd already know how it would manifest.

But Nadia was willing to gamble that Miles didn't know about hope stealers. After all, he hadn't known all the rules around saving lives, he didn't know how to steal wishes, and he didn't seem that au fait with the black market.

"When did you make your wishes?" Nadia pressed. A powerful enough heart secret from Miles would activate the wishing jar, allowing her to extract and trap the wish sitting so temptingly inside him. Her ticket to true freedom from the debt.

He flicked a grain of salt across the table. "One when I was eighteen, and the other one was . . . a while after."

"I guess it's hard to wait to make a wish when you're eighteen and there are so many things you want." She cradled the jar in her palms, praying she'd feel that telltale warmth when Miles spewed a secret that was strong enough. The secrets he was sharing so far hadn't been emotionally weighty or specific enough, unless she'd missed her chance when he'd spoken of his mother's cancer and his inability to wish her disease away.

Miles cracked his neck. "I'm not a very patient person. Mom was. She saved her wish for later in life, but I just dove right in."

"What did you ask for, that first time? Was it to always look flawless?"

Flattery had worked before, so might as well give it another go. Instead, he stared at her, flexing and unflexing his knuckles as though deeply unsettled. Or maybe he had early onset arthritis from shredding his guitar one too many times.

"What's with the third degree?" he muttered, his expression shifting toward suspicious—not all the way there yet, but turning into the neighborhood.

She laughed as brightly as she could. "Ah, sorry, occupational hazard."

"Huh?"

"When I'm not working my 'nighttime job,' I'm a marriage counselor. It was my way of rebelling—by getting a real job," she explained, cursing herself for admitting too much private information. Reckless and dangerous. If she had a wish of her own, she might have lost it by being so open. "I tend to accidentally interrogate people about their personal lives. I can't help it. When I start saying 'And how does that make you feel?' I give you my permission to throw that glass of water at me."

Thankfully, that small glimpse into her everyday life seemed to relax him a little. He stopped flexing his knuckles and instead steepled them on the table.

Miles smiled and nodded. "Therapy is so important these days. I'm not ashamed to admit I've had a session or two. Go ahead, ask what you like. Just as long as you're not going to bill me five hundred bucks at the end of this."

Nadia forced a grin. "I wouldn't be picking the cheapest thing on the menu if I charged that much."

"To tell you the truth," he went on, his voice taking on that hesitant, embarrassing ailment of a doctor's office tone, "my second wish was plain stupid."

Nadia clicked her tongue. "You didn't wish you could fly, did you? That just gets you a bunch of air miles, or a spammed inbox full of airline deals."

"No . . . I wished I could find what I was looking for," he replied sheepishly. "I never lose my keys anymore, but the thing is, finding what you're looking for ain't the same thing as knowing what you want. You get me?"

Nadia smiled as the jar warmed in her hands. She closed the lid with a practiced nonchalance, careful to maintain eye contact with Miles so he'd keep his focus on her and not her sleight of hand.

"The Wishing Tree got it twisted," she said. "Happens to the best of us." Or so she'd heard.

"Man, it felt good to get that out in the open." He sat back, unleashing a world-weary sigh.

"I totally get what you mean. You can *want* to find a million bucks, but that would only take you to a bank. The hard work has to come from you," she said, her insides flip-flopping like a tangled fish. Thanks to his shared secret about his second wish, his unspent third wish was now heating the jar in her hands. Now all she had to do was find a way to leave the restaurant without arousing his suspicion.

Miles nodded. "Exactly. I regret making that wish, although it comes in handy when I'm in a rush and nothing is where I left it, or the set list has vanished. But it also led me to the place where I'd find wish number three —saving your life." He grinned boyishly at her, and Nadia almost felt bad.

Almost.

Warm jar in hand, she dipped frantically into her satchel and took out her phone, as if it were buzzing. She pretended to slide an Answer icon and put the phone to her ear. "Mom? Mom, slow down. Yeah . . . yeah, I hear you. I told you where I was." She paused for effect. "You heard about that? Look, I'm on my way home. I'm fine, I didn't get hurt . . . Just take my word for it! I'm *fine*, Mom, just—"

She took the phone from her ear and stared at it, putting on her best panicked face.

"I'm so sorry, but you'd just have to know my mom. She's a wreck. I know I said I'd buy, but can you take care of the check?" Nadia skidded a twenty across the table and bolted.

She'd barely gone five paces when he said, "Hey, the tickle is gone . . ."

Nadia didn't look back. She heaved forward, sprinting through the gauntlet of the crammed restaurant, weaving in and out of the tables.

His voice bellowed across the room. "Hold up! Give it back!" The man had some pipes on him, that was for sure.

She shot out the door and raced across the parking lot to her Chevy. After fumbling for her keys, she threw open the driver door she'd purposefully left unlocked for her fast getaway and ducked into the seat, just as Miles burst out of the restaurant. Unfortunately for him, a gaggle of fans who'd been waiting outside swarmed him like flies on crap, brandishing phones at him for selfies. Unless he wanted to land himself in a lawsuit by shoving them out of the way, it would take him some time to get past them.

Fully appreciating her head start, she peeled out of the parking lot, leaving him with the bill *and* without a wish. Not to mention a lack of transportation. He'd have to call his chauffeur to save the day, or attempt a zombie apocalypse–style escape with those screaming girls trailing him back into town.

"Holy crap, holy crap, holy crap!" Nadia shrieked as she sped away, hardly able to believe she'd done it. The jar rested between her thighs, nice and toasty from the wish she'd thieved.

Chapter Eight

The adrenaline was finally wearing off—partly because Nadia had used up so much during the cemetery incident, and partly because she'd had enough time behind the wheel to put distance between her and the restaurant. She'd gotten away with it.

As if in celebration, Nadia's phone rang. She tipped the phone out of her bag. "Mom" flashed on the screen. After juggling the steering wheel and setting the phone in the cupholder, she swiped the Answer icon and put it on speaker.

"I'm driving, so you might not be able to hear me." Nadia's voice fought the tick of the rough engine as she answered. "But don't worry, I've—" She was about to tell her mom what she planned to do, only to remember that the Wishmaster might have their phones tapped. Maybe it would be better to just make the wish privately and save them all from the debt before anyone could talk her out of it.

Fortunately, Grace was already speaking. "Black Hat called and told me what happened at Bonaventure. Are you all right? I heard you lost the wish, but that's not important right now. We'll get another one, and everything will be fine. He said you were *probably* all right, but I need to hear it for myself. I almost had a heart attack when he said you got shot at."

"I'm fine," Nadia replied, touched to hear such concern from her usually self-absorbed mother.

"Where are you?" Grace's voice brimmed with worry.

Nadia checked the nearest street sign as it blasted by. "About ten minutes away, depending on traffic."

Everything in Savannah depended on traffic, trolleys, carriages, and the couldn't-care-less attitude of the respective drivers. As long as she didn't get stuck going around the squares, where so many fences and posts had been dinged over the years by overenthusiastic cars, she'd make good time.

"Drive safe, but try to get here as fast as you can." Grace sounded more unsettled with each passing word. "Your babcia isn't doing well, sweetheart. I put the phone on speaker like an idiot when Black Hat called, and when she heard what happened to you . . . well, she took a turn. I'm arguing with her right now, trying to get her to go to the hospital. She doesn't want to, since . . . you know."

Nadia did know. Given that her grandmother needed to be in the house to protect it and be protected by it, she always kicked up a stink at the merest suggestion of having to leave, since it left their home vulnerable to attack. Plus, Basha always claimed she was fine, even that time her ankle had bent ninety degrees, thanks to her other wish to never feel pain—a wish she had made, she'd told Nadia once, in the wake of a difficult childhood. That inability to feel physical pain made her getting sick all the more dangerous. Right now, Basha was probably christening the toilet bowl with her dinner.

"Will she go to the hospital when I get there, do you think?" Nadia asked.

Grace said nothing for a moment, then lowered her voice as if Basha might be listening. "You know she can be a mule sometimes. It's like wrangling a toddler to the dentist."

"Well, I'm coming straight there either way," Nadia confirmed, chancing a yellow light ahead. "I love you, Mom."

Maybe it was Miles's story, or maybe it was thinking about her grandmother being unwell, but she needed to let her mother know that last part.

"Me too," Grace replied.

As Nadia hung up, she decided right then and there that she couldn't risk telling her mother the truth, even if they were the only ones in the room. With how much more cautious Grace and Basha had become, they would undoubtedly try to dissuade her.

No, she had to take matters into her own hands if she ever wanted to clear the debt before Nick's resurrection deadline. She caressed the wishing jar in her lap. It would seem suspicious if she walked into the house with an obvious new lump in her satchel. Better that she absorb the wish into her body now and leave the wish trap in the car.

She pulled off the side of the road and coasted to a stop on a nameless side street. Taking a deep breath, she flipped open the jar and put her hand inside. The warm, tingly, almost liquid-feeling wish tickled her skin as it slithered into her palm. She took her hand out—and pressed it to her heart.

The reaction was immediate and intense.

"*Whoa*." Nadia tried to focus on breathing, but her heart pounded like her Chevy's engine at full throttle. "It's mine! It's friggin' mine!"

She cackled like a witch. She'd warned Miles about wishing to fly, but now she felt like she could actually sprout wings and soar up into the evening sky.

In the year since Nick's death, nothing—not her body, her soul—had felt so light. An overwhelming sensation of joy blossomed in her mind, sending her memories whizzing back to the early hours of a Saturday morning with him, tangled in the sheets and around each other. Their bodies, their breath, their ecstasy had never been more perfectly in sync than on that morning, while the sound of sultry jazz had floated in through the open windows like they were part of the music.

Her skin tingled with the remembered touch of his lips and fingertips, her cheeks flushing with the heat that no humid summer could replicate—the bedroom glow that made her feel feverish in the most delicious way.

"I feel you, Nick," she murmured, throwing the car in gear and hammering her foot down. Two quick turns later and she was barreling toward home. "You were right there, in our bed, and everything was perfect. After I make this wish, I'm going to get you back."

Now, all she needed was a candle and a match. It would be easiest to spend this wish before she got home, since Basha and Grace would be able to see the wish on her—not literally, but in every flush of joy in Nadia's cheeks, in the warmth of her glow. And if that wasn't enough, the telltale warmth of the compass coin in her mom's possession would tell Grace there was an unused wish under their roof. She had to do it now.

At the first set of traffic lights, she leaned over to check the glove box: old candy wrappers, a service manual, a flashlight, and an ancient bottle of Coke that appeared to be growing its own ecosystem. But no candle.

Basha must've done one of her random checks and removed the emergency candle Nadia could've sworn she'd put in there. Her mom and grandma liked to police her on the sly, which never failed to cause friction. She wasn't a child. It was another clear reminder of why she wanted to leave Savannah with Nick—maybe, with some distance, she wouldn't feel the urge to strangle her family members so often.

She swore under her breath, debating whether or not to run into a store for matches and birthday candles. On one hand, if she walked into the house with the wish, she was more likely to get found out. On the other hand, Nadia wasn't a heartless monster who didn't stop to see if her grandmother was on death's door. Plus, her paranoid brain kept delivering nightmare scenarios where Miles—or a rogue wish hunter—tried to gun for the wish while she was out in public. At least at the house, she'd be protected from any surprise attacks.

And she needed to get her head on straight. How had Miles phrased it? Everything had to be in sync, or it'd come out jumbled and wrong. Maybe with a musical metaphor that she was forgetting. She just needed to slow her ass down and have a long, hard think about how she should word her wish. This could be her only shot. She wouldn't mess it up by rushing.

The Wishing Tree vetoed any wishes directly related to gaining more wishes, which extended to wishing that you could sense unused wishes without a compass coin or steal them without a wish trap. That was a no-brainer that only rookies tried to swing.

However, the number one principle that all knowledgeable wishers understood was that wishes could only impact others indirectly, which was why you couldn't wish for all wars to end, or for your sick loved one to be magically cured, or for a particular person to fall in love with you. But you *could* wish to have incredible negotiation skills, or to have more knowledge than anyone else about lung cancer, or to be so charming that it would inspire people to swoon at your feet. All fair game. Wishes had to affect *personal* skills or circumstances—but it was up to the wisher to bring their desires to fruition.

Trying to brainstorm the best wish wording while weaving through traffic—and with her heart pounding—threatened to be a recipe for disaster. She needed time and space to think without the initial wish rush putting everything on fast-forward.

"Take deep breaths," she instructed, her voice like a self-help tape. "Focus on the things you can control. Picture the outcome you want, and the steps from where you are now to that end point. Ugh, I'll be telling myself to imagine a wave crashing on the rocks next."

The breathing helped. Concentrating on the inhale and the exhale, and the familiarity of the road ahead, she sensed the wish rush ebbing, allowing her mind to clear a bit.

She chewed on her lower lip as she tried to think of the best way to phrase her wish, building a pros and cons list in her head for possible outcomes. It was an old habit. The brainstorming began as a game that she used to play with Kaleena when they were small, when the wishes were more innocent. Now, like silly rhymes about how to remember the planets and how Henry VIII's six wives had died, that child's play had followed Nadia into adulthood.

She hung a right, bringing her onto the home stretch, and huffed out a strained breath. She'd have to be quick about it. Get in the house, make sure Basha was okay, race upstairs, find a candle and a match, then brainstorm a wish that would hopefully work.

Straightforward in theory, but in the world of wishes, the floor was lava and everything was guarded by an intricate web of laser beams.

$\backsim$

Nadia hurtled through the front door, expecting to find a dramatic scene to rival any soap opera. Instead, her mother was sitting in the den to the side of the kitchen, sipping on a frosted margarita as though she were on her first day of vacation.

"Did I miss the memo to stand down?" Nadia asked.

She hung back against the partition wall, keeping a safe distance in case Grace had the compass coin on her. One touch of that warm wooden surface and her mother would sense the unused wish inside Nadia.

Grace looked up with a casual shrug. "Your babcia insists she's feeling much better, after I told her you were okay. She stopped shaking and went up to her room, where I'm sure she's making some tea to calm her nerves."

Thinking of all the stores she could've stopped at to buy a candle and matches, Nadia bit the inside of her cheek to keep herself from saying something she'd regret.

"Are you sure, or is she just putting on a brave face?" Nadia cast a sly glance at the kitchen counter, but the compass coin wasn't there either.

Grace lounged back on the squashy sofa. "Do you think I'd be sitting down here, taking it easy, if I didn't know it was a false alarm?"

"Good point. Sorry." Nadia was being unnecessarily snippy, but in fairness, she *did* have a wishing debt to get rid of.

"Actually, I've got a bit of good news for you. It's why I'm celebrating." Grace fluffed back her wavy brown hair and jiggled the half-empty margarita glass at Nadia. "Black Hat says the wish still counts as number fifty, even though we didn't completely deliver it!"

Nadia frowned. "Did he sound like he was in a hospital when he called you?"

"Hmm? No, I don't think so. There wasn't any screaming or beeping. Though he did sound like he was talking through the worst stuffy nose of all time." Grace sipped her drink. "But think about how great that news is, Nadia! Why aren't you losing your mind right now? You look like you've been slapped with a pair of old panties."

Nadia forced a smile. "I'm just wondering what the catch is. I've never known Black Hat or the Wishmaster to be particularly benevolent."

"Always so cynical," Grace chided playfully, before patting the seat beside her. "Now, why don't you grab a drink, come on over here to your mama, and unload your traumatic tale so we can get around to the happy, smiling relief part."

Her mother hadn't mentioned the broken wishing box, so either she didn't know the full extent of the damage, or she was trying not to have her mood spoiled by doom and gloom after the win of keeping their tally at fifty. With so many more wishes to go, even that didn't feel like much of a victory to Nadia.

"I'm going to jump in the shower first, before my clothes decide to glue themselves to my skin thanks to all the rain and humidity," Nadia said with an awkward chuckle. "If they stuck a tiny AC unit to every gravestone in Bonaventure, that place would be heaven. But now that I think about it, it might be frowned upon to put fans on dead people . . ."

She knew she was rambling, but she couldn't stop. After she'd stepped through the house's invisible membrane, the giddy feeling of the wish in her chest had come back with a vengeance, turning her into a hyperactive mess.

Grace's eyes narrowed. "Do *you* need to go to the hospital? You're weirdly bouncy for someone who almost died."

"It's all the adrenaline," she said, wafting a hand through the air. "Makes the brain go haywire. My clients do this all the time after they've experienced trauma. One minute they're right down in a pit of despair. The next, they're climbing the walls, jumping around like they're kids again."

"Then you should definitely come and sit with me so some of your energy can rub off." Grace flashed a wink. "I might have a date tonight, and I could use a little extra pep to keep up."

Nadia pulled a face. "Well, I've got a date with the shower, because the only thing that'll rub off on you is this stench." She gave her pits a hard sniff to prove the point and escaped upstairs.

She crept along the hallway and paused outside Basha's door, which was slightly ajar. Through the narrow gap, Nadia could see Basha snoring softly in her antique rocking chair beside the tall windows on the far side of the room, facing the vista of a magnolia tree.

The last of the molten sunset snuck in through the opening in the heavy drapes made of blue velvet, and muted the jeweled tones of Basha's bedroom. In the daylight, it was a kaleidoscope of clashing colors, rich fabrics, and what Grace affectionately referred to as "a junkyard of useless crap." But to Nadia, it was a treasure trove of antiques and curios, accumulated from the days when her grandmother had dared to go outside for longer than a couple of minutes.

"Sleep well, and don't worry about me," Nadia whispered before darting across the hall to her plain but homey bedroom.

She closed the door behind her and bounded over her bed, then snatched up her laptop and a candle from her bedside table. The purple candle was supposed to smell of "Starlit Skies," but she had no idea what that meant. Space dust and the inside of an astronaut's suit, maybe? It had a subtle fruity scent with a hint of musk, and she never had to worry about forgetting to blow it out because Basha's second wish essentially made the house fireproof.

Nick used to scold her when she'd leave a candle burning, especially if he'd come home still wearing his uniform. "Do I need to show you the videos again? I swear, if you leave another 'One S'more with Feeling' burning, I'm banning you from the candle store. And then Mrs. Flaherty will go out of business, and it'll be sad times all around for everyone."

Nadia sat cross-legged on the floor beside her bedside table and opened her laptop. In this position, if anyone came in, she'd have a few extra seconds to skim the candle under the bed like a hockey puck and act like she was casually clacking away on her keyboard.

"Shit, I really am a teenager again," she muttered, setting the candle on the varnished floorboards in front of her as if she were at a very sad, very lonely birthday party.

For most people, blowing out candles was usually just a nice way to get some cake and a fleeting thrill. But the birthday candle tradition had started when wishing folk wanted to celebrate attaining a wish by sharing that happiness with their friends and family. After she made this wish, Nadia hoped she'd have more cause for celebration.

As she brought the head of the lighter to the candle wick and rolled her thumb over the sparking mechanism, her heart thudded in her chest so loud she almost feared Basha would hear. A meager wisp of smoke appeared. Undeterred, she rolled the metal wheel again and again, willing it to ignite.

At last, a flame appeared, and she hurried to touch it to the wick. It caught immediately, blooming into that elongated teardrop of glowing comfort.

"I wish I had an easier way to pay off my debt to the Wishmaster," she said aloud, her heart in her mouth.

It sounded promising. If she'd tried to wish the debt away in one go, it would be more likely to get bent out of shape by the Wishing Tree. This way, she wasn't asking for too much at once: assistance instead of a cure-all.

The flame flickered, but as she bent her head to blow it out, the candle snuffed itself out with an unsettling *whoosh*. No smoke, no residual scent, as if all the air had been sucked from the room. Puzzled, she moved her hand all around her, trying to feel for a draft.

"Did I do it?" She paused, but the wish rush still warmed her chest. "Guess not."

With determination, Nadia rolled the sparking mechanism and lit the wick a second time. She took a deep breath and repeated the wish, holding the air in her lungs until she was ready to blow the flame out. However, as she pursed her lips, the candle snuffed out again in that strange, smokeless snap. This time, it came with an added warning: a slight shock of pain in her chest, like static electricity.

She eyed the candle and pressed a hand to her heart. Maybe the wish wasn't potent enough because Miles had saved only *her* life, rather than evacuating a whole town before an earthquake or something. Perhaps the house itself could sense she was trying to go against Basha's edicts. Or maybe the Wishing Tree simply disliked the wish she was trying to make. But why? What was so off-limits about this particular wish? Was it because the Wishing Tree interpreted it as wishing for more wishes, like her mom had said?

A third try seemed like the quickest way to figure out the problem, though the flame extinguishing itself felt a lot like the equivalent of walking down a gloomy forest path littered with signs saying "GO BACK! DANGER AHEAD! NO, REALLY, TAKE ANOTHER STEP AT YOUR PERIL!"

Nadia rolled the mechanism again and waited for it to sputter into life before touching it to the wick. As it caught, she rattled a different variation of the wish off her tongue at lightning speed, hoping it might skirt the Wishing Tree "rules."

"I wish I had a shortcut to pay off my debt to the Wishmaster, where no one gets hurt," she said. After all, she wanted to resolve this family feud peaceably. Kaleena might've abandoned her and burdened her with this debt, but she was still Nadia's sister.

But just as Nadia moved to blow out the flame, a splintering pain forked through her entire body.

She hissed sharply through her teeth, wanting to scream, but aware that anything above a whimper would bring someone running. All she could do was hope the blinding pulse subsided. Through blurry eyes, she saw that the candle had extinguished itself.

"I guess you really didn't like that, huh?"

She needed to switch up the wording, since this was going down like a lead balloon.

Once the pain had ebbed, she rolled the sparking mechanism a fourth time—but nothing happened. She tried again, wondering if the Wishing Tree had the ability to screw with lighters as well as candles. Still nothing.

Frustrated, she held it to the light, then groaned. Out of fuel. Cursing under her breath, she hurled the lighter into the trash can.

She wasn't giving up. There were candles, matches, and lighters all over the house, which seemed a lot like mockery to her formerly wish-less state. The problem was, she could hardly retrieve a lighter without tipping her mother off that something was happening. Grace had already remarked on Nadia's mood, after all. Plus, her mother likely still had the compass coin. One false move and the opportunity would slip away—and Grace and Basha's surveillance would no doubt become even more oppressive.

A thought lit her mind like a camera flash. Basha kept matches in her bedside table, and she was fast asleep. Over the years, Nadia had seen her grandmother sleep through Fourth of July firework extravaganzas and Kaleena's emo phase that had zero volume control.

Nadia hurried back out into the hallway, pushed Basha's door open as slowly as she could, and slid through.

"Where did you go?" Basha mumbled in her sleep, the Polish words dulled by dreams. "I thought I knew where you were, but . . . and then the wasps came."

On the bedside table, an empty cup of tea with leaves crusted on the bottom explained why Basha had drifted off so quickly—part of her nightly ritual. Nadia crept the rest of the way to the bedside table and eked open the drawer. She had just opened the drawer wide enough to slot her hand inside when a shrill scream from downstairs echoed through the house.

For a second, Nadia's nerves unraveled. Then she reminded herself that the last time Grace had screamed like that, *The Bachelor*'s controversial final choice had been the root cause, and her heart slowed a bit. If her mom screamed again, *then* she'd start panicking.

"Is it Nazis? Is it Resistance?" Basha awoke with a start, still speaking her mother tongue.

Nadia closed the drawer as discreetly as she could and rushed over to her grandmother. The deceit struck a chord of guilt in her chest, even though she was doing this to benefit all three of them, not just herself.

"Nadia?" Basha's confusion faded. "What was that sound?"

"It's Mom," she replied. "She screamed. I was running past your door, on my way to check on her, when I heard you wake up."

Basha grabbed her cane and stuck out a hand. "Help me up. We go see what problem is. Is likely spider, but I deal with it. I do not mind spider, as long as is not too big."

Nadia helped Basha to her feet, and together they headed out to investigate.

"Mom? Mom, what's up?" Nadia called.

Grace stood at the foot of the staircase, in front of the window beside the front door. She was rigid with fear, eyes fixed on the front yard. Night had fallen, and the usual spotlight from the streetlamp outside was nowhere to be found, blanketing the garden in darkness.

Grace turned slowly, eyes wide. "I think someone was trying to look in through the window! They were just outside."

"The house won't let them in," Basha pointed out. "You think is Peeping Tom? Why? Surely all boys have seen what you have to offer." She snorted.

Grace ignored the gibe. "Maybe Croak has come back for another visit."

"What should we do?" Nadia asked, her mouth suddenly dry. If one of the Wishmaster's people had found out about her stolen wish, she was done for.

Grace stormed out through the front door, apparently unafraid of the potential danger. Nadia was about to follow, to talk some sense into her mother, when Basha's perpetually furnace-temperature hand wrapped around her forearm.

"Stay here, dziecko. I protect you from in here, she protect you from out there."

I don't need protecting. It sounded too childish to say out loud, so she bit it back. Instead, she stepped closer to the window and looked out, squinting into the darkness. A figure stood just past the gate, near Nadia's car. Grace approached the figure with her phone's flashlight raised, and as the light caught the turning face of the creepy shadow, Nadia's heart plummeted. With dawning horror, she realized who he was and why he was here.

After all, he *had* told her that his second wish had been to always find what he was looking for.

Frozen, mouth agape, Nadia frantically tried to decide what to do. At the same time, Grace and Miles started walking up the garden path, toward the door. Nadia needed to spend her wish *now*, but she still hadn't figured out the best wish to make, or the phrasing, or—

"Guess who just showed up on our doorstep, out of the blue!" Grace burst through the front door with a relieved grin on her face. "It's only Miles Hunter! Can you believe it? He says he's thinking about moving into the neighborhood because he wants a house with good bones and plenty of character." She flashed Miles a mortifying wink. "As it happens, I have both."

As Miles stepped into the foyer, Grace mouthed a dramatic "Oh my God" to Nadia behind his back. Saucy eye roll and everything.

"He's been looking at the Georgian Revival style to see if it's the right kind of old and reliable. On that one, I'm not sure I'm either, depending on the context." Grace exploded in a wild cackle as she pawed Miles's muscular arms. "I told him we'd give him the grand tour."

"Appreciate the hospitality," Miles said oh so casually.

As per the house's protective defenses, no one could enter without an invitation, but Grace had clearly extended one when she'd dragged him across the threshold. Nadia almost would've preferred to face Croak or Black Hat, rather than the man whose stolen wish was still burning a hole in her chest.

"This is Nadia, my daughter," Grace said perfunctorily.

The icy pit in Nadia's stomach grew even colder. Now Miles knew that she had even lied about her name.

"Surely you don't have a daughter that old?" Miles made a clear dig at Nadia as he complimented Grace. "I'd have thought you were sisters."

Grace beamed from ear to ear. "Flattery will get you *everywhere*."

"It's so nice to meet you . . . Nadia." Miles smiled, but the hard glint in his eyes said: *gotcha*.

Chapter Nine

"Do you drink?" Grace cooed. "Tell me you drink. I'm sure I can find a bottle of something spicy and expensive with our names on it. Or do you prefer something light and a bit fruity?" She fawned over Miles like she'd been starved of male company—something Nadia knew for damn sure couldn't be further from the truth.

Basha leaned on her cane. "Let the man get inside properly. You suffocate him!"

"As long as it's not Madeira, I'll have a glass," Miles said.

He seemed to be in the mood to appease everyone but Nadia. Had he somehow guessed that the other two women weren't in on her thievery?

"That stuff is too sweet for me," he continued. "It's like someone just thinned out some syrup and called it wine."

Grace erupted with laughter. "Say things like that, Miles—may I call you Miles?" He nodded, his eyes never leaving Nadia's face. "Say things like that, Miles, and the old money will faint right off their high horses."

"My daughter—she never speaks simple. Red or white?" Basha appeared equally taken by the musician as she grabbed him by the hand and pulled him farther into the foyer. Grace was dragged along with him, not quite ready to relinquish him from her clutches.

Miles shrugged. "White works for me, if it's dry."

"White wine it is. Surely the only dry thing in this house right now," Grace quipped as she reluctantly released her hold of Miles and hurried off to the kitchen to ransack the wine fridge.

Nadia cringed. She wouldn't have minded the house hurling *Grace* out into the front yard, for the sake of protecting Nadia's ears.

Miles stared at her, equal parts hurt and anger in his eyes. "Upset your mom is muscling in on your game? Nothing worse than someone taking what's yours, you know?" he muttered icily.

"Ah." Nadia wanted to reply with something more coherent, but really, what was there to say?

She thought of the wooden jar tucked under the driver's seat of the Chevy and hoped he couldn't read her face. Then again, with his ability to find whatever he was looking for, what difference did it make? He must've known where the jar was but figured out that Nadia had already absorbed his wish. Which was, of course, why he was standing in her house, staring at her like he wanted her to spontaneously combust. The wish was what he was *really* looking for.

Anger burned in her chest. She should've just bought the damn candles and a new lighter on the way home. It would've been easier. Basha had turned out to be fine, anyway. She wanted to blame Grace's frantic phone call, but there were bigger blockades at play. Namely, the Wishing Tree wasn't cooperating, and her wish phrasings were likely all duds. She needed time to think of something better, but time wasn't really on her side with Miles here. If she tried to sneak off upstairs, he'd call her out for sure.

"I should go and help my mom." Nadia shot Miles a tight smile and sprinted from the room before he could protest, leaving him in Basha's tender mercies.

In the kitchen, Grace clutched an armful of bottles. "Ah, perfect timing! Which do you think he'll like?"

"This is a bad idea, Mom." Nadia lowered her voice. "We can't put on some wine-tasting evening with a celebrity. If he stays here too long, the paparazzi might get interested in our 'barrier.' Some try-hard with a long lens probably followed him here."

Grace snorted. "I didn't see anyone, and I can sniff out a camera like a pig after truffles. Besides, it gives me time to show my best angle."

"And if you end up in the tabloids tomorrow, with the papers calling you Miles Hunter's new cougar?" Nadia blurted out, desperate to get that man out of the house as soon as possible.

Grace sighed wistfully, doing her best lovestruck debutante impression. "If only. I'd be swatting men away like mosquitos if I got a headline with that rock *god*."

"Have you ever heard a single song of his?" Nadia pointed out.

Grace tilted her head. "Does it matter?" She set the bottles down. "Anyway, I'm not saying I want him to play me like his guitar, but he can tune my pegs whenever he feels like it."

Nadia's gaze fixed on the wine for a moment. Miles must've been even more ignorant about the wishing world than she'd thought, since most wishers knew it was downright stupid to accept drinks from someone else. Although it could be put in any type of drink, Alexander's Tea was the proper name for the wishing bark infusion that diminished the abilities of a wisher. People often combined it with cinnamon to mask the bitter taste. The story went that Alexander the Great made a wish to be invulnerable, but someone slipped wishing bark into his tea, causing him to die young at the height of his powers. Nowadays, paranoia was the corner-stone of the wish-hunting world, and even Nadia's grandmother kept her tea-making supplies under lock and key up in her bedroom.

Nadia cast her mother a sly smile. Grace was thinking ahead more than Nadia gave her credit for. After all, she was the one who'd offered the drink, to see if he'd take it. If he hadn't accepted, sirens would've sounded in her mother's head about him being here on wish-related business.

"I'd go with the pinot grigio." Nadia gestured to a pale green bottle at the end of the row. "If he likes it dry, you might as well pucker his lips with that."

Grace covered her heart with her hand. "Stop—you're going to give a girl palpitations."

"How is that even remotely dirty?" Nadia frowned. "You know what? Never mind. I'll never understand the way your mind works, and I don't want to."

Grace uncorked the pinot grigio—no screwcaps here—and reached into the back of the cabinet for a small black bottle that contained the wishing bark infusion. As her mother dosed the musician's drink, Nadia turned on her heel and went back into the foyer.

"Where's my babcia?" Nadia scanned the foyer, but Basha had gone. Evidently, Miles wasn't as riveting as he thought he was.

He pointed up to the landing. "She said she felt tired, she was sorry she couldn't stay to shoot the breeze, and went off. I offered to help, but she refused."

"Maybe she knows you're a wolf in Louis Vuitton clothing," Nadia hissed. It was a hypocritical complaint, but she had to vent her frustration *somewhere*.

Miles patted his hoodie. "It's Fendi, actually, but I wouldn't expect you to know that. Thieves tend to be more into bootleg versions and don't really pay attention to who they're ripping off."

"Look, you need to leave," she said coolly. "Be pissed at me, fine, but you don't get to walk into my house and play nice with my mom and babcia. You're not welcome, and if this house had any sense, it would boot you out."

Miles moved closer, until they were almost nose to nose. "And you don't get to lay down the law to me after what you did. You're not the front man here. You're not even the bass player. So, give back what you took, or I'll go to Black Hat and rat you the hell out."

"I don't have your jar." She took a step back, the miasma of his cologne making her feel dizzy.

"You think I'm stupid?" He glared at her. "I know the wish isn't in the jar anymore. It's in you, and you're just buying time until you can use it. I bet you'd have done it already, if I hadn't shown up."

Nadia patted her chest. "You can't prove anything."

"Maybe not, but I don't think that's going to matter to Black Hat and company when I tell them you kept a wish you only got because *they* got screwed out of one." His lips curled into a grimace. "No honor among wish thieves, huh?"

He stepped back from her a second before Grace strolled into the room, which seemed ten degrees chillier than it had a moment ago.

"Here you go." Grace handed him a generous glass of white wine. "I hope Nadia is making you feel welcome?" She cast her daughter a warning look as if to say, *Don't you block me, girl.*

Miles transformed into a vision of charm. "Thank you, Grace. Just what I needed."

"Long day, huh?" Grace said, eyes glittering.

"Oh, you have *no* idea," Miles replied. He turned his attention to the room. "You've got a nice place here. But me, with a house this old, I'd be worried it might have some rot somewhere. You know, the kind that's really hard to scrape out."

Nadia took her glass from her mother. "No, I don't think there is. Since you're a *musician*, I wouldn't think you'd know too much about the business of old houses."

"In a house like this, the foundations are solid, and we've never had a problem with anything like that," Grace added obliviously, downing half of her glass while Miles sipped his politely. "Though it can get a bit damp—"

"I thought you were giving him a tour?" Nadia said, gripping the stem of her wine glass.

Grace grinned mischievously. "You're right, I was." She looped her arm through Miles's. "Let's start here. This is the entrance hall, as you can see." She led him to the staircase, and Nadia had a sudden fear that Grace intended to drag him to her bedroom, like a cavewoman.

"Are these Ukrainian?" Miles pulled back slightly, noting the Polish wood carvings and blue-and-white ceramics that littered every available space in the house.

Ukrainian? Which hole did you pull that one from?

Miles *knew* Nadia was Polish. She'd told him. Either he hadn't listened, or he was keeping up the innocent stranger act.

Grace smacked him lightly on the arm. "Lord, no, and don't let my mom hear you say that. We're Kaminskis, which admittedly sounds like it's from that sort of way, but it's actually Polish."

"I kind of guessed from your mother's accent that you weren't Old South." Miles smiled affably. "But Polish is cool, and 'Kaminski' is more interesting than 'Hunter,' that's for sure."

Grace urged him farther up the stairs. "My grandparents immigrated to the States after World War II, and we've been here ever since, adding some Polish flavor to Savannah."

Nadia waited for her mom to elaborate on what that Polish flavor might taste like, but to her relief, Grace let that one slide. As for the tale that Grace had skimmed over, there was a lot of missing narrative. Nadia's great-grandparents had moved to Savannah after running from rival wishmongers in Pennsylvania. Her great-grandmother was the one to establish the Kaminski Wishery as a family business, so Nadia supposed she had her to blame for her lifelong servitude.

She trailed the linked pair upstairs, where, to her further irritation, Grace insisted on leading Miles to Nadia's private sanctuary—the place where zero magic happened, including the wishing kind. Apparently.

"Ah, this is what I wanted to show you." Grace ushered Miles into the room, corralling around the base of Nadia's bed to the other side. "This is a painting of my grandmother. It doesn't do her any justice, and the eyes sort of follow you around the room, but Nadia likes it. Don't you, honey?"

The portrait was indeed one of Nadia's favorites. It depicted her great-grandmother in a rocking chair—the same one Basha now used—with a window behind her revealing the Polish countryside. And while it was true that her great-grandmother looked a bit stern, with dark, disapproving eyes and a dowdy black frock that made her look like something out of a horror novel, Nadia saw a lot of herself in that painted woman.

She folded her arms across her chest, as if to protect the wish. "I don't think Miles is going to want one for his house."

"I think this must be where my daughter gets her scowl from." Grace gestured to the grim shape of her grandmother's turned-down mouth. "Been doing it since she was a teen, so she's had plenty of practice over the years."

Nadia looked away from Miles, only to spot the candle on the floor. Her gaze flitted cautiously back to him, and she found him staring at the blackened wick of "Starlit Skies" as well. His eyes shifted toward her, and she met his steely glare, refusing to give any clue to his unspoken question.

While Grace prattled on, his eyes roamed the rest of the bedroom, then lighted on Nadia's bedside table. He reached over to pick up the book on top—*Assassin's Apprentice*, with its well-worn novelty bookmark of a peeking gnome sticking out from the middle.

"Don't touch that!" Nadia snapped, taking a step toward him.

Miles dropped it back onto the bedside table as though it might bite him, and Grace stared at her in shock.

"Sorry," Nadia muttered, shrinking into the churning sea of emotions in her chest. "Just . . . it's personal."

The book had been Nick's. He'd been meaning to read it since he was a kid but had only just gotten around to it a few weeks before he died. Now, it would forever be left unfinished, his bookmark commemorating the last page his eyes had graced. Nadia had scanned those two pages often, trying to guess which sentence might've been the final one he'd read before he'd switched off the light.

Grace recovered quickly. "I think that's the end of this portion of the tour." She weaved her arm through Miles's again and all but yanked him out of the bedroom. She crossed the hall to the room opposite, then knocked on the door.

"Mom," Grace said. "Are you sleeping? Miles should probably get an idea of the room sizes in a house like this."

Basha opened the door and peered out, leaning on her cane. "Ah, you still here."

"Afraid so." Miles flashed her a smile.

"Remind me, what sort of famous are you? Is movie star? Is politician?" Basha said. "It make big difference. The neighborhood is not so much a fan of politicians or movie stars. Nor are we. They make such mess when they film."

Miles chuckled, his demeanor relaxing. "I'm a musician."

"I do not listen to this modern music. Is noise."

He gave a small shrug. "I agree, honestly. A lot of 'bands' nowadays just use samples and autotune. Their songs might sell, but there's no heart there. No soul. And without soul, it's not real music."

Basha leaned forward with a serious look. "I have decided that I like you. You have good head on your shoulders." She nodded approvingly, but her expression morphed into one of curiosity as she turned to Nadia. "What is wrong with you, dziecko? You are this same way when this man arrived—look of a long-tailed cat in room of rocking chairs."

Nadia tried to flick the switch on her composed, marriage counselor mode. "I've just had a long day, is all. My tail is firmly tucked away, Babcia."

Grace shifted, and her eyes narrowed at Nadia, but she didn't say anything. No doubt the outburst in Nadia's bedroom was fresh on her mind.

Basha took Nadia's hand, patting it gently. "Is only to be expected. You must be shaken up. But I am glad you are all right. I worried so much I faint."

Obviously, they had zero idea that Miles had been the buyer at that particular sideways deal—and that Nadia would probably be dead, or on her way to the ER, if he hadn't stepped in to rescue her from a bullet to the heart. Instead, she had a ticking time bomb inside.

"We must talk more about your night. Nothing was damaged?" Basha asked pointedly, and it was all Nadia could do to keep her face neutral. She didn't want to deal with telling Basha that they needed to get a new wish trap from the Wishmaster just yet.

"I'll catch you up once Miles is gone, Babcia," Nadia said.

"That my cue?" Miles laughed, but it didn't reach his eyes. "Honestly, I should be hitting the road anyway. I've got to talk to someone about something that got stolen from me, and the longer I wait, the harder it'll be to get it back."

Nadia's insides twisted.

Grace gasped at his comment. "Really? That's terrible. Was it valuable?"

Miles sighed overdramatically. "Irreplaceable."

Well, he had that part right. People only got three wishes in their entire lifetime, and absorbing them into your body counted as a used wish, even if it got snatched. His third and final wish was now in her chest, and he would never get another unless he took the same wish back. No matter what, one of them would lose a wishing slot in their lifetime total.

And she wouldn't let it be her.

"I hope you get it back before it's too late, Miles." Grace put her arm around his shoulder and gave him a squeeze, pushing her boobs against his bicep.

Miles cast Nadia a significant glance. "Me too. I hate to be a snitch, but ain't nobody taking my stuff. I'll take this as high up as I have to."

Nadia tugged on the collar of her hoodie, feeling like it'd turned into a personal sauna of sweltering anxiety. He'd drawn between the lines with a big old warning: as soon as he left this house, he was going to Black Hat to tell him that she'd stolen his wish. Not Rebecca, not Clover Eyes, but Nadia Kaminski. And when you were "full named," like her grandmother always said, you were in serious trouble.

"Let me see you out," Grace insisted, dragging him away.

Basha waved. "Show that thief what you are made of!"

Nadia cringed and walked after Miles and her mother, trying to figure out what to do. As long as she was in the house, she was safe from Miles, invitation or no. But that safety came at a price. Within the house, she couldn't make her wish until Grace and Basha were asleep; that way, she could huff and puff through as many rejections as her body could take without them hearing and trying to talk her out of her plan to get rid of the debt.

She pressed her hand to her chest, reveling in that giddy spark, despite everything. It was pure, liquid hope.

Heading down the stairwell after the duo, she mentally cataloged more ways she could phrase her wish. She had to spend the damn thing as soon as possible—the longer she waited, the more risk there was of the Wishmaster discovering it.

Her eyes bored into the back of Miles's head as they reached the front door. No matter what, she couldn't let Miles contact Black Hat tonight. She needed to delay him—she just didn't know how yet.

"Can I walk you to your car?" Grace purred.

Miles took her hand and kissed it—the smooth devil. "There's no need. I walked here from my friend's a few blocks down. I'll have him give me a ride back to my house."

"I didn't think you actually *lived* in Savannah." Grace grinned, likely wondering if she could just "bump" into him. "I thought all you celebrities lived in LA."

Miles laughed. "I've got a summer home here, for when the LA life gets a bit too much. I'd blame it on the traffic, but that'd be a little hypocritical. Hometown boy is in my blood, I guess. Savannah will always call no matter where my feet tread."

Yeah, and you don't do your own driving, so what would you have to bitch about LA traffic for? In the midst of her internal jab, a thought came to her. Thanks to the wishing bark infusion in the wine, Miles's finding powers would be dulled, which gave her a slight advantage.

"I'll drive you!" she said, a little too enthusiastically. She lowered and smoothed out her voice. "I mean, it's the least I can do."

If her mother was jealous she didn't think of it first, she at least had the self-restraint not to bring it up this time.

"You sure?" Miles eyed Nadia suspiciously. She could almost see the cogs clanging in his head, as if he was coming up with a plan too.

"Of course. I'd hate for something to happen, you know." She smiled sweetly and headed out the door. "Wouldn't want you to get robbed again."

Chapter Ten

The instant the Chevy's passenger side door clunked shut,
Miles went for the figurative jugular.

"I bet you thought you played me real good, huh?" he
snapped at Nadia. "Did you spend the wish already? How did you steal
it? You think I don't know shit, but I figure it had a hell of a lot to do
with my damn jar! You stole my wish at the restaurant, right? Did
someone put you up to it? Are you working for that thug guy, or did
you and Black Hat come up with this?"

Nadia drove off at a sedate pace, only to put her foot down as soon
as she was away from the house and her mother's line of sight. He
could rant at her until he blew a lung, so long as it kept him busy.
Meanwhile, she needed to get to a store ASAP.

"Don't you go giving me the silent treatment, man!" Miles raged
on. "I don't do silence. So, you'd better start answering my questions. I
can find whatever I'm looking for, remember, and that doesn't stop at
the physical. I can *find* the answers. That's why I didn't call you out in
front of your folks. Figured you'd gang up with your mom and
grandma. And if your family kicked me out, I'd be watching through
the window as you blew a candle out at me." He trailed his fingertips
across the dash, creating a line in the fine layer of dust. "But maybe I'll

go have another glass of wine with your mom, or sit down and talk traditional Polish music with your grandma, and take my chances on what happens when they find out."

Nadia swerved in alarm, her nerves still a tangled mess. Of all the things he could've said, that was the one sentence guaranteed to grab her attention. After all, she wasn't entirely sure what she was going to do with Miles. She'd offered this ride, but really, could she let him out, knowing what he knew? He wasn't just going to let it slide, nor would he let her waltz into a store to grab the items she needed to make her wish.

"You planning to crash into something and hope I go through the windshield?" Miles hissed. "Stole my damn wish, my jar, and left me with the check. And after I saved your life!" He slammed back against his seat as Nadia took a corner a little too tightly.

"I don't want to hurt you," she said quietly. "I just . . . want you to go away."

"Just go away, huh? Yeah, I *bet* you wish that—you and a lot of other people!" He gave a wry, bitter grin. "Get ready for some disappointment, *Nadia*."

"If I said this wish was for something big, would you leave me alone?" She peered at the road and took a right, heading for the nearest grocery store. That gave her three minutes to bargain with him.

He snorted. "You obviously didn't care if my wish was for something big, so why should I care if yours is? You don't know what I wanted to use it for." He stared out the window. "And I ain't going through that rigmarole again. I have plenty of money, but my time is way more valuable, and I can't spare the hours to find a better wish seller, drop a load of cash, and hope I don't get shot at."

As Nadia reached the end of the road and made to turn left, dual reds and blues flashed in her face, and a cop waved at her. Police barriers blocked her path, and the crunched, smoking warriors of a two-car battle lay wounded beyond.

She could hardly believe it. It was like the universe itself was conspiring against her. Backing up, she returned the way she'd come.

"If you don't know the basics of wishing, you shouldn't be doing it," Nadia said, taking her frustrations out on him.

He side-eyed her. "Why? What don't I know?"

She should just tell him to buy another wish and have him find out the hard way that he'd been conned twice, but something stopped the lie from coming out. Maybe it was his tone when he'd mentioned wanting to make a big wish, maybe the guilt was finally getting to her, or maybe it was the fact that the universe seemed to be telling her this was a bad idea. Nadia stole wishes discreetly—without the target knowing—for a reason. This improvised thievery didn't suit her, and it didn't make her feel too good. She wasn't a brute-force thug like Dominic.

"You don't get another try," Nadia said. She sighed, knuckles whitening against the steering wheel.

He looked ready to strangle her. "What do you mean? Am I on a list of banned buyers now or something?"

Part of her regretted that she wasn't corrupt enough to send him on his way to another wishmonger, where he'd discover the truth for himself.

"Keep talking. You're the expert here, so educate me," he snapped.

"You've had your third wish. You don't get another," she said through gritted teeth. "I took it. If a wish gets stolen, then—*poof*—you just kissed it goodbye. Unless you can get the same one back before it gets spent by the person who snatched it." Of course, he still didn't understand how to actually steal a wish, and she wasn't going to fill him in.

"But I only had the damn thing for less than an hour!" Miles spluttered.

"Think of it this way," Nadia replied calmly, although her annoyance was about to boil over. "You have three blank slots for wishes. As soon as a wish fills that slot, the slot molds to fit that wish. After that point, only that key will fit into that keyhole."

"Pull over. Now!" he shouted, venom in his voice.

She shook her head. "I can't do that."

"So, what's the plan, then? Kill me so I don't tell anybody? You just driving around, deciding which river to dump my body in? The Wilmington's closer than the Savannah from here," he said sarcastically. "Is that why you offered to drive? Or—" His eyes widened. "Do you think

I'm going to take *pity* on you and just let you have it? You stole my last wish! No way I'm getting out of this car now."

She wasn't sure what she'd expected. Maybe she'd thought her honesty might soften him up, but perhaps Dr. Fitzpatrick had been right: honesty was never the best policy.

Nadia gave him an irritated look. "I told you, I don't want to hurt you. But you can't tell anyone about this, or I'll be the one getting dropped in a river."

"That's *your* problem, the way I see it," Miles shot back. "I think I'll call my publicist and tell him I've been kidnapped—the news would *love* to hear that Miles Hunter, local favorite and international headliner, is being held hostage by some rabid fangirl. Maybe that'd work in your favor. Who'd be able to get at you when you're locked up in a cell? But you're gonna give me back my wish first, so help me God."

She veered around a parked van, sending Miles crashing into the passenger door. "There are a lot of people out there who'd do anything to get a wish. I'm in the business of supplying them. You're not the only one who has someone on speed dial." She sucked in a breath. "I'm trying to give you an opportunity to play nice here. Your wish is gone. You've had two. Don't be greedy about it, and just agree to let this go."

Miles went silent for a moment, and Nadia contemplated her next strategy for when he inevitably tried to argue with her. It might make things simpler if she owned up to her reasons for wanting to keep the wish, but she wasn't going to bawl her eyes out to Miles about her endless debt and dead husband. It was just too personal. Besides, what if it didn't work? Better to have Miles believe she was ruthless and playing hardball.

"Look, everyone has a price. What's yours?" he said at last, surprising her with his softer approach. "You give me that wish back, I'll give you whatever you want."

He could've offered her a Gulfstream jet and a diamond the size of a bird's egg, and she wouldn't have taken it. She was just buying time until she could figure out how to incapacitate him for long enough— willingly or unwillingly—so she could make her wish.

"Give it up," she said. "The only way you'll get it back is to steal it from me, and that's not gonna happen. But go ahead. Try, if you want.

Show me you've got the skill to steal this wish out from under someone who's spent her entire life in this world, stealing wish after wish and getting *nothing* of her own."

Miles's gaze flitted down to the driver's side footwell. Who needed seat warmers when she had the wooden wishing jar burning a guilty hole beneath her seat? Both of them knew it, not that it was a real concern. She wouldn't have mentioned it if she thought he could actually do it. Since he was clueless about how to steal wishes, him having his jar was tantamount to giving him a nice ornament to stare at. But it might distract him for a while.

"Go ahead," she taunted. "Reach under the seat and get it, since I can tell that you can't stop thinking about it."

Leaning right over, with his face pretty much taking a crotch dive, he fumbled around beneath the threadbare, gray velour seat. Nadia sat stiffly, not knowing what to do with herself. Should she move her legs to the side so he wasn't using her thigh as a chin rest? Should she just pretend everything was cool and that there wasn't a man huffing and puffing so close to her nethers? It wasn't even a cheap thrill; it was just the most awkward thing to happen in a driver's seat, behind singing at the top of your lungs at a stoplight, not realizing the windows were down. Her mother, on the other hand, would've . . . That wasn't something she wanted to think about.

"Got it." He reeled back into his seat, turning the object over in his hands. "Now, how do I *really* use it? I know the blood thing you told me was an out-and-out lie."

Nadia scoffed. "You think I'm going to tell you? Ha. *You* figure it out. If you don't, the wish stays with me."

He smiled furtively. "You think you're clever, huh? I'm going to the Wishmaster. Someone will tell me how to make it work, and *you* can get whatever's coming to you." He started to pull open the door as Nadia slowed for a stoplight.

Panicking, she floored the gas pedal and ripped through the red light. She swerved to avoid someone about to make a turn, and swiped a utility pole, crunching his door shut.

"You could've killed me!" Miles shouted, his eyes wide.

Nadia's attention was fixed on the rearview to check for cop cars, but the only thing behind her was a blue BMW. She was already going to have a hell of a time explaining the damage to the car to her mom, and cops would only make things worse.

"Glad you're getting the picture," she replied more casually than her racing heart suggested. "So, what do you say we strike that deal before any other poles come along?"

He glowered at her. "I wish *this* Pole hadn't come along."

"Ah, you're a funny guy. I wouldn't have known." She half smirked.

Miles looked down at his wishing jar. "I'm not making that deal with you, not when you're guaranteed to win. You think I'm stupid enough to get tricked twice?" He put on a fake smile. "Come on, rich musician like me—there's got to be something else you'd take for my wish so we never have to see each other again. What would someone like you want, huh?"

"I won't know until you suggest it," she replied, hoping her vagueness would buy her more time.

His shoulders slumped. "With a house like that, you don't need property or money. Judging by your clothes and what you said about mine, you don't care about designer gear. You've got some janky chain around your neck, so you clearly aren't into jewelry either."

That one hurt.

She was about to reply, to make him think he had a chance of buying his wish back while she worked a way out of her dilemma, when her phone blared in her pocket. With one hand on the wheel, she took it out and slotted it into the cupholder. On the screen, the caller ID read "Babcia." Her heart nearly stopped. Her grandmother never called unless it was to be the bearer of bad news.

Hands shaking, Nadia ignored it and breathed a sigh of relief when the ringing stopped. But Basha called right back.

"Shouldn't you pick that up? Seems important," Miles said. "Maybe she knows, or maybe she's in trouble. Might be your fault. Trouble seems to follow you."

Nadia eyed the screen and let it ring off for a third time. What if Basha had learned of the broken wishing box and the stolen wish? Or what if she was sick again?

Miles tutted. "Damn, you are cold."

Stung by his words, she glanced at the blackened phone screen. He was right. If she didn't check in on Basha and something awful had happened, she'd never forgive herself.

She cursed under her breath as the phone buzzed again, then answered.

"Is everything all right?" Nadia asked, wedging the phone between her ear and her shoulder, swerving as she did so.

"I don't know which I regret more—saving your life or getting in this car with you. Again," Miles muttered.

Basha's croaky voice echoed through the phone. "Basha knows," she rasped, setting Nadia's nerves on edge. "You thought you get away with it. You stole wish, and you thought you could keep it for yourself."

Basha's words chilled her with the force of a Polish winter, and Nadia wondered if it might just be easier to crash the car into the nearest wall. Nothing could be worse than her grandmother's fury.

Chapter Eleven

Nadia slammed on the brakes and came to a dead halt in the middle of the road. A bleary-eyed partygoer stumbled off the sidewalk, banging on the hood as if she'd almost hit him. He bared his teeth at them like a rabid dog before lumbering off.

Miles braced against the dash. "Ground control to Major Kaminski! Are you *trying* to get yourself a night in a cell?"

Nadia took a rattling breath and pressed the phone closer to her ear again. "I'm sorry, Babcia. I didn't hear what you said—I was driving."

"I know you heard Basha," her grandmother replied in a tone so icy it could've brought on a rare Savannah snowstorm. "Make stop at church down the road."

Nadia's head twisted around. "How did you . . . ." She trailed off. There was no way Basha could be watching her. Not unless she could see through buildings.

"Make stop," Basha repeated. "This I command."

Nadia peered through the fuzz of the headlights and spotted the imposing, grayish twin spires that wouldn't have looked amiss in a gothic fairytale. Her grandmother must've guessed her general location, since she'd only left the house about five minutes ago.

Out of the corner of her eye, Nadia saw Miles reach for the door handle, and she stomped the gas. He wasn't getting away just because she was distracted. She pulled into the church parking lot, its stark-white façade and gold-bordered doorways shining even in the lamplight. She did a doughnut in the parking lot, trying to split the difference between driving fast enough to keep Miles in the car and making Basha think she really had stopped. Thankfully, the lot was empty, since evening had fallen and Savannah's visitors were more interested in sampling the bars than the holy water.

"Babcia, I was going to tell you about the wish. I just wanted to have some time to think first, and I didn't want to make you feel worse."

Really, Nadia wanted to scream that they'd left her with no other choice in finding some faster way to get rid of the debt. But when Basha was pissed, nothing made her explode faster than a raised voice or an accusation.

"I wasn't being deceitful," Nadia continued. "It happened by chance, and I wanted to help us with the debt—"

"You make no lie to me! You use wish for your own selfish needs. You are ungrateful, wretched dziecko! Are you in church parking lot? If is no, you will pray for hiding place in this world where I never find you."

Nadia's mind swirled. She couldn't convince Basha that she'd had good intentions—not until Basha calmed down, at least. But how did her grandmother find out about the wish? It made no sense. Did she have a second compass coin that Nadia didn't know about, which had warmed in the presence of the unused wish? If so, why wait to call Nadia out on that fact until after she had left the house? Had she seen Nadia trying to get the matches from the drawer while pretending to be asleep, but only now put two and two together?

She glanced at Miles, who was glaring at her as she started the second doughnut in the parking lot. It didn't matter how her grandmother had figured it out—the only question was what happened next. Basha had always made one thing as clear as crystal: she'd disown anyone who disobeyed her. And Nadia didn't have enough people left in her life to risk that.

I don't want that. Never that. Her family had saved her life; she wouldn't even be here, having this argument, without them. There'd have been no years of marriage to Nick, no brief exhale of utter joy amidst all the years she'd felt like she was holding her breath.

Guilt threatened to drown her.

Miles looked like he was debating about rolling out of the car, but he stayed put. "You gonna play it like that, then?" he mumbled, seemingly more to himself than her. "Fine. Maybe I'll stay right *here* until I get my wish back."

Nadia turned toward the driver's side door for some attempt at privacy. "I'm at the church, Babcia, but you need to listen to me. I—"

"Get out of car," Basha interjected, sounding breathless. "Go to church doors and apologize for betraying rodzina like this, after all we give you. Your whole life . . . so much we give, and you do such awful thing. Put us all in danger."

Basha may not have had a direct phone line to God, but the way she would pray by her bedside on tired knees and bent arthritic back without complaint undoubtedly commanded His attention. Her grandmother couldn't attend church anymore because of her house-protection duties, but with all the Catholic paraphernalia in her room, it might have been considered its own sanctuary—a metaphysical one to match the real one of the wish-enhanced house.

Nadia craned her neck to look up at the church through the windshield. "Okay, okay, I'm going. I'll beg forgiveness."

Maybe once she did what Basha asked, her grandmother would stop complaining long enough for Nadia to explain why she'd stolen the wish in the first place.

With a sigh, Nadia opened the door and got out, the phone still pressed to her ear. Miles's door squeaked as he followed her and headed up the sloping gray steps to the grand wooden doors, though he stopped halfway up and leaned against the railing. He tossed the wishing jar from hand to hand as if he, too, was trying to figure out his next move on the chessboard.

"I'm in front of the doors now," Nadia said, tilting her head up. She soon brought her gaze back down to ground level, the sheer size of the church giving her vertigo. "I don't think I can go inside. You want me to ask for God's forgiveness out here or what?"

"You no get flippant with me, dziecko," the voice on the other end of the line snapped. "Now, you tell Basha, did you steal this wish you hide from your family from the handsome guitarist?"

At this stage, Nadia saw no point in lying. "Yeah, I did. But it wasn't the wish I was selling to Black Hat, so you don't need to worry about it affecting our tally. That's what I've been trying to say." She glanced at Miles to see his reaction, but he just kept tossing his jar. "He —Miles—saved me from a bullet, so it was a different wish I stole from him. One that I created, in a roundabout kind of way, so it sort of belonged to me too. I'm just—"

The happy wish buzz washed away like footprints in sand. Nadia stopped short, the memory of their earlier conversation unspooling in her mind. Miles had never told Basha what instrument he played. Nadia herself only knew because of his chatter about "Memories of the Alhambra."

The hairs electrified up the back of her neck. "Who is this?" she whispered.

The call went dead.

Nadia spun around, trying to pick out any strange figures or suspicious cars driving past that might contain the spy. But it was nighttime on a Saturday in Savannah: *everyone* looked strange and suspicious.

Someone must've found a way to trick her. Spoofing a phone number was probably easy enough for anyone with a little technical know-how. But none of Kaleena's cronies that Nadia knew could *sound* exactly like her grandmother, "dzieckos" and all. Regardless, she had to get away from the church. She'd been led down the garden path, and here she was, stopping to smell the roses. She needed to get moving. Now.

Before she could form the thought to tell Miles to run, a tall woman with a slicked shock of blonde hair sprinted around the corner of the church. Nadia's hands raised automatically, her feet spreading as she sank into her hips, going instinctively into resting attack mode. It was the first thing she'd learned during her Krav Maga classes in college.

But the woman never touched her. Instead, the Amazonian vaulted over the railing at the top of the church steps, landed like a gymnast on the grass, and took off running away at full tilt. In the dim light, Nadia glimpsed a wooden locket dangling from the woman's hand.

Her heart sank. She knew exactly what she was dealing with: a wish trap.

"No, no, no, no," she said under her breath as understanding flushed through her. She'd revealed her secret about Miles saving her life and her stealing his wish, and that was plenty big enough for this hunter to steal the wish right out of her chest. No wonder the buzz had evaporated.

"Miles!" Nadia shouted. "She's stolen the wish!"

Miles jolted into gear. "The NBA all-star?"

"Who else?" she shot back as she leaped down the church steps and gave chase.

The vertically blessed thief hurtled toward a waiting car parked just up the street. The gleaming blue BMW was distinct enough to jog Nadia's startled brain—it was the same car that had almost followed them through the stoplight. She'd been tailed the whole time, but she'd been so distracted by Miles that she hadn't even realized it.

Cursing, Nadia sprinted toward the car. If she threw herself on the hood, would the thief stop, or just run her over?

From the right, a blur streaked past and covered the sidewalk in seconds, reaching the car before Nadia did. Just as the tall woman opened the driver's door, Miles slammed it shut again.

"Nuh-uh." He shook his head vehemently. "My wish isn't getting stolen twice in one evening."

The blonde woman stepped back—she didn't seem to want to mess with Miles. Nadia ducked down beside the BMW's rear bumper and whipped out the palm-sized folding knife in her jean pocket. She jabbed the blade into the back tires and smiled at the satisfying hiss as the rear quarter of the car sagged.

"Nadia Kaminski! Call off guard dog before I really lose temper!" the thief shouted in Basha's voice, confirming Nadia's suspicions—a wish had been used to allow this woman to mimic others' voices. Hell, the woman could probably impersonate *any* voice and had somehow managed to study Basha's vocal idiosyncrasies, right down to the chilling intonation.

Nadia popped up from behind the car. "How about you stop using my grandma's voice, then we can talk. You're not fit to have it come out of your mouth."

"Is not very friendly," the woman replied mockingly in Basha's voice before flashing a pristine smile, her eyes flicking between the two of them.

With a quick pivot, the woman charged at Miles, trying to wrestle him to the ground. Instead, he pushed her off him and sent her stumbling a few steps farther down the road.

Nadia slipped close to Miles, pulling up short a couple of paces from the thief. She raised her knife.

The woman's eyes narrowed as the blade gleamed in the streetlight. "You want fight? Is bad idea."

From the waistline of a pair of black cargo pants, the thief whipped out a collapsing baton. It clacked to its full length, the woman's knuckles whitening as she gripped the handle. This would certainly make things more interesting, but Nadia's classes had prepared her for weapons like these.

The thief swung clumsily at Nadia, who ducked under the baton's arc. Nadia saw an opening and slashed at the woman—more as a warning than anything else, but a bright-red cut appeared across the woman's cheek as she made contact. Every synapse in Nadia's brain was firing, every muscle tensing, and every nerve electric. The last thing she'd expected tonight was a knife fight. Despite everything, her lips curled into a wild grin.

The thief jerked back. "Don't be cocky, dziecko. First blood is no matter. Is only last that matters."

Why did this woman keep using Basha's voice? Maybe she was just trying to throw Nadia off—or maybe she worried Nadia would recognize her real voice if she used it.

The woman swung again, and Nadia slashed at her but realized too late that the swing was a feint. Nadia's blade sliced through air, and the woman brought the baton down hard on Nadia's hand. The force of the blow set her hand ablaze in pain and sent the knife clattering to the ground. Before Nadia could bend to retrieve it, the woman was on her again, delivering a blow to her shoulder that stung like a snakebite. The next strike was low, catching her just behind the left knee, sending her to the ground, tears of pain welling in her eyes.

"Hey!" Miles shouted as the woman advanced on him.

From the ground, Nadia watched him swing a haymaker at her, but the woman hit him with a body blow against his rib cage. He cried out and sank to his knees on the sidewalk next to Nadia, right hand on his possibly cracked ribs. He put his left hand on the concrete to keep from falling forward as he winced and moaned.

The thief towered above him and stepped on his outstretched left hand, tapping the baton menacingly on his wrist. "You try again, I break your fingers," she warned. "No more guitar for you, Miles Hunter."

In desperation, Nadia reached for her knife just beside the woman's left shoe. As Nadia's hand clenched around it, a shadow of movement darted above her, then—

A lightning bolt flashed across her eyes, and the world stuttered. She blinked and found herself on her side, eyes unable to focus. There were two thieves, two rock stars, two cars, two little tufts of weeds sticking out from cracks in the sidewalk.

"I thank for this." The thief bent over Nadia and patted her down. "Call it payment for your mother's treasonous calls to Atlanta."

It was only when she heard the jangle of her own car keys—a tangled mass of metal, where the kitschy, gift shop keyrings of famous monuments were crammed together—that Nadia realized what else was going on. The bitch was stealing Nick's Chevy.

Miles yelled something she couldn't make out. She couldn't see him, but she heard the pounding of running feet and muffled, incomprehensible shouts that made her feel as though she were underwater. Then there was the squeal of tires and the thud of something against metal. A fleshy thud.

Chapter Twelve

With the sharp, pounding pain in her head, Nadia's surroundings wafted in and out of focus. She blinked as a shape appeared above her.

"Are you . . . a ghost? Did you die already?" she asked.

"You're not *that* lucky." Miles extended a hand to her. "See? I'm solid. No ghosts here."

She reached out hesitantly. "Huh. Solid." She paused. "And sweaty. So sweaty."

"Funny way of saying thanks. You want me to leave you there or what?" Miles grasped her hand and pulled her to her feet, then dragged her arm around his shoulder to prop her up against the blue BMW.

Nadia side-eyed him, somewhat touched by the gesture. He could've left her there at any moment and saved himself from the chaos.

"Thanks," she said. "Really."

He led her to the front of the abandoned BMW, and she sat on the hood. For a moment, it looked like he was going to check her head, but he lowered his hand and sank down beside her. "No lie, though, you can kick some serious ass for a marriage counselor. I wasn't expecting you to be a secret ninja."

"The wishing business isn't all birthday parties and scented candles, you know." She shrugged, her head still pounding. "If you're a wish hunter, you've got to be ready to protect yourself."

"I thought the music industry was nasty, but wish-stealing is some filthy business, man." He gave a low whistle. "Compared to *that*, give me a pissed-off label exec any day of the week. Didn't expect to almost get killed twice today."

"Look, I really didn't mean to get you into this mess," Nadia said, hesitating on the edge of a real apology. If an innocent person had been hurt because of her choices, the remorse would've buried her. He hadn't left her lying on the sidewalk, and that was worth a lot.

Miles arched an eyebrow. "Not used to people coming after you when you steal their wishes, huh?"

She flushed a little. "It's always a risky business. At this point, you might as well give up trying to get your wish back. Honestly, the retaliation won't be worth it."

"So now you're all about honesty," he said dryly.

"I just want to give you a fair warning about what you might be getting into. My bark is worse than my bite, really, but I don't want you thinking that's true of anybody else in the wishing world."

"Already got that message in the cemetery when bullets were flying and when I got smacked in the stomach a few minutes ago." Miles's expression softened, and he looked at her like he had at the restaurant —like she was a person he was curious to know more about. "But I appreciate the heads-up."

"You don't know the half of it. This is sunshine and rainbows compared to what things used to be like under Adrian's rule. He used to give wishes to drug lords, rapists, murderers—anyone willing to pay up. Had a hard time letting go, which is why his crew is still sniffing around. Those three at Bonaventure were his."

"Think that giant was his too?" Miles glanced toward the road where the Chevy had disappeared a minute earlier.

Nadia massaged her temples. "I wasn't sure before, but this isn't Adrian's doing."

The thief's fuzzy last words filtered back into her head: *Call it payment for your mother's treasonous calls to Atlanta.* If that woman could mimic voices, it only stood to reason that Grace's latest call from Mr. Caldwell at the condemned house might've been another spoofed number designed to prove Grace's guilt.

The thought alone made Nadia's stomach sink as she added, "That thief is on the current Wishmaster's payroll, and that means we're in deeper shit than you know."

Miles grimaced. "Just what I wanted to hear."

Nadia pushed herself away from the hood—she couldn't keep idling here while that thief might be headed for Grace and Basha. The house's protective powers might not be enough this time, if the stolen wish was somehow used to counteract Basha's wish. She glanced at Miles, who was staring down at his phone as if checking for cracks. After the wishing bark infusion wore off, his finding powers would be incredibly useful for sensing any incoming threats from the Wishmaster. But how could she get him to come with her? Sure, he'd thrown himself into the fight, but she was under no illusions of what his motivations were. He just wanted his wish back so he could ditch Nadia as quickly as possible.

An idea came to her—one that would hopefully tempt him to follow her.

"I need to head home. My mom and babcia might be in trouble." She took two paces forward. "You should come too. I know you hate me right now, but you're in this as much as I am, and that means you're in the line of fire. So, we can lie low at my house until we can figure out our next move."

Miles scoffed. "People stop me for selfies on the street. There's no such thing as 'lying low.' Anyway, the Wishmaster will probably just break down the door, if they're really after us."

"There were no paparazzi outside the last time you came wandering into my house unannounced," she replied, struggling to bite back her sarcasm. "But I promise, it's the safest place for us. The house is protected by a wish that not even the Wishmaster can break through." *Yet.* She didn't want to think of the lengths Kaleena would go to conquer that obstacle, if she really wanted to dole out punishments.

Miles seemed to contemplate the idea for a moment. "All right, I see what you're saying. But I'll be watching you the whole time. I'm not letting you pull another fast one on me while I figure out what I'm gonna do about *my* wish. This isn't an olive branch."

"Then come on and keep up."

She broke into a sprint and took out her phone to dial her mom on the move, but the call rang through. Trying Basha's number and then the house number, she got the same endless chimes and no answer. She hadn't even stopped to check if Miles was following, but his footsteps pounded on the sidewalk behind her.

Her mind erupting with every worst-case scenario, she rushed past the live oaks and the giddy lovers trying to take nighttime pictures in front of the armillary sphere on Troup Square, maybe hoping their love would never be eclipsed. Perhaps there was a celestial sphere out there somewhere that had the exact moment marked for when Nick would be forever blocked from her life, steeping her world in a bereaved darkness.

Nick . . . It physically ached to admit it, but all thoughts of clearing the debt and reviving Nick would have to sit on the back burner for the time being. The woman who beat them up was a newbie that Nadia had never run into before. Was Kaleena expanding her operations? Or had her assumptions about the thief been wrong, and the Atlanta Wishmaster was making moves against the Kaminski family? Most troubling of all was the realization that the woman hadn't just seized a random opportunity to grab a wish. She'd known exactly where to look and who to trail.

For now, though, Nadia couldn't worry too much about that. She had to focus on stopping everything from imploding. If Kaleena took all of Nadia's wishes as punishment, her chances of ever making a wish for herself would disappear. But first, she needed to make sure Kaleena hadn't already gunned for Grace and Basha, thinking they had some part in this.

"Would you slow down for a second?" Miles yelled, but Nadia ignored him.

Finally, she turned onto her street, and her anxiety prompted her legs to move faster. Of course, there could be an innocent reason they weren't picking up the phone: her grandmother had her record player on too loud or she was pruning in the tub, and her mom had already headed out for her date and didn't want to be interrupted. But where the Wishmaster was concerned, it was better to be safe than sorry.

A minute later, Nadia came to the front gate of the Kaminski Mansion. The streetlight was still out, but she didn't need it to navigate the front path. As she was about to push open the gate, something caught her eye—a bronze glow underneath her feet. She jumped back as if she'd been shocked.

"Why are you—" Miles jumped back too, having just caught up.

Nadia's guts liquefied as the refreshed shape of the Zhar-Ptitsa's feather glinted menacingly up at her, just in front of the gate. It wasn't the faded echo of the first. That would've vanished by now. No, this was unmistakably strike two. The very thing she'd been scrambling to avoid.

She might not have been gone long, but news traveled fast.

"So much for me warning them," she whispered, terror crawling through her like freshly hatched spiders. Nadia finally remembered that Miles was standing beside her. "You should stay out here. I'll deal with this."

He eyed the sprayed feather on the ground. "What's got you so spooked? What is this?"

"It's a warning from the Wishmaster. One more and . . . well, the consequences won't be pretty."

Miles's face fell. "Who's it for?"

"Me—and them." Nadia tipped her head toward the house. "Seriously, you should just stay out here."

She pushed through the gate and headed up the front path, only to find Miles bounding after her.

"No way," he said. "The only reason I came here was to stay somewhere safe, remember? Plus, I'm not going anywhere till I have my wish back in here." He thumped on his chest.

Nadia muttered a curse. She deserved his distrust, given how she'd treated him before, but these were abnormal circumstances that would take too long for her to explain.

She sucked in a breath as they walked past the statue in the yard, its corroded face sending shivers down her spine. "I'm coming back out, Miles. I'm not trying to scam you here."

"Never said you were." He put up his hands. "But like I heard once, 'trust, but verify.' I'm coming in whether you like it or not. Besides, you don't look good, Nads," Miles said as they reached the porch steps.

She shot him a grimace. "*Don't* call me that. And just wait out on the porch for a minute. I'll come back out to get you."

She pushed past him and opened the door. But Miles slipped into the entrance hall behind her, ducking under her arm when she meant to slam the door in his face. Evidently, according to Basha and the house, he was still on the good list and welcome inside.

On a normal evening, there were always lights on, with the chatter of a TV, radio, or record player drifting through the halls. Now, the house sat in strange, dark quietude, as though it had been abandoned and was apprehensively waiting for its owners to come back.

"Mom? Babcia?" Nadia called out. She edged toward the kitchen and peered around the door, but there was no sound except for the droning fridge. "Are you here?"

She drew back from the kitchen and crossed the entrance hall to the living room on the right-hand side. It was what Nadia had always called the "showroom," since no one ever used it unless there was a special occasion. Usually, family gatherings took place in the den beside the kitchen. But if the Wishmaster had come, it'd definitely fit under the umbrella of a "special occasion."

Just not the good kind.

Taking a nervous breath, Nadia pushed open the living room door. Amber light enveloped the room in a hazy glow, as though a fire flickered inside—but the grate was cold and unused. Instead, the glow came from the antique brass lamps and the chandelier that had been dimmed to almost the lowest setting. With all the dark wood paneling and the drawn velvet drapes that sucked in what little light remained, the room seemed impossibly small, spotlighting only the red-and-gold jacquard couch in the center. Two figures sat there in silence, backs straight, hands resting politely in their laps. A chill rattled up Nadia's spine.

"Why didn't you answer?" Nadia asked, knowing it was a stupid question and aware of Miles peering at her from beside the doorway.

Grace said nothing. She didn't even look at her daughter. She just trained her eyes on the family portrait above the fireplace of the four remaining women in the Kaminski line, with one figure notably taped over in black.

"One of Wishmaster's people called and told us everything." Basha broke the silence, but there was no relief in it. "They explained truth—what happened at Bonaventure."

Out of the corner of her eye, Nadia saw Miles point toward the kitchen and creep away.

"You did not say the wishing box was destroyed," Basha continued. "You told lie."

Nadia shook her head. "I didn't, Babcia. I thought you already knew after Black Hat called Mom."

"You no speak." Basha raised a finger. "I speak now. You cannot be blamed for box breaking, but you should have told us yourself. But that is not all, as you know."

Nadia's stomach sank like a rock. She'd been dreading this conversation. Had Black Hat realized that Miles had saved her life and gained a wish—and then realized that Nadia took it for herself? Or had someone like Croak been watching them in Bonaventure from afar, unseen?

"You steal wish and keep for yourself, when you know we owe debt to Wishmaster." Basha clicked her tongue in distaste. "After all that was said earlier, you defy me, and you defy your mother. You think only of yourself and not the rodzina and what it would do to us."

Apparently, Grace had been instructed not to talk either. She only flinched and kept staring.

Nadia floundered. "I wasn't trying to defy you, and anyway, I don't have it anymore," she babbled. "I wanted to wish away the debt, Babcia! I saw the chance, and I took it. But someone stole the wish from me—someone who works for the Wishmaster."

"Foolish dziecko! What do I tell you? Keep head down, play nice, all will be well!" Basha groaned. "Now, you put me in dangerous position. You force me to act against Wishmaster. I have ways, do not mistake, but I no want use them. Wishmaster might retaliate and take our wishes, but . . . is last resort. If no options, I use. Even if our wishes are taken, it will save our lives."

Nadia fidgeted. "It's just two feathers, not three. We can still get back on Kal—I mean, the Wishmaster's good side."

Basha rose from her seat, shaking her cane at Nadia. "Is no 'just this' and 'just that.' Why did you no listen? I do not speak for good of my own health."

Rage festered inside Nadia, heating her face. Her grandmother was right—of course she was—but why couldn't Basha see the full picture? Why couldn't she understand that Nadia had been trying to do the right thing by freeing everyone from the debt? Sure, it came with the bonus of giving her free rein to resurrect Nick, but that wasn't her sole reason.

"I'll never get it right, will I?" Nadia retorted, her tongue no longer under her control. "I made this debt, and I wanted to fix it. I did what any of you would've done, given the opportunity. Don't pretend you'd have acted differently if an untracked wish fell into your lap."

Basha sighed. "I would believe if you were no clinging on to dead husband. Is not selfless act, dziecko. Basha is no stupid." Her eyes narrowed. "You go to place where Nick died yesterday, and you no think is strange coincidence? I ask you to obey and you disobey. You do it for him, not for us. If given choice, you would no pick rodzina—you pick him."

The sheer insensitivity in her grandmother's words struck a jarring chord in Nadia's chest. What did it matter what the endgame was, if the run-up helped everyone? Why couldn't she have more than one goal? In fact, she was starting to wonder what would have happened if she *had* managed to clear the debt with a wish. Would her grandmother have conjured up some other reason to stop her from bringing Nick back?

Nick *was* her rodzina, her family.

"Maybe if you helped us rack up wishes instead of hiding away in this house, we'd be done by now!" The explosive words burst out of Nadia before she could stop them. "But you wanted to delay us, didn't you? That way, you wouldn't have to pretend to be sympathetic and listen to me begging you to give me answers. It happened in *our* family once, somewhere in our history, so why couldn't it happen again? You say you care so much about the rodzina, but that's only when it suits you."

Basha raised her cane. "I beat sense into you right now! Is no our fault. Is all you and this foolish dream that you will no let die. You do this for him, no for us. Now you put us in danger!"

"This wouldn't have happened if you'd let me go to the Wishmaster to ask for a wish," Nadia nearly shouted. "Maybe there's still time. She doesn't hate me the way she hates you. If I beg her, maybe she'll help. If she says yes, then I won't need anything else from you. You'll never have to see your stupid, selfish little granddaughter again."

Basha jabbed the point of her cane into the floor, making a dent. "You no go to Wishmaster! You no make this worse!"

"I had a life without you, and I want it back. It's my right to make my own choices." Tears stung Nadia's eyes, but she refused to let them fall.

Basha turned her back on her. "Leave this house and take wretchedness with you. Is no wanted here. Is no welcome. We give and we give and we give to you, and you repay us with lies, insolence, and disrespect. I no have it in *my* house!"

A strange tug pulled at Nadia's waist, as if invisible hands were around her. She glared at her grandmother.

"Mama, no!" Grace yelled, finally finding her voice. "You both just need to calm down and talk about this when you're not so fired up. I really do think she was trying to do the right thing."

Basha waved a dismissive hand. "Two granddaughters, and both rotten as fallen apples from tree. I had hope for you, Nadia. You had promise, but you disappoint all same. Your core is no good either. Is moldy and spoiled. You same as sister, wanting only wishes for yourselves!"

"I asked for *one* wish, damn it!" Nadia fired back. "One. Not two, not three, just one. Am I not allowed a smidgen of hope after everything I've been through, or do you really only care about the business and debt? Don't you give a shit that my heart got ripped out and stamped on, and I'm barely breathing over here?"

Basha whirled around. "You no curse at me! I take soap to your mouth and scrub!"

Grace took hold of Basha's shoulders, only for the older woman to shuffle her off. "Please, Mama. Both of you, go to bed, and you can talk about this in the morning."

Basha pretended not to hear and glared at Nadia. "Perhaps my wish keep my Grace and me alive. But you make us forever prisoners here if Wishmaster threaten to take more than just wishes. You agreed with plan to take no more risks, keep head low. But now, another feather because of you!"

"You really can't see past your own problems, can you?" Nadia spat. "*Kaleena* was right all along."

Basha glowered. "Your rotten apple of sister will no save you. But perhaps she let your mother and me live when you have paid price for this."

"Mama, don't say that!" Grace jumped in again.

Basha aimed her cane at Nadia. "She make me this way. Both granddaughters—they destroy me! I take no more, Grace. I am done. Finished."

"We can come up with something. We can fix this," Grace pleaded. "But if you kick Nadia out, you're sentencing her to a life without wishes—and that's at the *very least*. We need her to stay protected here until we can strike another deal."

Basha scoffed. "She is dead to me anyway. Why should I care what happens, eh?"

Nadia wasn't even angry anymore; she was just bitterly, bitterly sad that her once-vibrant grandmother had turned into this. "Once upon a time, I thought you were queen of this household, Babcia. And you are. A tyrant queen."

"Will you stop winding each other up!" Grace begged, her harried gaze flitting between them.

"Wind up? I am not one bringing stranger to house," Basha said, and Nadia stiffened. "Yes, I know. I always know."

The door opened, and Miles stood just outside it, looking shocked and sheepish.

Basha rounded on him. "This is no your place, musician! Is no your home. Keep your nose out of family business."

Nadia waited for her to shoo him away or go into a meltdown about an "outsider" being privy to a wish-hunting conversation, but Basha didn't seem surprised at all.

"If you put your fingers in fire, you get burned," Basha continued, eyes narrowed at Nadia and speaking as if Miles wasn't standing right there. "Wishing world is no for you. I can see you are no prepared for such things."

"I wouldn't be in this mess if *she* hadn't stolen *my* wish!" Miles said. "That's some bullshit right there. I'm not 'keeping my nose out' until I get back what's mine."

Basha glared at him. "Then you are bad as Nadia. You no listen, and so you get in trouble. No one listens to Basha, and then cry when all goes wrong. If you steal unsanctioned wish, you find yourself in debt too."

"But it was *my* wish! I can't steal back what was already mine!"

Basha snorted. "You will see. Basha is always right. Wishmaster rules prevail."

Nadia shook her head. It was always the same with her. Basha couldn't even entertain the *possibility* she might be wrong.

"Not all of the rules are beyond compromise," Nadia said. "Not everything has to end with a debt, if it can be ironed out. Miles is a first-time offender, so he might just get a warning, or a suggestion that he leave town."

"I'm not leaving because some Wishmaster says I have to, and I'm not paying back a debt I don't owe," Miles shot back. "I haven't done anything wrong! You're all out of your damn minds if you think this makes any kind of sense. How can I steal my own wish? It's *mine*!"

Basha banged her cane on the ground, sending a shudder through the floorboards. "I have enough of this. Kick both out, now. I am tired of explaining rules to blockheads who no listen."

"Who are you talking to?" Miles asked, frowning in confusion.

Nadia groaned. "It's a long—"

A violent gust of wind pushed Nadia and Miles out through the living room door, their arms flailing. Grace howled for Basha to stop, but the sound got lost in the gale as the pair staggered back across the entrance hall, unable to fight the house's ejection. The front door swung open of its own accord a second before they would've been smashed against it, and with one last blast of Basha's anger, the house belched them out onto the porch.

The tornado winds ceased, and the door slammed back into the jamb. Thrown off balance, Nadia teetered on the top step of the porch, narrowly avoiding tumbling down the rest of them by grabbing the nearest column. Miles, on the other hand, had already landed on his back, half waterfalling down the steps.

"Ow! God, that hurts," he rasped, rolling onto his belly and pushing himself back onto his haunches. He arched his spine to a good ninety degrees, his hands splayed on his waist.

Nadia leaned into the pillar. "Anything broken?"

"I'm figuring that out." He twisted from side to side, the way she'd seen her mother do when Nadia was a kid, back in the days of spandex and aerobics.

She stared at the house, blinking back tears before turning her gaze toward the darkened street. Usually, occurrences that were considered "magic" manifested as something that could be logically explained: a door swinging back in someone's face, a freak lightning strike, a hint of déjà vu. The Wishing Tree relied on the brain's capacity to fill in blanks with a more believable explanation. If there were any paparazzi lurking in the shadows, Nadia figured they'd do exactly that and convince themselves that someone had shoved them both out of the door instead.

"So that's really it?" Miles asked as he rose unsteadily to his feet.

Nadia nodded. "The house won't let me back in now. Or you." She rubbed her eyes, pretending she was trying to dislodge some dust while discreetly soaking up a stray tear.

He laughed nervously. "The house has a mind of its own?"

"It's not the house, really—it's Basha. As long as she's in there, it's like she's *one* with the place, although they act independently." Nadia gestured back at the house. "I got mad once as a kid and tried to break a vase, but it just kept bouncing off the floor until Basha pushed me out the door. Back then, I'd beg to be let back in because I had nowhere else to go."

"She doesn't like to be challenged, I see," Miles noted wryly.

How much had he overheard in there about Nick? She tried to think if she'd even used the word "resurrection," but the hurt and frustration muddled her memory. At least Miles was polite enough not to pry into her personal drama.

Nadia followed him down the garden path. "I knew she'd be mad, but . . . I don't even want to talk about it right now. It'll just get me pissed off again."

"Is the Wishmaster really coming for me?" Miles asked.

"It's definitely possible. But, like I said, you might get let off for being a first-time offender." She frowned. "Although, knowing the way the Wishmaster handles things, I wouldn't count on it."

She took out her phone and checked for any threatening voice mails, but her mailbox was empty. With no safe house and no car, she wasn't sure where to head next. Her insides tightened with a strange, clenching loss as she remembered the taunting jangle of her keys. Nick's Chevy was probably gone for good now.

Sure, to most people, it was just a car, and it wasn't like she had no insurance to cover the theft. But it wasn't just a car to her. It was a well of memories: road trips across the state and that satisfying crunch of gravel when they arrived at their B and B or campsite for the night. Parking up on a grassy roadside for no other reason than to take in a beautiful view, or to paw over each other like they were teenagers, fogging up the windows. And the late-night snack runs to the store, asking what the other wanted. It was like that woman had driven off with a box full of Nadia's most precious possessions.

Nadia stared at the sidewalk. "I guess we'll just have to walk to the nearest street corner and figure out what to do next."

"What's this 'we' stuff, Nads? I'm set. I texted my ride while you were all in there yelling at each other." Miles nodded to the side of the road opposite the house, where a black Mercedes with tinted windows waited, its headlights on. Maybe he'd been too distracted talking to his chauffer to listen to much of the conversation after all. He spread his arms wide. "Now, are you gonna come along or what?"

"How come I get an invite now?" she said suspiciously, eyeing the ride. "Not that long ago, you were going to call your publicist and say I'd abducted you. Why the sudden change of heart? Don't tell me you've taken pity on me after hearing that screaming match?"

Miles snorted. "For someone with an advanced degree, you're not so sharp."

"Well?"

"You figure it out."

She thought through it, although the pounding in her head didn't make it easy. What did he have to gain from this arrangement?

"You're okay with me tagging along now because you realize you need my expertise. Is that it?" Nadia said. "You could *find* your wish again, but you don't know shit about the way the business works, so you know that if you want to have any hope of getting your wish back —and not having your fingers broken—you need me along."

He smirked. "Fine, you got it. I need your help with this whole wish trap thing, even if I know you're just going to try to do me dirty again in the end. But we'll see."

"Lucky for you, I have a heart of gold," she replied with a straight face.

"Ha! You ever thought about comedy? I know what's in it for you— you want me to use my finding powers to help you out. I didn't want to have to offer something I know you wouldn't have been able to resist."

Nadia snorted. "Oh yeah, what's that? I'm not my mom, remember."

Miles chuckled. "Obviously. A private concert was what *I* was talking about. What were you thinking?"

Nadia felt color rising in her cheeks, and the fact that Miles stared at her intently only made it worse.

He shrugged. "Maybe I'd have considered it, if that's what it took." He flashed her his best deep, troubled rock-poet look. "I could've made you believe in love again. Even if it was just until the sun came up."

Nadia faked a mini vomit. "Does that really work on women?"

Miles laughed. "More than you'd think."

An idea struck her as he moved to cross the road. A wish trap was her only means of getting another wish to help her escape this whole mess. Or at least a way to resurrect Nick, if she had to run out of Savannah and start someplace new, away from her family's constant judgment and threat of punishment. Maybe it was time to make a deal.

"I've got a proposition for you." Remembering his earlier words about a night with him, she hastened to add, "A *real* proposition."

"Okay, shoot."

She took a deep breath. "If I help you get your wish back *and* I promise not to steal it again, then you'll help me 'find' a way to escape punishment from the Wishmaster."

He turned to her, his eyebrows arched. "I thought that was a given. What's the catch? What else do *you* get out of it? 'Cause I don't buy you suddenly turning into Mother Teresa."

She nodded to the pregnant-esque bulge in his hoodie pocket. "I get to keep your wishing jar."

He frowned. "You want this jar? *My* jar?"

Nadia understood his skepticism, but it truly was a genuine offer. Given that Miles could easily find her whenever he wanted, there was no point in gunning for his wish again. But she might as well try to gain something of value from this exchange that would last her beyond their reluctant partnership.

"My wishing box is broken, remember?" she explained, eager to strike a deal before she got into his car. "And once you have your wish back, you won't have any need for your jar. But it'll give me a shot at getting my two remaining wishes."

His nose crinkled. "Now it sounds like you're just trying to convince me not to trust you."

"How can anybody trust *anyone*?" she answered, employing some of her marriage counselor expertise in framing questions. "But we have to. When there's a lion around, the antelopes have to stick together."

Miles eyed her curiously. "I get I'm supposed to be the antelope in that little bit of poetry, but what does that make you, then?"

"We're *both* antelopes, fighting a mutual lion—the Wishmaster who stole our wish." She put on a rehearsed smile, hoping it would make him more open.

"Sounds exactly like what a lion would say. Open up that mouth. I want to see those fangs. Besides, it's *my* wish. Not *ours*."

She nodded guiltily. "As I said, I promise I won't steal that wish from you again, since it's your last. I . . . I've been dishonest and unfair toward you, and I'm sorry. I'm trying to make it up to you." The admission was harder than she'd expected. She'd encouraged similar words from her clients many times, but it was easier to encourage someone else to apologize than to do it herself. "Believe it or not, that's not the sort of person I am. Sure, I'll lose the space your wish would've filled, but I'll still have two more wishing slots left."

Miles looked at her, skepticism still written across his face.

She sighed. "Fine, how about this: it'll be easier for me to find a second wish if you aren't tailing me indefinitely, trying to get revenge because I stole your wish. This way, we both get a clean break."

After a moment of staring at her without speaking, Miles patted his jar-shaped tummy. "I'm probably a sucker, but for some reason, I believe you. You'd better not be lying again." He turned his head sharply, his eyes creasing. "But I've got an additional rider on this contract."

"Which is?"

"You tell me how the jar works before I give it to you—which isn't happening until I get my wish back and spend it so I know you can't steal it *again*, by the way—and maybe we can go our separate ways . . . on friendlier terms. But first, we need to stop yapping and hitch our wagons to this ride, and fast. Feels like I'm losing the thief's trail already."

Nadia shrugged. "Deal."

As they finally crossed toward the Mercedes, the burly beefcake who got out of the driver's side looked like a bouncer told he was attending a wedding on short notice. His suit was at least two sizes too small for his gym-pumped body, and the collar looked like it was about to burst from trying to contain his thick neck. He had a kind—albeit overly tanned—face and a friendly smile.

"So, you need me after all? I thought you said you were good tonight, man," the driver joked. "I was about to crack open a cold one."

Miles went in for a bear hug, with a resounding back clap. "Sorry to drag you out, Jack. Things changed. You know how it is."

"I do. That's why I'm always ready to run to your beck and call." Jack smirked, and Miles laughed, but Nadia heard a note of irritation in the driver's voice. Jack eyed her. "And who's this? I'd guess supermodel, but that's not your type these days. You still got a type? It's been a while."

Jack turned to Nadia and whispered conspiratorially, "It's a goddamn tragedy. Used to be the best part of my day, drivin' home Victoria's Secret angels and famous actresses. Can't name any names, of course. These days, though? Nobody."

Nadia stuck out her hand. "I'm Nadia. Not a supermodel. More the thorn in Miles's side."

"Not the first one I've met." Jack laughed brightly and turned to Miles. "Ain't that the truth?"

Miles grimaced. "This is a different kind of situation."

"That's what you always say." Jack opened the back door of the Mercedes, then nodded perfunctorily at Nadia. "Ma'am." She climbed inside. "Sir," he said with exaggerated politeness to Miles.

Miles shook his head as he slid onto the cool leather seats, but he waited until Jack was in the driver's seat before he spoke. "C'mon, how many years have you been driving me? You know I hate that 'sir' shit."

Jack's laugh sounded forced again. "Fine, Miles. You're the boss after all."

"Anyway, don't worry. You'll be home again in no time. Not gonna be an all-nighter."

"You always say that too." Jack rolled his eyes. The poor guy had probably been looking forward to his night off, though Miles didn't seem to notice his annoyance.

"Got a favorite song of his you want to hear?" Jack asked Nadia, looking at her in the rearview mirror.

She shook her head. "Nah. Not sure I know any of them. I'm more of a country fan." That wasn't strictly true, but the withering glare Miles gave her was worth it.

Jack laughed. "Oh man, I like you."

"All right, everybody done trying to clown on the guy who owns the car?" Miles snapped. "Just get going. I'll let you know where to turn."

Jack sighed. "This again?"

As the car accelerated smoothly down the street, Nadia watched the childhood home from which she'd been cast out recede into the night. That was the past, it seemed. Now, she was completely alone.

Miles humming a tune to himself as he stared out the window offered a correction: she wasn't *completely* alone. She had one person in her corner.

Maybe.

Chapter Thirteen

Leaning up against the tinted window, Nadia peered out as the car sailed down East Broad Street, passing Mother Mathilda Beasley Park. It wasn't as well-known to outsiders as places like Forsyth Park or Bonaventure, but it ought to have been. It was named after Mother Beasley, the first African American nun in the state of Georgia, and that fact alone made it one of her favorite parks.

On a normal day, the park made her smile, but not tonight. It reminded her of so many Saturday mornings with her mom, grandma, and sister, where hours flew by like minutes while they conjured up stories across the two playgrounds. The jungle gyms would transform into castles, Nadia defending one while Kaleena defended the other. Sometimes, they were ships, or fortresses in the sky, or stables for the imaginary horses they rode around the park's trails. And sometimes, they were just jungle gyms.

Growing up ruins everything. She'd heard about mother birds kicking their chicks out of the nest as a fly-or-fall test. But no documentary had ever warned her that you could fly away from the nest, only to return as a grown bird years later and get hoofed out when the grizzled old hen didn't like how you behaved.

It hurt to get thrown out of the house like that, with no attempt at compromise or understanding. Finally, her worst fear had come true: she was truly alone, with nobody to turn to. And that loneliness was a peach pit in her stomach—spiky and rough, and sprouting fronds of fear that slithered up into her ribs, squeezing her chest until she couldn't take a full breath. It felt a lot like grief, but of a very different kind. Perhaps it would be even harder to resurrect her dead relationships than it would be to revive Nick.

Nadia concentrated on Miles as a distraction and lowered her voice so Jack wouldn't hear. "Can you still sense the thief? How does this finding thing work, anyway?"

Miles shrugged. "I can feel her, but the path's fuzzier than usual right now. It's hard to explain. Like, it's not GPS precise. It's more of a feeling, like Hot and Cold. You know, that kids' game, if you used to play that."

"Does that mean you're feeling warm right now?"

"Yeah. The warmth ain't as strong, but maybe that just means she's still running." He paused and took out his wishing jar. "Now, part of this bargain is you teaching me how to use this thing, remember? We've got time."

"Now? Here?" Nadia nodded toward the driver's seat.

"Don't worry about it. He'll just think we're talking about a new album or something. Hit me with lesson one."

She folded her arms across her chest. "Well, once you open the wish trap, you have to coax someone into sharing what's called a heart secret. Something they wouldn't tell anyone else. It has to be emotional enough to release the wish. The Wishing Tree decides what kind of secret is big enough to do that."

"Sounds . . . vague." He squinted down at the jar.

"Welcome to the business," Nadia said. "Stealing wishes is all about knowing what to ask and how to ask it. If you're too direct, people clam up. You have to ease them in and build rapport until they feel comfortable enough to let things slip."

"Ah, now the marriage counseling makes sense." He smirked. "But seems like that might violate some sort of professional code of ethics. Should I report you to some medical board?"

"I don't do it just to steal wishes," she said, straightening in her seat. "I genuinely like helping people. My reconciliation rates are high because I care."

"Okay, so how do you *know* if a secret is strong enough?" Miles asked. "You can't just guess, or you'd get it wrong half the time and end up wishless."

Nadia gestured toward the jar. "The wood stays cold if it's too weak, and it warms up if it's strong enough. It's not a subtle heat either."

"How close do you have to be to steal a wish in the first place?" He seemed eager, as if she were unpicking the threads of the universe for him.

"You have to be quite close, which is why that thief called me out to the church. She was nearby with her wish trap. You can also get someone to put a piece of paper, with the heart secret written on it, into your wishing jar or into your hand. But it has to be verbal or hand-written, if you're thinking you can get some old flame to text you a secret. That doesn't work." She smiled thinly. "The Wishing Tree hasn't moved into the digital age."

Miles scratched his chin. "What if you were listening outside a confessional box?"

"That's blasphemy, and you'd get run out of town," she retorted.

"How about if you hung around one of those trees that people tie their wishes and secrets to? If you took one, would that work?" He looked hopeful. "Or could you ask a kid? Kids are always spilling secrets."

Nadia raised an eyebrow. "And you were calling *me* underhanded before."

"Yeah, I guess that'd be a bit shady." He dropped his chin to his chest. "But what if the kid had saved someone's life, so they had a wish to spare? Some kids would have something like a heart secret, but you might get one who's just had a happy life so far. Would the gauge for what's 'big enough' of a secret go down for them? Or what if you walked past someone who was telling someone else a secret over the phone?"

Nadia sighed. "Look, this isn't math or chemistry. You don't add two parts of this and one part of that and get the same outcome every time. There are some rules that can't be broken, and some that can be bent near ninety degrees. It's hard to quantify. And you're not going to learn everything in five minutes that I've spent a lifetime studying. So, I'll keep it simple. The only thing you can rely on is the heat of the wish trap."

"But hold up—what if you had already *spent* my wish, not just absorbed it? Could I have gotten it back?"

"I see you're already planning ahead for when I betray you," Nadia said dryly.

He gave her a look. "Gotta keep my options open. So people can do that, then?"

"Hope stealers can, yeah." She figured she might as well go all in at this point. "They specialize in guessing people's wish wording, though it's harder to steal a used wish, in my opinion. You need the exact wording *and* a piece of wishery paper, which is tough to find these days. You write down the wording, burn the paper, and the wish goes into a wish trap. Still counts as one of your three if you absorb it, though."

"I get what you're saying." Miles rubbed his chin. "Then they can have whatever power the other person had—and equally as strong."

"More often, people just let the wish disappear, especially if it's the wish of someone they have a grudge against," Nadia said.

"Now that's just wasteful. And petty as hell."

She shrugged. "Not when you've been on the receiving end of some crappy wish-given ability and want revenge without outright murdering them. It's a common punishment in the wishing world."

"Then let's hope—" Miles suddenly perked up. "Ooh, I'm getting that good feeling! Jack, go back around the block!"

The driver nodded. "You got it."

It was the third time they'd gone around, but Nadia wasn't going to argue with Miles's feelers—although she suspected his senses were still dulled from the wishing bark–infused wine he'd drunk, courtesy of her mother.

"Agh, it's gone again," Miles grumbled as they did another circuit. "Can you go around once more, Jack?"

Jack cast a withering look back through the rearview mirror. "Sure. Whatever you want."

"It keeps slipping." Miles tapped his temple, as if it might help to center his feelers. "What's wrong with me? It's never like this."

Nadia contemplated mentioning the wishing bark, but Jack cut in before she could.

"He did this when I first got the job," he said. "We were in LA, and he wanted to find Lionel Richie's house. I said he could just get one of those StarMaps, or whatever they're called, but he was dead set on just looking for it. I thought he was nuts, but he's paying my bills, y'know, so you do what you gotta do."

Nadia smiled. "Lionel Richie, huh?"

"What?" Miles shot her a wounded look. "He's a legend. A musician can like a lot of music, Nads. Just because they play rock doesn't mean that's all they've got on the turntables."

"Anyway," Jack continued, "I'm driving around and around Beverly Hills, thinking I'm going to get pulled over for curb-crawling or something, and Miles goes, 'Got it! Turn that way!' So I do, and it's the same damn street we've been driving up and down for the last half hour. But then he starts sniffing, like he's going to smell the wealth of Lionel Richie, and I'm already thinking about handing in my notice."

Nadia laughed. "And then what happened?"

"He sticks his head out the window and starts pointing wildly, so I pull up to this place and press the intercom. He takes over, saying he's this up-and-coming musician who wants to have a mentoring session or something." Jack looked back at Miles. "Should I tell her the rest?"

Miles shook his head, his expression unamused. "No, go around the block again."

"Seriously?" Jack's brow wrinkled.

"Do I look like I'm joking?" Miles turned to Nadia as the driver did his bidding. "Basically, I got laughed off the street. Security asked if I knew how many people tried that line every day. I gave them my name and everything, but they said they'd never heard of me. If ever you need humbling, go to the house of someone super famous and try to get past their security."

After going around the same block three more times, Jack's irritated sighs grew more and more frequent.

"Can't you just tell me where you want me to go?" Jack grumbled over the sound of the radio. "You must have some idea. I don't think you're going to find a celebrity down this street."

Miles rubbed his head and whispered to Nadia, "I don't understand. I could feel my wish—it was right there—and then it vanished. It keeps happening."

"If your wish is at the Wishmaster's headquarters, I might have an idea why," Nadia replied. Although they'd both been speaking quietly, she hoped the low music would further mask their conversation from Jack. "It's notoriously hard to find, and even harder to remember. I've been there once, but if you put a gun to my head and asked me for the directions, I wouldn't be able to tell you. There's some kind of wishing afoot there. Like my . . . family's house, but on a bigger scale."

Calling the Kaminski Mansion her house hadn't felt right since she'd moved out for college, but now that she'd been literally thrown onto the street, it didn't feel like it belonged to her anymore at all.

"And your finding skills might also be on the fritz because of the wine my mom gave you," she added hesitantly. "You shouldn't take drinks from wishing folk. Nine times out of ten, it's infused with Alexander's Tea—a concoction that dulls wished-for abilities, albeit temporarily."

Miles's jaw dropped. "You people *drugged* me? Of course you did. There's literally nothing you won't do."

"Maybe you should try changing what you're looking for," Nadia suggested as a peace offering.

"Now you're going to tell me how to use *my* finding ability?" he huffed, but she could see a thought pass across his eyes. A few moments later, and now on their umpteenth circuit of the same block, Miles punched the air. "Yes, there it is! Jack, take a right!"

Jack exhaled. "Finally."

Nadia had no idea where they were headed, and Miles didn't seem to want to elaborate.

A few minutes after that, Miles leaned forward through the gap in the front seats. His mouth twisted into a grimace as he muttered to himself, "Really? Here? Why here?"

"Want me to park around back?" Jack asked.

Miles sighed. "No, just get us close to the front. We'll jump out."

"Front of what?" Nadia asked as she leaned over and looked out Miles's window. "The Scrapyard?"

She'd heard about the place—a dive bar and live music club that tried to stay under the tourist radar in order to retain its hole-in-the-wall status.

"You back to slumming like the early days?" Jack asked with a chuckle.

Miles shook his head. He mumbled the truth so that only Nadia would hear it. "Believe me, I hoped I'd never have to come back here, but that's what I get for bumping into the likes of you. This is where the heat is."

The place was hidden away inside an innocuous-looking one-story building with a black metal *S* on the roof and a tiny plaque by the door that read *The Scrapyard*. Beneath a tangled canopy of lights, the local crowd milled about on the outside patio, where smokers and over-heated partygoers went to cool off. This wasn't Nadia's kind of Saturday-night scene at all, even when Nick was alive, although he'd loved mosh pits.

"Let me guess—this is where you warbled through your first open nights in front of an ambivalent crowd determined to talk over you?" Nadia teased.

Miles clasped at his chest. "Too close to the bone, man." He took a shaky breath. "I used to play here with my band when I first started out. I was just a kid then. I also broke up with my high school girlfriend in the parking lot, who also happened to be the lead singer of said band. So, yeah, I've got some history here."

With a decisive push, he opened the door and got out. Nadia scooted along to his side and clambered out behind him, but by the time her feet were firmly on the sidewalk, he was already at the bar's entrance with his hood up and his sunglasses back on.

"That really doesn't make you look incognito," she muttered, darting after him.

After buying tickets from the woman at the door, they ventured deeper into the bar. A mesmerizing optical bombardment of blue and orange neon lights snaked across the ceiling and walls. Nadia squinted against the glare of jangling arcade games, and the olfactory hit of greasy food threatened to overwhelm her. "Seven Nation Army" bumped through the speakers at a surprisingly sedate volume, but she figured the decibels would skyrocket once the band got onto the raised stage at the back of the club.

"You need to take those sunglasses off!" Nadia said over the background music.

He pulled his Ray-Bans to the bridge of his nose and peered over the rims. "I don't want to be noticed."

"Then look like a normal person!"

Reluctantly, he took them off and folded them back into his hoodie pouch, alongside his wishing jar. "Do you want a drink?"

"No, I want to know why we're here." She waved a hand around the bar. "What tingles are your Spidey senses giving off?"

He pulled her around to a nook between the bar and the hallway that led to the bathrooms. "I was thinking of *how* to get the wish back, not just finding the wish itself," he explained. "Even if we could find the headquarters, following the thief straight back to the Wishmaster would land us in shark-infested waters. Maybe literally. So, I focused on wanting to find a way for us to actually steal the wish. And now we're here, so I'm following my nose."

"Is this your way of telling me you have no idea what we're doing?" Nadia eyed him warily.

He shook his head. "My finding skill is sort of like listening to a record and picking out the different strands—I might notice a harmony, or the twang of a bass guitar, or a bit of a flute, and it's up to me to figure out what I'm hearing. It doesn't give me specifics. I only have a sense of where to look, but not what I'll find there or what to do with that information."

"The ever-nuanced ways of the wishing world," Nadia grumbled. Maybe the wishing bark had really fritzed Miles's finding skills, or maybe she just needed to trust in the process.

Miles scanned the room. His eyes flitted from side to side until they zeroed in on a dark-haired man laughing with a nervous-looking older woman at a table in front of a *Ms. Pac-Man* game. The woman appeared even more out of place than Miles had when he'd worn his sunglasses, with her floral blouse buttoned up to the neck and a vintage Chanel jacket that she'd yet to remove despite the close heat of the bar. The man turned slightly, giving Nadia a glimpse of the wishbone flower tattoo on his neck.

"Shit," Nadia muttered. "The guy over there is another one of the Wishmaster's. Goes by Croak."

Miles's eyes widened. "I hope that's not because he makes people croak?"

"He's an intermediary, like Black Hat," she replied. "He'll recognize me in a heartbeat, so we need to be careful."

He tilted his head toward the older woman. "What about her?"

"Probably looking to buy a wish. Does she seem like a Saturday-night regular to you?"

He pursed his lips. "Does everyone in the wishery business get to pick their own code names, or are they handed out?"

"We pick them."

His mouth cracked into a smile. "Mine would be something like 'the Axe,' maybe."

Nadia rolled her eyes. "Listen, if we screw this up, the Wishmaster might have somebody hit you with a literal axe and keep your hands as a trophy. So let's just focus, okay?"

Miles held up a hand. "Gotcha. No code names. Total seriousness from now on."

The outside crowd filtered back in as a skittish, wide-eyed techie flitted around the stage like a trapped squirrel, tapping on the mics and checking the drums. A second later, the overhead music was turned down, leaving only the sound of shoes on the wooden floors and the murmured conversations bouncing around the bar.

Using the crowd to their advantage, Nadia and Miles weaved through the throng of eager bodies and snuck along the wall of arcade games to take a seat behind the two conspirators. On the way, Nadia swiped a bar-branded hat off the wall and jammed it onto her head, trying to tuck her hair under the edges. She'd just about finished when she slid onto the chair, with her back to Croak.

Miles looked like he was going to put his shades back on, but Nadia swatted his hand.

"What did I just say?" she hissed. "The hood is enough."

"Lenny Kravitz does it." But he folded them away again.

Nadia settled back against the chair. Despite the chatter around them, she managed to pick out Croak's voice and snatch the gist of what he was saying to the woman. Nadia assumed the Wishmaster had chosen this location—somewhere public, and somewhere way out of the client's comfort zone—to make her hurry through the meeting and agree to anything the intermediary offered.

"Once you've made the transaction, you meet one of our people at the drop-off point, and everyone goes home happy," Croak said.

The buyer sounded like she was rattling her jewelry with anxiety. "Are you sure this is all legitimate? I mean, can it really be real, this wishing business? You're not trying to con me in a very elaborate way, are you?"

Most first-timers shared the same concerns, and for good reason. It wasn't an easy pill to swallow, finding out that there was something akin to magic in this world after believing that fairy tales and strange happenings were the stuff of conspiracy theorists and daydreams.

"I get why you'd be worried, but I showed you it's all legit," Croak replied. "Seeing is believing, right? You'll get what you're paying for. Simple as that."

The woman made a nervous sound halfway between a laugh and a throat clearing. "It's just so difficult to wrap my head around. A wish coming true . . . Isn't that what everybody wants?"

"That's why you're one of the lucky ones," Croak said. "Once the money clears, yours will be ready. My colleague Valhalla will be the one at the drop tomorrow morning. You can't miss her. You'd see her head above any crowd, and she'll be steering the whole operation."

Miles leaned forward. "I got that feeling again. Major heat. Valhalla has got to be our thief."

Nadia nodded.

"And what time should I meet this woman?" the buyer asked.

"Val will be expecting you tomorrow morning—exactly at nine twenty. You'll have to go through that whole process I explained earlier." Nadia heard Croak slide a piece of paper across the table. "This is the address, and you'll need that other info on there. Don't lose it."

A button clicked open. The buyer had put the slip of paper in her purse. Nadia exchanged a conspiratorial look with Miles. In order to get the intel *they* needed, they'd have to pickpocket the buyer for that slip of paper.

Chapter Fourteen

Nadia had assumed Croak would leave after handing off the address to the buyer, but instead he slouched back in his chair, taking a swig of his drink. His eyes were fixed on the stage. Clearly, he was sticking around for the show, and the older woman next to him was pinned in by chairs on all sides, so she was forced to stay too.

"I need you to distract him while I talk to the buyer," Nadia whispered to Miles. "Can you manage that? Knowing him, he's probably wearing something expensive, so spill some beer on him."

"I don't have a drink."

"Then mock him—he'll hate that."

The crowd's raucous cheers nearly drowned out her words. Nadia's gaze shifted toward the stage as a tall, beautiful Black woman wielding an impressive mother-of-pearl guitar took hold of the mic. Gold eyeliner highlighted the almond shape of her eyes, while another gold line down the center of her lips added to the rock goddess vibes.

"How are we all doing tonight?" Her silky voice reverberated around the club, followed by a squeal of feedback. "You going to get on that, Jim? The only feedback I want tonight is cheers and hollers."

The crowd whooped and started up a chant. "Monique, Monique, Monique!"

"Aw, y'all remember me. I'm touched." The singer smiled, her eyes twinkling. "Here I was thinking I'd be six songs in before y'all knew who you were here to see."

The slightly tipsy crowd erupted in a cacophony of whistles, howls, and bawdy cheers.

Nadia nudged Miles hard. "What's up with you? Get focused! You look like you've seen a ghost."

"Yeah, ghost of lovers past," Miles muttered. "Remember the high school girlfriend I mentioned?" He nodded to the stage. "That's Monique. I had no idea she was still doing shows here."

Nadia looked back at the singer. "If she sings anything like she holds the attention of a room, you never should've let her go."

He cast her a withering glare. "My mom always said the same thing."

"Take me home, Monique!" one man called out, no doubt emboldened with liquid courage.

Monique flashed him a grin. "Aw, honey, you know that ain't one of my songs. There ain't no country roads, and this ain't West Virginia."

The crowd laughed, and the man ducked down behind his friend, chastened.

"Are you ready to scream your lungs out and dance like y'all have got no bones?" Monique shouted. "Don't be making any jokes there, sugar—I got my eye on you." She pointed to the man who'd called out, and the crowd lost their minds. "Make some noise for Monique and the Cosmos Mariners!"

Nadia smiled at the undeniably Savannahian name, thinking of the poet Conrad Aiken and the inscription on his stone bench tombstone from which they'd clearly taken inspiration.

After a compulsory "one, two, three" from the band's drummer, the music kicked in, and it became twice as hard to hear anything. Nadia fought to keep her ears attuned to Croak and the buyer. Monique's fingertips danced across the frets, and she bit her bottom lip in concentration before lunging toward the mic and breaking into the first lines of the song. The sound that came out proved to be as silky and rich as Monique's speaking voice and bolstered by one hell of a powerful belt.

"Wow." Nadia gaped at the woman despite herself. "You *really* shouldn't have let her go."

Miles huffed. "Well, *I'm* still focused on the mission."

He got up and plucked an abandoned drink from beside a *Street Fighter* arcade machine. With surprisingly convincing fake-drunk accuracy, he toppled into Croak and spilled the rancid drink all over him, including the discarded ball of chewed-up gum that had been floating in it. Croak shrieked and jolted to his feet like he'd been challenged to a duel.

"Hey, asshole, do you have any idea how much this cost?" Croak jabbed a finger into Miles's chest, probably not realizing that Miles was wearing a small fortune.

Miles drunk-snickered. "Polyester cleans easy, my man. No harm, no foul."

"P-Polyester!" Croak's cheeks flushed. "This is hand-sewn silk, you moron! Limited edition Dolce & Gabbana. It cost me fifteen hundred bucks, and I'm going to get every dime out of you."

Miles shrugged, blinking both eyes at different times like a true inebriate. "I've got, like, thirty bucks on me. But ain't no way that cost no fifteen hundred dollars."

Nadia had to admit that Miles was doing a mighty fine job of distracting the intermediary. Croak hadn't even given his buyer a second glance; he was too panicked about his precious shirt.

"Asshole!" Croak looked about ready to start throwing fists, but a bouncer moving through the crowd nearby seemed to make him think better of it. Instead, he stormed toward the bathrooms.

Nadia twisted around and slid into the seat that Croak had vacated. The buyer gave a startled yelp and clutched her hands to her chest like she thought Nadia might steal the rings off her fingers. In fairness, after all that had gone on this evening, Nadia probably looked in need of a shower.

"Sorry about my friend. He gets so clumsy when he's had too much," Nadia began, her tone remorseful. "That's a lovely blouse, and I'd feel terrible if your jacket was ruined. Is it an original Chanel? I saw one just like that when my husband and I were in Paris a few years ago." Hopefully, the touch of emotional truth would encourage the woman to open up more herself. It was just like in Nadia's office, except here they were having the conversation at a near yell to be heard over the music.

"Oh . . . He didn't spill any on me," the woman said. "And thank you for saying that about my blouse. My granddaughter called it hideous a few weeks ago, so I wasn't sure if I should wear it again."

The buyer's hands relaxed back onto the table, one placed elegantly over the other. Nadia imagined that this woman had been a debutante in her day, which meant her purse would be to the side of her chair, a short distance from her daintily folded legs. Those were the protocols —always keep one's purse within reach, but not in a place that would be in anyone's way.

Nadia smiled warmly. "It suits your complexion. I'm always telling my grandma she needs to wear brighter colors."

It pained her to talk about Basha, even in an imaginary sense. In reality, her grandmother loved pairing a bold print with her favorite black clothing. Kaleena used to wear Basha's fancy jackets around as a kid and pretend she was a fashion designer, bossing the family cat around. Back before the days of wish debts.

"Aren't you a dear." The buyer's eyes shone, making Nadia feel doubly guilty about what she was going to do. "And you have a very keen eye, spotting my jacket. I bought it many moons ago when I was in Paris, actually. I don't travel so much anymore."

Nadia put on a sad expression. "How come?"

She probed her foot toward the older woman and wiggled the toe of her shoe until she found the handbag strap. Fortunately, with Monique and the Cosmos Mariners bringing the house down, there was no way the buyer could've heard the handbag dragging in Nadia's direction.

"Oh, I have no one to adventure with these days," the woman admitted. "My husband passed a few years ago, and my children and grandchildren have their own busy lives to attend to. They don't want to be escorting around an old coot like me, and I wouldn't want to slow them down."

Nadia nodded sympathetically. "My husband died too. A year ago."

The buyer gasped. "Oh no, that's . . . terrible! You're much too young to be a widow."

While pulling the handbag closer with her foot, Nadia took out her necklace and showed the woman her rings. "I can't even bring myself to wear mine anymore, so I just put his and mine on this chain where they can be close to my heart." She gestured to the buyer's hand, empty of that circle of holy matrimony. "You feel the same?"

"For years, I kept meaning to get it resized." The buyer rubbed the ringless finger. "Then, after he passed, I didn't see the point anymore. Why wear a wedding ring when it will only be a constant reminder of what has been lost?"

Real tears stung Nadia's eyes. "I couldn't have put it better myself."

"That really is tragic, dear." The older woman shook her head sadly. "What was he like, if you don't mind me asking? My Frankie was handsome until the day he died. A great bear of a man, he was. So big and strong I always thought it was impossible that he'd be the first to go."

Nadia lifted her foot and brought the bag into her lap, keeping everything under the table. Tilting her head to one side as though contemplating the woman's question, she unclicked the magnetic button fastening and dipped her hand inside. Rifling through the contents of a—thankfully—meticulously clean bag, she found the slip of paper in no time and palmed it underneath her thigh.

"He was everything to me," Nadia said as she reversed the bag-stealing procedure. "I'm not sure there's any other way I can put it. He was my husband, my best friend, my therapist, and everything in between. Though he was a pretty terrible chef."

The woman laughed. "I'm sorry, I don't think I caught your name."

"Rebecca Aiken." Nadia put out her hand.

"Dolores Lea," the buyer replied in kind. She shook Nadia's hand, her grip surprisingly firm.

Nadia should've felt bad for abusing the woman's trust, and in several ways she did. But she figured she was doing Mrs. Lea a favor. Obviously, the older woman was seeking to change her life through this exchange with Croak, but Nadia doubted Mrs. Lea was prepared for the consequences of any wish she might make. She was too green, too trusting, too sweet.

And because of that same naïveté, Mrs. Lea would probably think she'd lost the slip of paper and call up Croak, who would undoubtedly switch the drop-off location for security purposes. Nadia cursed inwardly. That would put Nadia and Miles back at square one. She'd have to take a photo of the paper and return it to Mrs. Lea's purse before she was any the wiser.

Mrs. Lea put her hand on Nadia's shoulder. "I wish I had a grand-child like you, Rebecca. I wish I could be noticed. I used to be celebrated as a rare beauty and was on every party list in half of Georgia. But now it feels as though I have been left to rot before my time, and . . . I wish I could relive some of that youth and feel seen again, instead of being a nuisance that nobody wants to deal with."

"I'm sure that's not how your family feels." Nadia patted the woman's hand. "I'll probably have to take my friend home in a moment, but can I get you a drink before I go? One for the road, if you're not staying?"

Mrs. Lea chuckled. "This is Savannah, dear. It'd be rude not to accept a drink."

"What's your poison?" Nadia took the paper from under her thigh and stood, slipping it into her pocket as though she was adjusting her jeans.

"I'll have a bourbon if you don't mind. Neat."

Nadia hesitated. "Can I say something?"

"Of course, dear." Mrs. Lea nodded.

"Why don't you tell your family how you feel?" Nadia sighed. "I know that probably sounds patronizing, but sometimes we get scared to ask people to keep us company, in case we're rejected. So we avoid it, even if it means being lonely."

Mrs. Lea looked uncertain. "I'm not sure I should burden them."

"It won't be a quick fix, but . . . face your fears. Your family won't know you need support until you tell them." Nadia put on a grin, though it came with a jab to her heart, thinking of Basha. "And if they act like brats, you take every dime of their inheritance and you spend it on yourself. All of it."

She turned and weaved through the crowd toward the bar. After catching the attention of a bartender, she ordered a bourbon for Mrs. Lea and then shifted her focus to the slip of paper. She set it on the bar, whipped out her phone, and took a picture.

As she waited for the drink to arrive, she read the words that Croak had written, to double up on committing it to her memory. It included an address that seemed vaguely familiar, as well as the words "rain/basketball." Nadia had enough experience in the world of wishmongers to know a password when she saw one.

Maybe it was the latest password into Mata Hari's Speakeasy, which changed weekly so only those "in the know" would have the means to get in. A gimmick, but an effective one. The only problem was, the address didn't match up. She'd have to look into it when she had better cell service.

"Is that everything?" The bartender pushed a red plastic cup at Nadia.

She nodded. "Yeah, thanks."

Taking the drink, Nadia headed back to the table. All the while, her mind whirred, trying to figure out how she could put the paper back in Mrs. Lea's purse without the woman realizing anything was amiss.

Inspiration struck just as she approached the table.

"Oh, I think you dropped a receipt or something." Nadia bent down and pretended to snatch the piece of paper from the floor. "My husband was a tax accountant, so I've had it seared into my brain that you've got to keep every last one of these suckers."

Mrs. Lea pressed a hand to her chest. "Oh, my dear, thank you! I would've been lost without that."

"A big purchase?" Nadia asked as she handed the folded piece of paper back to its original owner.

"Yes, you could say that." Mrs. Lea quickly picked up her purse and put the note into a zipped inside pocket. "You know, I'm so very glad I met you tonight. I should thank your friend for spilling that beer over my . . . associate."

Nadia put the bourbon on the table. "Does this mean you'll think about confronting your fears?"

"I daresay I will." Mrs. Lea raised the red cup to Nadia and downed the contents in one go without even flinching. "Ooh, I needed that as well."

Nadia patted Mrs. Lea on the shoulder. "Good luck to you, and thank you for taking a moment to talk to me. I'd say we both feel better for it."

"I wholeheartedly agree." Mrs. Lea already looked more cheerful.

Nadia nodded. "I better get my friend home. Good night, Mrs. Lea."

"And to you."

Praying the older woman took her advice so she wouldn't feel like a colossally terrible person, Nadia headed for the bar's entrance. She was almost there when Miles appeared at the end of the bathroom hallway, waving a frantic hand—a signal that Croak was coming. A moment later, the man himself stepped out of the men's room, still wiping his jacket. Scowling, Croak leaned against the wall and surveyed the crowd, probably looking for Miles. For his part, Miles darted to the side and pulled his hoodie tight. Nadia froze. There was no way she could leave now without crossing Croak's line of sight, and Kaleena probably had an APB out on her. She couldn't risk it.

"That was 'Whiskey in a Teacup,' and I love all of y'all for dancing along with me!" Monique's voice boomed through the club. "There ain't nothing sadder than dancing alone, especially when you're under a spotlight!" She stooped to pick up a plastic cup of beer and took a swig.

The room thrummed with energy, the crowd getting rowdier by the second, cheering on their Mistress of Ceremonies as she took another gulp of her beer.

"I ain't downing this for no one. You want me to wreck this velvety voice? Anyway, I ain't planning to be carried out of here. When I leave, I'm going to be crowd-surfing out!" Monique teased, and the crowd erupted in agreement.

Nadia sank back against the wall, wedging herself between *Donkey Kong* and *The House of the Dead*. She cursed under her breath, knowing just how close she was to freedom.

"Hold the music, hold the music, hold the music!" Monique

shouted, waving her hand at the crowd to quiet them. "Is that *Miles Hunter* I see, or am I more liquored up than I thought? Hey, Jim, get that spotlight on the door!"

The technician did her bidding without delay. Nadia cowered further into the wall in case the spotlight's glow bled into where she was hiding.

Fortunately, Croak seemed too fixated on the surprising developments to notice Nadia. She figured he was wondering if he could actually get his money back, now that he knew who'd spilled the drink. Miles tried to hide his face in the edge of his hood, his expression horrified.

"It *is* Savannah's golden boy!" Monique crowed, lapping up the crowd's attention. "I heard you were in town, but I never got your call. Let me guess—you lost my number again?"

The crowd booed at Miles's expense.

Monique cackled. "Aw, don't be too hard on the guy. He's a bona fide celebrity, don't you know? And he definitely doesn't charge five dollars for his concerts, so you've got yourselves a bargain tonight." She opened her arms wide. "That being said, my fine ladies, gentlemen, and nonbinary beauties, take in this moment, 'cause it's probably the only time you'll see Mr. Miles Hunter without having to glimpse him through a sea of black suits!"

The crowd cheered and laughed, their heads twisting back to see if Monique was telling the truth or yanking their chain. Gasps and whispers spread through the club.

"Is that really him? Damn, he looks as good as his pictures," someone in a group of women said.

Monique whipped her mic cord around like a lasso. "But what you might not know, and what the tabloids won't tell you, is that this *Rolling Stone*-gracing, supermodel-chasing, music chart–effacing rock star is *my* ex-boyfriend."

The crowd transformed into a herd of lowing cattle, directing their low "oohs" at a mortified Miles.

"And don't get it twisted—I'm the one who broke up with *him*! I was one chart he couldn't climb, though he tried soooo hard," she continued, to an explosion of hoots and hollers. "Best thing I ever did for you, wasn't it, honey?"

Miles shuffled awkwardly, and though he and Nadia had no love for one another, she wished she could've hustled him out of there, body-guard-style, as fast as possible. But Croak was still standing close to Miles, and she couldn't think of a way to get them out without revealing her presence.

"Pussy got your tongue, Miles?" Monique teased, sauntering across the stage. "Then let me tell y'all the story of Miles Hunter. The untold scoop. After we broke up, *he* goes on to this stratospheric solo career and becomes Mr. Billboard. I like to think he did it to spite me. Funny thing is, he used to play lead guitar for us. But like John Lennon supposedly once said about Ringo Starr, though I'll bend it for the occasion, 'He wasn't even the best guitarist in the band.' I let him take lead because we were seeing each other, and his singing—yow, y'all sing better than he ever did! But now *he's* a rock god. NME's words, not mine. So, either he's a fake, or he sold his soul to the devil way back when."

The crowd oohed again, putting Miles on the spot. Nadia couldn't imagine having that much attention on her; even experiencing it secondhand threatened to make her break out in hives.

"Why don't you play with me, for old times' sake?" Monique suggested. "Any song of your choosing. I'll even let you fiddle with my guitar."

To Nadia's surprise, Miles walked forward, and the crowd parted to let him through. When he reached the stage, he clambered up and held out his hands for Monique's guitar. She gave it to him, wearing an amused smile.

"Do you know any of my songs?" he asked into the mic.

She burst out laughing. "You kidding? I turn the radio off when your voice comes on."

The crowd chuckled, but a lot of them looked at Miles with eager eyes. They'd come here to see a local band who, by the looks of it, had stayed local, and they were getting an internationally renowned celebrity for the price of their entry ticket.

"I don't need it, honey," Miles mimicked. "When I sang with you, I was still a boy. It took you breaking up with me to turn me into a man, and that's where I found my voice and my talent. You should know it's hard to shine when you're always standing in someone's shadow."

Monique gave him a soft, private smile, her tone suddenly sincere. "Well, the spotlight shines brighter when you're used to the dark, you know." Then she bounded back into performer mode, grinning to the crowd. "Let's see what this big shot has got to show for us!"

Miles put the guitar strap over his head and took a fresh pick from the mic stand. "All right, I'll choose a different type of crowd pleaser, since this is a one-off." He strummed a chord and smiled. "Band, play with me if you know it. And you folks, sing along when it feels right! This is for my country music fan." He looked out into the crowd and met Nadia's eyes, his lips turning up into a smirk. Her stomach fluttered unexpectedly at the public ribbing, even if the crowd didn't get it.

He jumped straight into the opening chords of "Friends in Low Places," prompting Monique to let out a howl of glee. Cheek to cheek with him in front of the mic, they started singing with a fresh, rock-and-roll spin on the Garth Brooks classic. Miles took the melody while Monique boosted it with some flawless harmonies, wagging her arms in a comical interpretation of a line dance as the band caught up.

At the end of the first verse, the two singers gave each other a friendly nudge. By the time it got to the chorus, the crowd had started to sing along, toasting with their cups of beer and whiskey and cheering whenever the lyrics mentioned it. With each repetition, the crowd grew louder and louder, until even Nadia got a little swept up in the moment. Despite the circumstances, a small bubble of happiness swelled in her chest—not quite the same as the wish rush, but pleasant, nonetheless.

A brief reprieve she was only too glad to enjoy after a day from hell.

But she wasn't the only one feeling the party spirit. Apparently giving up on being able to corner someone as famous as Miles—or perhaps just planning to send him the bill—Croak wandered away from the bathroom hallway to mingle with the same cluster of pretty women who'd been marveling at Miles's good looks. Nadia took advantage and slipped out of the club.

On the street, she spotted Miles's black Mercedes parked up against the curb where it was guaranteed to get a ticket. Not that she cared. She ran straight for it and tried the door handle, but it wouldn't budge. Confused, she peered into the front passenger window to find the driver's seat empty. Jack had clearly wandered off, which meant she'd have to wait until Miles's impromptu concert was over. By the sound of the deafening cheers that exploded a few minutes later, she figured she wouldn't have to wait too much longer.

"Hey! Where did you go?" Miles called, running out to meet her with the ovation still in full swing. "I thought you left without me."

She smiled. "I had to take my chances while Croak was listening to your Garth Brooks impression."

"Did you like that?" He beamed, his face the picture of elation.

She gave a slight shrug. "I kind of had fun. It looked like you did too."

"I like more intimate concerts in smaller venues, but they don't pay the bills, and the managers don't like it when I come up with 'wild' ideas. That might've just changed my mind, though." He tilted his head back and drew in a deep, satisfied breath. "If Prince did it, so can I."

She side-eyed him. "Yeah, but Prince was an icon."

"Give me time," he retorted.

Nadia leaned back against the car. "So, that was the ex, huh? You didn't know she was still playing here?"

"I'm just glad she's still playing anywhere. She always had a stellar voice." He gestured at Nadia. "Enough of that. Did you get the address? I only got up onstage to buy you some extra time. I wouldn't have risked getting in trouble with Monique, except I knew it would piss off that Croak guy and keep him distracted longer."

She nodded. "I had it before you wandered onstage. We have to get there at nine twenty tomorrow morning. There was a code on it too, but I don't know what it means." She showed him the picture on her phone.

"Well, if it makes you feel any better, I'm getting that warm, wishy-wish feeling from it." He folded his arms across his chest. "See, I told you there was a reason it led me here. We couldn't have gone to the drop-off point without the password."

Nadia glanced back at the bar's doorway, eager to get moving. "The trouble is, Jack isn't here."

"I'll get him. Watch." Miles tugged on the door handle a few times until the ear-splitting screech of the alarm filled the air.

Nadia gaped at him. "What did you do that for!"

"You'll see."

A moment later, Jack came running out of the alley next to the bar, stubbing out a cigarette as he went. He was flushed, his forehead slicked with sweat. Nadia wondered if he'd met a special someone down that hidden passageway and enjoyed more than a rush of nicotine.

Jack swept his hair back as he approached. "Sorry about that. I thought you'd be gone a whole lot longer." He raced around to the driver's side and got in, killing the alarm and popping the locks to the back seats.

Nadia's gaze lingered a few seconds longer on the alleyway, hoping to see the face of the backstreet lover who'd gotten the driver so hot and bothered.

Sly dog. It seemed like Jack had bigger rock star tendencies than Miles did, if he could pick someone up in such a short span of time. Maybe Jack had offered to take them for a ride in his souped-up Mercedes sometime.

Her heart jarred in her chest as her gaze trailed back to the bar's entrance. Croak had emerged, and he was staring at them. Her head snapped back around, but there was no way he hadn't seen her. Muttering every expletive under the sun, she tugged on the door handle. If Jack had just stayed put, Croak wouldn't have seen her with Miles.

"Clover Eyes!" Croak said, walking toward them.

Nadia yanked open the back door and dove inside, with Miles hopping in after her.

"Drive!" she barked.

Jack turned around in his seat, scowling.

"Give him a break," Miles said, "he—"

Nadia stabbed a finger toward his window. "Croak just saw me!"

At that moment, Croak's voice vibrated through the windows. "Looks like you've chosen a side, Miles Hunter! If you think fame and money can save you, you've got another thing coming." He continued his approach to the car, spurring Miles to take a less subtle approach to getting the hell out of there.

"Shit! Jack, *go*."

The engine growled to life, and they rocketed away from the curb, leaving Croak in their dust. Nadia bit back a snarl in Jack's direction. It wasn't really his fault, but if he'd stayed at the car, they'd have been gone before Croak saw them. If Valhalla hadn't told the Wishmaster already, then Croak would—it was now abundantly clear that Miles Hunter and Nadia Kaminski were in cahoots.

"Shit, shit, shit," Miles muttered as he scratched his temple. He tapped his fingers on the window ledge. "Nothing we can do about it now. He didn't see you with the buyer, so I reckon we're still good. If not, I can feel things out and we'll try a different track, but that's tomorrow's problem. Either way, I'm getting my wish back. When someone steals from you, they'll always try to take more the next time, so you got to show them you don't mess around—and you take back what's yours. So long as their guns aren't bigger than yours, and there aren't more of them."

Nadia pursed her lips. "I hate to break it to you, but there are more of them. And most of them have guns."

"I'm being philosophical here, not literal," he retorted. "And I wasn't born yesterday. There's only one criminal underworld, you know. The only difference between groups is what product they're moving. They'll fleece you for all you've got if you let them, but I'll be damned if they're going to punish me for trying to take back what I earned."

Jack looked through the rearview at them. "I'm not gonna ask questions about what's going on, but we running the tires off the Mercedes tomorrow too?"

Miles yawned. "Yeah. Come around about quarter after eight."

"Will do," Jack replied. "We goin' far?"

Miles batted the question away. "Don't worry about it. Man, what a day it's been." He turned to Nadia. "You want Jack to drive you back to your—oh, damn. I'd forgotten about that."

The red in Nadia's cheeks rose. "It's fine. You can just drop me off at a hotel or something."

"You don't have anywhere to go, do you?" he said. "I've got plenty of spare bedrooms." He offered her an olive-branch smile. "Rock star, remember?"

"I thought you preferred 'musician'?" she replied, contemplating her options—or lack thereof.

Miles chuckled. "I was trying to be self-deprecating so you'd be comfortable."

"*That's* your idea of self-deprecating?" She shook her head, but in the end, she knew she had no choice. She used to have enough of a social life to avoid a hermit label, but ever since Nick died, she'd drifted further away from all the people she'd once called friends. "Fine. I'll stay in your swanky penthouse, or wherever you live when you're in Savannah."

He nodded to Jack. "Might as well end the day weird, since that seems to be the pattern."

A thousand quips pinballed through her mind, but only one word tumbled out. "Thanks."

Miles grinned at her. "You've sure been telling me that a lot today."

For once, she decided to keep her snarky comebacks to herself and gave him a genuine smile of gratitude. He deserved that much, especially considering how he'd swallowed his ego and sung Garth Brooks for her.

Chapter Fifteen

From the outside, Miles's opulent summer home looked like a lighthouse had mated with an Arabian palace—all stark-white exteriors with arbitrarily placed rounded domes and polished marble.

"My actual house in Malibu is homier," Miles had insisted self-consciously as they'd pulled up to the imposing beast. Even the driveway had taken a few minutes to drive along. "I wanted a 'historic' home in Savannah, like yours, but this one is more private. I gave up style for security."

After they'd arrived, Miles left her to sit alone in the lounge while he prepared a nightcap for both of them. Nadia perched stiffly on a rigid leather couch, terrified of moving a single cushion out of place. She gazed out the giant windows at the glinting water beyond the spiral-shaped pool, which looked like it might unfurl and dive into the river at any moment. Plenty of women would probably die for the chance to be where she was, but she'd only agreed to have a drink with him in hopes that it would help her sleep. After what had happened with Basha and Grace, she needed something strong to keep her mind from wandering back home.

She observed the jagged sculpture to the far side of the lounge. It appeared to be an angel of some kind, crafted out of knives, which didn't exactly scream "make yourself at home." On the opposite wall hung the so-called fingerpainting that Dr. Fitzpatrick's wife had created, which at least provided a splash of welcoming color.

"Here you go." Miles plopped down beside her on the couch and handed off a strangely shaped glass filled with a dark, reddish-purple liquid. The vessel reminded her of a tiny teapot, with a serpentine spout curving upward.

She eyed it. "Uh, how do I drink it?"

"With your mouth," he teased and got a cold glare in return. "You sip it through the glass straw. I got these as a gift, though I don't remember who from. A fan, probably, who read in an interview that I like port. They know more about me than *I* know about me."

Nadia pulled a face. "You washed them first, right?"

"Thoroughly," he confirmed. "Well, my housekeeper did. At least, I assume she did."

She resisted the urge to roll her eyes. Instead, she put her lips to the built-in straw and sipped up some of the heady, sweet port. Once she drank some more, the liquid coated her throat and took away the urge to splutter.

A smile spread across her face. "You know what, that *is* good."

"I told you," he replied proudly. As he sipped his own drink, Nadia suppressed a laugh. From her angle, it looked like he was puffing on an antique pipe.

They drank in silence, and before she knew it, the glass was empty. Her body felt looser, and even the couch seemed a little cozier as she sat back against the cushions she hadn't dared to touch. She supposed her tolerance must've gone down a fair bit; she had tried to avoid booze as much as possible since Nick died, in case it led her down the slippery slope that her grandfather, Basha's husband, had helter-skeltered down.

The thought of Nick brought wishes to mind, as it always did these days.

"Have you figured out what you want to spend your third wish on yet, if we manage to get it back?" Nadia asked.

Miles looked up from where he'd been staring a hole in the floor.

"Actually, yeah. The whole thing with Monique got me thinking." He lifted his chin confidently. "I'm going to wish for love."

Nadia groaned. "Wishes can't make someone fall in love with you. You wish for that, you'll end up with a bad case of the unrequiteds."

He leaned back. "Yeah, yeah, I know all that. My mom used to say you can only make *yourself* more lovable to a person. But by then, you might not even recognize yourself." He shuddered. "That freaks me out, man, to think of losing myself to another person that way. What I *want* is to find the perfect girl and live happily ever after, forever and always. All that good, mushy shit."

"Earth to Miles—you already made a finding wish," she reminded him. "That'll serve you better than a love wish. Take it from an old pro who's seen a lot of wishes *and* loves, good and bad. A love wish will just cause you tears, and maybe the need to run away from folks who find you a little too adorable."

Miles sipped the rest of his drink. "Nah, that's where you're wrong. The 'find anything' wish can help me find a woman who'll fall in love with me, but it won't give me the rest." He grinned. "I thought about wishing for a magic tongue, but I already have that."

"Bad idea, even as a joke. There are a couple of outcomes to that: verbal diarrhea, a tongue with a mind of its own, or one that lets you deliver some stinging comebacks. The last one sounds all right, but sometimes, saying exactly what you want at the right moment comes with a slap of guilt afterward," she informed him, watching reflective shards from the sculpture knives flash against the far wall.

Miles laughed. "You know that's not what I meant."

"I chose to think you weren't heading into arrogant asshole territory," she retorted, the discomfort sneaking back in.

He lurched back up and waved his hands at her. "Nah, nah, nah, don't get me wrong here. That was me lightening the mood, since things were getting a little too real." He paused, his expression turning serious. "What I really want is to have a happy, lifelong marriage with the sexiest, smartest, funniest woman on the planet—in that order."

"What about kindness, sincerity, generosity? And what if she's already married, whoever this impossible woman is? You'd be screwed then."

Nadia tapped the side of her port sipper, contemplating whether he was greedy or just trying to find fulfillment like everyone else. Even with fame and fortune, he still needed more. But she wasn't sure if love would fix that either. From her counseling sessions, she'd learned that some people, no matter what they did, wound up disappointed.

He shrugged. "True love, whatever that is, is worth fighting for. Anyway, you're not going to change my mind. This wish I've got in mind feels . . . different. It feels right."

She decided to humor him. "Oh, and why's that?"

"Unlike my other wishes, I actually *earned* this one by doing a good deed. That's why it has to be used on something special," he replied, surprisingly earnest. "How about you? What are you so desperate to wish for? I mean, you were gearing up to fight tooth and nail to get that wish back from that Amazonian chick."

"Valhalla, and she's not a chick. She has no beak or feathers. She's a woman," Nadia corrected.

Miles saluted. "Apologies. No offense intended." He hesitated. "But that wish must be pretty important, if you were willing to risk a crack to the head or worse."

"Well, I was trying to wish away my debt to the Wishmaster, but that wish was really just a means to an end. There's a bigger one that I want."

He arched an eyebrow. "I'm listening."

"I haven't had enough to drink to spill my guts yet." Nadia turned her gaze back out to the starry night and watched the reeds sway in the breeze.

Miles took her glass and disappeared, only to return with a full measure each. "You drink this while I guess what your deal is." He put the sipper in her hand and sat up on the couch with crossed legs, like a teenager at a sleepover preparing for some juicy gossip. "Are you sick? Did you get a bad diagnosis and you're trying to heal yourself?"

"Close, but no cigar," she replied, wondering if that might be the answer to her wish-wording conundrum. If she wished to have her broken heart healed, would the Wishing Tree give Nick back? No, there'd be way too many variables.

Miles took a sip of his drink. "Are you in trouble with the law?

Does it have something to do with some student loans you need to pay off?"

"Nope and nope."

He tilted his head up toward the skylight. "You want a talent? Or you want to be able to read minds to make your job easier?"

"Getting colder by the second." She sipped more of her port, her eyelids growing heavier.

He leaned forward and stared at her hard. "Do you want to have the power to grant wishes so you can help your clients? Can you do that? Would the Wishing Tree allow that?"

"Now you're just looking for inspiration. And no, you can't do that." She sighed, feeling the urge to unburden herself. "Look, I don't know exactly how much you heard at my house, but I'm trying to find a way to bring my dead husband back to life."

Miles froze. "I *definitely* missed that part. It got pretty heated, so it kind of just blended into one big screech toward the end."

"He was murdered," she went on, staring down into the maroon liquid and watching the viscous trail cling to the glass as she swirled it.

Somehow, it was easier for her to say that he'd been murdered than it was to say that he'd died. There was culpability in a murder, even if there hadn't been any justice in her husband's case. She didn't even realize the bomb she'd dropped until she saw Miles's stunned expression.

"He was a firefighter," she continued. "A hero, really, though I used to tease him for having that complex. Anyway, there'd been a spate of arsons in the months leading up to his death. A year ago, he was called to another suspected arson, and he never came home. His supposed best friend, Chris, shot him in the back—he was a firefighter too. Another fire truck got there in time to stop the house from burning down, but Nick had already lost too much blood."

A moment of stilted silence passed before Miles spoke. "Why would his best friend do that?"

"Your guess is as good as mine," she replied bitterly. "Chris never made it to trial. He hanged himself in his cell. My guess is, Chris was the one responsible for the other arsons and Nick somehow found out.

Nobody will ever know for sure. The only thing I *do* know is that he was guilty of murder. Otherwise, why would he kill himself?"

She neglected to mention the accusations that had come out after Nick's death—that *he* had been the serial arsonist. The sheer outrage that anyone, let alone the courts, could even suggest it made her want to punch a wall. Sure, firefighter arson was a known phenomenon, but her Nick would never do such a thing. He'd scolded her for leaving a candle burning while she napped, for Pete's sake. Looking down, she noticed that her hands had curled into fists.

Miles went strangely quiet, his expression sorrowful and sympathetic. "What was he like?"

The question threw her but also touched her in an unforeseen way. She'd fully expected him to flip the conversation back to himself and how she'd intended to use the stolen wish.

"He was mine, and I was his," she said quietly. "While I was always a tortoise, head forever tucked into her shell, he was universally adored and a social butterfly who dragged my tortoise ass out of the house and taught me how to have a good time."

Miles gave a subtle nod, as if to say, *it's okay to keep talking about him.* After the years with Grace and Basha, his willingness to listen was unfamiliar and made her feel a bit nervous, but the port had already loosened her tongue.

"There was this one time, at a Christmas party, where some guys were going around offering up Chatham Artillery Punch," she began. "I took a cup of it, not knowing what it was, and he swiped it from me before I could take a sip." She laughed at the memory. "He drank the whole thing so the guys would think I'd done what no one dared, and he shoved the cup back into my hand. I've never seen him so drunk in all the years I've known him."

Nadia paused. Verb tenses were weird when it still felt like he should be alive.

She took a deep breath and continued. "There was one point where he started prowling across the room on all fours, howling like a wolf and tugging on a man's pantleg with his teeth, hissing and spitting. He raided the buffet table and started flicking shrimp at a bunch of older women to see if he could 'get the prawns in the purses.' His words. Then he started smooching a lamp because he thought it was me, threw up in a potted plant, and passed out on the dance floor. It took four men to carry him out, because he woke up and tried to fight them all. The hangover lasted three days, and he wasn't even over thirty then."

Miles stared at her, his mouth agape. "What the hell is Chatham Artillery Punch?"

"You haven't heard of it? The old Savannah regiment concocted it. It's been nicknamed the 'killer of time' and 'vanquisher of men,' if that makes things clearer," she explained, smiling.

"Is it made with sunset rum or something?"

"Well, basically, you mix a whole bunch of booze—brandy, whiskey, rum, champagne, lots of sugar, and maybe lemon to mask the taste—in a horse bucket, then you serve it. It's apparently floored many an American hero, though only the oldest member of the Chatham Artillery knows the actual recipe."

Miles offered a sad smile. "Sounds like your husband was the life of the party."

"He was, but I loved the quiet, at-home, cuddles-on-the-sofa him too." Her eyes prickled with tears. "He really cared about people, you know? I'd come downstairs and find the front door wide open, and he'd be out in the neighbor's garden pulling up weeds, or mowing the lawn, or fixing a broken sprinkler. There was nothing he wouldn't do for me or anyone who needed help."

Her goal of reviving Nick and running off into some distant sunset together, with the debt settled and no chains weighing them down, had never felt further away. Somewhere along the line, that goal had morphed into avoiding confrontation with her sister. And though she was already deep in the self-pity quagmire, she'd veered herself off course by taking the wish. But who wouldn't, in that position, with a panic-inducing deadline clanging in their head?

Miles dipped his chin to his chest. "I can see why you'd want him back. I don't even know him, and I wouldn't mind meeting the guy."

"I *know* I can make it happen," Nadia said. "There has to be a loophole in the Wishing Tree's rules that'll let me bring him back."

He raised an eyebrow. "How do you know?"

"It's happened before, in my family. My great-great-uncle was rumored to have brought his daughter back from the dead," she said, bristling with nervous energy. "I've only heard about it in bits and pieces, mostly from my sister, Kaleena, who heard it from my mom and my babcia."

Kaleena. Her name slipped out every now and again, but never within spitting distance of her mother and grandmother. Nadia couldn't remember when the shift had begun, when her sister had become a nameless entity in the Kaminski household. One day, Basha had simply refused to use Kaleena's name again. Grace had slowly followed suit. Time, and the threat of being cast out, had deleted the name from Nadia's tongue, though it came back unbidden every so often. Those in the Savannah wish-hunting circle called her sister "Wishmaster" with such a fervent, almost religious devotion that Nadia spent half the time thinking of her more as a distant figurehead than a sibling she'd once laughed with over silly pranks and bedroom fashion shows.

Miles drained the last dregs from his sipper with a slurping sound. "For real? Do you think there's truth in you having a resurrected relative?"

Nadia shrugged. "Mom and Babcia were always tight-lipped about it, since they're against the whole idea of necromancy in general. But the story feels too personal to our family history to be made up."

"Sounds riskier than wishing for love, if you ask me." He sprawled out like a cat. "But I won't judge if you don't."

She was slightly tipsy from the port, but an idea ignited in her mind. "You! It's you!"

"Huh? What?" His hands shot to his chest like he was protecting his modesty.

She sipped the last of her port to give herself that final dose of courage. "It's you, dummy! You're my key." She set the sipper down and clapped her hands together. "*You* can *find* a way for me to bring Nick back!"

Miles's mouth dropped open. "Holy shit, you're a genius! I knew that port would get some neurons firing. Aw man, imagine if I could do that for you. You've been a royal pain in my ass, but at least now I understand why. Hell, *I'd* have stolen my wish if I were in your position."

"You'll do it?" She bounced up and down, giddy as a kid on a trampoline.

He cricked his neck and flexed his arms. "Leave it to the maestro, Nads. One loophole, coming up. Fresh out of the kitchen." He closed his eyes tightly, apparently putting his feelers out. His eyes flicked back and forth beneath his lids as Nadia waited for a hopeful outcome. His forehead crinkled and his lips puckered inward, his fingertips tapping an unsteady rhythm on the stiff leather.

All of a sudden, Miles cried out in pain. His hands flew to his temples and pressed against them hard, like he was trying to keep something inside his skull—or stop something from getting out. His face contorted into a mask of agony, and his lips parted, releasing a rasping whisper.

"It feels like guitar strings pulled to . . . the breaking point and then . . . past that." He gasped and his eyes shot open, revealing a few thread veins in the whites of his eyes that hadn't been there before.

Nadia touched his knee. "Are you okay? What happened?"

She recognized the twisted pain on his face. It seemed the Wishing Tree didn't just reject wishes; it also rejected using wish-given abilities to seek answers to forbidden wishes.

"Apparently, the Wishing Tree . . . doesn't want anyone finding a . . . loophole," he managed to get out, groaning and massaging his temples more gently.

The disappointment swept in like the tide, rushing through Nadia's veins and dousing the flame of hope that'd flickered in her chest. She could've smacked herself for allowing the optimism in, but when it came to Nick, she couldn't help it. She had to cling to anything that came along that could improve her chances of resurrecting him—no matter how painful it was when the bubble burst.

"Is the Wishing Tree a metaphor?" Miles asked, squinting at her. "Or is it, you know, *really real?* 'Cause I feel like I just got smacked with an actual branch."

His question reminded her of her childhood, when she'd asked similar ones like "Where did the Tree come from? How old is it? Who found it? Where does it live?" and Basha had replied again and again, "Nobody knows, dziecko. Is myth. Is legend. Is Wishing Tree. Simply is."

Still, it had some level of sentience, considering the kick it had delivered to her body when it rejected her, as well as the jolt Miles just received.

She gave Miles's knee an awkward pat. "I'm so sorry. I wouldn't have asked if I'd known it would do that. But thanks. Can I get you an Advil from the kitchen or something?"

"You're giving up already?" he said. "Here, let me try again. Maybe now that I know what's coming, I can withstand it. I reckon it's like getting the hang of a really complicated solo—once I've done it a couple of times, it'll be second nature."

Nadia shook her head vehemently. "No, don't. I'm not getting blamed for your brain turning to scrambled eggs. Thank you for the offer, but . . . don't."

"We just need to have a jamming session with it," he continued, his enthusiasm undiminished. "You know, approach it in a few different ways. Reword it or bog it down in a bunch of jargon, like the lawyers and the contracts I'm always dealing with. Something that doesn't sound like I'm looking for a loophole while leading me straight to it."

Nadia sighed. It wasn't worth putting herself through another hope rollercoaster. "Really, thank you, but don't wreck your head for me. I don't want someone else getting hurt on my behalf. The guilt would bury me."

"You're not what I thought you were," Miles said unexpectedly. "I'd have gone a lot easier on you if you'd just been up-front. Don't get me wrong, though. I get why you'd want to keep that kind of thing to yourself. It's fresh still. You keep opening a wound, and it ain't never going to heal."

Nadia nodded. "You're not what I thought you were either."

"The way I see it, we're all two people in one body: the person we show the world, and the person we show in private." Miles shrugged.

"There's probably a third too: the person we only show ourselves. That's the hardest one to face, I think."

"You sure you didn't take a couple of psych classes?" She laughed softly.

Miles smiled. "I read a lot. I've got a big library at my house in Malibu, but I don't have too many books here. Just paperbacks I buy at the airport." He met her sad gaze. "You'd think a wish hunter, somewhere along the line, would've written some volumes about making difficult wishes work."

"They did, but wish hunters got mixed up in witch trials across the world, so it became a safety thing to not keep records." Nadia turned her face away and stared at a vein of black that threaded through the white marble floor. "I just wish my family would tell me the truth about the resurrection in our history. Then, at least I'd have a vague path to follow."

Miles gave a low whistle. "You come from one messed-up family, Nads."

"You don't even know the half of it. Or even a third of it, for that matter." She shot him a disapproving look. "And please, for the love of all that's holy, stop calling me Nads. It sounds like testicles."

He chuckled. "I hadn't even thought of that." His expression turned thoughtful. "I've been wondering . . . If you've got such major beef with this Wishmaster, why don't you just, you know, leave and get your wishes somewhere else? It's not like they've got an invisible wall around Savannah." He hesitated. "Or do they?"

Nadia sank deeper into the couch. "They might as well. There's no place I could run to where the Wishmaster wouldn't find me, not until I've settled things. That's why I need your wishing jar—so I can steal another wish and use it to somehow get myself out of this mess."

"Ah, I get you."

Nadia paused. "But I kind of feel like I *should* stay here and straighten things out with the Wishmaster, if only because she's my big sister."

"What?" His eyes almost bugged out of his head. "You didn't feel like mentioning that sooner?"

"I didn't think it was all that relevant," she said with a shrug. "It's not like she'd listen to me if I begged her to give back your wish. She prides herself in being a hard-ass."

Miles gave a low whistle. "When I was a kid, I hated being an only child. Now, I feel kinda lucky. Was she always like that?"

"No, and that's the worst part. This Wishmaster persona of hers was made, not born, and I don't know what happened to turn her into what she is now." Nadia shook her head in frustration, livid that there were all these holes in her knowledge that no one had ever tried to help her patch up. Every attempt she'd made over the years of getting an explanation from Grace or Basha about the sudden rift in their family had come to a dead end.

"I guess there's no leniency for being blood, huh?"

Nadia mustered a stiff laugh. "Apparently not, and I don't feel like getting on the wrong end of her third wish."

"What do you mean? She wish for some scary superpowers?"

"I have no clue what she used any of her wishes for. Rumor has it, though, that she's got this unspent third wish that she's threatened to use on anyone who crosses her. That's what Black Hat told me once, anyway. When we were kids, she was always smart when it came to wish wording, so you can bet it'll be just as nasty as she wants it to be."

Nadia's heart suddenly ached. Kaleena never used to be that vindictive. Her sharp attitude had always come from a place of love. She'd been the kind of person who'd yell at the neighbor kid for taking a baby bird from its nest and then stay up nights raising the hatchling to adulthood.

She sat up, her muscles tightening at the turn the conversation was taking. "Anyway, we should both get some sleep. We've got an early start to get to the drop-off point, and we'll need to be sharp for it. There's no telling what might be waiting for us."

Miles fidgeted uncomfortably. "Guns ain't really my thing, but we should be armed in case things get nasty again. I've got a revolver in the safe, but I don't make a habit of carrying it around. Might have to make an exception tomorrow."

"I've still got this." Nadia pulled out her tactical folding knife and eyed the blade, losing herself in the dull sheen. She was no knife-fighting expert, as Valhalla had proved earlier, but the facts were these: she wanted to live in a world with Nick in it, and this deal with Miles led to that possibility.

And the one benefit of falling out of her family's good graces was that she had little else to lose.

Chapter Sixteen

Since Basha had kicked her out with nothing but what was on her back, the next morning, Nadia had to borrow a couple of items from Miles's "lost and found" conquest box, which he'd assured her had all been washed and dried by his poor housekeeper—a woman Nadia had yet to see.

"I can't believe you took a woman home who wore an 'I Heart Georgia' T-shirt," Nadia grumbled as they walked east along River Street. Jack had parked up on the western side of the Hyatt Regency so the duo could approach their destination on foot. That way, they'd look less suspicious, and Jack would have time to prepare for his role in the rest of the plan, which would have him driving something a little less . . . wheely.

Miles grinned. "I can't believe you wouldn't wear it. What's more incognito than a gift shop T-shirt? You'd fit right in as a tourist."

"Standing next to you, I could wear a clown suit and I still wouldn't stand out." She gestured to the black jeans and muted greige sweatshirt that Miles had picked as his undercover getup. Sure, it was simple, but on him it looked runway fresh. Plus, he had those stupid sunglasses on again.

As for her, she'd gone with a pair of faded blue jeans—the super tight kind favored by her mother—and a plain white V-neck. Over the top, she had a wine-colored Art College zip-up sweater. The entire outfit had come from the cast-off box that she'd vowed never to speak of again. But at least the new ensemble made her feel a little fresher and would help her avoid immediate detection from the Wishmaster's crew.

After last night, an easiness had developed between her and Miles that had still been there when they'd woken up—separately, of course. Nadia had worried it might be like the awkward first day back at work after an office Christmas party where too much festive spirit had been consumed and memories were a bit foggy. But that morning, he'd had a smile and a coffee waiting for her while jazz had floated through his fancy sound system. It wasn't quite friendship, but perhaps "accomplices" was a fitting term, given the occasion.

"You still have the jar, the candles, and the lighter with you, right?" Nadia asked.

Miles patted the crossover bag across his chest. "Jar's right in here, and I've got Pomegranate Noir, along with English Pear and Freesia. Oh, and Lime Basil and Mandarin. I thought a variety would be good."

"You realize it doesn't matter what it smells like? It doesn't change the potency of the wish, though Pomegranate Noir sounds like it could do a fair bit of damage." She should've known he'd bring ridiculous candles, but they'd do the trick if they had to make the wish straight-away to avoid it being stolen back in its unused form again.

Miles shrugged. "You never know, the perfect scent might be the key to wording the perfect wish."

Nadia had given him the task of bringing the candles and lighter as a way of proving that she could be trusted not to steal his wish again. It was also why he was the one carrying the wishing jar. All they needed to do was steal Valhalla's wooden locket of a wish trap before the buyer could absorb it and spend the wish, but it was smart to have Miles's backup trap. Still, part of Nadia hoped Mrs. Lea wouldn't show up today at all after their heart-to-heart conversation the night before.

They turned left onto the River Street walk as they reached

Morrell Park: a rectangle of grass and trimmed shrubbery with a few spread-boughed trees set right on the riverfront. Here, tourists took out their phones for a photo opportunity with Florence Martus—the famed Waving Girl who had waved her handkerchief to passing ships and was now immortalized as a statue.

Nadia hoped the statue would be a good omen today. She looked ahead at Waving Girl Landing, the address on Croak's note, and checked the time on her phone. It was 8:56, which meant they had twenty-four minutes to scope out any people waiting to board the riverboat and prevent Mrs. Lea from picking up the wish.

Closer to the landing, Miles paused and leaned up against the boardwalk railing. Nadia stopped with him and cast a sly side-eye toward the riverboat landing.

"Do you think we'll have to actually get on the riverboat?" Miles whispered, though there was no one else around.

Nadia shrugged. "Seems like nine twenty is a pretty specific time to give. I figure the buyer is supposed to get on the nine twenty riverboat, which is where the pickup will happen." She frowned at him. "Why? Don't tell me you get seasick. I thought you had a jet boat."

"*Jack* has a jet boat, and he's never gotten me on the damn thing. Not yet, anyway." Miles shivered, looking a touch green around the gills. "I'll swim in a pool, but being away from shore . . . Let's just say there's a reason I don't own a yacht."

Nadia groaned in exasperation. "You could've told me that sooner. Just try not to throw up. We've got one shot at this." She opened her phone and brought up the picture of the note. "I still can't figure out what this *rain/basketball* thing is supposed to mean as part of the password. Usually it involves more than just a couple of random words. I've had to use them at wish exchanges before."

"My finding skills aren't really doing me any favors with that. But we're in the right place for the wish. I feel all warm and fuzzy when I look at that riverboat." He nodded to one in the near distance—a vision of green, white, and creamy yellow that reminded Nadia of a tugboat. She preferred the riverboats that looked like wedding cakes, with the rotating paddles.

"It's got to be an added layer of security," Nadia speculated aloud. "After what happened at Bonaventure, the Wishmaster won't be taking any chances. Then again, using a private meeting place for the drop-off would've been the safer choice, if that was the concern."

Miles canted his head. "Maybe they've been compromised, or they're worried about having spies in their private drop-off zones."

"Could be," Nadia answered. Kaleena was obsessed with secrecy, the epitome of a better-safe-than-sorry kind of person. "Or maybe they're just trying to avoid using known meeting places. I've never had a drop-off on the riverfront—too many people around."

Nadia suspected there might be another reason for this location, but she kept it to herself. Since they'd fought Valhalla, the Wishmaster definitely knew that at least two people were after this particular wish. Putting the drop-off on a riverboat, just after rush hour and before the tourist influx, meant there wouldn't be many people getting on—an easy way to narrow down the number of people her goons would have to look out for.

Fifteen minutes later, one of the multi-decked wedding cake steamers chugged up to the landing, bearing the name *Georgia Queen* in red letters on the side. For a fleeting second, Nadia's heart leaped with childish excitement, but she quickly scolded herself. This wasn't a leisure cruise. She had a job to do.

"Come on, this is us." Nadia weaved her arm through Miles's and put on a goofy, tourist-esque smile as she led him to the landing. She pretended to point out various landmarks across the river and leaned into him, as though they were lovers taking a stroll.

"What are you doing?" he hissed.

She peered up, batting her eyelashes. "Blending in. We're tourist lovebirds."

"Then pull out your phone and take some selfies. Nobody points or *oohs* and *aahs* anymore."

She wanted to point even harder and *ooh* even louder, but he wasn't wrong.

Nadia slipped her phone out of the front pocket of her borrowed jeans and pretended to snap a photo of them. She deliberately shot the pictures at unflattering angles to annoy him, but it turned out to be pretty hard to take a bad picture of Miles. He huffed and tried to take the phone from her, but she elbowed him discreetly.

"This was *your* idea," she reminded him. "Now look at me as if I'm one of your fancy guitars."

He chuckled. "I see you more as a pair of big cymbals. You come in when no one's expecting it and scare the shit out of people."

After purchasing tickets from the little hut, the pair wandered down the landing and onto the waiting riverboat. Once aboard, Miles steered her up three sets of steps and across the top deck, toward the squat, yellow-painted box at the front. She didn't know too much about boats, but it looked like it might be the captain's "bridge."

"Have you got your knife ready to go?" Miles murmured, patting his crossbody bag. She presumed he was feeling around for his revolver.

Nadia fumbled at her back pocket. "Yeah, how about you?"

"Let's hope it doesn't come to that, eh? If anyone snaps a picture of me waving a gun around, my publicist is going to murder me."

She raised an eyebrow. "Because that's the main priority here—you not getting the paparazzi sicced on you."

Truth be told, him getting recognized *was* fairly high on her list of concerns. If a stranger called attention to Miles, one of Kaleena's intermediaries would definitely notice, and they'd know that Nadia was here too. But it worked the other way as well. If one of the intermediaries saw *her* first, they'd know Miles was here. Among the Savannahian wishmongers, she was basically a celebrity herself as the Wishmaster's sister.

Still, she didn't mention that worry to Miles. She didn't want him to get cold feet and back out now that they were already on the riverboat, especially since he was the one with the exit strategy and the finding ability.

"And you're sure Jack's in position?" Nadia bristled with nervous energy, her throat dry as sandpaper.

Miles took a deep breath. "I texted him while you were buying the tickets. He's got the engine running, ready to catch us when we . . . ugh, don't remind me. This wasn't what I had planned for today."

"Were you supposed to be shooting for the cover of *GQ*? Is there a supermodel you haven't slept with, awaiting your call?" She flashed him a smile to try to cheer him up. "And please tell me that bag's water-proof. A soggy candlewick won't do us much good."

Miles laughed, but it sounded hollow. "Don't worry, they'll stay dry. This thing is limited edition and made of military-grade something or other."

As they approached the bridge, a burly bouncer appeared in front of the entrance. Nadia's eyebrows went up. They were definitely in the right place. She and Miles made a show of leaning over the railing to look at the water below. Pretending to wipe some schmutz off Miles's cheek, Nadia turned them both around, backs to the hired muscle. She raised her phone and snapped a selfie, framing the bouncer instead of her and Miles. She opened the pic as she pretended to huddle into Miles's side, and magnified the image to check if she recognized the muscle.

She panned the image around the screen with one finger until she could see the windows of the captain's bridge, but they were all tinted black, preventing anyone from peering in. With a sigh, she handed over her phone to Miles, who stowed it away in his bag for safekeeping.

"Do you know him?" Miles asked, tucking a strand of hair behind Nadia's ear in melodramatic, rom-com fashion.

She shook her head. "No. Small mercies." She gave Miles a playful slap on the chest and blinked in surprise. It was like hitting granite. "He doesn't look like one of the Wishmaster's cronies. The Wish-master likes things covert, and this guy stands out."

"I'm warm," Miles muttered. "This has to be the place."

Nadia frowned. "Then we just need to stand here and stop the buyer from coming upstairs. If that guy *is* one of the Wishmaster's meatheads, the buyer will be going straight for him."

"I'll take care of that." He lifted her hand to his lips and kissed it, only to make a sour face afterward. "Ugh, you could knock out a horse with the sanitizer on your hands."

She giggled girlishly, hating every moment of the charade. "What are you going to do?"

"Use my mojo to find the buyer and block her from coming upstairs. I might even whip out my celebrity charm if things get hairy."

Nadia smirked. "Her name's Dolores Lea. You could pretend you know her, if you're really struggling."

"Oh yeah, because that's believable," he said. "If anything happens up here, just bang on the side of the boat, or scream, or something. I don't know how these missions tend to work."

With that, he walked away, though he made sure to keep hold of her hand until the last moment, like he was an old-timey soldier going away to war. Hopefully, the bouncer had bought their puppy-love couple act—otherwise she'd just giggled for nothing.

As the riverboat pulled away from the landing, Nadia kept up the pretense of staring down at the water. Another couple came up the stairs to the top deck. Neither person was Mrs. Lea.

Nadia clenched the deck's railing as the couple walked up to the bouncer. What if the couple worked for Kaleena, and one of them had wished for the ability to disguise themselves?

"Can we go in front of the captain's cabin to take pictures?" a young woman with long blonde hair asked the bulky guard.

The man shook his head. "You can't obscure the view, or the captain won't be able to see. I suggest you get down to the lower decks. Looks like rain is coming our way."

Nadia felt a flicker of doubt. Maybe this was a normal security guard after all, hired to stop people from blocking the captain's view, and she was wasting her time up here. She supposed there was only one way to find out.

She waited for the young couple to head back down to the lower decks, then drifted toward the bouncer in what she hoped looked like a casual fashion. He barely showed a hint of acknowledgment and kept staring forward.

"Excuse me." She cleared her throat. "I'm here to speak to the captain."

The guard's expression remained blank. "The captain is pretty busy right now." He tilted his head skyward. "It's getting gray and cloudy out there. I hope the weather holds out for the cruise. Think it's going to rain?"

A eureka moment sparked in Nadia's head. He'd used the word "rain" with that couple before. And there was no such thing as coincidence in the wishing world. It had to be the password from Croak's note, and "rain" was part of this feeder line, to gauge if she was acting on behalf of the buyer or not. Anyone who wasn't in the know would think the bouncer was small-talking about the weather, but she'd cracked it. All she had to do now was slip the second word into her answer.

"I friggin' hope not. I'm just here for my grandma. My buddies and I were planning to play basketball at the park a little later on," she replied, hoping there wasn't some set phrase she was supposed to say instead of just fitting her word into a sentence. Like an "eagle flies at midnight" kind of thing, followed by an exchange of sleek metal suitcases and terrible Russian accents.

The guard's face relaxed. "Would you like to meet the captain?"

"I'd be honored." Nadia smiled, her heart pounding a mile a minute. She wasn't quite sure what she'd pulled off, or what she'd face on the bridge, but she couldn't help feeling a swell of satisfaction. Even if this *was* only stage one.

"I'll just see if the captain is ready for . . . visitors." The bouncer gave an awkward head-bob of a bow and disappeared inside the bridge, leaving Nadia to her jittering nerves.

She'd been waiting for a couple of minutes when Miles bounded back up the stairs to the top deck. He skidded to a halt at the head of the steps and rushed out the words "I'm sorry!" in a way that was anything but discreet.

"What for?" Nadia snapped.

"The old woman is on her way up here," he replied, rapid-fire. "I tried to tell her it was out of bounds, but she said she had someone to meet."

Panicking, Nadia split her attention between the bridge door and the stairwell. If Mrs. Lea saw her, it wouldn't take long before she realized she'd been duped.

"Why didn't you stop her?" Nadia ran a stressed hand over her hair.

Miles flashed her a withering look and pointed to himself. "You wanted me to put my hands on an old white woman?"

At that moment, the bouncer emerged from the bridge. His eyes narrowed, then widened as he seemed to really see Miles for the first time. His mouth opened, but Nadia didn't wait to hear what he'd say. She charged through the still-open door, shouting a strangled "good luck" to Miles as she slammed it behind her and yanked the bolt across.

Panting, Nadia pressed her back flat to the locked door that rattled into her with the percussion of the bouncer's concerned fists. The handle spasmed violently but held, which was good in one sense—but it also denied her exit, and she had no strategy on how to make one. The bouncer would be prowling like a wolf out there until Nadia reemerged, unless Miles figured out a way to handle him. She was definitely flying by the seat of her pants now.

At the controls, a figure turned to meet her. But the captain could've kept their back to her, and Nadia still would've known who it was. The height gave it away.

Valhalla. And she was wearing the wooden wish trap locket around her neck.

Still revved up on adrenaline, Nadia pushed off from the door, lunging for Val and knocking her into the controls.

"I wondered if it'd be you," Nadia snarled, reaching for the locket.

Val grabbed Nadia's shoulders and kept the locket out of her reach. "Croak said you were up to something. Never thought you'd be stupid enough to come here." Her voice, thankfully, wasn't Basha's this time, but instead had a higher, smoother tone.

"Not stupid if . . . it . . . works."

Nadia grunted as she managed to wrench free of Valhalla's grip. The woman tussled with her across the bridge, and they slammed against one of the windows. Nadia clawed at Val's chest, desperate to rip that locket off her.

Val threw Nadia off, sending her slamming into the wall. They eyed each other for a moment, Nadia plotting her next attack.

"What'd they feed you?" she said through labored breaths.

"Jealous? Didn't grow much in your sister's shadow?"

Val lunged for her, and Nadia kicked her hard in the knee. Her opponent stumbled forward, shrieking in pain. Nadia snatched the locket while the taller woman tried to regain her balance, then sprinted to the bridge door, unlocked it, and darted through.

She almost collided with Mrs. Lea as Miles trailed behind the older woman, sputtering in exasperation. Mrs. Lea's eyes caught Nadia's for a moment, and Nadia recognized the look of crushing confusion, but she didn't stop to wallow in the guilt of what she'd done.

"I'm really sorry," Nadia called, running past.

Tying the locket's chain into a knot at the back of her neck, she took the stairs to the lower deck two at a time. But when she was halfway down, she jolted to a stop—Miles wasn't with her.

She turned at the sound of muttered curses and Miles shouting, "Do you know who I am?"

Nadia darted back up the steps to the top deck, and her eyes widened as she took in the scene. Things were spiraling out of control. The bouncer had Miles almost bent backward over the railing, twisting his right wrist at a grotesque angle. Miles dipped his left hand into his hoodie, and Nadia caught the briefest flash of the gun.

The bouncer shook him, and the gun flew from Miles's grip. It disappeared into the Savannah with a pathetic splash that was barely audible over the paddle wheel churning through the river.

"Hey! Get off him!" Nadia yelled, racing toward Miles.

At her words, the bouncer took his attention off Miles for a second, but that was all they needed. Miles smashed the bouncer in the jaw with a left hook, and the man staggered backward. Shaking his fingers, Miles ran toward her. Now it was time to get off the boat and hope that Jack was where he said he'd be.

Nadia climbed the railing and was just about to leap when an iron grip closed around her left arm and snatched her back aboard. Before Nadia could even scream, Val had her in a headlock. The blonde woman's massive hand closed around both of Nadia's necklaces: the locket and the chain that bore her wedding rings.

Reaching wildly as she lost her balance, Nadia grabbed Val's shirt at the collar as she fell backward, slamming the taller woman hard against the railing. For a brief moment, it felt like they were both suspended in midair—until Val lost her balance and followed Nadia over the edge and into the murky water below.

Chapter Seventeen

Nadia's stomach twisted as she fell, gravity seeming to stagnate. Just above her, Valhalla slammed into the riverboat hull on her way down. Then the cold, grayish water closed around Nadia. A dagger of pain jabbed the length of her spine, and the river engulfed her, swallowing her whole.

Ignoring the shock from the chilly water and the panic in her brain, she clawed her way to the surface. She wasn't about to drown in the Savannah River. Not now, not ever. She gasped and spluttered as she broke the surface, then treaded water and coughed out the dirty river muck.

Nadia looked around frantically, and her heart leaped when she spotted the wooden locket floating only a few strokes from her.

She swam toward the wish trap in a messy attempt at freestyle and grabbed for the pendant. She missed it once, then twice, her depth perception still foggy from the impact to her neck and head. Finally, third time lucky, her hand closed around it, and the warm viscosity of the wish undulated between the locket and her palm.

Relief swept through her.

A loud splash interrupted her momentary victory. Val had surfaced much too close for comfort. But the blonde enforcer seemed to have forgotten Nadia, instead struggling to make her way toward the shore; she must have hurt herself in the tumble over the side.

Nadia remembered her promise, but she couldn't risk losing the wish. Not again.

With a quick, inward apology to Miles, she flicked open the locket and pressed her palm to its center, letting the strange tingle of the wish sink into her hand. Then she pressed the wish to her heart. The giddy, bubbly wish rush was back, in stark contrast to the cold and foamy Savannah.

There'd be hell to pay later, but right now this felt good with a capital *G*. It was no wonder there were rush addicts in the wishing world, usually coming in pairs, who bounced a wish back and forth between each other without using it so they could feel that tingle over and over and over again. That had a tendency to turn nasty, though, when one of them finally decided they wanted to use the wish, but that wasn't the road she was headed down. She was just glad to have it back.

Now all Nadia had to do was wait for two things: Miles and their ride.

The bruiser from the riverboat threw a life preserver overboard to Val, who clung to it for dear life. Nadia grinned as she swam away, still high on the wish.

"When the Wishmaster finds out about this, you're gonna pay, Clover Eyes," Val shouted from behind her. "But it won't stop there. Basha and Grace are going to pay too. You're *done*."

The giddy rush disappeared, along with Nadia's grin.

I'm going to be sick. She inhaled and exhaled, trying to fend off the nausea. She needed Jack to get here pronto.

Nadia watched as the bouncer lifted Val from the water—and then she spotted someone clambering up onto the railing overhead, a cross-body bag strapped over their chest. Quite an audience congregated behind the latest candidate for the Olympic diving medal.

Miles pushed off from the railing and arced perfectly through the air. Streamlined as a swordfish, he sliced through the water with barely a splash.

"Show-off," she grumbled, though the spectators seemed impressed, with many a mouth hanging open.

Miles spy-hopped right beside her. Treading water, he flashed her an anxious grin. "Just keep bobbing—we'll be out of here soon." He put his fingers to his mouth and whistled sharply in three loud bursts. Passengers gawked from the upper decks, snapping pictures and chattering excitedly with one another.

"Keep facing me so they can't get a shot of your face," Nadia said. "I do *not* want to be in the tabloids as your soggy sidepiece."

"All the commenters will say it's Photoshopped, even if they can get a picture. Believe me, I know how these things work," he assured as the riverboat chugged away.

Nadia's teeth chattered, the shock of the cold and the threat finally getting to her. "How long is Jack going to be?"

"You hear that sweet music?" Miles curved a hand around his ear, while Nadia's eyebrow knitted together.

"No. What am I supposed to be hearing?"

Miles beamed. "That, Nads, is the bass note of the cavalry."

Sure enough, she heard the grumble of an engine approaching as a boat zipped out from behind a massive freighter churning down the river.

"How the hell did he hear you whistle?" she asked, dumbfounded.

Miles laughed. "I texted him before I jumped. The whistle was just for show."

The speedboat rocked in the riverboat's wake, and Jack pulled the watercraft alongside them with a Bond-esque skid. From the helm, he looked down at them, grinning from ear to ear.

"How's that for a time trial? Just gotta hope the river cops didn't see me," Jack said proudly as he held out a hand and dragged them both aboard.

Soaked through and shaking like a wet dog, Nadia huddled into one of the boat's black leather seats. Miles, on the other hand, seemed totally unaffected by his plunge into the murky depths and had come out of the water looking like he was shooting for a six-page spread. He went in to give Jack a grateful hug, but the other man put his hand on Miles's chest.

"Keep the river water to yourself, boss," Jack said with a laugh. He growled in time with the engine, and they zipped away from Valhalla and the riverboat, although Nadia knew that escaping her trouble with the Wishmaster wouldn't be so easy.

"You okay?" Miles asked as he slid into the seat next to hers. "You hit the water pretty damn hard. Did you get the locket?"

Nadia took a deep breath before answering. "No, it snapped off, but I managed to get to it in time. But . . . I also had to absorb the wish before she could steal the locket again. But it's still yours, I promise," she hastened to add, knowing it was the right thing to do. "I'm not going to use it—I just needed to make sure she didn't get it."

"You bullshitting me?" Miles asked, arching a dubious eyebrow.

She shook her head. "It's yours, I swear, but we'll have to wait to use your wishing jar." She frowned, realizing exactly what that would entail. "And I'll have to tell you a heart secret, which I'm not really looking forward to doing, to be honest. I'm usually the one coaxing out the secrets, not the one giving them up. Well, not intentionally."

He stared at her. "I don't have the jar."

"What?"

"That bouncer has it. I took it out to get my phone, and he wrestled the damn thing out of my hands before I knew which way was up. I thought you saw." He pinched the lingering river water out of his nose. "I was lucky to get away with the candles."

The guilt in Nadia's chest swelled. "I guess I missed that."

"No sweat," he said, though his clenched jaw suggested otherwise. "We can drive to my dad's place in Atlanta after this. I think he still has my mom's jar. And I'll let you have it afterward, like I promised, if you keep your end of the deal."

"That works." Nadia leaned back into the seat as the boat pushed forward, slicing through the water. "It's just one thing after another . . ."

"So, this secret—are you going to tell me you wear mismatched socks? Too late. I already know. I saw those on the floor this morning, so that ain't going to cut it." He chuckled, evidently pleased that he was still going to get his wish back *and* get Nadia to cough up a secret.

She glared at him. "You leave that up to me." She glanced back up the river, where Val and the riverboat had disappeared. "We don't have long until the Wishmaster brings a major crapstorm down on us."

"Another one?" Miles frowned. "Is the giant off to tell tales?"

Nadia nodded. "Valhalla is probably on the phone right now. We're in uncharted territory," she admitted. "I don't know what comes next, but it's not going to be good."

Once Miles got his wish back, she'd have fulfilled her part of the bargain, and then she'd ask him to use his finding powers to help her uncover the best way to ensure that Grace and Basha stayed protected. And with a new wish trap in hand, she could try to find two more wishes before Kaleena caught up with her—one to fix this mess and another to resurrect Nick.

Reflexively, she reached for the reassuring solidity of the rings she wore around her neck, only to realize with a horrifying jolt that they weren't there. She patted around her neck and chest, trying to make them reappear. But there was no mistake.

They were gone.

"My rings!" she cried out, her heart leaping into a panicked rhythm. "We have to go back! I've got to find them!" She grabbed Miles's shoulders, tears spiking at her eyes.

He took hold of her arms. "What's wrong? What are you talking about?"

"My rings, Miles!" she choked out, feeling as though the entire world were melting like wax around her.

Those rings were her gravity. Mrs. Lea had said she didn't want the constant reminder of what she'd lost with her wedding ring, but Nadia did. She *needed* that reminder so she could remember why she was doing all of this.

"What rings? You don't wear rings," he replied calmly, grabbing her hands to keep her from flailing.

She wanted to rake at her throat, but she couldn't get her hands out of his grip. "My rings—I wear them around my neck." Her breaths came in a burst of hyperventilation, somewhere between a hiccup and a gasp. "My husband . . . my ring and his. They're not there. The chain must've snapped when I fell."

"Okay, take some nice, deep breaths. You don't need to worry. I'll find them for you later," he said soothingly. "They're not gone, they're not lost, they're just waiting for you, okay? I'll get them back, but you said it yourself: we've got the Wishmaster on us, so we can't stick around here for too long."

"Thank you," Nadia stammered. "You'll go back for them? You really will?"

He let go of her hands. "I will. I know what it's like to lose something that belonged to somebody who's not here anymore. I'll get them for you—I promise."

Miles's reassuring smile turned into a frown as he eyed the riverbank.

"Jack?" he shouted above the engine noise and the wind. "Where you going, man? Are you taking us all the way back to my house? You know that's way slower, right?"

Puzzled, Nadia followed Miles's line of sight—they'd passed the jetty closest to the Hyatt parking lot. Had he missed the drop-off point? Did he see some river cops, maybe, and decide to just keep going?

"Making a quick detour, then I'll loop back," Jack yelled. Despite the volume, he said it a little too casually for Nadia's liking. She might not have been able to get out of the water looking like a million bucks, but she knew how to read people. Her stomach twisted.

Something was up.

"How much does he know?" Nadia asked Miles, only loud enough for him to hear. "We got away too easy, Miles. It's not a detour. Something's wrong!"

He gave her a bewildered look. "How hard did you hit the water? Jack's my guy—he wouldn't stab me in the back. And he doesn't know anything about wishing stuff."

"Listen to me, Miles!" Nadia hissed. "Something's not right here. We're on a *river*—what possible detour could he be taking? It's not like he's dropping by a boat-thru for a burger and a damn milkshake."

Doubt flickered across Miles's face, his gaze turning toward his driver. "Hey, Jack, no detours. That ain't what I pay you for. Drop us as close to the parking lot as you can get, give me the keys to the Mercedes, and we'll be good."

"It won't take long," Jack called over his shoulder. "Trust me. Have I ever let you down before?"

Nadia flashed Miles a "see?!" look.

"Nah," he said to Jack, sounding tense. "Take us straight to the dock by the Hyatt."

"Sorry, Miles. Gotta do this thing first."

"And I'm telling you I want to go straight to the dock. I paid for this boat, and you're going to drive it wherever I say. That's kinda your job, Jack," Miles snapped, fear glinting in his half-narrowed eyes. "If you don't, then step away from the wheel and I'll drive my damn self there."

Jack shook his head. "That's not how this is gonna go."

Miles stood from his seat as if to make a move, but Jack turned halfway toward them, left hand on the wheel—and a small pistol in his right.

Miles froze.

"I need the two of you to sit down and shut up," Jack spat. "I know that'll be hard for you, Miles, since you're a big fan of the sound of your own voice, but if you don't, *I'll* shut you up."

Nadia's stomach lurched. Jack was probably already looking forward to his briefcase of cash . . . or a promised wish. She thought about what she'd seen at The Scrapyard: Jack, all sweaty and distracted, coming out of the alley and crushing a cigarette under his shoe. Who had gotten to him? Val or another of Kaleena's lackeys? It could've been anyone. Who knew what wishes they were up against? For every Val able to duplicate a voice, there was a Miles who knew how to find things or any other number of variations. No matter how it had happened, in the end, someone had turned Miles's friend into a traitor.

Miles sat down in his seat, eyes full of rage, while Jack kept the gun casually pointed in their direction, alternating between keeping an eye on them and the river ahead. When Jack looked forward for a second, Miles gave Nadia an expectant look as he unclipped the strap of his crossbody bag, unzipped the top, and let the whole thing fall to the floor next to her seat.

"I thought we were friends," Miles shouted when Jack turned around.

Jack snickered as he gave Miles a bitter smile. "You never thought of me as a friend. I'm your driver, nothing else. You just said it yourself five seconds ago. You had this coming, Miles, but you were too full of yourself to see it."

Miles nudged the bag with his foot, and Nadia's heart skipped a beat when one of the scented candles rolled out of it. She looked back up at him, her eyes wide.

"What about all the bonuses and tickets I've gotten you over the years?" Miles said, nodding discreetly to Nadia even while he kept Jack's attention. "All the girls you've met? All the places we've been? Don't forget who paid for everything you own, you son of a bitch."

Jack snorted. "There's always more rich people, Miles. And after this, *I'm* gonna be one of 'em."

Nadia reached down, grabbing the candle and a lighter from the bag. She straightened up before Jack had the chance to look her way.

This wasn't how she'd envisioned spending her first wish, and it would mean that Miles would truly lose his third wish for good, at least in its unspent form. But they didn't have many other options. She needed some way to get them out of this—and quickly.

Chapter Eighteen

"You know what, I don't think this has anything to do with me," Miles told Jack. "Do you got some kind of inferiority complex? Is that what this is? Didn't get enough attention as a kid, and now you're projecting that onto me?"

Nadia cringed at Miles's clumsy attempt at psychoanalysis. Didn't he know those sorts of questions would just put Jack on the defensive? But she appreciated that Miles was trying to buy her more time by getting Jack riled up. She brought her knees up so she could ready the candles and lighter without being seen, her heart rampaging in her chest.

Jack snorted. "Greedy people like you at the top take everything, while the rest of us can't catch a break. I'm always doing everything you don't want to do, whenever you want it done. And you never think twice about calling me to do your dirty work when I finally get a day to spend how *I* want."

"You want to explain that? 'Cause I'm stumped about how I've been 'greedy' at all by asking you to do your *job*," Miles shot back, sounding genuinely pissed off.

Jack waggled the gun, as if to remind Miles who had the mic.

"Well, you keep all the important shit to yourself, for one thing,"

Jack explained, ignoring Miles's comment. Clearly, he'd been building up to this for a long time. "While I was havin' a smoke by the club, this guy in a funny black top hat comes up to me. I figure he's a weirdo looking for a couple dollars or a hookup, but he tells me he's got dirt on you that I'm gonna want to hear. I'm kinda pissed on account of you ruining my night, so I give him my number, just to see if he's got what he says he does. Figure it's worth *something*, right?"

Nadia fought an irritated noise from escaping her throat. Black Hat. That little bastard. There were no true allies in Savannah's wishing world.

"So, when you and Nadia were at the house, I get the call," Jack continued. "This guy tells me to meet him, so I go out to the place. Two guys—the one with the hat and that Asian dude who came out of the club. They told me something *veeeery* interesting." He gesticulated with the gun, putting Nadia on edge. "Said they could hook me up with the same stuff you got—y'know, whatever this drug is that y'all are taking to make yourselves super powerful and creative. The Asian guy showed me some weird shit to prove it. This is my ticket in, Miles. I'm havin' what y'all are havin'.'"

"None of this is what you think it is, and if you think *I* treat you bad, wait till you see how the people you're working for now are gonna treat you," Miles said. "You gotta listen to me, man."

Jack snickered. "I can handle myself. Look where you are right now." He waggled his gun again. "You're not talking me out of this. That guy made me promises, and I'll *make* him keep 'em."

While they bickered, Nadia balanced the candle in her lap, and the wish rush fizzed through her again. The problem was, while she needed an out for this particular situation, she wasn't about to waste a wish—one of only three she could ever get—without it also getting her closer to Nick. She just couldn't. Whatever she wished for would have to pull double duty.

After another moment's thought, the wording came to her.

A thrill bounded through her veins as she brought the lighter to the crooked candle wick lying nearly smashed into the wax. She leaned over the candle to block the wind of the racing boat. A roll on the sparking mechanism and the flame awakened at once. She touched it to the wick—only to be met with a dismal hissing sound and a few disheartening spits. Dampness met her thumb and finger as she pinched the wick to straighten it out. The bag must've sprung a leak while they were in the water.

Nadia dug her fingernails into the wax in a futile attempt to reach the dry part of the wick. She would've broken the damn candle in half if it wasn't encased in glass.

"Fame and fortune—if that's what you're after—don't make a person happy." Miles glanced at Nadia as he continued to lecture Jack. "Wouldn't make your life any better, except you'd have to live with the fact that you stabbed your friend in the back to get it."

"That's rich, coming from you," Jack retorted. "What you've got wasn't from hard work either, was it? That's right, that Cronk guy told me *all* about it."

Puzzled, Nadia looked up from her wax-clawing, but Miles wouldn't meet her eyes. She didn't have time to ponder Jack's words too much, though, as he veered the boat toward a small, empty dock a little way up the river.

"Jack, I—" Miles began.

"Shut up. Maybe you can try talkin' to *them*." Jack nodded at two figures approaching the dock, dressed in police uniforms.

With their window narrowing by the second, Nadia frantically tried to get the stupid candle to light. But every time she tried, she got nothing but hisses and sputters. Panicked, she gave up on that candle and rummaged another one from the bag. She took Pomegranate Noir in her hands and gave the lighter another go.

She rolled the sparking mechanism again but startled as Jack turned and their eyes met.

"What are *you* doing?" he snapped, wrenching the lighter and the candle out of her desperate grip. "You going to MacGyver a bomb or somethin'?"

Jack sneered as he snatched Miles's bag and tossed it overboard, where it hit the water with a splash. He turned back to the wheel and maneuvered the boat the last bit of distance to the dock. Miles cast a distraught look at Nadia.

They'd lost their last chance.

Words from Basha years ago sprang into Nadia's head. "Is no good to think of wishing as cure-all. Is good for some things, not everything. It will stab you in back more times than it helps. You remember this, you never have problem."

Neither the words nor the thought of her grandmother helped Nadia's feeling of helpless desperation.

"Come on, Jack," Miles pleaded. "This is bad business." He gestured at the riverbank where the "cops" waited. "These guys are serious. They might *kill* us!"

Jack shook his head. "That Crank guy promised that neither of you would get hurt," he said, but his voice faltered. "It was just gonna be a negotiation."

"They're lying," Nadia replied, not even bothering to hide her fear.

Jack's gaze flitted from his former employer to the "cops" on the jetty. "I don't want you to *die*, man." He paused, the irony that he had a gun trained on Miles completely lost on him. "I'll handle it. I've got a way with words."

"Just keep driving the boat! You're not going to talk them out of whatever they want," Miles protested.

Jack didn't reply.

Just shy of the dock, he reversed the engine, bringing the jet boat next to a mooring post. The bump of waves to Nadia's right offered a tempting escape, but the pistol still hanging from Jack's hand was more persuasive. The two fake officers waited ahead.

Folding his arms across his chest, Jack puffed himself up like a bull-frog. "All right, I've delivered. Now give me my 'wish' or whatever you guys call it. And remember, you promised nobody was going to get—"

A knife pinwheeled through the air almost too fast to see.

Jack collapsed onto the deck with a thud and rolled over, scream-ing. Jabbed into his left eye was a thin-bladed throwing knife that had buried itself just deep enough to somehow not kill him. The gun landed somewhere underneath him.

Nadia recoiled in horror and looked away, not daring to meet Miles's eyes. The blade had come from the still-raised hand of the female "officer"—a willowy young woman with braided dark hair and cold eyes as devoid of emotion as a shark's. Nadia recognized her as

Calypso, another of the Wishmaster's inner circle, rumored to have wished to never miss her target.

Not much of a rumor anymore. That kind of perfect aim, taking his eye and *only* his eye, was proof of a wish-given skill if ever Nadia had seen it.

"The only reason you're alive is because I spared you," Calypso said coolly. "A millimeter to the left and that blade would be lodged in your brain. Demand something else, why don't you."

Jack moaned in response.

"No?" Calypso spat. "Good. Now, shut the fuck up and get out of here. And I'll be watching, so don't do anything stupid. Cross me again, and the next one goes through your heart."

Nadia could only stare at Calypso, fear melting all words off her tongue. Yes, Jack had betrayed them, but he hadn't deserved to suffer like *this*.

Miles knelt over his driver, his expression panicked. "Jack! Hang in there, man." He glared at the Wishmaster's goons. "What the hell did you do that for?"

"Because we felt like it. Now, let's go," replied Calypso's male counterpart, a lackey Nadia didn't recognize. He was small and mousy, with a pair of thick spectacles, but if he couldn't offer the Wishmaster muscle, then he had to be wielding some other valuable skill.

A blur of black uniform slipped across the dock as the mousy man shot forward at inhuman speed and pinched the back of Miles's neck. Nadia didn't know what he'd done, but it couldn't be good. Miles seemed frozen in shock while Calypso walked toward him with her arms outstretched.

Nadia scrambled away, ready to throw herself back into that sweet, murky Savannah River if it meant saving herself.

"Get back!" she warned the bespectacled man. "Don't touch me."

Before she could blink, the officer was behind her. His hand snapped around the back of her neck, his pinched fingers cold and slimy against her skin, as if he were dripping poison into her. She tried to shuffle farther back so she could tip herself into the water, but her limbs wouldn't move. In fact, her whole body felt weirdly relaxed, like she'd been drugged.

"You don't give orders," he whispered as he picked her up and threw her over his shoulder with surprising strength.

Nadia tried to speak, but her jaw had gone slack, her mouth refusing to cooperate. And yet, she could still feel the unspent wish buzzing around inside her like a lost bumblebee trying to find the hive. How long would she be able to keep it before Kaleena pulled a secret out of her—and the wish with it?

Chapter Nineteen

Still woozy, Nadia and Miles were dumped into the back of a windowless van and left to roll around like discarded scaffolding in a builder's pickup. Nadia wanted to curse or yell as they bounced around during the drive, but her mouth stayed frozen, as though she'd just come in from subzero temperatures and her body hadn't caught up with the warmth yet.

She didn't need Miles's finding power to know where they were headed: the Wishmaster's headquarters. Her inner "oh shit" instincts were strong.

Going there would bring a decisive end to her hopes for a brighter future. Kaleena would force two more wishes into her and take them back. Nadia would feel the high of each, and the all-consuming low of knowing she'd never get to use them for herself. No Nick, no desperate reunion after a year apart, no faraway place for them to grow gray and old. She really had kissed him, held him, told him she loved him for the last time. There would be no second chance. The one thing that had kept her in the wish-hunting game since he'd died was her dream of settling the debt and starting fresh, but her plans had diverged so massively—all because she'd seen an easier route and tried to run with it, hoping there'd be no fallout.

Nadia wanted to sleep forever. It was all too much to think about.

Ten minutes later, she managed to coax a wiggle out of her toes and fingers—a positive sign that whatever the pinching guy had done wasn't permanent. A few minutes after that, instead of feeling like a mosquito encased in hardened amber, she felt more like a bug who'd gotten caught in a puddle of honey. A little sticky, but all the parts were moving.

When the van finally came to a halt, their captors bundled them out with sacks over their heads. As Nadia tried to get her legs working again, she half walked and was half dragged inside some sort of building, then down a hallway, judging by the change in sound.

While she was still trying to get a grip on what was happening, her escort jerked her sharply to a halt, and a door clanged shut behind her. Rough hands snaked over her body, patting her down. Someone took the tactical folding knife from her back pocket. Both her and Miles's phones were already at the bottom of the Savannah, thanks to Jack throwing the bag overboard.

"Hey!" Miles sniped nearby. "Hands off."

A moment later, the hood came off, revealing a stone-faced Calypso. Nadia looked around as best she could without making it obvious. The inside of the building looked like an old bank, with pillars and archways running along the sides of a central hall and bright daylight shining in through square-hatched windows. Marble, polished to a high shine, explained the slipperiness underfoot. The only furniture was a few benches that seemed like they'd been thrifted from a railway station, and a single reception desk at the far end of the hall—all devoid of people.

"Well, this is a sight I'd hoped to never see again," Nadia muttered, her voice odd and unnatural as her mouth and tongue struggled to remember how to function.

Calypso smirked and turned to the mousy man. "Come on, Folgers. We're running behind schedule." She took hold of Nadia's arm and frog-marched her down another hallway. Folgers—Nadia scoffed at the code name—grabbed Miles and dragged him along behind them.

Every time they turned a corner or went through a door, Nadia's mind became fuzzy, as though it was trying to forget what it had seen.

Whatever wish had been used to keep the Wishmaster's headquarters hidden made it impossible to place where she was. Once or twice she thought Calypso had retraced her steps, but the wish made it hard to tell. Being here was like remembering a long-forgotten dream—she only recognized the place after seeing it again, and even then she wasn't completely sure.

"I see you trying to look around. Go ahead," she heard Folgers tell Miles with a chuckle. "Won't help you any. You won't remember shit about this place. Just know you're seeing someplace most people never do. Enjoy it while you can."

The headquarters felt like part prison, part high-security vault. Given the way Adrian had been driven into hiding, Nadia understood why Kaleena never met clients at all, preferring to send wish-laden intermediaries out to do it in public. In addition, the highest-potency wishes were stored in the most heavily guarded parts of this building. Those that surfaced for sale usually went to auction, and top-shelf ones sold for seven figures, though that had been under Adrian. Kaleena seemed to be hoarding those wishes for her own purposes now.

Their guards kept them moving quickly, and the wish protecting the building didn't seem to bother those in the Wishmaster's circle. They emerged into an archaic-style hallway that reminded Nadia of enclosed cloisters, with curving white windows and dirty gray tiling. Beyond the crosshatched panes, she could see the street, where people walked by in ignorant bliss. To them, this building was probably like Narnia—one day, it was there, and the next, they'd forgotten all about it. She imagined there were commuters who walked past this place every day and still didn't notice it, thanks to the illusion.

Miles started to say something, but he got cut off by a smack from his captor. Nadia's cheeks flushed with a guilty heat—that he was here at all was her fault. Calypso and Folgers dragged them along a concrete corridor and paused at a huge steel door with a hefty lock wheel.

They'd reached the vault, and never before in her life had Nadia so desperately wanted a door to stay closed.

Calypso pressed her hand to a scanner beside the door, then stared into a retinal scanner, which chirped approvingly. Kaleena clearly wasn't taking any chances with security, though Nadia thought it was a little overkill given the protecting wish, the security cameras in every room, and the hired muscle.

The door's indicator lights turned green, and Calypso spun the lock. As she pulled the vault door open, she smiled cruelly and gestured inside. "Welcome to your room."

"These things are airtight. We'll suffocate—"

Nadia's protests were cut off as Calypso shoved her inside, followed shortly by Miles.

Calypso pointed to a vent overhead in the vault that, judging by the weld marks around it, had been retrofitted to prevent exactly what Nadia feared. "The Wishmaster wants to talk to you," she explained. "And what the Wishmaster wants, the Wishmaster gets, so trust me when I say you won't suffocate. At least until then."

"When?" Nadia asked, taking in the vault's bare steel walls. "Today? Tomorrow?"

Calypso shrugged.

"I can't wait long," Miles protested. "I need to piss, like, yesterday."

Folgers slid a rusty metal bucket into the vault with his foot.

"Enjoy your stay. If you need anything at all, just shout." Calypso gave them a wicked grin and shut the vault door with a muffled thud. As the locking bolts slid closed with an ominous *click*, all Nadia could think of was a closed coffin being lowered into a grave.

Nadia wandered over to the far-right corner and sank down against the wall, feeling heavy to her bones.

Miles's foot flew back like he was going to give the bucket an annoyed kick, but he seemed to think better of it and began to pace instead. "Hey, Wishmaster, what the hell do you think you're doing?" he shouted up at one of the security cameras in the vault. "I. Didn't. Steal. Anything! *My* wish got stolen!"

"Watch it," Nadia warned, trying to ignore her own despair.

He rubbed the back of his neck where he'd been pinched and turned to face her. "I don't care. It's the truth. I'm here because supposedly I stole a wish from . . . myself? Man, come *on*!"

Nadia rested her head against the cold concrete. "If you keep quiet, *you* might get away with a lighter punishment. The real beef is with me, you know."

That seemed to placate him. He gave up on his pacing and took a seat near her, which she thought was a bit odd when there was so much space.

"Do you think Jack's all right?" Miles asked, after a few minutes of silence. "I can't get that image of him out of my head, with all that blood running out of his eye." He shuddered. "I know he did us dirty, but he didn't deserve that."

Nadia nestled her chin between her bent knees. "That's on him. He got himself in that situation. You tried to give him a heads-up, but he didn't listen."

"Whoa. Foreigner must've written 'Cold as Ice' about you," Miles said, staring at her in disbelief.

She sighed. "It could've been way worse for him. He's lucky to still be alive. And to have another eye left." She mustered some sympathy and tried to form it into a comforting smile, but Miles had sunk back into his pit of guilt.

Of course, she understood why he felt responsible. Jack wouldn't have gotten involved in the situation if it hadn't been for Miles, just as Miles would be sitting pretty with a brand-new granted wish if she hadn't tried to outfox him. Like the roots of the Wishing Tree itself, everything had a funny way of connecting, and not always for the better.

Miles stared up at the ceiling. "Guess we could be in here for a few days. Weeks, for all we know."

"My clients will think I've ghosted them." Nadia felt a pang at the thought of the couples who would take her disappearance to heart. Of course, depending how the next interaction with her captors went, she might end up *actually* ghosted, so there was that to worry about too. "I need to call them somehow, just to let them know . . ."

Miles gave her a sympathetic look. "Maybe they'll figure you had a family emergency or something."

"Maybe," Nadia murmured.

It was definitely true, in all kinds of ways. But the vise around her lungs tightened. She thought of a couple she had been counseling who had recently lost a child—stillborn at thirty-nine weeks. The wife had suffered miscarriage after miscarriage before that baby, so they'd put everything into that little boy who *almost* made it. The love they shared for each other became lost somewhere in the wreckage of all that tragedy, and it was Nadia's job to help them sift through the debris until they found it again. Tears welled in her eyes. Who would be there for her clients come Monday, when her door was closed and her phone went straight to voice mail?

Sometimes, she envied her clients' wishless lives, since all her world seemed to do was screw things up. Or, rather, she screwed things up because of this wishing, stealing, deceiving side hustle.

Miles had fallen back into a comfortable silence, only the whir of the vents filling the empty cube of maddening steel walls.

"Why didn't you make the wish back on the boat? I bought you plenty of time," Miles said ten minutes later. "It wasn't easy for me to give that up, you know. I mean, that was my last one, and I was really going to use it on something good! I could've stomached losing it if it'd gone to saving my ass, but here we are, ass unsaved."

Nadia met his accusatory gaze. "Three words: wet friggin' wick. Your designer bag wasn't as waterproof as you claimed."

Miles groaned and put his head in his hands.

"The wish is still here." She patted her chest, then murmured, "And I know it couldn't have been easy for you, after thinking you were finally getting it back. I'm sorry it didn't work."

"Well, I doubt either of us will get to keep it now. But I'm gonna *find* us a way out of here eventually, if my name ain't Miles Clarence Hunter."

"Clarence?" Nadia raised an eyebrow.

"Clarence is a *great* name. Best saxophonist in the world was Clarence Clemons, God rest his soul." Miles made the sign of the cross.

She made a subtle gesture toward the security cameras. "Careful what you're saying. And not just about the sax player. Bad things happen to people who give away their own game." She turned back to him, lowering her voice to a barely audible whisper. "Anyway, if your . . .

exit strategies were so infallible, we'd have escaped before we even got here."

She was careful not to mention "finding" in case the surveillance picked up on it.

"Sometimes, it takes time," he muttered back. "And sometimes, exits can't be found because they don't exist. But I'm working on it."

Nadia frowned. "Are you getting any tingling in your waters?"

"I don't know what that's supposed to mean, but I *do* know that the warm and fuzzies seem to be pointing toward one thing . . . or person."

"Huh?"

"Apparently, you're what I'm looking for," he replied. "I mean, you're my ticket out of here. Well, you've got something to do with an exit, anyway, but it's figuring out *how* that's the hard part."

Nadia groaned. "You mentioned that at The Scrapyard. That nuance kind of pisses me off."

"You're a counselor! Nuance is what you do, I thought. But you know what pisses *me* off? The whole damn wishing world." He smoothed a hand over his close-shaven head. "How does it even make any sense that I'm getting the rap for wanting to take back my own wish? I didn't do anything wrong, but I guess that's the justice system for you, even in this underground, shady, cloak-and-dagger business."

They fell silent again, and Nadia found her thoughts drifting, as always, to Nick.

If she didn't make it out of here alive, at least she was one step closer to holding him in her arms again. It wasn't what she really wanted, but she'd take it if that was all she could have. As she'd silently told him a thousand times, death wasn't going to part them. She'd left that out of the vows for a reason.

Miles sighed. "I'm never getting my third wish. I guess my happy marriage just wasn't meant to be."

His words, so close to where her own thoughts were, snuck past her guard. "You don't *really* need a wish for that," Nadia retorted, only half realizing that she'd said it out loud. "You can find a fulfilling relationship on your own. Part of your problem is thinking that a wish will bring that to you when you could just put yourself out there."

Miles waved her away. "*You* don't know how many bad dates I've been on, how many times I've had my heart broken, how many hearts *I've* broken, or how many women turned out to be gold diggers."

"Isn't that the trade-off for being Savannah's most eligible bachelor for so long?" Nadia said, resting her chin on her knees.

He shrugged. "Doesn't matter, anyway. If that wish is gone for good, that's my destiny. Three down, none left." He tipped over to one side slowly, wincing the whole way down to the floor beside her.

"You all right there?" she asked.

"My neck is killing me. I feel like one of those assholes sprained it while they were dragging me around, or Mr. Pinchy dislocated something." He flexed his fingers. "Though the old magic makers are almost back to normal."

"Good to focus on the positive where you can."

He chuckled. "I feel like that's the therapist in you coming out: 'yes, let's focus on the growth here.' Is that what you do for your clients?"

"Close enough." Nadia smiled, amused despite herself.

"Been a while since I've been to therapy." He folded his hands behind his head. "Is this where you drag out my deepest, darkest secrets and tell me I've got unresolved mommy issues?"

She cocked her head at him. "That depends. Do you think you have unresolved mommy issues?"

He closed his eyes. "Not really."

A thought popped into Nadia's mind. Or rather, the destination they might've been headed toward if Jack hadn't screwed them over.

"You mentioned your mom's wishing jar on the speedboat, and you said she was the one who wanted to help you figure out how to really use it," she said in her dulcet counselor tones. "Was she the one who came from a wishing line? Did the two of you ever talk about what you wished for?" The wishes people made always intrigued her.

For a while, he didn't reply. In fact, Nadia was beginning to wonder if he'd fallen asleep. Nick had always been able to fall asleep within a few minutes—a trait she'd envied, since she tended to have a billion things racing around in her mind when she laid her head on her pillow. Even back then.

"I have no idea if we'll get out of here alive," he said, startling her, "but I kind of feel strangely at peace with that, somehow. Like I can give my last confessional to a professional—ha, that rhymed—and free my soul from any heavy burdens before I drift on up to the heavens with my angel wings." His tone was joking, but his expression looked tense.

Aided by the gift of experience, Nadia knew it was best to wait and let him fill the silence.

"My first wish, I admit, I spent on something selfish," he went on. "My mom's wish was the opposite—she used her heirloom for a greater good, though I'd be lying if I said she didn't influence my decision. I wanted to make her proud, you know?"

Nadia continued in her patient silence.

"Growing up, I'd spend every available hour listening to records on my mom's old vinyl player. Even now, nothing else comes close to the sound of vinyl." He sighed wistfully. "I'd play them again and again, picking out the different instruments, listening for those hidden melodies and bass notes and that kind of thing. But the guitar . . . Man, I'd wear some records out by going back to the solos and trying to figure them out on the acoustic that my dad bought me one Christmas. I must've been ten or so.

"I sucked at school. I was always, like, third last to get picked in sports, and I had the singing voice of a strangled cat. But when my fingers strummed that guitar, I felt like I was actually halfway decent at something." His brows lowered in consternation. "But I wanted to be better. I'd practice and practice, but it was like I plateaued at mediocre. The gap between my talent and my aspirations used to frustrate the hell out of me, to the point where I almost smashed my guitar against a wall once. I didn't want to be playing gigs at The Scrapyard forever."

"I can imagine that was exasperating, especially considering your passion for music," Nadia prompted, wanting to hear more about his life. She'd spilled her guts at his house. She figured she should let him return the favor, in case this was where they parted ways for good.

"It sounds cheesy, but I idolized these famous guitarists and wanted to be on the same level as them. I wanted my name up in lights, you know?" he went on. "My mom thought I was there already, but that's what moms are for—to cheerlead your mediocrity."

Nadia smiled. "That's not cheesy at all. It's understandable. And I've seen you play—there's nothing run-of-the-mill about it. Your mom was right."

"That's the problem. I never used to play like that. It all came from a wish." He took a deep breath, putting Nadia on edge in case he blurted out the wish itself in the monitored room. "And my star basically rose from there."

She exhaled a sigh of relief.

"My voice and playing improved until I could shred with the best of them without really trying too hard," Miles continued. "It was like my fingers knew exactly what to do without getting muddled the way they used to. Then, I got discovered and signed, and I rocketed to international fame." He tapped his fingers on his chest. "Monique assumed I'd been holding out on her and the band and that my fame was overhyped. She'll never know how close to the truth she was."

"Have you felt unworthy of your stardom, then?" she asked.

Nadia was genuinely curious. It seemed Black Hat and Croak had made an educated guess when it came to the "dirt" on Miles they gave Jack. When someone was rich and famous in the wishing world, it wasn't hard to guess what they might've wished for. But until Jack had mentioned it, Nadia hadn't even considered that Miles's talents might be wish-given, because his love for music seemed as deep rooted as his Georgia upbringing.

He tilted his head, his eyes still closed. "Sometimes, I feel like the people I grew up with—my dad and mom especially, at least when she was alive—look at me like people must've looked at Robert Johnson."

"Robert Johnson?" Nadia asked.

"The way the story goes, back when he was working on a plantation in Mississippi, he had these big dreams of becoming a famous blues musician," Miles explained. "You can understand why that might've been tricky for him. Anyway, some guy tells him to take his guitar to this crossroads at midnight—you know, 'cause the spooky stuff always happens at that time. Midnight comes, and this big Black dude appears and tunes Robert's guitar. That dude was supposedly the

Devil, in case you didn't catch that. So anyway, the Devil plays a couple of songs on the guitar before giving it back to Robert, who then becomes this guitar god. Like me, one day he was mediocre and then —*bam!*—he became a master pretty much overnight. All for the price of a soul."

"Or maybe he made a wish, like you?" she suggested.

Miles shook his head. "Nah, I doubt it. He just had immense talent during a time when Black men weren't supposed to be good at anything, so people started telling these tall tales to make that reality seem plausible. They did him dirty in a lot of ways. Like, if they were going to make up a story, why did it have to be this Faustian thing instead of it being an angel or the Lord Himself who gave Robert his talent?" He pursed his lips. "I'll tell you why. Back then, the Lord wasn't supposed to be generous to Black folk either."

"Is that a sticking point for you—that Robert Johnson had a naturally extraordinary talent?" Nadia asked.

He made a quiet thinking noise. "I guess I feel like my story is closer to selling my soul to the Devil, and I hate that. I *wish* I could've had my talent naturally without wishing for it." He paused. "That's why I told Jack that you don't get automatic happiness when you wish for things, because . . . you sort of miss out on the journey and the sense of pride you'd get if you made it to the top under your own steam."

"I understand that," Nadia said softly.

He gave a small nod. "Wishing for good health or to get out of poverty is a worthwhile wish, because it's not inherently selfish," he continued. "Those are things I can get behind being given rather than earned, for the most part."

"It's very noble that you tried to stop Jack from repeating what you view as your mistakes, though I'd argue that your music has brought comfort to many, many people. There's good in that," she pointed out.

He shrugged. "Maybe, but it's not something I built for myself. You know, like eating vegetables you grew in your own garden. I robbed myself of that. Worse, I robbed myself of the chance to try to get there on my own." His face fell. "Now, when I play, I'll never know what's my actual skill and what's just . . . magic, or façade, or whatever you want to call it. All because I wanted to be an all-around guitar god, like my idols. Although I still haven't mastered 'Memories of the Alhambra.'"

She turned her gaze toward the wall opposite, seeking questions in the void. "Wouldn't you feel the same way about a good relationship? Surely, you'd want to earn that too, instead of wishing it into existence? I can imagine that not knowing if someone actually loves you or if it's the magnetic draw of a wish would be worse than not knowing if your talent is yours or wish-given."

Miles sighed. "It's *me* I want to change, not someone else. I don't mean my personality or my face or anything, but the intangible parts of me, if that makes any sense. I want to be a better man, and I don't know if I have it in me to do that on my own." He cleared his throat, sounding a bit embarrassed by the admission. "Aaaand that's enough of *that*."

"I don't mind," she said honestly.

He coughed, dipping his head. "Well, thanks for listening. I don't normally talk to people like this. Must be your counselor vibes making me all like 'think about your childhood traumas' and that sort of jazz."

"My brand of psychology isn't as intrusive as tha—"

The vault lock made its clattering rotation. The door wheezed open and Val strode in, one arm in a hospital-blue temporary sling.

Cold fear grabbed Nadia. Val had reason enough to beat her senseless after the riverboat fiasco. But the tall woman merely gestured for them to stand, and they dutifully obeyed.

"The Wishmaster is ready to see you now," Val instructed, but when Miles moved to the door, she shook her head. "No, just her."

Miles shot Nadia a glance, her own concern reflected on his face. Not twenty-four hours ago, she'd have given anything to lose him, and now she'd rather have walked on hot coals than be separated. What if she got hurt and needed to find a way out? What if *he* got hurt while she was being interrogated? She'd told him they might go easier on him, but that had been nothing more than speculation. Kaleena wasn't called a ballbreaker for nothing. And Nadia couldn't do anything to help her newfound conspirator except try to bargain with Kaleena— which would've stood a better chance of success if she wasn't already in debt. She had briefly talked to her older sister only once or twice in the three years since Kaleena had become Wishmaster.

Stretching the stiffness out of her legs, Nadia gave Miles what she hoped was a parting nod of reassurance and followed Val out of the vault. In sulking silence, the blonde bruiser led Nadia back through the maze of hallways, giving her no choice but to contemplate Miles's fate and all the dire consequences that wishing brought.

Aware of Val's eyes boring into her, Nadia broke the silence. "Remember, you were the one who grabbed *me* and tipped us both overboard. Not to mention stealing the wish from me."

"It hurt like hell to pop this shoulder back into place," Val grumbled.

Nadia shrugged, happy that both her shoulders worked perfectly well—at least for now. "I repeat, *you* came at *me*. That wish wasn't yours to steal, so you brought all your pain on yourself. If you're looking for sympathy, you're barking up the wrong Kaminski."

Val slammed Nadia up against the nearest wall. "I wasn't doing it for myself, you stupid bitch. I need to earn back *my* third wish, or my wife will—" She stopped herself.

Nadia blinked in surprise at Val's sudden outburst. "Is that what the Wishmaster has on you? Your—"

"No." Val's tone cut off further discussion, and a ripple of annoyance passed over her angular, Scandinavian features. Now that they weren't actively trying to kill each other, Nadia could actually get a good look at the woman. She had a strong jaw, cheekbones to make a sculptor weep, and eyebrows so fair they were almost invisible. Honestly, she wouldn't have looked out of place with braided hair, war paint on her face, and a shield and sword in her hands, rowing to victory on a Viking longboat.

Val released her grip and stepped back. "Get moving." She shoved Nadia along another narrow, identical corridor. "And don't think you'll be getting any special treatment. Nobody here cares who you are, least of all the boss."

～

When they reached a windowless corridor, Val stopped by a wooden doorway. She opened it, revealing a wide stairwell that coiled down to some deeper level of the headquarters' labyrinth. As Nadia reached for the banister and peered over the edge, she immediately regretted it. Vertigo had never bothered her before, but not knowing how far down the staircase went made her stomach twist uncontrollably.

That, and not knowing what waited for her below.

As they made their descent, the steps banged and creaked. With Val behind her, Nadia didn't have much choice but to keep going. The bottom of the staircase led to another gloomy hallway lit by dim lamps. Val gave her a prompting shove, and Nadia tried keep her chin up and her shoulders squared as she marched toward a wide doorway at the hallway's end. Val skirted past her and opened it.

Soft, ambient light spilled into the grim corridor, though Nadia didn't find it remotely inviting. She wouldn't have taken another step if Val hadn't forced her.

The lavish chamber had two floors, with the second forming a gallery of sorts, thanks to an elegant balustrade of carved, swirling marble that made Nadia think of sea serpents in constant battle. Velveteen drapes were tied at every section of the galleried upper tier, presumably to give privacy when needed.

The upper gallery of Ionic columns created a shadowed walkway on all sides, giving the chamber a Southern Gothic feel. The entire floor of the lower level was crafted from smooth, pale oak and covered in plush white rugs that made it look like there'd been a polar bear massacre. The white was the first comforting thing Nadia saw. It was unlikely she'd be tortured in this room—blood would be a pain to get out of those rugs.

In the center of the chamber stood a long dining table draped in a silken tablecloth, with high-backed golden chairs spanning both sides. Lanterns with real flames hung down from the upper gallery, and a chandelier of candles and bronze vines took pride of place, suspended by a sturdy iron chain. More lanterns were placed along the length of the dining table, in a medley of ornate black iron vessels. Alongside them rested centerpieces of vivid red, burnished orange, and coral-hued flowers that stood out against the neutral tones of the rest of the room.

"Somebody wished for interior design mojo, I see," Nadia remarked.

"I suggest you don't talk," Val shot back.

Nadia didn't plan to, her attention fixed on the lanterns. Maybe she could run to one and make her wish before Val or Kaleena could stop her. If she wished for invulnerability, she might make it out alive, but she sensed that the particular wish in her chest wasn't potent enough for that kind of request. That called for a saved-a-bus-of-orphans level of potency.

A woman emerged from the lower gallery with a book in her hands, interrupting Nadia's fevered ideas of escape. Her Slavic features echoed Nadia's own, though she'd gone for a smart-casual attire of black jeans and a flowy, silky blouse instead of the damp lost-and-found clothes Nadia had on. Approaching the dining table, she set down her book and smiled.

Val pushed on the back of Nadia's head. "You bow to the Wishmaster."

"There's no need for that. We're family, after all," Kaleena replied in a mocking tone. "It's been too long, little sister."

Chapter Twenty

Nadia met her sister's amused stare. Kaleena's hazel eyes mirrored her own, and they shared the same long brunette locks, though Kaleena's had been primped into wavy submission. While they both had strong jaws and defined eyebrows, Kaleena's cheeks were plumper, with a hard dip beneath that gave them a hollowed appearance. And Kaleena was far paler in complexion, but Nadia supposed that was expected when someone refused to ever crawl out of their underground bunker.

At thirty-eight, Kaleena could've passed for late twenties, maybe younger, though she carried herself with a maturity and gravitas that no twenty-something possessed. Her hourglass silhouette, aided by a pricey outfit, oozed power and bolstered the confidence in her stride. A rose-gold watch glinted on her left wrist in the dim light—one Nadia was surprised to find she recognized. She'd bought that watch for Kaleena as a birthday gift years ago, the metal now chipped in places.

"You've been quite the busy bee," Kaleena continued when Nadia made no attempt to respond to her "little sister" remark. It was just another power play, minimizing Nadia's stance with a carefully chosen, false endearment. "I'm happy to see you return to the hive after trying to steal a drop of honey for yourself. A girl after my own heart. It's just a shame you can't enjoy the sweet taste of it to the fullest."

Nothing about Kaleena's cheerful cadence made it sound like she was actually glad to see her sister. It still baffled Nadia how much Kaleena had changed. The moment she became the Wishmaster, her entire personality had twisted. It was uncanny, like the title had created a whole new version of the sister Nadia had once looked up to.

"You can go, and don't let the door hit you on the way out," Kaleena addressed Val bluntly. A smile formed on her lips. "I mean it—the hinges need fixing. You should probably get maintenance on that."

"Yes, Wishmaster." Val bowed and shuffled backward out of the majestic double doors, as though she were in the presence of legitimate royalty.

"Take a seat, little sister," Kaleena instructed, gesturing to the end of the long dining table. Luxurious cashmere throws were draped over two of the high-backed golden chairs at the far end. Presumably, they'd been fastidiously arranged for this meeting—the chairs pulled out ever so slightly, the throws positioned just right, and a bespoke cream-and-gold glazed teapot set out with two matching cups, the faint hint of cinnamon in the air. Everything was far too casually perfect not to have been the product of careful preparation.

Nadia held her ground, despite the cacophony of thoughts that echoed in her head. "Thanks, Kaleena, but I'll stand."

Her sister rolled her eyes. "It's a pretty name, for sure, but it's *Wishmaster* now, as you well know. That's who I am, and you can thank Basha for that. But I could wear a name tag, if it would make it easier for you?" She went to the dining table, pulled out the chair to the left of the table's head, and flourished a melodramatic hand across the vacant seat.

"I'd say you've got a lot to thank our babcia for," Nadia said, reluctantly sitting down. "You wouldn't have a thriving little business here if it weren't for the wishes we pour into your enterprise."

Kaleena took a seat at the head of the table and swept a perfectly manicured fingertip toward the teapot, ignoring Nadia's comment entirely. "Normally, I'd offer my guests tea, but seeing as you have no spent wishes, there'd be little point. Unless you like the bitter taste? That would suit you, since I am sensing a lot of bitterness."

"How do you know I haven't spent the one I took from Val already?" Nadia shot back, hating how the sister she'd once adored had become so blasé, with a constant need to assert dominance.

Nadia still remembered the times she'd perched by her big sister's stereo, ready to push down the Record button when a song came on that Kaleena wanted on cassette for her crappy first car. Or when they'd built a fort out of blankets and scarfed down a whole tin of Polish cookies that they'd stolen from the kitchen one Christmas Eve. Or when, albeit reluctantly, Kaleena had helped Nadia build an entire town made out of books for her bevy of toys to live in, then humored her for hours with conjured dramas that would've rivaled any soap opera. The stuffed rabbit being caught in a love triangle with the hand-knitted squirrel and the knockoff Ken doll had been a particular highlight.

Now, after years of barely any contact, Nadia couldn't help but feel abandoned. Like an iceberg, Kaleena had broken off and drifted away from the family glacier, and while Nadia could understand the desire to cut ties with a sometimes suffocating homelife, she wondered if her sister understood just how hard it had hit Nadia to have her one ally drift away from her as well.

Worse still, Kaleena had never shown a sliver of remorse for shouldering them with an immense debt, even when the wish had been needed to save Nadia's life. It wasn't that Nadia had expected a handout, but 101 wishes seemed excessive to demand of your supposed loved ones. She had always suspected that Kaleena wanted to make an example of them to prove her ruthlessness as Wishmaster—to show that she didn't make exceptions, even for her own family.

Kaleena smiled, though it reminded Nadia of the fixed, eerie smirk painted on porcelain dolls. "One of my associates can sense the number of wishes a person has remaining. You have three, little sister, so let's not pretend, hmm? We're not children anymore, though I'll always be sad that you missed out on your growth spurt. Do you still hem all of your jeans, or have you finally started shopping in the petite section?"

Instead of smarting off like she wanted to, Nadia shrugged and said, "I thought I'd find out what you already know, instead of going over old ground. That'd just be boring for both of us."

"I'd forgotten how funny you could be," Kaleena deadpanned as she took a wooden compass coin—emblazoned with her wishbone flower insignia—from her pocket. She rolled it effortlessly across her knuckles. "I don't even need one of these coins to tell that you've got an unspent wish inside you, nor do I need an associate to give me your total." She flicked the coin upward, watching it spin before it came back to land between two knuckles. "You've become quite the renegade. The wishing grapevine is rife with gossip about what you've been up to at Bonaventure and on the river."

"All good things, I hope?" Nadia replied dryly.

"It's curious to me," Kaleena said, rolling the coin again. "You've always been the loyal, reliable, steadfast Kaminski child. Why would you suddenly flip the script like that, betraying your family after years of toeing every line? Don't mistake me, I'm impressed that you followed in my footsteps, but it does pique the old interest. Or did Basha put you up to this?"

Kaleena flipped the coin into the air again. Perhaps this was some heads-or-tails scenario, and Kaleena was waiting for it to land on the side she wanted. With every upward toss, Nadia's nerves skyrocketed. She had no escape route. Those doors were shut, and even if she could get past them, she'd have a mind-boggling labyrinth of evasive hallways to navigate before she could even think about reaching the outside world. And after that? Still more of Kaleena's minions waiting to drag her back, kicking and screaming.

"Mom and Babcia had nothing to do with me taking that wish," Nadia said. "I made my own choices."

Her sister gave a low hum. "I'm sure you believe that. You've seemed perfectly happy to do their bidding up until now. And you were even living with them under the same roof. It's obvious where your loyalties lie."

Nadia was a little taken aback. Her desire to pay off the debt hadn't been some act of loyalty to their grandmother. Yet Kaleena eyed her as if she were a lowly agent of the real enemy—as if she might report back to Basha about this meeting.

"Is that the reason you've never once contacted me directly these past three years? Why you've never answered my calls?" Nadia asked carefully. "Because of some misguided paranoia about Babcia?"

Kaleena's eyes widened. "You think it's misguided? How adorably naïve. There's a reason I put 'This is not a game' at the top of the debt contract. Our grandmother—and by association, our mother—will do whatever is necessary to avoid paying what I'm owed. Now, we need to talk about what *you* owe me."

Nadia tried to prevent the spike of fear from showing on her face. She'd rather beg and plead for clemency than let this debt consume the rest of her life. It was time for her last, and only, trump card: trying to get Kaleena to soften up through their shared past.

"Do you remember that violent drunk guy we stole a wish from when we were kids?" Nadia began. "That must've been around twenty years ago now."

Kaleena stopped flicking the coin. "What about him?"

"He could've killed you, but you refused to stop trying to pry that wish out of him," Nadia went on. "We were young and stupid then, with no real idea of how to steal secrets. But you kept plying him with booze, asking him every question under the sun to try to snatch his wish. Even when he grabbed you around the throat, you kept asking him things."

They'd been ten and seventeen years old, having only just started to capture wishes on their own, after their dad left. Working as a mismatched team, they'd used their young charms to coax people into giving up their heart secrets: Nadia would play the sobbing kid who'd temporarily lost her mom, and Kaleena would prey on sly-eyed men whom she'd caught gawking at her. But this one memory was the clearest in Nadia's mind, since it was the first time she'd realized how dangerous the wishing world could be.

Kaleena had asked the man if he'd ever put his hands around his daughter's neck when she'd pissed him off. He'd let go of her so fast he nearly fell over. Kaleena had still been gasping for air when he'd drunkenly blurted out, "I put her in the hospital." He'd had tears in his eyes, and so had Kaleena, although hers had probably been tears of victory.

"Do you remember what you said to me that day, after we took his wish and left him sobbing?" Nadia pressed, certain there was some fragment of her compassionate big sister left in this cold-hearted woman.

"I'm sure you're going to tell me," Kaleena replied, looking entirely unmoved.

"You said, 'Someday you'll learn that certain people can't be trusted with power, and it's our job to make sure they don't get to keep it.' *That* was why you refused to leave, even when it got dangerous. You couldn't allow that wish to stay with that man because he might've accidentally used it and hurt someone innocent." Nadia waited to see some glimmer of softness in those hard, hazel eyes, but it didn't come.

Instead, Kaleena tilted her head. "And what, may I ask, was the point of that sweet little anecdote? Are you trying to pluck at my heartstrings?" She pretended to strum what appeared to be a tiny, invisible harp.

"You might not be that person anymore, but there's still truth in what you said back then," Nadia replied. "The reason you stayed until you had that guy's wish is the same reason you're so paranoid about who you let close—you can smell when someone might become corrupt with power." She paused. "But I wonder if you can smell it on yourself."

It was a risky move to criticize the Wishmaster so openly, but maybe if her sister saw the hypocrisy in all this, she would change her mind about the harshness of her punishments. People really were capable of changing for the better—Nadia believed that to the depths of her soul, especially after all she'd seen in her counseling office.

"I *know* who I am." Kaleena chuckled. "I permit corruption in neither my enterprise nor myself. Nor do I seek power. I enforce order. Save me the lecture, little sister. I'm not one of your clients."

Nadia's cheeks burned, though she wasn't sure why. "I understand the need for order, and there's more of it now. It's less violent than when Adrian ran things, but . . ." She trailed off as Kaleena's mouth turned up at the mention of his name.

"But?" Kaleena prompted.

Nadia sighed nervously. "There's order, and then there's vindictive-ness." She swallowed past the lump in her throat. "I'm not trying to usurp your place or mess things up. I just want one thing: to revive Nick, to have him back, so I can live the life that I thought I was promised when I married him."

"Nothing is promised, unfortunately," Kaleena replied, with maybe the faintest drip of sympathy.

Clearly, nothing could persuade Kaleena to dig into her humanity. All of Nadia's usual counselor tactics of appealing to pathos, logos, and ethos weren't working at all on her big sister.

Nadia leaned forward. "I know, but that doesn't mean it's out of my reach."

"I liked Nick," Kaleena said, resuming her coin-play. "How could anyone not? He was the kind of guy who saved runaway strollers and would mow an old lady's lawn without her asking, but they're usually the ones with the darkest demons. I imagine you've got countless psychiatry textbooks that say the same thing."

Nadia's expression hardened. "He didn't cause those arsons. There was nothing dark about him. He was good, he was sweet, he was kind, and . . . now he's gone."

"Perhaps you didn't know him as well as you thought, then," Kaleena said flatly. "We've all got sides we hide from others, don't we?"

A spark of anger ignited inside Nadia. Oh, so now Kaleena, who'd been living in her hidden lair for years, thought *she* knew something about Nick that Nadia didn't? How could her sister possibly know anything that Nadia didn't when it came to her own husband? She wanted to lunge across the table at her sister, to bash her face into that exquisite marble, to rip every last piece of expensive fabric to shreds.

Gripping the edge of the chair, she took a steadying breath.

"I don't care what he chose to keep from me. He's my Nick either way," Nadia said at last. "Babcia wouldn't let me bring him back. She says I have no right to want anything because our debt was my fault, and that should be my only priority."

If there was one thing Nadia hoped would get her sister on her side, it was Kaleena's raging hatred of Basha.

"*I* made the stupid mistake of crashing the car. *I* was the one who needed a spare organ in a tight turnaround," Nadia went on, keeping her head down. "*I* was the one who forced Babcia and Mom to get into this debt, to save my life. It doesn't matter to them that I didn't ask to be saved. I'm grateful, sure, but if I'd known it would cause this much hassle, maybe I'd have asked them not to bother."

Kaleena straightened, a glint of rage in her eyes. "Ah, so that's the tale they wove, is it? I assumed you'd stayed because of your loyalty to the rodzina—Basha's old chestnut. If I'd known they'd lied to you, I'd have gotten you on my side before all this happened . . ." She clicked her tongue. "But that doesn't matter now. What you need to know is this: that debt is Basha and Grace's responsibility, not yours."

Nadia's stomach lurched, a prickling unease replacing her former anger.

"What do you mean?" Nadia asked, but that flicker of real emotion had vanished from Kaleena's eyes. The car accident story was the only one Nadia knew, and since she'd been unconscious, it wasn't like she had any memory of it. But what if her family had kept her in the dark about some part of what happened?

"Your recent behavior and interference aren't something I can overlook," Kaleena said. "You're focusing on how *you've* been wronged and what *you* want, when you're in no position to bargain. If you wanted to use a wish, you should've come to me and asked. As I said, the debt is Basha and Grace's. I would have allowed you your wish. We're sisters, after all. That comes with a few perks—if you come to me on a good day."

The unease swelled in Nadia's stomach. Basha and Grace had warned her against asking the Wishmaster for a wish, claiming there'd be hell to pay if she did. Yet Kaleena just said that she would've given her permission. If Basha and Grace had lied to keep Nadia from asking for a wish, had they lied about the cause of the debt too?

Or was Kaleena the one lying? After all, it was easy enough for her to claim that she would've allowed Nadia to spend a wish, even if it was only an empty promise. But Kaleena had no reason to tell Nadia that she *didn't* owe a debt when the opposite would clearly benefit her as Wishmaster.

"Then where did our debt come from?" Nadia asked in a small voice.

"*Their* debt. Not yours."

The room seemed to close around Nadia. "But how did . . . ?"

Kaleena wagged a finger. "The cause isn't for me to say. You'd only believe it if it came from Basha, and I feel she *ought* to be the one to come clean, though she and Grace have been lying so long they've probably started to believe it."

"So, it's really . . . not my debt?" Nadia needed to say it aloud to try to process it. If it was true, then she now understood why her wish to clear her debt hadn't worked. Why would it, when the debt wasn't hers to begin with?

"Nope, but you took their debt on, never doubting them for a moment," Kaleena continued. "Then you went against the rules—you stole a wish 'off the books' after already flubbing an exchange, and you plotted to attack my associates. I was hoping you'd decide not to go through with it so that I wouldn't need to drag you in here, but you went and proved me right. You endangered Val, resulting in a client losing the product they'd paid for . . . I don't think I need to go on." She placed her hands on the table in a slow, measured way. "It's bad for business, little sister, and you have to face the consequences. No perks there, I'm afraid."

Nadia scratched her temple. "Then why did you send a feather, and why did Croak say he was watching me closely?"

"Not closely enough, it seems." Kaleena sniffed. "But I've been having him watch you for the past year. I knew you'd be a wreck after Nick passed, and I couldn't come and check on you myself when you moved into that den of iniquity, so I sent Croak in my stead. As for the feathers—one was yours, one was theirs. The latter came about because they were scheming to have me overthrown, and I can't stand a mutiny. There's too much cleanup afterward, so I thought I'd nip it in the bud. Still, let's skirt back around to your feather and your transgressions, since that's why we're here."

Nadia had hoped their bygone sisterly bond might save her from a brutal punishment, but it had always been a long shot. On to plan B: an all-out, hands-clasped-together, prostrate-on-the-ground, pleading desperation.

"Then let me buy this wish!" Nadia said in a rush. "I can get you a dozen more. Two dozen. You know that. Look how many we've already stolen for you!"

There was no movement on the Wishmaster's face as she replied. "That's a given."

"Or take this one!" Nadia blurted out, not quite on her knees yet. "You can have it back. Forget I stole it from you in the first place." She sagely avoided mentioning that the wish rightly belonged to Miles. This was about saving both of their hides—hers and Miles's—and if it cost him his last wish, then at least he'd have his life and his freedom.

Kaleena raised an unimpressed eyebrow, every hair immaculately in place. "Well, thank you for the kind offer, but you didn't really have an option of *not* returning it." She mustered a half smile. "Still, I appreciate you reducing my workload. I would've hated to have to drag you to extraction, especially if you'd planned to wail and scream. Embarrassing."

Nadia's skin crawled at that putrid little word: extraction. It made her think of teeth being yanked and alien objects being plucked out of wide-open carcasses on a surgical table.

"I messed up. I know it. But if you let me keep this one, I'll work twice—"

"I'm more concerned with quality over quantity right now," Kaleena said. "And I have something else in mind, if you're *really* determined to prove you won't break the rules again." She fell silent, an expectant tension twanging between them.

Nadia swallowed. "What is it?"

Her sister smirked. "You are going to use your wish for me."

The chair's soft cushioning and layers of fuzzy add-ons felt suffocating, keeping Nadia trapped in her seat. "What?"

"Should I repeat it to you in Polish? I thought my meaning was clear enough. Or are you asking what I want you to wish for?" Kaleena took a purple tea light out of the nearest lantern and flicked it back and forth between her fingers, as though taunting Nadia about the imminent loss of her wish.

"Well, maybe I need it simpler," Nadia replied, her throat constricting.

"There's a certain . . . skill that no other associate of mine has been able to use." Her eyes met Nadia's, her pupils reflecting the flickering flame. "I think you'd be the perfect candidate for it."

"So, you actually want *me* to use the wish?" Nadia floundered.

"It saves having to bounce it around other people." Kaleena nodded to Nadia's chest. "That wish has been through enough bodies."

"What's the skill? What do you want it for?" Nadia asked with narrowed eyes.

"Oh, this and that." Kaleena wafted a hand through the air. "But I have three very important tasks in mind. Succeed in all three, and you'll have your freedom. No more debt, no more servitude, no catch beyond those three little tasks. And maybe we can get together for brunch once in a blue moon and take that wander down memory lane that you crave."

Nadia got the feeling there *was* a catch and that those three tasks wouldn't be remotely small, but she held her tongue. After all, this was the kind of "out" she'd never expected to get from her sister, queen of the zero-tolerance policy.

"And when I say you'll be free, I mean it," Kaleena continued, her tone softening. "You can do whatever you like. Take wishes from whomever you like. Try to resurrect a couple of people if you want, though I'm not going to be making any bets on you succeeding in that anytime soon."

Nadia shook her head. "There's an enormous 'but' here, and it isn't mine."

"Hilarious," Kaleena said. "Think of it as terms and conditions—a form of motivation. I'll have to give you two more wishes, take them back, and hold them as collateral until the job's done. Standard protocol so you don't get tempted to steal wishes for yourself instead of me, especially given that you now have a history of that. I want no Nick distractions."

Nadia rubbed her thumb against the pressure point in her palm to try to quell her nerves. "But you would give them back in their unused state, right?"

"Of course." Kaleena looked momentarily offended. "In this business, my word is my bond. I'll return the wishes when the three deeds are accomplished. I could even give you a guiding hand about how to use those last two to find a way to revive your dearly departed, if that's what you really want. Call it a sisterly sweetener."

If anything, it was sisterly aspartame: pretending to be sweet while it made your guts gurgle and sent you sprinting for the bathroom. But Nadia could sweep past all the sarcasm and incongruity to see the very real hope that Kaleena was dangling in front of her.

"What's the wish? How do I know it won't counteract any kind of resurrection wish?" Nadia said, trying to soften the edge of desperation in her voice.

Kaleena shrugged. "I can't tell you what the wish is until you accept." She ceased her private game of finger hockey with the tea light and skimmed it toward Nadia like a fiery puck, as if confident that Nadia wouldn't try anything funny with her current wish. "The offer's there, little sister, and you won't get a better one. Either it's this or you scrounge up *another* one hundred and one wishes for the next . . . however many years of your Nickless life."

The mere thought of giving up decades to wish hunting made Nadia's body go slack with despair. Three tasks sounded a whole lot better than running around like a headless chicken trying to coax out secrets while never getting to use a wish for herself.

Sorry, Miles. At this point, he wasn't getting his wish back either way. The least she could do was accept her sister's offer and throw his freedom into the bargain too.

"If I do it, will you let Miles go?" Nadia said quietly.

"Ah, a bold move, and very admirable. But no," Kaleena replied. "No one gets out of a debt. Order must be maintained, no matter who the offender is or why they did it."

Nadia wanted to push the subject more, but what if she only caused more trouble for Miles by doing so? It wasn't worth the risk. Her only choice was to settle for the deal she'd been given. Nadia swallowed hard. "Fine. I'll do it."

"Excellent." Kaleena pulled a piece of paper from her pocket and pushed it across the table to Nadia, leaving it curled up beside the tea light.

Nadia resisted the urge to glower, though she couldn't help sending livid thoughts toward the Wishing Tree. Sure, it could stop people from resurrecting loved ones who had only good intentions for necromancy, or prevent people from wishing they were dead. Yet somehow it hadn't come up with a way to stop people from forcing others to make wishes that benefited them. To Nadia, it seemed the Wishing Tree had some major reprioritizing to do.

"Say the words on the paper out loud," Kaleena instructed, oblivious to Nadia's inner raging. "Those exact words. No deviation. If you make a mistake, you'll wish you'd never been born."

That was another wish prohibited by the Wishing Tree—for obvious logistical, genetically cataclysmic reasons—but the threat was clear enough, regardless of the wording.

"Do you know how painful it is to have a used wish taken?" Kaleena pressed. "Agonizing, I hear. They don't call it 'hope stealing' for no reason. And if you try any funny business, I'll force you to spend two wishes, then I'll steal them back and let them disappear into the ether."

With shaky hands, Nadia opened the piece of paper. It read, in elegant cursive, *I wish to be the perfect spy for Kaleena Kaminski*. She had no choice but to obey, or else she'd lose her ability to wish *and* face that torturous extraction.

Nadia looked up at her sister, whose expression remained an enigma. "This could manifest in so many different, twisted ways."

She read it again, fearful of its simplicity. True, the Wishing Tree tended to outright ignore any wishes longer than a handful of words, and multipart wishes never worked, but every word was open to interpretation.

"Didn't you see the name on the paper? The wish manifests the same way each time because it's based on what *I* want in a spy, not whatever's in *your* head." Kaleena pincered the piece of paper and dropped it into her other palm, ready to crush it. "I hate to rush you, but time's a-ticking." She clicked her tongue, emulating the sound of a clock.

The wish's wording could hurt Nadia, alter her forever, but what was worse? An uncertain outcome, or the certainty that she'd never get Nick back if she didn't do this? She lunged for the paper and all but clawed it out of Kaleena's hand. It startled Nadia how cold her elder sister's skin was, as though she were carved from marble.

"I'll do it! I'll make the wish!" Nadia gasped. "I promise, I'll do it." She hated the groveling tone of her voice, but that was exactly what Kaleena wanted, with all her "little sister" and "Nickless life" business: control over her.

"Go on, then," Kaleena said, eyeing her palm as if expecting to see scratches.

Nadia unfurled the piece of paper and read aloud without hesitation in case she lost her nerve. "I wish to be the perfect spy for Kaleena Kaminski." Then, closing her eyes, she leaned forward and blew out the tea light.

As a wisp of smoke spiraled upward, a peculiar warmth tingled across Nadia's chest, up her throat, and into her skull, where it bubbled around in her brain. Then the heat dispersed, taking the wish rush with it. She waited to feel empty, or unusual, or changed in some way, knowing the manifestation couldn't be far away. The effects were usually instantaneous, or at least within a twenty-four-hour window. How long would hers take?

At first, nothing seemed outwardly different. She hadn't transformed into a cyborg with guns for arms, and she wasn't feeling a sudden urge to have her martini shaken, not stirred. Her eyes couldn't see through solid walls, and her ears weren't hearing a dog take a piss against a fire hydrant twelve blocks away. But there was an odd darkening around the edges of her vision, like the room was vignetted, skewing her sight to the point where she felt like she was looking through a fishbowl.

"Two people have tried this before," Kaleena said, watching her with interest. "Hopefully, you'll be lucky number three."

The use of past tense didn't escape Nadia's notice. What the hell had happened to those previous wishers? Presumably, they weren't around anymore. Or, if they were, they probably weren't the same as they'd been pre-wish.

Before Kaleena could elaborate, the imposing double doors sprang open and Val stormed in with a face like thunder.

"We had a runner, Wishmaster, but we found him before he got far." Val bowed her head, breathing hard as if she'd sprinted the whole way there.

"Bring him to me," Kaleena instructed. "Though tell me—how did he manage to get out?"

Val winced. Nadia got the impression that Val didn't want to answer the Wishmaster's question, but the answer came nevertheless, as though it had been squeezed out of her like the last blob of toothpaste in the tube. "He tricked the guards."

Craning her neck to get a look at the empty hallway behind Val, Nadia felt a ripple of anxiety about the "him" they were referring to. What if Miles had tried to escape on his own, after getting some kind of epiphany from his finding ability? She wasn't annoyed, just worried. After all the time they'd spent together recently, she couldn't help but feel responsible for him, especially after getting him into this mess in the first place.

But she had no idea if the favor she'd just given her sister would go any way toward saving Miles from the Wishmaster's punishment. He might've dug himself a hole that she couldn't airlift him out of. Had she condemned him to a terrible fate?

"He's already been taken to the cellar for extraction," Val went on, her breath leveling. "I can take Clover Eyes back to the vault, if you're done with her?"

Nadia still had no clue what her wish had wrought. Dread percolated down through her chest and into her stomach. Although . . . she *did* feel a bizarre sensation as she looked into Val's eyes. Detachment. Floating. But it was gone in an instant.

Kaleena scraped back her chair and stood with a smile. "This is the perfect opportunity to test-drive your new wish, little sister."

Chapter Twenty-One

Nadia kept her eyes down as Kaleena and Val marched her back through another maze of blurry optical illusions masquerading as hallways.

"How deep does this place go?" Nadia asked after five sets of stairs and a seemingly endless series of identical corridors. Overhead, huge chrome air-conditioning pipes and fans whirred nonstop, pushing fresh air through the labyrinth.

Kaleena checked her watch. "As deep as I want it to. Give me a white rabbit and a pipe-toting caterpillar."

"All this Wishmastering has turned you into the Cheshire Cat," Nadia muttered.

When they reached the end of a wide hallway, Kaleena punched a lengthy code into a keypad, in addition to using a hand and retinal scanner. A green light winked on, and the hefty steel blast door ahead opened wide.

Nadia highly doubted that anyone could ever break into this place, although some foolhardy thieves had probably attempted it. People who'd wished to shape-shift or break any code could crack a lesser gauntlet of defensive obstacles in no time, but by throwing the whole box of tricks into the security protocols—including the building's weird distortion trick—it made any type of break-in close to impossible.

Beyond the door was a totally different aesthetic. Kaleena led Nadia and Val into an annex with a curved stone ceiling and a single wooden door in the wall opposite. A smattering of handwoven rugs covered the pale gray flagstones, and sprays of white lilies adorned several ornamental tables while purple lavender-scented candles flickered all around.

Kaleena pulled an old-fashioned skeleton key from her pocket and slipped it into the lock on the wooden door. It turned with a rusty grating sound before she pulled on the black ring and opened the door wide.

"Val, stay here," Kaleena instructed. "Little sister, come with me."

Nadia followed dutifully, only to gasp as she entered the next room. This was *the* room—the chamber a thousand wish hunters would give their left arm to snatch a glimpse of. And though Nadia had always wondered why it was called the "wishing cellar," it all made sense as she took in the view.

The ceiling curved down to the flagstone floor like the one outside in the annex, and every wall was covered in sturdy wooden racks that hugged the contours of the vast, semicircular space. Shadowed passageways led off in all directions, presumably to more curving caverns like this one, where wishes were stored in place of vintage wines. At least, that was what Nadia assumed was contained within the gunmetal gray safe-deposit boxes that adorned every rack. Each one had a number engraved on the front.

"Wishmaster."

The voice brought Nadia's attention back to the center of the room. Thanks to the dimmed halogens buried in the stone walls, she hadn't noticed they had company until that moment.

Kaleena twisted the nearby dimmer switch, bringing three figures into view. Nadia's heart stuttered in her chest. Croak stood sentinel over a zip-cuffed Miles, who sat hunched in a chair and wore a tense, faraway expression. It took Nadia a moment to place the third figure—

a man strung up by the neck with a rope attached to a ceiling hook, his feet dancing a frantic jig to keep his tiptoes on the wooden chair beneath him.

Dominic—Adrian's henchman who'd attacked them at Bonaventure.

"Nadia . . ." Miles said, relief in his voice, though she couldn't quite tell whether the relief was because she was okay or because he didn't seem to be paddling up shit creek quite as fast as Dominic was.

Kaleena strode toward Dominic, her elegant boots clicking ominously across the flagstones.

"You've tried so hard to get in here, and yet now you can't get out," Kaleena mused, resting a hand on the chair that was between Dominic and a slow, strangled death. "I'd admire your perseverance if I was the sort of person who admired irony. But I'm not."

She rocked the chair slightly, and Dominic's eyes widened as he fought to keep his footing on the slippery, varnished wood.

"You've been like a pesky sand gnat to me for years now, always crawling into crevices where you don't belong," she continued, her voice chillingly calm. "You were small enough for me to ignore. But now, here you are, trying to take what doesn't belong to you, and I can't have that. Adrian's not in charge now, Dominic. There's no more begging for forgiveness when you never asked for permission."

"No, we just have to lick your boots . . . every time we want a wish!" Dominic spat, his words tangled in the rope around his throat. "I'm sick of being treated like . . . a second-class citizen."

Kaleena tipped the chair forward, forcing Dominic to kick out to try to gain purchase on its flimsy back.

Nadia observed the situation with a mixture of alarm and pitilessness. Dominic had held on to the misguided hope that Adrian would somehow return to power and grant wishes to whoever agreed to serve him. Kaleena was far more selective with whom she let work for her, handpicking only those she deemed worthiest to receive wishes. The way Kaleena had pincered the wishing world of Savannah with strict rules and held unspent wishes as collateral—something Adrian had never done—hadn't earned her widespread devotion, but it certainly earned her *fear*, and plenty of hate to go along with it.

But what was Miles doing here? Nadia had assumed Val was talking about him when she'd said someone had tried to escape, but now Nadia wasn't so sure. Maybe they'd been referring to Dominic. Either way, she guessed that her recent accomplice had been brought here for the same reason she had: the show. Kaleena wanted Nadia and Miles to understand the consequences of crossing her. Perhaps that meant Miles would be let off with a slap on the wrist if he assured the Wishmaster he'd behave.

Or maybe that was just wishful thinking.

Miles eyed Nadia curiously, as if trying to sense the wish inside her —the one that no longer existed. A guilty warmth tingled across Nadia's face, and she hoped that he'd forgive her when he found out the circumstances.

"You and your friends wanted to make a wish to oust me, didn't you?" Kaleena asked. "Why don't you tell me all about it. If you were going to go to such lengths, you really should've aimed for a more potent wish."

Dominic managed to steady himself in an awkward en pointe. His eyelids flickered with anger, but the rest of him had turned waxy with anxious sweat. "You . . . murdered Adrian!" he said in a garbled voice, the rope still tight around his neck. "I know it, even if . . . no one can prove it!"

Nadia stilled. She'd assumed Adrian was still alive and had been lying low, licking his wounds. But *dead?* Maybe she shouldn't have been all that surprised, but to think that her own sister was capable of such violence filled her with a sinking sense of unease.

"That isn't what I asked," Kaleena replied. "Adrian was already on borrowed time during his spell as Wishmaster. If I hadn't usurped him, someone else would've. But I wouldn't stoop so low as to kill him." She crossed her arms. "Perhaps you've forgotten what Adrian was really like. Murder was his MO. He made a lot of enemies that way. Maybe one of them caught up with him."

Nadia didn't believe it. Maybe Kaleena hadn't murdered him herself, but she had clearly been more involved than she was admitting, judging by her cavalier attitude.

"You planned it. I know . . . you did," Dominic hissed.

"Whatever makes you feel better," Kaleena said with a shrug as she walked to the wall and typed a code into a keypad. Part of the wall slid to the side, revealing a series of narrow wooden drawers. She pulled the top one out and removed a slip of wishery paper, fashioned from a gossamer-thin strip of papyrus-like material. Like the wooden wish traps and wishing bark infusion, the unusual paper came from the Wishing Tree itself. The few times Nadia had seen wishery paper, it always had that same subtle, silvery sheen.

Dominic's nostrils flared as he saw the paper.

Kaleena wafted the slip like a tiny flag. "I'm going to take your used wishes, Dominic. What, did you think I was really going to hang you? Not when there's greater value in the living."

Dominic struggled more insistently. "No, you're just . . . a common . . . hope stealer!"

Nadia almost snorted at the hypocrisy. Adrian had his own squadron of hope stealers when he'd been Wishmaster. Although Nadia had never seen it done, she'd heard rumors of hope stealers ripping used wishes out of their enemies and reselling whatever they had wished for to someone else. It was the ultimate insult to take someone's spent wishes and leave them powerless.

"You . . . can't!" Dominic gasped around his noose. "You don't . . . know the wording of . . . my wishes."

Kaleena sauntered up to him and stepped onto the chair so she could whisper into his ear.

Dominic's petrified face said everything: the Wishmaster knew.

As Kaleena stepped off the chair, Dominic thrashed against his bonds and noose—the last act of a desperate man. Nadia's stomach churned at his panic and despair. He was no saint, true, but he didn't deserve torture and humiliation on top of what was likely going to be his execution.

"No!" he cried. "No, you . . . can't! Please! Don't! I'll do anything, just don't . . . take them away!"

Kaleena walked to one of the ornamental side tables and took a pen from the embedded drawer. In her elegant cursive, she wrote something before folding the wishery paper in half. Without so much as a glance at Dominic, she dropped it into the flame of one of the purple candles that flickered around the wishing cellar.

The paper burned in an instant, and Dominic screamed. His veins lit up, silvery lines pulsing up and down his limbs, splintering up his neck and into his face. He flailed and twisted, a fish dangling from a hook. Two square wooden boxes were hinged open on one of the side tables—wish traps for capturing his wish-given abilities, Nadia was sure.

"I suppose you'll be more careful with guns, now that you're no longer bulletproof," Kaleena said above the din. She closed the wooden boxes simultaneously with a casual flick of her wrists. "And you won't be weaseling out of any more scrapes with your second wish either, which is bad news for you, especially right now."

Nadia shuddered, squeezing her eyes shut so she wouldn't have to watch Dominic's face.

"You know, I never understood why so many of Adrian's followers chose to be bulletproof, since it's so easy to guess the wording," Kaleena mused. "There are a thousand other ways a person can meet their end, anyway: stabbing, drowning, strangulation, electrocution, et cetera. I suppose asking for invulnerability is riskier than keeping it simple; it could manifest differently. And you never did get a potent enough wish, did you, Dominic?"

"Make it . . . stop!" Dominic howled, the silvery spiderwebs of his veins turning an unsettling shade of black. His body bucked and spasmed, his face deepening to purple as the rope tightened around his neck.

Kaleena went to the cleat on the wall and unraveled the rope, lowering Dominic to the ground. He collapsed in a sweating, gasping, writhing heap, his eyes rolling back into his head as he unleashed one final, tortured scream. Then he passed out, though Nadia suspected there'd be more pain to come—physical and emotional—when he woke up again.

"This isn't like you," Nadia said quietly, unable to keep the words from escaping her mouth. "You never used to be this cold."

Kaleena dusted off her hands. "If I seem icy, it's only because I have to keep putting out other people's fires."

"You don't have to be cruel." Nadia knew she was treading on dangerous ground, but she couldn't help it. It needed to be said. This was nothing but a demonstration of the Wishmaster's power, and it proved how close she was to becoming Adrian, despite her proclaimed differences from him.

"When you're in my position, then you can tell me what's necessary," Kaleena replied, unmoved, as her attention turned to Miles.

Nadia's heart leaped into her throat. "Don't! He only wanted his wish back!"

"Calm down before you embarrass us both." Kaleena sighed. "Now, Mr. Miles Hunter, you don't need to look at me like that either. I won't steal *your* wishes—as long as you steal another wish to replace the one you took. And do me an added small errand for trying to attack my associates."

Miles stared right back. "I shouldn't have to do anything. Like Nadia said, I was just trying to get *my* wish back. *My* rightful wish that I made by saving a life."

"Ah, but it's what you did afterward that requires due penance," Kaleena said, wagging a finger at him. "One wish, that's all. That's a bargain considering all the trouble you've put me through."

Miles scoffed. "I *had* to do those things to get my wish back—which I'd already paid you for, remember? Plus, I didn't see your people intervening to give me back what I'd earned."

Kaleena dragged the spare chair over and sat down across from him, knee to knee. "I don't want to hurt you, Miles. I only hurt people who want to hurt me, and you're not one of them. But I'm afraid you still have to pay for what you've done. Besides, you have so much more to lose than merely being bulletproof like Dominic. What would it be like for you, I wonder, to go from being 'an all-around guitar god' like your idols, as you so helpfully put it, to being a mere mortal like the rest of us?"

Nadia's jaw dropped; she remembered Miles saying those words in the cell, but she hadn't realized they were the exact wording of his wish. Judging by the horrified expression on his face and the way he sat bolt upright, they were. But how could Kaleena have known with such certainty? He could've used any number of other phrasings, like wishing for fame, or wishing for musical talent, or wishing to win Grammys, or just wishing to be a guitar god without the "idols" part.

"How did you—?" Miles lurched to his feet, but Croak shoved him back down.

Kaleena shrugged. "I have associates with a variety of talents. But thank you for confirming that they were right."

Miles stared dead ahead, and Nadia could almost feel the dread coming off him in waves.

"You don't have a lot of options, Miles." Kaleena's voice softened as she continued, but there was no warmth in it. "You bought another wish from me a few years ago, and now that you've lost your third, you have no more to spend. I don't care how you spent your other wish, but that first one certainly seems *very* important to you. I doubt you'd be able to keep your career without it."

Miles opened his mouth to speak, but he couldn't seem to form any words. Nadia's heart went out to him. His whole life—his whole identity—had to be flashing before his eyes.

Nadia's own wish crept into her head. She didn't want to serve someone like her sister, making new deals and paying off another debt. She'd already spent the last three years of her life toiling for Basha and Grace under the pretense that she owed them something, though she no longer knew if that was anywhere close to the truth. She was tired of being wedged under other people's thumbs. But what could she do? She was fresh out of options too—Kaleena had seen to that.

"One wish? And one errand?" Miles's mouth set in a grim line.

Kaleena nodded.

"And your goons will stay off my incredibly pert ass for the rest of my born days?" It should've comforted Nadia that Miles hadn't lost his sense of humor, but it didn't. She knew a defense mechanism when she saw one.

Kaleena mustered the ghost of a professional, unamused smile. "That's the deal."

"I don't really have a choice, anyway. Fine. Whatever it takes to get clear of you bunch of backstabbers," Miles replied. Nadia wasn't sure if his barb was aimed at her too. She hoped not.

"I need to hear a 'Yes, I'll do it.' I don't like vague responses," Kaleena prompted.

Miles adopted a childish expression, and his reply matched. "Yes, O powerful and mighty Wishmaster, I'll do it."

"Excellent." Kaleena turned her attention back to Nadia, beckoning her with a small flick of the hand. "Now, I need you to check on our unconscious friend over there. Get a good look into his eyes."

Nadia didn't fully understand the point of the request—she wasn't that type of doctor, after all—but she obeyed, slowly approaching the slumped figure on the ground. His chest rose and fell with small, jagged breaths. She crouched at his side and peered down at his half-lidded eyes, only to shake her head in surprise as that strange fishbowl, shutter-lens sensation warped her vision once more.

"Take his hand and say a good, wholesome prayer for him," Kaleena instructed, perching farther forward on the edge of her chair.

A surge of uncertainty shot through Nadia. What was going to happen, exactly? Regardless, she wasn't really in a position to refuse.

Nadia reached for Dominic's hand. The moment her warm skin touched his clammy palm, an electric shock jumped into her fingertips and shot up her arm in a startling spike. Her hand jerked back like she'd put her fingers in a live socket, though Dominic didn't seem to be affected. He lay still, his breaths uneven.

"Did you feel it?" Kaleena asked with an undertone of excitement.

Nadia gulped. "I felt . . . something."

"Val!" Kaleena shouted abruptly, making Nadia jolt for a second time.

Val lumbered into the room, eyes flitting as though expecting to find a fight. "Yes, Wishmaster?"

"Take Dominic to one of the vaults as planned, and make sure all the emergency exits are locked. *Especially* that one at the back," Kaleena commanded.

As Val dragged Dominic out, Nadia and Miles locked eyes. Immediately, the world became a fishbowl again. Nadia's vision narrowed and distorted, filling with kaleidoscope shards of refracted color, as though someone had placed strange lenses over her eyes.

Croak yanked Miles out of the chair and hauled him toward the exit, following Val's lead. As Miles passed her, Nadia reached for his zip-tied hands on impulse. As their skin touched, a fresh bolt of lightning forked up her arm. She couldn't explain the feeling, but she sensed it was connected to the wish Kaleena had forced her to make. Miles glanced at Nadia with haunted eyes one last time before Croak pulled him away.

"I knew you'd keep yourself together," Kaleena said, now that they were alone in the wishing cellar. "You are my sister, after all. Apple of my eye. Or rotten apple, as Basha would say."

Nadia did her best not to shudder. "What does this wish do? I don't understand."

"All in good time." Kaleena took out her phone and watched the black screen intently. "If I try to explain, it'll just confuse you. Think of this as on-the-job training."

Nadia wanted to grab her sister and rattle the answers out of her, but there was no point. Kaleena would call for backup, and Nadia would wind up back in a vault before she could even get out the words "What the hell is wrong with you?" She contemplated the wording of the wish, trying to figure out how it might have changed her.

Kaleena's phone rang.

"What is it, Val?" Kaleena answered on speakerphone, implying that she wanted Nadia to hear the conversation.

"It's Dominic," Val replied flatly. "He escaped out the emergency exit at the back, and he's headed down the street. I sent Tiger and Bones after him, but he's pretty quick for his size."

Nadia expected a volcanic eruption of fury from her sister, but instead, Kaleena chuckled in delight.

"Perfect," Kaleena said. She hung up and turned to Nadia. "Now it's time for your test run."

Nadia frowned. "Test run? What are you talking about?"

"You never used to be this slow." Kaleena tutted. "It should be obvious by now—if not, your wish intuition should kick in shortly. Think of Dominic. Put him in your mind's eye."

Nadia didn't want to, but it was like someone saying not to think of pink elephants and being unable to stop the mind from conjuring up the image. As her thoughts focused on Dominic, her vision warped into that same fishbowl lens, fractured with rainbow shards. The vignette around her field of vision spiraled inward, the whole world twisting in a vortex, and she found herself being sucked right out of her body and into that spinning cyclone.

Chapter Twenty-Two

Heart pumping overtime and adrenaline flowing like electrified motor oil, Nadia felt every burning tendon of a body unused to running so fast. But it wasn't her body. Not unless she'd gained over a hundred pounds, hairy forearms, and totally different anatomy in the span of a few seconds.

What the hell? She knew the words were hers, but they didn't come out of whatever mouth her mind—or her being, or whatever astral echo of a person she'd become—was attached to.

Stop! Go back! Just stop right where you are! Freeze, damn it! She tried a bevy of commands, but nothing worked.

Through eyes that could've used a trip to the optometrist, she saw the familiar lichen-covered benches of Oglethorpe Square as the body her mind was piggybacking on charged along the center path, startling a sweet older couple. Nadia had the urge to turn around and apologize, but her bodily host kept running.

She was an unwilling passenger, along for the ride.

That wasn't quite right. She *was* Dominic, in a way. Every ache and twinge, each breathless gasp pulling in the mossy smell in the air, the smack of shoes on concrete that filled her ears—all of those sensations were shared. But not his mind. If he was still in there with her—and he must've been, considering someone was deciding when to turn and when to look around—she couldn't feel his thoughts.

To make matters even more frustrating, she was so close to home. If she could just commandeer Dominic's mind, she could run to the Kaminski Mansion and . . . She drew a blank. What could her mom and grandmother do for her? Basha would still be pissed, and Grace would still be picking splinters out of her ass cheeks from sitting on the fence. Plus, after what Kaleena had said about the car accident, how could Nadia trust them?

Dominic pounded on down Abercorn Street, past Nadia's favorite Thai place, the tantalizing aroma of lemongrass, garlic, and Thai basil flaring through Dominic's nostrils. He cut straight over Oglethorpe Avenue, the pedestrian crossing light on red. Car hoods came a little too close for comfort, and horns blared their disapproval, but Dominic charged on.

His feet thudded against the sidewalk, the black-painted railings of Colonial Park Cemetery on his left. He ran past weather-stained head-stones and yellowed grass that had scorched beneath the Savannah sun. Dominic glanced over his shoulder, as if he thought one of Kaleena's lackeys might charge across the field of dead people, vault the fence, and knock him flat before dragging him back to the Wishmaster's headquarters.

A valid concern, honestly.

Dominic's incessant head-turning was starting to make Nadia feel dizzy, and their shared neck bristled with imminent whiplash. His eyes fixed forward again, his breath so loud in their mutual ears that it drowned out her every thought.

Passing the corner of the cemetery, Dominic stuck out a hand and hailed a cab. One stopped abruptly at the curb, ignoring the stoplights and the traffic behind. Dominic threw himself into the back.

"Corner of West Forty-Eighth and Bulloch," Dominic wheezed, sinking back into the leatherette seat as though it were the only thing holding him together.

His words were final proof that not only was he in here with her, but he had no idea she was his passenger. She doubted a cab ride address would've been the first thing he said since she'd joined him if he sensed her in his head.

The cab driver gave a subtle nod and pulled away from the curb. Dominic settled into his seat, likely thinking he was safer with every yard he put between him and the Wishmaster. He closed his eyes, leaving Nadia with only the stench of his sweat and the vibration of the cab. Soon enough, he was snoring softly.

Locked inside Dominic's sleeping head, all she could do was think. *You're wanted by the Wishmaster! Hello? Earth to Dominic! This isn't the time to be snoozing!*

His eyes only opened again once the cab pulled up on the corner of West Forty-Eighth and Bulloch, where adobe bungalows with fenced-off gardens lined the street. A nosy neighbor eyed the cab from his bike as he cycled past.

"That'll be sixteen dollars," said the driver, holding out an expectant hand.

Dominic pulled himself from the car in a fluster as he delved into his pocket and took out a crumpled twenty. "Keep the change." He flung it over the driver's seat and stepped onto the sidewalk, gazing up at the full-canopied trees—a small moment that surprised her, especially as he closed his eyes once more and let the warm breeze wash over him. A man enjoying a freedom he never thought he'd have again.

Finally, he seemed to realize that though he had escaped, he was still in trouble. He broke back into an exhausting, lumbering run down West Forty-Eighth before stopping about halfway along the street. He paused to catch his breath, clutching at his searing sides, then he turned down a gap between two houses. At a cabin-like structure at the back, he dragged himself up three rickety steps toward a black door. There, he knocked.

"What day is it today?" a harsh, raspy voice slithered through the heavy-duty door.

"Independence Day," Dominic replied, panting so hard Nadia feared he might have a coronary. If he did, would she be stuck in this body? How did this spy thing work? *Could* she go back to her body, or was this a one-time deal? The idea of being permanently trapped inside

Dominic's body . . . Surely, Kaleena wouldn't have done that to her. Would she?

Bolts scraped back and the door opened, allowing Dominic entry. Inside, the safe house—or whatever this might be—was drenched in shadow. An anemic lightbulb dangled from an unfinished ceiling, casting a dim glow around an equally stark room. Nadia waited for Dominic to look at the person who'd let him inside, but the bastard kept his eyes down, almost as though he knew Nadia was watching. Though, of course, that shouldn't be possible.

"What brings you here?" asked the same person who'd called for the code. Nadia didn't recognize the voice, but it sounded like it belonged to a middle-aged woman with a penchant for smoking, especially judging by the cigarette stench.

Dominic leaned up against the wall. "The wolves are after me." He dabbed his sweaty brow with his sleeve. "Meet me at the terminal in three days. Get everyone. We need to ditch this city and scram into North Carolina before the Wishmaster puts us all in the ground, like she did with Adrian."

"I had a feelin' this day was comin'." The stranger sighed. "You best get your ass out of here before they come searchin'. Three days—we'll meet you. But you can't stay here."

Dominic nodded. "I know. I just came to warn you." His breathing evened out, giving Nadia a reprieve too. "In the meantime, act natural. Don't give anyone any reason to think you're loyal to someone else. The Wishmaster thinks it's just me, Tony, Lemmy, and Mike who's still fighting for Adrian, and I don't want her doing to you what she's done to me."

"What's that?" the voice inquired.

Dominic waved a hand through the gloomy air, the dust tickling his nostrils. "I'll tell you all about it when we scram. Right now, I need to keep running. You'll be safe enough here, so long as you and the others stay low."

"I'll get the word out," the accomplice promised.

Dominic pushed himself away from the wall, dislodging a flurry of sawdust, and headed for the back door. He drew back the sturdy bolt and slipped outside, taking a few strides across a barren wasteland of a backyard, before he lurched into another painful sprint through the unfamiliar neighborhood.

I don't want to go to North Carolina! I don't want to stay stuck in this body! Nadia had no idea how long this little trip into Dominic's mind was supposed to last, and she didn't have a guidebook on how to get back to herself. And as Dominic's heart rate skyrocketed once again, his thighs burning with every juddering impact of his feet against the tarmac of the main road, Nadia's panic exploded. What if there was no way to return to her body? What if she had to stay stuck in this head until he died, or her body died—whichever happened to come first?

Amid that wrenching panic, she became aware of the "thread" of her real self pulsating in her thoughts like a homing beacon. Whether it had been ignited by her terror or not, she didn't know, but she wasn't going to turn down the lifeline. All she could do was focus on it and hope that something would come of finding that center of herself again.

Take me back. She tried to picture herself through an outsider's eyes, the way she'd pictured Dominic.

No sooner had she imagined her brunette braid, the moles that speckled her face, and her green irises with rings of brown, her vision warped back to that disjointed fishbowl lens and didn't stop until she felt reality itself warp with it. Her line of sight narrowed to two pinholes, and then the twin circles of darkness whirled into a black vortex. In that twisting weirdness, she felt some part of herself being sucked out of Dominic's body, and she had to hope she would end up back in her own.

Nadia staggered forward, her hip colliding with a hard edge. It took her a full ten seconds to realize she was completely corporeal again: her limbs, lightly downed forearms, passable cardio threshold, twenty-twenty vision, and familiar anatomy were entirely her own. She could've sworn she had been in the wishing cellar when her "test run" had started, but now she was somehow back in Kaleena's luxurious galleria.

"What . . . what was . . . that?" Nadia tried out her voice, the familiarity washing her in cool relief.

Kaleena was perched majestically on a cream-colored armchair, not far from the long dining table. The chair reminded Nadia of an oyster shell, thanks to its segmented upholstery and scalloped-edged wood trim, though Kaleena was no pearl. In fact, Nadia wouldn't have minded crushing her back into sand and dirt.

"Yeah, I'm waiting for her to come back. She's still—" Kaleena, phone pressed to her ear, stopped talking as she watched Nadia. A second later, she resumed. "She's still on autopilot. Keep me informed."

Nadia stared down at her hands, flexing and curling them as though she'd never seen fingers before. She had no idea how much time had passed, or how she'd come to be back in this room, but she definitely didn't remember walking all that way—or being carried. It puzzled and concerned her in equal measure. If she couldn't recall what her own body had done while her mind had been elsewhere, did that mean her "shell" had just been doing its own thing all this time? How could it even function without her mind present? These were philosophical and neuroscientific questions that she couldn't even contemplate answering, as she was still managing the sensation of having a mouth and fingers that did what she wanted them to do.

Seemingly out of thin air, Val appeared at her side, making her jump in alarm.

"Holy hell!" Nadia shouted. She had zero recollection of Val coming back after escorting Dominic and losing him, but she supposed she should just add it to the growing list of things she couldn't remember.

"Ah, you're back!" Kaleena smiled, still on her call. "Hold on a moment."

Nadia pointed at herself. "You want me to hold on a moment?"

"No, not you," Kaleena said to her and then spoke into the phone. "Yes, I want you to hold on while I find out what she knows." She turned her attention fully on her sister, holding out the mouthpiece of her phone toward Nadia. "Tell us what you saw and heard."

A thought tiptoed into the back of Nadia's skull. Her sister had put her out on a test run, but perhaps this was Nadia's opportunity to do some experimentation of her own. She was supposed to be the "perfect spy," but no matter how detailed the wording, there was always a chance that a wish could be misconstrued through the prism of the Wishing Tree. Maybe that meant the wish had loopholes that Nadia could use to her advantage. It hadn't said anything about being perfectly *honest* with Kaleena, after all.

"I saw Dominic running through Oglethorpe Square and down toward the cemetery. From there, he took a cab and . . . backtracked to the river." The words flowed off Nadia's tongue without a hitch, with only the slightest bump of her own hesitation. "He met someone at a safe house, though I didn't see the person. I only heard them talking. They're planning to run to North Carolina in three days."

Kaleena clapped her hands in triumph and returned her attention to the person on the phone. "You heard that? Good. That means we'll finally be rid of these termites, in three short days. I know exactly the traitor who has a place up in North Carolina. Yes . . . mm-hmm. I'll be there in a few to talk logistics." She hung up and unleashed a satisfied sigh, then got to her feet.

"Sounds like that was what you wanted to hear?" Nadia said coolly.

Kaleena grinned. "Oh, it was. And now, I have to head out so I can do the fun part." She paused. "But you need to go back into Dominic, to keep an eye on him."

Nadia swallowed. "I thought I'd done my part?"

"The spying doesn't stop until I say the job is done, little sister," Kaleena replied, walking toward the exit. "If you're worried about your body, don't. Val can keep an eye on you while you keep an eye on our target. I'd say we could chain you up, but that's a touch medieval for my tastes."

Val smirked. "I'll be right here in case—sorry, *when*—you come back from your trip to Dominic."

"Oh, I'm coming back," Nadia muttered, trying to buy herself some time before she had to enter that disorienting vortex again. It had left her feeling on the verge of vomiting.

"Then chop, chop!" Kaleena ordered, already halfway out the door. "Get your front-row seat before it's gone."

Val's snarling face was only inches away from Nadia's. "You heard the Wishmaster. Get on with it."

Nadia sent a glower at Val to tell her to drop dead, then thought of Dominic again. This time, the unsteadying fishbowl blur was a mere flicker as her mind flew out of her dearly beloved body and hurtled back into Dominic's.

At first, she wasn't sure if she'd landed in the right lump of flesh. She'd left Dominic running on the road, but now they seemed to be inside a building, where an eerie gloom swallowed up the only vision she had to rely on—his. A strong saline smell, with a bottom note of rancid fish and a middle note of something distinctly chemical—chlorine, perhaps—bombarded their shared nostrils. If she could've hurled, she would've. Underneath those overwhelming stenches, however, she could make out the subtle, earthy tang of rotting wood. Maybe they were near the waterfront.

No! I lied for you, and you came here anyway? What the hell is wrong with you? She wanted to grab his brain and shake it, but her hands were back at HQ.

Had hearing the word "terminal" somehow influenced the lie she'd chosen? She immediately wished she'd said a park or a shopping mall, or literally anything else that didn't remotely involve the river. Maybe the "perfect spy" part of the wish made it so that any lie she tried to tell Kaleena was swapped with the truth. That was a terrifying possibility she'd have to keep in mind for the future.

Dominic must've taken a cab as soon as she left. Either that, or there was a bit of time-bending to go along with the mind-bending. Nadia cursed herself inwardly as she watched a flame ignite in front of her. Dominic's lighter. It didn't do much in the way of illuminating the dark space, but it was better than the alternative.

Following the distracted flit of his eyes, she realized he was searching for something. In front of him stood an angular mass draped in a blue tarp. His meaty hands reached for the bungee cords that held the plasticky cover in place and tugged them free with the frustration of a man who knew he was on borrowed time. When he stopped to smear at his forehead with his sweat-soaked sleeve, Nadia couldn't blame him. It was stuffy as all hell in here, and she would've given her wandering body for a cold drink.

What's under there, eh? What would someone like you hide in a warehouse like this? With a touch more light on the situation, she glimpsed the high, corrugated sheet metal ceiling of the building and the hulking dark shapes of other tarped goods. Something about the warehouse felt less than legal, but maybe that was just the vibe Dominic's shifty behavior gave her.

He yanked the tarp away with a grunt and set to work, sifting through a stack of moldering crates that looked ready to crumble. After drawing a hunting knife to use as a pry bar, he levered the lids of the nearest crates and started scrabbling around inside, only to swear like a sailor every time he came up empty.

Guns . . . I bet it's guns. Maybe she missed some part of his code earlier. What if he had no intention of running? What if that actually meant launching an attack against the Wishmaster? Nothing would surprise Nadia after the last couple of days. She wanted to scream into Dominic's mind that attacking the Wishmaster was essentially a death sentence. But he'd made his own bed when he'd hitched his wagon to Adrian. Hell, he'd tried to kill her. It wasn't like she owed him a warning.

And yet, thwarting Kaleena's plans seemed so much more satisfying than seeing Dominic walk into fatal danger.

At a slight scuffing sound, Dominic whipped around, and Nadia was keenly aware of the primordial fear that surged through him. His adrenaline spiked, turning his legs to jelly. As a man who had once been bulletproof, how long had it been since he'd truly felt afraid?

He moved his trembling hand slowly inside one of the crates, where his fingertips closed over something rough and cold and slightly indented—a pistol.

Don't you dare get yourself killed while I'm in here! She shuddered right along with him as his gaze settled on a crack of light that she could've sworn hadn't been there before. It was a door that'd been left ajar.

On feet that weren't made for delicacy, Dominic crept toward the far side of the warehouse, where the dim green light of a fire exit glowed. Nadia experienced every ebb and flow of his nauseated stomach, the constriction in his throat, and the rasp of his breaths. The only time in her life Nadia had ever been more afraid was the day she opened the door to find police officers with their hats held against their chests, as if they were already standing graveside at Nick's funeral.

Dominic had just reached the fire exit when—

The hammer strike of bone yielding to a bullet.

There wasn't time to register anything other than the strange sensation of the bullet tearing through the back of Dominic's skull and the floor rushing to meet his still-open eyes.

Inside the prison of his mind, Nadia screamed. But there was no one to hear her.

Chapter Twenty-Three

Time and space took a fleeting hiatus in the aftermath of Nadia's unheard scream. She tried to focus on her body, but the pain and the shock—and the echoes of Dominic's turbulent emotions still surging inside her—made concentration impossible. In the impenetrable blackness that followed his collapse to the ground, face down in the fishy, salty sludge, she floated in an expanse of nothingness. Not part of him, but not part of herself anymore. A double out-of-body experience.

Is this what death feels like? Is there just . . . nothing, after the spark goes out? With no gateway into Dominic's dying mind, she couldn't sense his experience of this earth-shattering moment. There was only the fear from his last, rattling breath, and the awful stillness of a body that no longer had a purpose to serve.

Is this how it was for you, Nick? Did you think of me when that bullet went through you, or was there no time? Are you out there, or am I just dreaming every time I feel you around?

The darkness took on an unfamiliar weight, as though someone else were there in the shadowlands with her. They were almost within her reach, yet she had no hands to feel for them, whoever they were. Was it Dominic's mind, migrating from this world to the hereafter? Or was it someone else, some other soul who'd slipped through the veil for a moment?

Before she could dwell on it to the point of insanity, she felt a familiar pulse—her own heartbeat. Her eyes flew open to the atmospheric glow of her sister's private domain. This time, Nadia was perched on that clamshell armchair, her T-shirt sticking in all the wrong places, drenched through with sweat. A firm hand rested on each of her shoulders.

"The wanderer finally returns," Val grumbled—the owner of said hands. "Whatever autopilot your body went into kept trying to get up and walk around. It didn't like me trying to stop it, so I had to use a bit of force."

Nadia didn't care. At least she was back. Her body felt cold and clammy, every breath like sucking down a fireball that seared in her lungs. And though she gripped the armrests as tightly as she could, nothing stopped the violent tremble in her fingertips, or the sick, detached sensation in her stomach, like the universe hadn't quite stitched her back into place properly.

Val eyed her warily. "What's wrong with you?"

"I just . . . watched someone . . . die," Nadia said, gasping through her words. "No . . . *I* just died. I felt it. I felt myself hovering in . . . I don't know where."

Val went to the dining table, poured a glass of water, and brought it back to Nadia. When Nadia didn't immediately reach for it, Val said, "Relax, there's nothing funky about it. It's just water."

Nadia took a tentative sip, spilling half of it as her hands shook. "There's nothing, Val. It's . . . black. Endless black."

"Nobody knows what really happens until it's their turn," Val replied, and Nadia appreciated the flicker of humanity in her gentle tone. The tall woman crouched in front of her. "But looks like you get to stay on the carousel ride for a little while longer, at least."

Nadia shook her head. "I felt pretty fucking close to getting tossed off."

"Well, you're handling it better than the other . . . trial runs we've had." Val smiled encouragingly, though Nadia had a feeling she'd wanted to say "guinea pigs" instead. "First time somebody tried it, they couldn't handle being in other people's minds. Now she's enjoying the psychiatric services up at Georgia Regional. Well, maybe 'enjoying' isn't the word. Second time, our guy got addicted to the voyeurism of it and refused to leave the last body he inhabited. He's probably still there, eagerly awaiting a flash of skin in a mirror. We don't know for sure. We got his body down in one of our vaults—just an empty husk that sits in the corner and has to be tube-fed so he doesn't waste away."

Nadia squeezed her eyes shut, debating whether or not to rant about the fact that her own sister was willing to risk the same happening to her. She decided against it. "I'd say I'm much closer to that first one."

Val shook her head. "You've shown a lot of promise, and the Wishmaster is certain it'll keep working because of what you do for a living. Being a counselor and everything, you must know how to exist in other people's heads without it breaking you or consuming you."

Nadia creaked open her eyelids and shot Val a sour look. "I don't get *inside* their actual minds, Val. I ask questions, I listen, I advise. I don't slither around people's brains like a frigging parasite."

"You do now," Val replied. "Welcome to the inner circle, where your wish is the boss's command."

Nadia had never desired to be anywhere near the Wishmaster's tight-knit group of devout puppets. More than ever before, she wished she could go back to the parking lot outside Bonaventure and sincerely talk herself out of doing anything stupid, shunning any temptation that came her way. But there was no wish for time travel—that was another entry on the Wishing Tree's banned list, for the same reason you couldn't wish someone had never been born. No grandfather paradoxes allowed, thanks very much.

Her thoughts flitted bitterly toward Kaleena's wording. Nadia still wasn't sure that the "perfect spy" could lie without consequence. Nothing Kaleena did was left to chance; everything was meticulously thought out, way ahead of time. Did it also mean Nadia couldn't use the power on Kaleena, or did it mean Nadia wouldn't be able to use this ability for personal purposes? The limits would need to be tested —and sooner rather than later.

Figuring now was as good a time as any, she focused in on her sister, certain that they'd at least accidentally touched. Then again, she couldn't remember feeling a skin-to-skin jolt. Nadia's vision distorted for a few moments, but it was like a broken shutter lens that wouldn't open all the way. No matter how hard she strained her eyes and tried to will that wrenching vortex to whiz her away into Kaleena's head, she got nothing but throbbing temples, aching eyeballs, and a disappointing answer to her questions.

Nadia turned her attention on Val, knowing she could be useful as a fly on the wall around Kaleena, but got the same busted-shutter feeling.

"What else did you learn from these poor bastards?" Nadia asked instead, figuring insight would be almost as good as actual experimentation. For now, at least.

"Based on experiments with earlier, um, *subjects*," Val said, "touching people seems to be the way to get a connection up and running. You can't just hop inside anyone's mind unless you've established that physical catalyst first. Once you've touched them, you can get into their head whenever, no matter the distance."

Val kept a distance of her own, making Nadia wonder if *she* had to be the one to touch her target to make that mind bridge. Val had had her hands on Nadia's shoulders when she'd zoomed back from Dominic's corpse, but Nadia hadn't initiated any skin-to-skin contact with Val, so that was another aspect that would require some knob-twiddling.

Miles . . . Realization pierced her jangled brain, like she had a rod sticking out of her head and lightning had just struck. She'd touched his hand in the wishing cellar and experienced that warping shutter-lens effect. He might've been locked up somewhere in this rabbit hole of a building, but based on what Val had said, that distance would mean nothing to her, since that epidermal direct line had hooked up the cell towers of their minds, so to speak.

She cast an anxious glance at Val, but really, what could the woman do if Nadia left her body on a whim? After all, Nadia worked for the Wishmaster now too, whether she wanted to or not.

Nadia went ahead and thought of her coconspirator.

The marble and velvet furnishings swelled in her periphery, while

Val, who'd gotten to her feet in front of Nadia, seemed to teleport into the distance, as if Nadia were simultaneously looking through the small and wide sides of a pair of binoculars. The vignettes darkened the edges of her vision, then whorled inward, turning her world into two tiny dots of light. She spun with the darkness and sucked in one last breath as her mind disengaged from her body, letting the now familiar, but no less terrifying, vortex suck her out of herself and fire her through time and space to a different mind altogether.

Her vision cleared like the sea calming in the eye of a storm, and her disembodied mouth unleashed a startled gasp that only she could hear. Kaleena stood front and center in her private room, her expression cold and humorless.

". . . need her to come with me," Nadia heard Miles say. "I mean, there's gotta be some kind of wishing rights, where I get to see what my wish was used for. Partial custody, visitation, that kind of thing."

Nadia's disconnected heart sank as she paused to feel out Miles's emotions. She might not have been able to crack into his thoughts, but a strong current of disappointment made his chest—and, by proxy, hers—feel heavy. His shoulders were slumped too. This was a man who knew his third and final wish had already been spent. All hope gone. No takebacks. No do-overs. No wishing for the love of his life, no matter how impossible that wish might have been. His sorrow was palpable, even if he managed to keep it out of his voice.

"Grace likes you. She trusts you. That makes you—and you alone— the best candidate for the job," Kaleena replied. "Or perhaps you need more motivation?"

A torrent of unease made Miles and Nadia's shared stomach squirm. "Hey, I'm all for getting out of this debt you've lumped on me, though I'll never agree I deserve it." He spoke with a confidence that belied the discomfort inside. "But I'm guessing you forgot I got kicked out of Grace's digs on my literal ass. Without Nadia there, Grace won't trust me for whatever you've got in mind."

"Would you prefer to be on a task that requires less talking and more dodging bullets?" Kaleena retorted.

Miles put up his tied hands. "I ain't trying to get out of what you're putting on the table." He paused, his Adam's apple bobbing. "Hell, I'll even tell you what I used my second wish for, if it proves that I'm not digging in my heels here. I was stupid with it. I wished for a bunch of Grammys. Worth it? Nah, but the after-party was killer. Could've used some of that Chatham Artillery Punch, though, if you know what I mean." He laughed tightly, and Nadia guessed he hoped to protect his finding wish with a lie Kaleena might believe.

And the fact that Miles had remembered her sad ramblings about Nick made her astral being swell with gratitude. With no one in her family on her side, he'd shown that *he* was, even though his wish was gone.

Kaleena's eyes narrowed, and Nadia shivered alongside Miles. "I feel like you're being a little too eager here. Nobody likes a suck-up. Not even me."

Miles squared his shoulders. "You're all about exchanges. I gave you the goods about my second wish in exchange for you putting Nadia on this 'errand' with me. It won't work without her, and I don't feel like getting hauled back into this room later just to say I told you so and then having you try ripping out my first wish for being right."

What's he doing? Why is he trying so hard to get me in on this? She sensed a nervous energy in him.

"Fine. You've made a good case, and Grace *is* sharper than she seems." Kaleena gave a casual shrug. "Nadia will work with you this time. Just get me what I want. And you still owe me a wish to complete our bargain, once I decide where you'll be most useful."

A wave of relief rolled through Miles like one of the jazz crescendos he'd talked so much about, only Nadia didn't know what would happen when this drumroll ended. If Kaleena had plans that involved Grace, then that spelled nothing but chaos, and it would entail slicing the ropes of family ties that were already in pieces.

"Get up. Since you've pulled Nadia into this, we'll need to discuss the plan of action with her. Won't that be so much fun?" Kaleena shot Miles a withering glare before striding up to the door of the prison vault and going through the triple-threat security measures.

What's wrong, sis? You think I might be the slightest *bit uncooperative because you sent me out into Dominic's mind, fully knowing that he was going to get a bullet to the back of the skull with me inside his head?* If Nadia hadn't just heard Miles put so much on the line to get her out of the Wish-master's headquarters, she might've slipped back into her body and picked up the closest thing to a baseball bat she could find. But if he could grin and bear it after losing his wish, she supposed she would have to as well.

Concentrating on the thread of her own body, she retreated from Miles's mind in that eerie black, tugging slipstream, and she slid back into her familiar form. Her vision opened on the marble floor to find her feet in the process of pacing. Abruptly, she stopped and whirled around to see Val a few steps behind her.

"I gave up trying to stop you," Val said flatly. "You've been trying to psychoanalyze me for the past ten minutes. *That*, I couldn't stop. Where did you go?"

Nadia arched an eyebrow. "I didn't go anywhere. That was me, not the autopilot."

"Uh-huh," Val said.

Nadia didn't care if Val believed her or not. As far as she was concerned, this was a huge win. Nadia had been able to see through Miles—a person she'd touched and mentally zapped into—despite it not being for Kaleena's benefit. Perhaps the Wishing Tree had inten-tionally screwed Kaleena over, and none of her previous "spies" had attempted such a loophole, given how quickly they'd traveled on a downward spiral.

Before she could even think about running a victory lap around the long dining table, if only to confuse Val further, the gigantic double doors whispered open across the marble. Kaleena strode in with Miles and Croak flanking her, though the former still had his hands zip-tied.

"Sit down," Kaleena instructed, with no preamble. "I have another task for you."

Nadia feigned ignorance. "So soon? But I just got back."

"If I were running off your snail-paced clock, I'd be waiting years for your debt to be fulfilled."

Kaleena sat down at the head of the table, where Nadia joined her a moment later, trying not to scowl. Miles took a seat opposite Nadia, the two of them exchanging reassuring looks. Kaleena flexed her hands until her knuckles cracked, as though reminding her little sister of what those hands could do if she failed.

"This will be your first of the three jobs I mentioned," Kaleena explained coolly, tipping her head toward Miles. "You can thank *him* for that."

Nadia smirked. "Thanks."

"No problem," Miles replied, with half a smile.

Kaleena ignored the aside. "Your task is to retrieve something that was stolen from me years ago—by everyone's favorite charlatan, Basha."

That was the catch Nadia had been waiting for. Not only would it be difficult to steal anything from Basha, given that the walls basically had ears, but it also felt like a true betrayal. Even though Nadia had been unceremoniously booted out of the house, that didn't mean she wanted to cause more trouble or actively deceive her grandmother and mother, especially not under the Wishmaster's orders.

Kaleena had no love for their mom, but she didn't outright loathe Grace the way she did Basha. And though Nadia didn't yet know what it was she was being sent to find, this felt like a textbook case of child-hood trauma rearing its head in adulthood. She had seen enough clients to know that getting that final word rarely brought about inner peace. Only time, therapy, and years of conscious healing could do that, but Kaleena appeared more than happy to keep her old wounds fresh.

And now, as Wishmaster, she was planning her revenge.

Chapter Twenty-Four

"There it is," Kaleena said. They sat in her Tesla a few houses down from the Kaminski Mansion, which was backlit by a molten, early-evening sun. Golden hour. The Wishmaster and Val sat up front, with Miles and Nadia in the back.

Kaleena peered through the windshield at their family home, giving nothing away in her body language. "Funny how it never changes. Same old, same old."

Nadia leaned through the gap between the two front seats, muscling past Val's bulky shoulder and looking at her sister. "How does it feel, being here again?"

"Like going to the dentist," Kaleena replied, settling back into the seat. "It's an occasional necessity, but I'm not thrilled about it. Truth be told, I'd rather have a root canal."

Nadia imagined that the final argument that had led to Kaleena severing ties with their mother and grandmother had happened within those walls. It seemed that, for the Wishmaster, the house was the tangled, withered branch in an otherwise flourishing tree of success.

"But you've been thinking about all this for a while, haven't you?" Nadia asked.

A few hours had passed since their planning session in Kaleena's war room, and while Nadia's memory of the headquarters had faded to vague flashes of expensive finery, gloomy corridors, and towering pillars, the task ahead remained clear as crystal. The sheer depth the Wishmaster had gone into, covering every possible outcome, suggested that this wasn't some off-the-cuff idea that had suddenly come to her. Kaleena had been refining her plans until the perfect pawn came along—someone who would be invited into the house, rather than a brute-force infiltrator.

Kaleena turned around and gave her a hard stare. "Don't try to be clever, Nadia."

Nadia's eyes widened in feigned ignorance. "I'm not. I'm curious, that's all. Like, how many people have tried this before? How many times have you had one of your people here without any of us knowing? What's the harm in telling me—it's not like I can go back in time and forewarn anyone. If I could do that, I'd go back to Bonaventure and save *myself*."

Kaleena shrugged. "A couple of mommy dearest's boy toys were mine, but she'd always offer them drinks infused with wishing bark. If they didn't drink, she sent them packing." She snorted. "That one acts like an airhead, but she's a fox in more ways than one."

"That one"? You mean our mom. Even after being on the receiving end of her own family scrap, Nadia still couldn't understand how someone could just detach from everything they'd ever known.

"I'm not saying anything against her charms, but I always wondered where she found so many young guys. Makes sense that some of them were working for you," Nadia conceded, reading a flicker of bitterness on Kaleena's face.

"She's an attention whore who cares only about herself," Kaleena spat. "She made it easy to get spies in there, and I pity the poor bastards who drank what she was serving up. But she's as tight-lipped as Basha, even after her daily pitcher of margaritas."

Val stifled a snort and turned her amused gaze out the window, her wide shoulders shaking with silent laughter. Nadia scowled. Sure, her family wasn't perfect, but whose was? Miles wisely stayed quiet.

"Look, I'm not trying to burst your bubble," Nadia said, "but I still don't think it's going to work. They're not going to invite me in. Even if Mom wanted to, Babcia won't allow it. She wants nothing to do with me."

Kaleena's eyes narrowed. "Is that really what you're worried about, or are you trying to backpedal because you don't want to act out against Basha? Let's not forget, her lies about *her* debt are why you're here. You don't owe her anything, but you *do* owe me."

The car accident—that massive blip in Nadia's memory. She remembered driving in the dark and pouring rain, trying to blink in time with the windshield wipers so she could see the road ahead of her. Then, there were glaring lights, so bright she couldn't look at them directly. And then . . . nothing. Absolutely nothing, until she woke up in the hospital. She lacked even the finest thread in the fabric of that memory, although she had a scar to prove that a surgery had happened to replace her liver. Nick had been at her bedside at the hospital too, of course, but he'd only ever recited the story that Grace and Basha had told him—he hadn't known what had happened behind closed doors.

"Maybe if you told me how she lied, it might inspire me." Nadia waited, hoping her sister wouldn't be able to resist slandering Basha. But Kaleena just turned her gaze out the window.

"Our grandmother is a selfish old crone who deserves every ounce of misfortune that comes her way, and she's been slithering free of responsibility for so long. It's finally time for her to pay for all the misery she's caused," Kaleena said, with unsettling calm.

Miles leaned between the seats. "Have you ever tried therapy?"

"Get moving," Kaleena retorted, taking the child lock off the back doors. "Any inane questions you have about our, frankly, hysterical family history, I'm sure Nadia will answer them on the way to the house. Although, since you've met Grace and Basha, you've probably gotten the gist. And maybe Basha will answer some of your questions while you're in there, Nadia. But don't let your curiosity get in the way of the mission. I won't accept failure."

What if I don't like what I hear? Nadia wasn't Basha's biggest fan right now, but in the tug-of-war between her sister and grandmother, she still wasn't sure where she stood. While part of her had a fragile hope that this "secret" might be a lie, Kaleena would never set something up without knowing there'd be a payoff.

"You'll get what you asked for," Nadia said as she got out of the car.

Stealing back something that had belonged to Kaleena seemed like a fair price to pay to stay breathing and get closer to bringing Nick back, and it wasn't like Kaleena had asked her to hurt anyone to get it. The house, and Basha's protective wish, would ensure that things didn't turn violent. It would be a quick in-and-out stealth job. No harm, no foul.

Still, the "getting in" part bothered her. What if the house, and Basha, stuck up a dismissive middle finger, rendering the mission a dud before they'd even begun?

Out on the sidewalk, Nadia dug her hands into her pockets and set off at a casual pace, resisting the urge to glance back over her shoulder at Kaleena. She knew it was pointless, but part of her wanted to see some glimpse of fear, or nostalgia, or sadness, or . . . *something* on her sister's face other than anger and resentment. Instead, she focused on the path ahead, with Miles drawing parallel at her side, his arms tucked into his sweatshirt pouch like it was a muff.

"Are you pissed at me for using your wish?" Nadia muttered, listening to every beat of her footsteps.

Miles laughed. "There's so much to be pissed off about, man, that everything has sort of canceled everything else out. Right now, I'm feeling pretty zen."

"I'm sorry I dragged you into this by stealing your wish in the first place. Really sorry, actually," she murmured.

He nudged her in the arm. "Hey, you've got a messed-up family— that was bound to give your social graces a hit."

Nadia chuckled wryly as she watched the sidewalk pass underfoot, counting down the flagstones until she reached the gates of the Kaminski Mansion.

"Man, there's so much more I want to know about this whole wishing world," Miles said, then puffed out a breath. "Later, we're sitting down with some port, and you're going to give me the whole thing—studio outtakes, B sides, and all. Fair?"

She nodded. "If there is a later."

"You think we're going to get booted out on our asses again?" He cast her an anxious look.

"Honestly, I don't know. My babcia could win medals in stubbornness." Nadia cricked her neck, trying to relieve some of the gathering tension.

Miles chuckled, but it faded as quickly as it had emerged. "Will you tell me what my wish got spent on? Your sister threw some bones during her planning lecture, but no one stopped to explain what she meant by you being able to spy on people."

"I'll give you the details later," Nadia promised. "For now, just know that it involves my body and my mind . . . separating. Kind of like astral projection into somebody else's body. I'll probably need to use it in there, so be ready for some weirdness when it comes. Apparently, I start wandering around and acting like a robotic version of myself."

Miles raised an eyebrow. "That does sound freaky. But I'll try to make sure your body doesn't get stuck in any corners or something."

Reaching the black wrought-iron gates, Nadia paused with her hand on the metal. The syrupy air smelled of incoming rain. Swollen gray clouds stampeded across the early-evening sky, mimicking the onset of night as it darkened the world around them to an unnerving sepia. Her exhaustion finally caught up to her, weighing down her steps. The morning's icy plunge into the Savannah River felt like it had happened a month ago.

Nadia pushed open the gate, and they walked along the garden path, trampling the perennial weeds that slunk up through the stones to taste the sunlight. Drawing in a deep breath, she climbed the porch steps and passed the rickety love seat that swung in the warm breeze as though a phantom couple nestled together, waiting for the rain to fall.

She knocked on the door, not daring to try her key. Like a vampire, she needed an invitation. It was the only way to reset the house's rejection protocols, and that permission had to come from one of the Kaminski family members already inside.

A few moments later, footfalls approached. Nadia's muscles seized up as she feared it'd be Basha. After everything her sister had said about the car accident, and the potential lies she'd been drip-fed, she wasn't sure if she was ready to see the old woman just yet.

The door creaked open, and the orange porch light shone on Grace's tired, makeup-free face, revealing every wrinkle, every mole, every fine crease in her pursed lips. It took Nadia a second to realize it was actually her, since her mom never left her bedroom without her war paint on.

Grace's expression morphed into one of shock, then her features crumpled into a mask of relief. "My girl . . . You came back. Thank the Wishing Tree, you came back. Get in here, sweetheart! Get your blessed backside in here!"

Grace opened the door wider and yanked Nadia into the house. Miles lunged for Nadia's hand, clearly worried he might be left outside if he didn't stay connected. As their skin touched, Nadia waited for the fizz of her spying ability to jump between them, but it didn't come.

So, it's a one-time reaction. One touch and the connection is made. Nadia couldn't dwell on it for long as Grace threw her arms around her and held her tight, stroking her hair and swaying her from side to side as though they'd been apart for months. Nadia let go of Miles's hand and put her arms around her mom, unable to resist the temptation of a motherly hug.

"I thought that was it," Grace murmured, pulling away. "I thought both my sweet girls were gone forever."

Nadia tried not to snort at the idea of Kaleena being a "sweet girl," but her mother's genuine concern filled her with a welcome warmth. "I wouldn't let things end like that between us, Mom. Really."

"I've been going out of my mind," Grace continued, solely focused on Nadia, as if she hadn't even realized Miles was there. "About fifty times, I've put on my jacket and gotten my keys, ready to head out and find you. But your babcia insisted on us staying put for safety. You know how she is."

As though that was some blanket excuse? It was one vital point that Nadia told her clients time and time again—that the only way to move forward and make reparations was to accept responsibility for past dick moves. Making excuses stunted any future growth, yet Nadia had taken it as gospel for years that her grandma could be forgiven for just about anything because "you know how she is."

Well, not today.

Nadia took her mom's hands and gave them a squeeze, immediately feeling the electric spark of a mental connection jumping between them. The fishbowl lens distorted the grand entrance hall and made Grace's eyes bulge like a treefrog before Nadia blinked away the weirdness. As long as she didn't think of Grace, she wouldn't wind up inside her head. At least, she hoped those were the parameters, though she still hadn't had much time to experiment.

"Where is she?" Nadia asked flatly.

Grace dropped her gaze. "Upstairs, sleeping. I think the past couple of days have tuckered her out."

Nadia bit back a scathing retort.

With an alarmed gasp, Grace hurried to cover her face. "I wish I'd known you were bringing company, Nadia. I'm out here naked-faced, looking like worn-out leather, with lips as pale as my bare behind."

Miles laughed awkwardly. "You don't look any different to me."

"Well, I'll take that as a compliment." Grace kept hold of Nadia's hand, behaving a bit more soberly than usual. "Now, why don't we stop loitering around the door like we aren't staying, hmm?" Grace glanced nervously up at the curving stairwell. "Let's shimmy on through to the kitchen—get you both feeling right back at home with some snacks and a drink."

Grace grabbed Miles's hand and tugged the pair of them away from the entrance hall, through the left-hand doorway that led into the kitchen-slash-den. All the while, Grace kept glancing at the staircase, as though expecting Basha to appear at any moment. Nadia shared her fear. No amount of rehearsal or preparation could ready her for facing her grandma and the questions that called for some serious answers.

"Settle yourselves down! You're not in court. Don't stand on ceremony," Grace insisted.

She ushered them around the partition wall toward the comfy, well-loved sofas in the den—the same sofas that rested right in front of the blackboard bearing the chalk scratches of the Kaminski debt. Nadia was almost overcome by the sudden urge to erase every tally, as if that would let her regain the years she'd spent paying back a debt that wasn't hers.

Eyeing one another, Nadia and Miles did as they were told, sinking down onto the largest sofa with perfect, stiff synchronicity. They tipped closer together, thanks to the aging dip in the middle of the squishy cushions, sitting there like clueless teenagers who were in each other's rooms for the first time.

Meanwhile, Grace barreled around the kitchen, tore packets out of the cupboards, and wrenched them open, cascading them into waiting bowls. Nadia spied potato chips, pretzel bites, and salted nuts—she could only imagine the incoming jokes. Though she had no intention of eating, her stomach growled. When *was* the last time she'd eaten anything? Her mom hurriedly set out two glasses, pouring white wine into both. Then she yanked open the refrigerator door and plucked out a ready-made margarita.

Nadia gave Miles a discreet elbow in the ribs, as if to say, *You know not to drink that, right?*

He nodded in reply, but that didn't mean they were out of the woods. Now that Nadia had a spent wish, she couldn't trust anyone, not even her own mom, when it came to taking drinks she hadn't prepared herself. She couldn't have the wishing bark infusion dampening her spying abilities, especially right now.

Grace carried everything over like a waitress and laid the food and drinks out on the low, scuffed table in front of the sofa. She scooted in right next to Miles.

"I remember you liked your wine dry, Miles," she said, handing the glass to him. "Nadia will drink anything. She's like her mom that way. Though we both love our margaritas, don't we?"

Nadia eyed her mom warily. Where were the lewd jokes and the flirtations? "Are you feeling all right?"

"It's been a tough few days for us all. I can tell that *you* haven't been getting much sleep." Grace gulped down a mouthful of margarita while Nadia waited for the obvious quip that didn't come. Instead, her mom seemed pensive. "Did you have a friend to stay with? I haven't slept a wink either, and not because I hit the jackpot."

Nadia picked up her wine glass and pretended to take a sip. "I spent the night with Miles." Her stomach lurched as she realized what she'd said. "I mean, I crashed at his place. He let me stay over, in my own bedroom. He's got, like, a million rooms."

"Made sure to give you the one with the best view too," Miles added.

Grace looked between the two of them and then turned to Nadia. "And here I was, thinking you were flicking through channels and guzzling down dinner from a vending machine, when you were being spoiled rotten by a rock star." She jiggled excitedly. "Tell me more. How was it?"

Miles grinned. "We got a little tipsy. I showed her my art collection."

"I bet you did, you sly devil!" Grace cackled, while Nadia simmered with utter embarrassment. Miles seemed to be taking a tiny slice of revenge for having his wish stolen.

"I have an enormous art collection," Miles purred, thoroughly enjoying himself. "It might be the biggest in Savannah, and I ain't being modest."

Grace gave him a playful smack in the arm and glanced at Nadia. "Is that why you look so tired, honey? Were you up all night, staring at his 'art collection' and having a good time?" A forced, too-bright smile curved up her lips, as though she wanted to believe her daughter had been all right, instead of the alternative.

"I drank because I got kicked out of the house, and I *crashed* at his place because I had nowhere to go and no friends to call," Nadia muttered. How could her mom be so blasé, acting like everything was peachy? Did Grace somehow suspect that Nadia had ulterior motives for being here? She tried to study her mom's expression for any hint of suspicion, but Grace's reactions seemed genuine.

"Well, that's awful nice of you, Miles. I could tell you were a good soul the moment you came through the door. Thank you for taking care of my girl." Grace's cheer evaporated, her cheeks reddening. "So, does that mean the Wishmaster didn't come for you, then? I've been fretting like a wild thing, thinking the Wishmaster might have taken everything out on you. But you're here, and you seem to be in one piece, and . . ." She trailed off with a stifled hiccup.

A painful silence followed as Grace turned her face away and pretended to look at a snagged thread on a nearby cushion, but Nadia knew she was trying not to cry. Her mom could put on a brave face better than anyone, yet it had to have stung, knowing she could've stood up to Basha and sided with Nadia, but she'd been too afraid of getting her own ass kicked out. Maybe she didn't suspect anything was amiss with Nadia after all, and was only trying to make amends with her forced cheerfulness.

A slow *tap-tap* splintered through the uncomfortable quiet, followed by the disconcerting shuffle of slippered feet. Nadia turned toward the kitchen door, which was just visible past the partition wall. The entire house seemed to tense, the air so thick it threatened to choke her.

Basha had arrived.

Chapter Twenty-Five

Nadia tried to slow her angry breaths as Basha stopped beneath the arch that separated the kitchen and den. Her grandmother wore the same haughty expression she always did, never acknowledging the hurt she'd caused—the lies about the debt, the constant piling on of guilt, the way she'd kicked Nadia out of the house without remorse. What could Nadia possibly say to the person who had torn her family apart? Well, she had to take the high road now and pretend everything was just fine. At least until this mission was over.

Basha's keen eyes homed in on Grace, narrowing with displeasure. "Why you let this traitor into house?" she hissed, spit flying with every word.

Nadia forced herself to remain stone-faced and silent. Miles shifted in his seat beside her, probably not all that excited to have a front-row seat to another potential family screaming match.

"We can't just leave her out there, Mama," Grace said quietly. "It's not safe. The Wishmaster—"

"I kick ungrateful beast out again," Basha shouted. "You do this once more, I kick you out too!"

Grace seemed to shrink into herself again, and Nadia saw red.

After all the groveling Grace had done to "keep the peace," how dare Basha treat her like that? Screw staying calm.

"You want to die alone, is that it, Babcia?" Nadia said in a low voice. "Just go ahead and push away everyone who's ever given a shit about you, then."

Basha wouldn't even look at her. "I am only one who does what is best for rodzina."

Nadia jumped up, shaking with adrenaline, as if everything she'd ever wanted to say but dammed up for years was finally ready to rush forth. She'd regret her own outburst if they got kicked out again before she could get what Kaleena had asked for. But the past three days had been a microcosm of the last three years: a constant cycle of Basha's sneering disappointment, Grace's cowardly silence, and Nadia always, *always* pushing her own life aside to do what they wanted.

"You do what's best for *us*, do you? Then why did you lie about my car accident? Why did you lie about the Wishmaster not wanting to grant me a wish?" She tried to speak with a controlled calm. "Maybe I'm wrong, but the thing is, I don't think I am. You're all about control, Babcia. And I think you've been controlling me, all this time, since that accident."

Basha stared at Nadia, her hand quaking on the glass ruby at the top of her cane. And in that silent fury, Nadia heard everything she needed to know.

They *had* lied. Kaleena had told the truth.

"Who told you such story?" Basha spat at last.

"I ran into Croak." Nadia let her anger fuel a plausible lie. "He saw me get kicked out and thought he'd twist the knife a little harder by telling me what he'd heard from the Wishmaster. So thanks for letting me learn about it in the worst possible way."

"Nadia—" Grace began.

"You made me think that I owed you something, when none of this debt is mine." Nadia pointed a defiant finger at the blackboard and its chalk tally. "I know you lied to me about the debt—both of you. You said you got into this mess because *I* needed a liver, but that's not true, is it?" Her voice cracked, but she didn't care. She wanted her grandmother to see her pain. She wanted Basha to take accountability for the torrent of confusion, heartbreak, and betrayal that collided within her.

"I never wanted to lie to you!" Grace cried, leaping to her feet and reaching for Nadia.

Miles stood and put himself between mother and daughter. A simple gesture, but one that meant a whole lot to Nadia. She didn't know if she could handle her mom touching her and trying to calm her down when she wanted to stay mad.

Nadia swallowed thickly. "Then why do it?"

"Because the debt was too much. We needed your help, and we'd never have hope of paying it off if it was just your babcia and me," Grace replied, the words rattling off her tongue in desperation. "We didn't want to tell you about the debt at first, but then after your car accident, your babcia told me it'd be better to keep you in Savannah anyway. You had all these . . . ideas of going to live in far-off cities, and she said . . . she said you wouldn't be safe there. She said you'd only be safe here, and that we had to make sure you didn't leave. Can you blame me for wanting to keep my daughter home instead of a thousand miles away?" She visibly floundered, looking to Miles as though he could—or would—help her out of this hole.

"You put the weight of our family's survival on my shoulders, when I hadn't done anything to deserve it," Nadia seethed, balling her hands into fists. "You laid on the guilt to stop me from wishing for myself, and not *once* did you show a sliver of remorse. You were happy to make me run around, stealing wishes for this damn chalkboard, when that debt wasn't even mine! Wasn't the accident enough of a trauma, without you making me feel guilty for getting injured?"

Grace tried to get past Miles, but he moved and blocked her. "The accident was part of *why* we had to keep you in Savannah. If you'd gone off the road in Maine or something, we wouldn't have been there to support you afterward. And that would've been hard on Nick too, caring for you all by himself. It wasn't just about the debt. We wanted to protect you. Don't you see?"

"No, I just see two really shitty people who've put someone they're supposed to love through hell for their own benefit." An angry tear rolled down Nadia's cheek, and Miles gave her a look that told her he was fine with leaving whenever she wanted. In the back of her mind, Nadia knew they had to stay until the mission was finished, but she needed real answers more than she feared Kaleena's wrath.

Grace gave a strangled cry. "Nadia, honey, it's not like that."

"Then explain it to me," she shot back.

Grace buckled. "I didn't want to do it," she whispered. "Like I said, when you had your accident, we . . . we were already in debt to your sister. We hid it from you because we didn't want you to worry."

"Say no more!" Basha barked, but Grace continued regardless, swept up on a wave of obvious guilt that needed relieving.

"Your liver is an ordinary transplant. You got lucky with a donor on such short notice, but not through wishing," Grace choked out, sobbing into her hands. "Mama came up with the idea of using it to keep you in Savannah, to help us with the debt. I wanted to ask you for help, hoping you'd volunteer, but Mama said guilting you would keep you from leaving and saddling the two of us with all that debt to recover on our own."

"Quiet, dziecko! You go too far," Basha spat at Grace.

Nadia bit the inside of her cheek to stop herself from unraveling. "And what did you do to Kaleena, huh, to make her lay a debt like that on you both? Did she find out a lie like this too?"

Basha slammed her cane into the floor. "She is no innocent! She did her duty for rodzina and did not like outcome, so turned on rodzina." Her mouth twisted in a grimace. "I no force her to do anything she wasn't prepared to do. We were all in danger. We had no choice."

"What duty? What are you talking about?" Nadia asked, confused.

Both Basha and Grace hesitated.

"Did this have something to do with Adrian?" she pressed, her voice tight. "*Did* Kaleena kill him?"

Dominic had certainly seemed to think so, and while Nadia had once believed that Kaleena wouldn't take such drastic measures, the day's events had been more than enough to convince her otherwise.

Basha lifted her chin. "Adrian did not like us speaking out against his wickedness. He want us gone. He fear I try to dethrone him." She sniffed. "Is what I wanted. I no lie. So, I make wretched dziecko take care of problem. I ask her to use potent wish she wanted to keep for herself. We were running out of time, and she got rid of him. I no expect her to demand debt in return—selfish beast. I no expect her to be Wishmaster either. Was supposed to be me, or someone with experience. She take the title for herself, and still does no forgive me. Where would she be if no for me, hmm? All this mess—is her doing."

Grace leaned on Miles like she couldn't hold herself up. "It had to be done to save our family, honey. You have to understand the kind of threat we were under during that time. Adrian wanted to eliminate us, not just control us. We *had* to act, or you and your sister would've been his next targets, once he stole our used wishes and the wishing box from us." She paused. "I would have done it, but I had no wishes left. My third was stolen by your deadbeat father."

"So . . . you never had a third wishing slot you could've used to save me in the first place?" Nadia trembled all over with a rage more overwhelming than anything she'd felt before. But there was pity too. Pity for her sister, and the things that'd driven Kaleena to become the cold woman she was now.

"Oh, it's all so crystal clear. She had an unused wish ready, didn't she?" Nadia continued, everything coming together in her mind. "The one she'd been saving since she nearly got strangled by that drunk guy. The one she used to obsess over, dreaming about how she'd spend it, and how she'd word it when she did. She held on to that wish for years, and *you* made her spend it to find a way to kill Adrian. I'm right, aren't I?"

It was no wonder Kaleena hated Basha. Hell, Nadia was having a hard time finding a single redeeming quality. That wish had meant everything to Kaleena, considering how she'd fought so hard to get it. Most seventeen-year-olds would've spent it there and then, but not Kaleena. She'd been as meticulous then as she was now, and she'd vowed to Nadia that she wouldn't waste it on something trivial.

"I'm going to save this until I know, without a doubt, what I want to do with it," Kaleena had told Nadia after taking the wish into herself. "And I'm going to word it so perfectly that the Wishing Tree won't be able to mess with what I want."

In fact, Basha had only let her keep it, without raining down a hailstorm of consequences, because Kaleena had promised not to use it until the right time came. Evidently, to Basha, that had been mistranslated as "when the right time came for the family to force her into using it for their own ends."

Grace nodded feebly. "And Adrian had a thing for her, so we knew he'd allow her past his defenses."

Nadia gasped in disbelief. "Are you kidding me? What the hell is wrong with the two of you? You used her as some kind of honey trap!"

Basha sniffed and observed the facets of her cane-topper. "I did what rodzina needed for protection in long run."

"I didn't want to do it!" Grace repeated, clutching on to Miles's shoulder. "Your babcia made me. *She* was the one who coerced your sister into making the wish, and then sent her into the lion's den. I would never!"

Basha shuffled forward a couple of steps, shaking her cane at Grace. "Ungrateful liar! You knew stakes—he die or we die. You wanted him gone. You convinced that wretched girl! You no blame me, when you did as much as I did!"

"I would never put my girls in harm's way," Grace shot back, blubbering. "You told *me* lies to get me to help you. And then you pressured me while I was out of my mind with worry, when Nadia almost died. I didn't know what I was agreeing to!"

Nadia wanted a concrete answer to what Kaleena had actually done, but they were hurling insults in such vague terms that it was impossible to decipher. And though she had a million questions, she didn't have time to ask them now.

Miles caught her eye and nodded toward the clock on the den wall, clearly sharing her thoughts. Kaleena had given them until the hour to grab the item and hand it off to her, and they were fast running out of minutes.

"Quiet!" Nadia roared.

Basha and Grace fell silent, both blinking in shock at the unexpected outburst.

"It's obvious we've got some healing to do." Nadia chose that moment to approach Basha and touched the top of her hand that held so tightly to the ruby head of the cane. Basha didn't pull away, and the fizzing spark leaped between them, unnoticed by the older woman.

"And I didn't come here to start a slinging match. I came here for the rodzina—to warn you."

Basha's eyes crinkled. "What kind of warning?"

"The Wishmaster said she'd give me another chance," Nadia replied, aiming for calm, "but she let something slip that I thought you, specifically, would want to know."

Basha tilted her head. "What she say?"

"The Wishmaster has already been here and taken 'what she wanted.' I don't know what that is, but I'm guessing you do." Nadia drew her hand away from her grandmother.

Miles hurried up to join the charade. "You should've seen her face! I haven't seen someone that smug since the Grammys."

Basha didn't appear to be listening to him, though. The old woman had paled, glancing distractedly at the kitchen door.

"I'm sure the Wishmaster was only bluffing," Grace said. "There's no way she could've gotten inside without an invitation, and the house would've hit back if there was a break-in." She paused, her expression anxious. "But maybe we should take stock of our valuables so we can all rest easy."

Nadia focused on her grandmother. "Mom's right. You should." She sighed, making it just dramatic enough. "I'm going to head out and leave you to it. I only stopped by to give you that warning and make sure you were both all right. See, Babcia, I still care about the family, no matter what's been done to me."

And my sister.

Nadia bit her tongue on the last part, in case she gave away the anger and hurt that still simmered inside. A betrayal of such magnitude, regardless of Basha's platitudes about "good intentions," wouldn't be forgiven quickly. Nadia wasn't even sure it could *ever* be forgiven.

Grace pushed Miles out of the way, letting Nadia know she meant business. "Why don't you stay awhile?" she blurted out. "If the Wishmaster *has* been in the house, we don't know if she might come back. You'll be safer here, so . . . please don't leave right away. You could even spend the night, unless you've developed a taste for rock star mansions?" She flashed a wink at Miles, but it came off fake, like she was trying to maintain a mask of bravado that was rapidly slipping.

"What about Miles?" Nadia had a feeling she already knew the enthusiastic answer, though the prospect filled her with discomfort. Honestly, she wanted to be anywhere but here, with so many thoughts and questions buzzing around in her mind. But Kaleena had been clear: if Grace offered up the chance for Nadia to stay overnight, she had to accept, if only to lull their mother into a false sense of security while Nadia took the item.

"Well, *of course* I was talking to the pair of you." Grace gave Miles a playful slap on the arm. "Apparently, you come together these days." There was that forced cheer again, with Grace trying to sound more like her usual self.

Nadia ignored the innuendo. "Miles, that work for you?" She let her gaze flit toward Basha. Her grandmother was being way too calm about the idea that something might've happened to their valuables. When Basha moved, it would be Nadia's time to move too.

"Sure, it'd be my *pleasure*." He waggled his eyebrows, and Nadia resisted the urge to pull his hood down over his face so she wouldn't have to put up with his subtle payback.

"You're a peach, Miles Hunter," Grace said. "A delicious, delicious peach! And when in Georgia . . ." She edged closer to him.

Nadia folded her arms across her chest, still discreetly splitting her attention. "We've got a guest bedroom, but I'll warn you now—it doesn't have a lock, so you might want to wedge a chair against the handle to stop unwanted visitors from creeping in."

"Or you could share, to save on laundry?" Grace chimed in, making Nadia's eye twitch.

"When have you ever done the laundry, Mom?" she shot back. "Anyway, if you've seen his house, you'll know he likes a lot of space. Too much, some might say. It's like an aircraft hangar."

Miles skirted away from Grace. "The guest room is fine by me. I'll even throw the sheets in the machine in the morning—save you a job."

"When have *you* ever done the laundry?" Nadia repeated.

Before Miles could make excuses, Basha hobbled toward the kitchen door, the end of her cane following the stepping-stones of old dents in the floorboards. "I leave you all. I need peace of mind. Is too noisy."

Peace of mind? Basha wasn't one to abandon an argument before she'd won it. Perhaps she had the capacity to retreat after all. Or perhaps "peace of mind" was her own personal code for "I need to check on some of those valuables in private."

"Good night, Babcia." The words lodged in Nadia's throat, but she needed to feign politeness, even if she didn't feel like being nice.

Basha didn't bother to reply. She just *tap-tapped* out of the room and into the entrance hall, where Nadia listened for the departing drumbeat of her grandmother lumbering up the stairs.

As the sound disappeared, one word popped into Nadia's head: *showtime.*

"I need to take the weight off my feet." Nadia stretched her arms and padded back over to the sofa, settling onto the comforting cushions. "Wouldn't it be good if there were a way to just leave your body plugged in somewhere for an hour to recharge?" She cast a pointed look at Miles, signaling to him that she was about to do that "weird" thing she'd warned him about.

His eyelids cranked wider, as if to say, *Now?*

Nadia gave the faintest nod and faked a yawn, closing her eyes like she intended to doze off. A second later, the cushions gave beside her as Miles dove down, and she heard him pat the empty seat beside him.

"So, Grace, how come a bona fide fox like you doesn't have a Mr. Kaminski? Let me guess, there's no man in Savannah who can handle you?" Miles said silkily, not knowing the floodgates he was about to open with that dangerous statement.

But he'd have to fend for himself, as Nadia was already warping away to sneak into Basha's body.

Chapter Twenty-Six

Her vision settled on the jewel-toned Aladdin's cave of Basha's room. The view appeared blurrier than Nadia had expected, considering how her grandmother's notoriously sharp gaze didn't miss a thing. At first, Nadia wondered if there were tears at work, fogging up the lenses, so to speak. But even after Basha had blinked a few times, the blur prevailed.

I told you to schedule an eye doctor appointment, Babcia. They do house calls. Despite having everything she'd known ripped out from under her, thanks to Basha's lies, Nadia couldn't help the instinctively caring thoughts that came into her mind.

Basha turned and closed her bedroom door, locking it with an antique iron key the size of a tablespoon. As it turned in the lock, she rested her hand against the warm wood of the door and drew in a stilted breath that sounded almost like a sob. In that slow exhale, Nadia felt an unbearable weight press down on her grandmother's chest. The old woman's hands shook, and her subsequent breaths rasped out in shallow gasps. Basha hung her head and closed her eyes, a riptide of grief threatening to send her to her knees.

I knew you couldn't be that cold. You give out tough love like nobody's business, but you've got a heart that cares. If you could just swallow your pride and admit that you were wrong, you'd save yourself—and everyone else—from so much pain. Nadia wished she was physically in the room so she could say that to her grandmother. Being inside Basha's body wasn't a heal-all salve to the wounds she'd inflicted on the family, but it allowed Nadia into a carefully hidden part of her grandmother: the remorseful, vulnerable side.

"There is no time for this," Basha muttered to herself in Polish. "I can't fix what is broken now. Focus, Basha. Be stronger than this."

Pushing away from the door, she hobbled over to the bedside table, which was adorned with ornate jewelry boxes and a bronzed lamp shaped like a hunched monkey. The silken, amethyst-colored lampshade muted the bulb's glow to a moody red. Basha pulled out the top drawer—the same one Nadia had tried to steal matches from—and tiptoed her fingers to the very back, pressing down until Nadia heard an unusual *click*. A false bottom slid back into the bedside table, revealing a box of matches and a series of keys nesting in a row of square organizers.

So that's why I couldn't find the damn matches! Nadia supposed she ought to have known Basha would have some tricks up her sleeve.

Basha plucked up the smallest key and shuffled over to the closet on the far side of the room: an antique armoire with intricate black vines carved across the varnished surface of the weighty double doors. Nadia and Kaleena used to hide in there as children, when their grandmother was busy, and pretend it was a gateway to Narnia, complete with the silky fur coats that Basha hadn't been able to resist at the thrift store—and that Kaleena had always yelled at her for buying. Even now, whenever Nadia smelled mothballs, it reminded her of being tucked away in that closet, listening to the hushed sound of her and her sister's breathing in the darkness.

Opening the closet doors wide, Basha disappeared inside, pushing away sparkly evening dresses that hadn't been worn in decades. Nadia felt the rise in her grandmother's heart rate as she slotted the small key into a tiny indent in the back of the armoire—the kind that a person would only know was there if they'd had it designed themselves.

Basha removed the key and wedged her thin, gnarled fingers into a crevice in the wood, huffing and puffing as she slid a secret panel backward. A damp wheeze of stale air gusted out, but Basha wafted it away with her heavily ringed hand and proceeded through the gap, her bones creaking as she bent to get through.

Are you kidding me? All those years Nadia had spent pretending this was a gateway of some kind, only to find out that it literally was.

Beyond the gap lay a cramped nook, with a structurally questionable set of stairs leading up into the attic. Panting hard, Basha gripped the pale banister and hauled herself up every dusty step until she reached a doorway. She might not have been able to feel pain, but she hadn't wished for good cardio. Nadia was terrified that her grandmother might fall and break her neck, or plummet straight through the rickety stairs. But Basha made it, grunting the whole way.

Turning a ceramic knob decorated with periwinkle flowers, she pushed through into a small attic space, which was stuffed to the rafters with the spoils of Basha's hoarding endeavors. Nadia gasped inside her mental hideaway, marveling at the treasure trove of hand-woven rugs, oil paintings, and wooden furniture. How had she never found this place, after all the exploring she'd done as a kid? It made her feel like she'd lost out somehow.

"Now, where are you?" Basha paused to catch her breath. "I know you are here."

Nadia's astral heart jumped for a second, thinking her grandmother was talking to her.

A moment later, Basha limped over to an old briefcase perilously balanced on top of a stack of ancient side tables that were missing a variety of legs. With trembling muscles, she tugged the briefcase off the tower of tables and set it down on top of a derelict dollhouse that looked remarkably like the Kaminski Mansion. There, she rolled the dials of a combination lock: 1-7-0-1-4-5. Nadia quickly memorized it and figured it might be the European way of representing January 17, 1945, a date that was no doubt significant to her grandmother and the world's history.

Basha pushed open the briefcase clasps and lifted the lid. If Nadia had had her own eyes, they would've been wide as saucers, unabashedly excited to find out what was inside. She spied a worn leather-bound journal; various coiled necklaces, with rings cushioned on top like jeweled eggs; and a square wooden box. The box was crafted from the same rust-colored heartwood as the box Nadia had broken at Bonaventure, with a wishbone flower burned into the lid and twisting fronds curling down the sides. It had to be the wish trap Nadia had been sent here to find.

What's so special about this one, sis? She'd assumed the Wishmaster had an abundance of traps to call her own, but it seemed Kaleena had a personal connection to this particular one.

"Lying wężowej!" Basha muttered, slamming the briefcase lid shut and rolling the dials back into a random sequence.

All the way back out of the attic, down the stairs, through the closet, and into the bedroom, Nadia could feel Basha's prickles of anger. She didn't like to be hoodwinked, though Nadia wasn't sure who her grandmother had meant to call a lying snake. If Basha suspected her of being on Kaleena's team, it would mean a one-way ticket out of the house—for good this time.

What did you expect, Babcia? You made Kaleena use a wish she'd saved for almost two decades. Did you think she'd take that lying down? You know her better than that. Nadia's thoughts warred with one another, flitting from understanding to bitterness to sorrow to betrayal to hurt to forgiveness, then all the way back around again in a never-ending carousel of emotion.

She watched as Basha returned the key to the hidden compartment, where she picked up another key. With it, she shuffled over to her private stash of tea supplies and opened the jade-green safe, taking in a deep breath as the pungent aroma of spices, tea leaves, and herbal infusions washed over them both. Apparently deciding it was too early for her nightly ritual, Basha closed the safe again, settling down into her chair instead.

You won't find a fix for this in the bottom of a teacup, anyway, Babcia. Reluctantly, Nadia concentrated on her own body and jumped ship. After she twisted through the black vortex, her vision soon cleared on the chalkboard. It seemed her autopilot body had behaved itself and stayed put.

"Sorry, did I drift off?" Nadia contrived another loud yawn. "I must be more tired than I thought. I feel like I just went off to some other place entirely."

Grace refilled her own glass. "Don't worry about it, honey. Miles and I have been having ourselves a fine old time while you've been snoozing."

"Your mom was just telling me what she likes to get up to on Tybee Island." Miles gulped, flashing major help-me eyes at Nadia.

"Oh, come now, when did I go back to being Nadia's mom? I like it when you call me by my name." Grace giggled, clearly a few sheets to the wind.

Nadia patted herself down, hoping she wasn't veering into melodrama territory. "Crap, I think I left my phone at your house, Miles. I was supposed to call the bank before closing to get them to approve my new card. Damn it. I'll have to do it tomorrow."

It might've sounded like an inane anecdote, but there was a secret code in those words that Miles knew to expect. "Approving the new card" meant the box had been found, while "calling the bank" meant they were ready to move on to phase two. Fortunately, Grace was too lost in Miles's startled eyes to realize there was something fishy going on.

"I'd lend you mine, but I've got a bunch of VIPs on here," Miles said. "And I ain't risking any of my DMs getting leaked." He used the excuse to take out the phone that he'd borrowed from Kaleena, tucking it right up to his chin so Grace couldn't snatch a peek. "Speaking of which, I should give my housekeeper the heads-up about where I am. She'll worry her sweet self sick if I don't turn up at home tonight."

Grace sat back, her mouth pursing in displeasure. "This housekeeper lives with you? How old is she?"

"A few years older than you, I reckon, and she lives at my place. Her grandkids stay over a lot too." Miles typed hurriedly, sending word to the head honcho.

Grace paled. "Are you saying I'm old enough to be someone's grandma?"

"You are, Mom," Nadia interjected sharply, feeling a little insulted by her mom's obvious horror. If things had panned out the way they were supposed to, Grace might've *been* a grandma by now.

Miles slid the phone back into his pocket. Nadia waited for the next part to play out, tapping her foot in agitation.

Grace's phone buzzed, prompting her to almost upend what was left of her margarita onto poor Miles. He dodged the green spray while Grace fumbled around one-handed for the phone. She pulled it out and gasped as her eyes fixed on the name that flashed on the screen. Even without seeing it, Nadia knew it read "Wishmaster." It used to be "Kaleena," but that got changed under Basha's insistence.

"What's wrong?" Nadia asked, knowing full well what was happening.

Grace set down her drink and clutched the phone with both hands like she had a live bomb in her palms. "It's your sister." She gulped. "I should answer it, shouldn't I?"

"That's up to you," Nadia replied, praying she did.

Grace twisted her neck back and looked at the kitchen door. "I should ask your babcia first. She'll know what to do." Without waiting for further advice, she sprinted to the entrance hall. "Mama? Mama, can you come down here a sec?"

"What you yell for? Is no need!" Basha shouted back a few seconds later.

"The Wishmaster is calling, and . . . Mama, I don't know what to do!" Grace answered, pacing back and forth between the kitchen island and the doorway.

Basha thudded down the stairs, and Nadia shared an anxious glance with Miles.

"Answer phone!" her grandmother barked. "Don't hop like frog in hot water. If she is calling, we get these terms over with, then be done with her! Good riddance!"

Grace hesitated, her fingertip poised over the screen.

"Answer it!" Basha snapped again, appearing on the threshold. Her eyes were ringed with red.

Grace swiped her finger in a sharp jolt, as though the screen might singe her. Rather than hold the phone up to her ear, however, she tapped the Speaker button and skimmed the device onto the center island, as if trying to put some distance between herself and her eldest daughter's voice.

"It's not wise to keep me waiting." Kaleena's mocking tone breezed through the speakers. "The two of you are already on thin ice, given your recent behavior."

Basha clacked over to the island. "What behavior? We do nothing."

"Come now, you know that's not true," Kaleena replied. "Do you expect me to believe that Nadia acted alone, considering our delightfully fucked-up history? You made me use a wish. Why not her?"

Basha straightened, hands clasped on her cane. "She is bad as you! Is not my fault you are both wild and disrespectful!"

"As bad as me?" Kaleena choked out a cold laugh. "You need to take a long, hard look at yourself, Basha. I think you'll find that you're the common denominator, while the rest of us got caught in your—"

Her last words were smothered by an earth-shaking blast that made Grace drop to the ground, while Nadia's hands flew to her ears. Miles, on the other hand, didn't even flinch. Clearly, the years of thunderous drum solos and heavy guitar had made him immune.

"The boiler!" Grace yelped. "Is it the boiler? Or are we under attack? Was that a *bomb*? What's going on! Kaleena, did you do this?"

"I don't know what you're talking about, but it sounded pretty loud," she replied casually. "That almost burst my eardrums."

"You make threat?" Basha shrieked, her cheeks turning red with fury. "As if you could do anything while we are in house!"

Kaleena laughed. "No, *there* go my eardrums."

That was Nadia's cue, though her hearing had taken on an underwater fuzziness. "I'll go and check the damage," she shouted, probably too loud.

With Grace still huddled on the floor and Basha about ready to take her cane to the phone screen, neither of them responded to Nadia as she rushed away from the kitchen. She hoped Miles would ensure that Basha and Grace stayed put as planned.

Nadia bounded up the stairs. Her shoes screeched to a halt outside Basha's room, and she darted through the door, making straight for the bedside table. Her fingernails scrabbled along the back of the top drawer until she found something smooth and metallic. She pressed down and was rewarded with a *click* that allowed her to slide the false bottom back to reveal the nesting keys. Nadia reached for the smallest one, just as Basha had done without knowing she was being watched, and sprinted for the vintage armoire.

She threw open the door and slotted the key straight into that tiny opening to the far-left side, which was hidden behind a forest of dusty fur. Turning the key in a full circle, she dug her fingers into the hair-thin crack down the side of the closet's back until it rolled away, opening up the passage to the attic stairwell.

After she bounded the final stretch upward, she burst into the house's last mystery, seeking out the briefcase that Basha had left on the old dollhouse. With shaky hands, she turned the combination lock and popped open the surprisingly well-preserved clasps.

This isn't yours, Babcia. It was the only comfort Nadia could take. Sure, her grandmother had royally screwed her over since the car accident, but robbing an old woman—and family, no less—would never sit well with her.

Nadia grabbed the wish trap and tucked it under her arm, then closed the briefcase and turned the combination lock back to the numbers Basha had left it on. She might've stopped to open the box if Kaleena hadn't explicitly instructed her, before they left, not to do so if she didn't want to turn her debt into a lifetime one.

She barreled out of the attic room and down the stairs, before slipping through the secret door and closing it behind her. It took some juggling skill to get the small key out of her pocket so she could lock up again.

With frantic breaths, she emerged from the closet and immediately froze. A faint knocking permeated the silence. Her eyes flitted toward the half-closed bedroom door, but if Basha or Grace wanted to step inside, they wouldn't bother to knock. So where was the sound coming from?

"You try to blow hole in my house? You think you can do as you please?" Basha howled from downstairs. "I never allow you inside!"

Nadia frowned as the knocking continued. She shut the armoire doors and scanned the bedroom, noticing a strange shadow stretching across the patchwork of brightly patterned rugs. Another knock made her twist her head toward the window, and a yelp of alarm escaped her throat.

Kaleena waited on the other side, perched at the top of a ladder, knuckles raised to the pane.

Nadia froze. This wasn't part of the plan.

Chapter Twenty-Seven

Nadia crept toward the window and mouthed, "What are you doing?"

"Open up," Kaleena replied, pointing to the curved handle inside.

Nadia did so, edging the window wide. "How are you here when you're on the phone with—" She stopped short as understanding dawned. *Val* was the one talking to Basha, using Kaleena's voice, while the real Kaleena had scaled a ladder to retrieve her beloved wish trap. "Are you coming inside, or are you going to hover out there like a Peeping Tom?"

"Give it to me." Kaleena eyed the rust-colored box under Nadia's arm. No pleases, thank-yous, or gratitude whatsoever. Just a hunger that Nadia hadn't seen before.

After a moment's hesitation, Nadia handed the box over, validating the exchange with thoughts of getting her own wishes, bringing Nick back, and teaching Basha that she couldn't manipulate everyone and not bear any of the responsibility. A hard life didn't give you the right to mess with everyone around you, consequence free.

"Hello, my friend," Kaleena cooed to the box, before returning her attention to Nadia. "Where did you find it?"

Nadia furrowed her brow. "Is that important?" She didn't know why, but the thought of telling Kaleena about all of Basha's secret hideaways seemed tantamount to telling her the color of their grandmother's lingerie.

"It is if you want to bring your debt down to two jobs," Kaleena replied, her hair uncharacteristically disheveled from the wind.

Nadia looked back over her shoulder. "She's got a secret drawer full of keys. This one"—she dangled the small key off her little finger —"opens up a false panel in the back of the closet. There's a staircase up to the attic, where Babcia has a locked briefcase. The wish trap was inside it."

Kaleena leaned forward on the ladder, using both hands to open the wooden box as her arms hung over the ledge. Resting the base on the windowsill, she dipped her hand inside and took out a folded piece of silver wishery paper. She smiled to herself, then replaced the slip of paper and closed the lid tight. In that moment, Nadia cursed herself for not checking the contents before Kaleena came a-knocking, regardless of the threat of an endless debt. What was written on that paper that the Wishmaster wanted so badly? A wish, obviously, but what kind? And whose?

Nadia opened her mouth to interrogate right as a cry went up.

"Where is worthless dziecko?" Basha's voice bellowed through the house.

"My Polish is rusty these days, but I think she's talking to you." Kaleena waved a hand at the door. "You should get back downstairs before she comes looking for you. With her creaky legs, I'd say you've got a couple of minutes."

"Then you should get your ass off this ladder!" Nadia hissed, tugging at the curtains.

"Leave that. Basha will know you've been up here if you touch her precious curtains," Kaleena instructed, sticking her hand through the window to show her rose-gold watch. "Clock's ticking, little sister. Get moving."

Nadia whirled around and ran back the way she'd come, pausing by the bedside table to put everything back the way it was. Taking a steadying breath, she looked over her shoulder to find Kaleena climbing down the ladder. Satisfied, Nadia took off out of the bedroom, the exchange made. There was no taking it back now.

In the hallway, Nadia instinctively grabbed a szabla off the wall: a slightly curved saber used by Polish hussars for centuries in cavalry clashes that rang across Europe. Basha always claimed it was the real deal and that it had been passed down through her family for generations. Nadia was no weapons expert, but she was pretty sure the Nazis would've had something to say if they'd found a Kaminski with a sword like this stashed away. Still, at least it looked like she'd tried to arm herself against intruders.

Wielding it clumsily, she jogged back into the kitchen.

Basha spun around, fist raised. "This is war. Before, I say yes to having Kaminski in power over stranger. But Wishmaster has gone too far this time! You fight with us, or you fight against us."

Grace was now perched on a barstool, looking as shaken up as her favorite margarita. Even Miles, who stood awkwardly on the lip between the den and the kitchen, seemed unsettled.

"I promise to get remaining wishes for debt, but she no listen!" Basha stabbed a finger at the now-blank phone screen. "She rant and rave, and call me all names under sun! She leave us no choice. We overthrow her and put someone new in her place, like we did with Adrian. It can be done. Basha knows how." All of a sudden, she appeared to run out of steam, staggering into the side of the island and bracing her hand against it. "We talk fighting tomorrow. We make plan then. My bones . . . they are too weary tonight. The house will protect until morning. The Wishmaster no reach us in here, as long as I stay inside."

Grace lifted her head. "I'll take you up to bed, Mama."

"You are good girl. Only good girl." Basha held out her hand for her daughter. "I have my tea. I feel better soon." Together, they lumbered out of the kitchen, the stress of the evening evident in their identically hunched shoulders.

None of this felt right. Nadia had expected to feel relieved, and a touch guilty, after the box had been handed off. Instead, dread roiled inside her belly, along with an overwhelming heave of growing horror.

Of course, she hadn't really had a choice, but she regretted giving the wish trap to Kaleena all the same. It boiled down to that slip of wishery paper and what was written on it that the Wishmaster wanted so desperately. *That* was the cause of Nadia's internal upheaval, because it meant this wasn't about a wish trap at all.

"Nice sword. Is a certain somebody up there with her head missing?" Miles asked, walking up to her and eyeing the saber.

Nadia blinked absently. "Sorry. I picked it up on the way. Seems like overkill now that I'm looking at it." She set the saber against the nearest barstool.

"You okay?" He put his hand on her shoulder. "You were definitely checked out for a while there."

"Better than having to listen to my mom serenade you."

He laughed, but it sounded like the kind of chuckle someone made with a gun to their head. "So, are we good to go? Is she—"

Nadia put a stern finger to her lips. "Not here. Follow me." Leading the way, she took him up to the guest bedroom, wincing as she passed Basha's closed door. From within, she heard Grace singing softly in the language of the motherland. Basha had to be feeling worse than Nadia thought, if she'd asked Grace to sing.

Pressing on, Nadia didn't stop until she and Miles were inside the guest bathroom. There, she shut the door and turned on the shower, then settled down onto the closed toilet lid.

"Do you need some alone time?" Miles asked hesitantly, looking perplexed.

She rolled her head in her hands, too nervous about what she'd done to play into his banter. "Can you sense where Kaleena is right now?"

"Uh, not really, no," he replied after taking a moment to put out his feelers. "There's, like, a tiny bit of Marco but not much Polo."

Nadia's head shot up. "Be more specific, please. My head's about to explode."

"Feels like she's back in the car. Farther away, maybe." He leaned up against the bathroom counter. "Not close at all, if that's what's got you freaked."

Nadia unleashed a sigh of relief so intense it made her ears pop. "Thank God for that."

"So, I'm not the only one feeling like I ate bad shrimp." Miles fanned himself as the bathroom started to steam from the running hot water. "That was some ridiculous shit, Nads. Kaleena never mentioned she'd be bringing her own pyros. Gave me some nasty flashbacks, man. I almost got third-degree burns when a fire jet thing went off too early once while I was onstage. My faux leather jacket starts bubbling, right, and I have to throw it off before it melts into me. The fans just thought it was part of the show."

He'd gone and called her "Nads" again, but she figured the slipup was just due to nerves, and she found it didn't annoy her as much as it had before.

Nadia leaned back against the toilet tank. "For all that time we spent planning, there were things she didn't tell us." She explained to Miles what had gone down in Basha's bedroom, throwing in a detail or two about her ability and how she'd known where to find everything. "Did my body try to do anything while I was out?"

"Not really. You kind of fell asleep, snoring and everything. I wouldn't have had you down as a heavy bass kind of snorer. More of a piccolo whistler."

He readjusted his elbow on the bathroom counter, sending a glass jar of cotton rounds skittering off the edge and onto the floor. The smash shivered through Nadia as the shards fanned out, and her frightened gaze met Miles's sheepish face.

"Ah, damn it!" he said. "Was that expensive? Some Polish heirloom or something? I can buy you a new one, even if I have to get it from the Smithsonian."

Nadia shook her head slowly. "That shouldn't have happened."

"It was an accident, man. I didn't mean to," he protested boyishly. "Seriously, tell me what it cost, and I'll get you a new one. Or one like it. Close as I can get."

Her voice hardened. "No, you don't understand. *That* shouldn't have happened in this house. Basha's protective shield, mechanism, spell, or whatever you want to call it doesn't allow things to break."

I invited her in . . . Nadia's stomach pitched. At the window, she'd asked Kaleena if she was going to come inside. To the house, that was as good as opening the damn front door and welcoming someone inside with all the bells and whistles. A memory flash of seeing her sister put her arm partway through the window ramped up her fear. Kaleena had flaunted what she could now do, and Nadia had been too stressed about getting caught to notice.

She leaped up and raced out of the bathroom, bombing through the guest bedroom and out into the hall. Gasping for a full breath, she rushed to Basha's room and edged the door open. Her grandmother lay curled up in the four-poster bed, a teal satin blanket draped over her and an empty cup sitting on her bedside table. Her mother, meanwhile, was nowhere to be seen.

Careful not to wake the old woman, Nadia tiptoed to the window and checked the latch. The window itself had been drawn into the jamb, but the handle was turned upward in the "open" position. Kaleena must've closed it to create less suspicion, but that didn't mean she'd entered the house . . . right? Nadia fervently wanted to believe that was true, but if it was, then why had Kaleena demanded to know about the key drawer and the location of the briefcase? Her heart threatened to pound right out of her chest as she thought of Basha's tea safe and the other keys that were hidden in that drawer.

Kaleena . . . what did you do? The Wishmaster knew about Basha's evening ritual. She would've known where to go and what to switch out to replace Basha's usual tea with a bark-infused version that would diminish her wish-given power. Evidently, Kaleena had made one brief stop after tricking Nadia into thinking she was heading back down the ladder.

Nadia gasped. "I left the window open. I let her in." She steadied herself on the window ledge.

She was about to turn and run to her grandmother, to try to wake her, when Miles appeared behind her, blocking her way. "What's going on?" He wasn't joking anymore.

"I don't know," Nadia whispered. "But it's bad. Really bad."

Miles's gaze darted toward the window, his nostrils flaring. "Do you smell that?"

Nadia whipped around, catching the orange flicker of strange light somewhere below the sill, near the back door of the house, joined by the faint whiff of smoke that she'd thought was one of her grandmother's sticks of incense.

"It's fire." She gripped the window ledge until her knuckles whitened. "The house is on fire."

Chapter Twenty-Eight

Flicking an internal switch to survival mode, Nadia concentrated on her mom and hoped her autopilot body wouldn't throw itself out of the window. She zipped straight into Grace's head, staying no more than a couple of seconds to find out where her mom was, before popping back into her own familiar mind.

"Miles, get my mom from the study—three doors down. Grab her and get out of the house! And call 911!" Nadia urged, immediately stepping back as she realized she'd gotten a little too close to him.

He stared at her like she had something in her teeth.

"Now, Miles!" Nadia said. Nick's voice rang in her head: *in a fire, it's the smoke that'll kill you first.*

Miles jolted into action. "Gotcha." He ran for the door, only to turn on the threshold. "What about you?"

"I'll deal with my babcia." She hurried to the bed, shaking the old woman's narrow shoulders gently as Miles disappeared out into the hallway.

"Babcia? Babcia, you need to wake up!" Nadia gripped Basha as hard as she dared. Her grandmother might've had a tough-as-old-boots outer shell, but her thin arms were like matchsticks, and Nadia didn't want to break anything.

"Babcia! Wake the hell up!" Nadia hoped a bit of bad language might coax her grandmother out of her stupor.

At least she knew Basha's unconsciousness wasn't because of Kaleena's tea tampering. If Kaleena had poisoned the tea, the house would've made Basha throw it up, or would've flung the cup out of her hand. No, the tea switch had been done to *disarm* Basha's wish, since that didn't exactly harm her.

But there was only one logical reason for Kaleena to numb the protective wish—she was going to kill Basha. Her grandmother had been right. This was war, and the Wishmaster had launched the first attack.

"Wake up!" Nadia grimaced as she grabbed a glass of water from the nightstand and chucked it at Basha's face.

The old woman's eyelids fluttered open, her expression groggy while Nadia pulled her up into a sitting position. "What is going on, dziecko? Why you splash me? You make threat too?"

"There's a fire, and we need to get out before it spreads," Nadia said, ignoring the sharp-tongued comments and trying to tug her grandmother off the bed.

But Basha fought back with surprising strength in her stick-thin arms and vein-knotted hands. "That is what Wishmaster wants. If we stay in house, we will be fine. Is a trick. I no fall for it."

Nadia tried to move her again, terrified she might wrench her grandmother's arm out of its socket. "Kaleena found a way around your wish, Babcia. She managed to put a dose of Alexander's Tea in your stash. The house isn't protected anymore, and neither are you."

Basha scooted to the end of the bed. "I must save my things," she said, using one of the four posts to lever herself to her feet.

"There's no point, Babcia. The wish trap in the attic isn't there anymore." Nadia resigned herself to telling the truth, if only to get Basha moving. "Kaleena came here to steal it, and she did. So, move your ass downstairs and get out of the house!" Regardless of the bad blood between them, she wouldn't let her grandmother die.

Basha gaped at Nadia with watery eyes. "You betray me?"

"Let's not argue about betrayals here," Nadia shot back, grabbing Basha's arm and pulling it around her shoulders. "We have to leave.

Now." She wasn't sure if the fire had started only at the back of the house or if Kaleena had set every exit ablaze.

But Basha clung on to the bedpost, her nails digging into the wood. "I get briefcase. I rather die here than go without it."

"Fine, but I'll get it. You'll take too long." Huffing out a frustrated breath, Nadia ran to the bedside table and popped open the false bottom. That one action revealed everything about the part she'd played, but she could dwell on that later, preferably before they were incinerated.

Once she snatched up the key, she raced for the dresser, going through the motions until she was up the attic steps. She grabbed the briefcase off the dollhouse, surrounded by furniture, stacks of books, rolled-up rugs, and baskets of clothes that likely wouldn't survive the coming inferno. Despite the bad memories, she loved this house and the treasures within it, and Kaleena was taking a wrecking ball to it all. Nadia had never wanted this outcome, but she'd given Kaleena the tinderbox to make it happen.

Shaking off dark thoughts, she barreled back down the stairs and ran over to Basha, pushing the briefcase into her grandmother's hands.

"You know, the way you feel about this damn briefcase is *exactly* how I've felt about Nick this whole time." Nadia couldn't stop the bitter words from tumbling out.

Basha let go of the bedpost, both her arms wrapping around the briefcase as she looked at Nadia with sad curiosity. And then, she said six words that Nadia had never expected: "It was my *mama* who succeeded."

"Pardon?" Nadia blinked, torn between dragging her grandmother out of the room and digging deeper.

Basha sighed, setting the briefcase on the bed and quickly unlocking it. At first, Nadia was going to scream at her for wasting more time—Nadia hadn't lied about the missing wish trap, after all— but Basha seemed to be looking for something else.

"The person who came back to life, dziecko—it was me. No some forgotten member of rodzina long ago." Her thin fingers curled around a battered journal, then she tossed it to Nadia, who only just managed to catch it. "The rest of story is in there. My mama's diary."

Nadia looked down at the plain brown leather, so frozen with confusion that she couldn't think of anything to say. Was this some trick her grandmother was playing? It seemed impossible that Basha could have such a rapid change of heart.

"You might find answers in those pages," Basha added, her voice oddly thick with emotion. "Answers to help choose right wish. Is no guarantee, but is start."

Nadia slammed the lid back down on the briefcase and clicked the locks, then shoved the briefcase into Basha's arms. Taking hold of her grandmother's wrist, she tugged the old woman toward the door while she ruminated on what she could possibly say about this unexpected gift.

"Why, Babcia?" she said at last, pulling Basha down the hall. "Why didn't you just give me this when I first asked for help?" A bittersweet choke of sadness bubbled out of Nadia's mouth. "Do you . . . Do you understand how different things might've been?"

"I understand." Basha gave a small nod, following Nadia along like a scolded child. "But I have reason. Reviving someone is dangerous—it comes at steep cost to wisher. My mama paid steep price. I no want you to sacrifice something of yourself to bring Nick back. I no bear to see you hurt in such way. But is your choice. Is no mine. Journal is . . . apology."

"Thank you, Babcia." Holding the journal in her hands was enough for Nadia to push aside her bitterness and blame, if only for the moment.

Reaching the top of the staircase, Nadia spotted Miles and Grace bursting back through the front door, hightailing it through the thick black smoke toward the stairs. Nadia shoved the journal down the waistband of her jeans.

"What the hell, Nadia?" Miles panted as he stopped at the bottom step. "We ran outside, but you didn't come!"

"Babcia needed to get some things." Nadia gestured to the briefcase, which Basha was readjusting in her arms.

Miles bounded up the stairs and scooped Basha over his shoulders, briefcase and all. "Problem solved." He took a few deep breaths in the clearer air, Grace catching up behind him.

"The showroom is burning—and the backyard," Grace said, her voice shaking. "We need to go out the front. That's the only exit now."

"Trouble is, we've got company," Miles said.

"Kaleena . . ." Basha muttered. It was the first time Nadia had heard her grandmother say that name in years.

Miles nodded. "Yeah. She's out there." He jogged down the stairs carrying Basha, with Grace and Nadia running after him.

Thick black tendrils of smoke curled upward, turning the entire entrance hall into a seething mass of poisonous haze. More smoke belched from underneath the door to the showroom, and though she couldn't see the flames, Nadia could hear that telltale crackle coming from the kitchen.

She pulled the neckline of her T-shirt over her nose and mouth. It wasn't much, but it'd give her a few extra seconds. At her side, Grace followed suit, while Miles dipped his chin into the collar of his sweatshirt and put his sleeve over Basha's mouth. Wielding the old woman like she weighed nothing, Miles ran toward the entrance hall.

"Stop! Put me down," Basha called out when they were halfway across.

"Is the smoke getting to you?" Miles asked, having no choice but to set her down once she started flailing.

Basha lumbered toward Nadia, her free hand gripping Nadia's wrist. "Tell Wishmaster that you could no save me from flames. Tell her I was stubborn as mule. Tell her I locked myself in bedroom and refuse to leave, to protect house. Tell her I no believe about the tea." She brought Nadia's hand up and kissed it gently.

And before anyone could stop her, Basha turned around and hobbled away as fast as she could, through to the already burning kitchen, heading for the back door.

"Babcia!" Nadia tried to shout, but the smoke caught the back of her throat, making her cough violently. She watched her grandmother avoid the flames to reach the door that led out into the garden—though most of the garden had become a forest of towering flames with a snowfall of gray ash.

Basha turned the doorknob, flinching as a searing gust of burning wind swept through the hallway, dispersing the smoke momentarily. Before Basha vanished into a narrow break in the inferno, Nadia glimpsed a scorched line of livid red along her grandmother's palm— and realized that the tea would've also dulled her wish to never feel pain.

Chapter Twenty-Nine

"We have to bring her back!" Grace spluttered, eyes streaming from the smoke. "She won't make it out there!"

Nadia could barely speak through the choking fumes, but fear made her force out the words, if only to stop her mom from running out into that blaze. "She knows what she's doing. We have to save ourselves!"

Apparently sensing the flight risk, Miles darted forward and swept Grace into his arms. Ordinarily, she'd have gone wild for this kind of heroic display, but not this time. Strangled sobs hiccupped out of her throat as she pounded her fists against Miles's chest, her reddened eyes fixed on the kitchen door and the terrifying furnace beyond it.

"Let me go!" she cried. "That's my mama! She'll die!"

Nadia held on to her mom's hand as the trio plowed through the dense smoke, unable to see anything ahead of them. They were relying solely on Miles and his finding skill to get them out before the smoke finished them off.

"I know it's hard, but you can't say a word to Kaleena!" Nadia stressed, squeezing her mom's fingers. "Babcia always does her own thing. Death isn't reckless enough to take her, so focus on that."

Nadia heard the door wrench open, but the smoke only billowed with renewed aggression, as though it knew it was losing its prey. Following Miles's pull, her grip firmly on Grace's hand, she sensed the change in texture beneath her shoes—they'd made it outside. But the wooden slats of the porch groaned underfoot, the agonized creaks seeming to say, *Hurry! We can't hold much longer!* All around, flames licked up the side of the house, catching on the wooden shutters and making the gray paint bubble, though it couldn't do much about the brickwork and the Ionic columns just yet. The blaze had to devour the guts of the house first before it grew hot enough to destroy the masonry.

They stumbled down the porch steps and along the garden path, past the defunct fountain, then slowed as the air cleared. Nadia let go of her mom's hand and stooped, feeling like she might be sick as she clutched on to her thighs. Sucking in deep breath after deep breath, and coughing out rattling exhales, she could feel the tight, oppressive weight of all that smoke sitting in her lungs.

"Oh man . . . oh man . . ." Miles wheezed, banging on his chest after he set Grace on her feet.

"Kaleena?" Grace's whisper severed any relief Nadia might've had that they'd escaped unscathed. Grace drew air through a clenched hand, like she was holding an invisible paper bag, her eyes wide with shock and sadness.

Nadia followed her mother's stunned gaze to find Kaleena standing at the iron gates with her arms crossed.

"A warning might've been nice," Nadia said curtly as she approached Kaleena. Miles and Grace trailed her at a distance. "You know, a 'by the way, you might burn to death if you don't vamoose' or something."

Kaleena pursed her lips. "Where's Basha? This is her day of reckoning—I wouldn't want her to miss it."

Mom, stay calm. Remember what I said. Nadia tried to catch her mom's eye, but Grace couldn't stop staring at her eldest daughter.

All of a sudden, Grace stepped forward and slapped Kaleena across the face. Nadia flinched, and beside her, Miles looked as if he might run down the street.

"This is your fault," Grace hissed at the stunned Wishmaster. "Your babcia, my mama, is dead because of you! You didn't have to forgive her—you made it blatantly obvious you never would—but you didn't have to kill her!"

Nadia smothered her shock at the real despair written across her mom's face. Maybe Grace truly believed Basha wouldn't make it through the back garden blaze and that it wasn't just an act.

"Don't you dare put your hands on me again." Kaleena stepped away from them, her left cheek an angry pink. "And how, exactly, did I *kill* her?"

"Babcia wouldn't come out, Wishmaster," Nadia said, jumping in. "She locked her bedroom door from the inside, and we couldn't break it down. You know how thick the doors are in there. She thought you were bluffing about numbing her wishes. She wouldn't believe a word, and . . . she stopped replying to us, after a while."

"With the smoke so dense, it probably got to her before the fire could," Miles added, his face a perfect mask of solemnity.

Kaleena's eyelids flickered with annoyance. "I suppose it doesn't matter how the job gets done, as long as it's done." She recovered quickly from her obvious disappointment. "Now, once you two have stopped hacking up your lungs, it's time for us to make a move. Our work here is done." She waved a hand at Miles and Nadia, deliberately drifting over Grace.

"Tell me you didn't help with this . . ." Grace grabbed Nadia's shoulder, forcing her to turn around. Her mother looked more vulnerable than Nadia had ever seen her.

"I didn't have a choice," Nadia mumbled. "She's the only one who can help me get Nick back."

Grace's cheeks flushed with a splotchy red. "At the expense of your babcia?"

"I tried to get her out, Mom. I didn't know she was going to refuse," Nadia protested, feeling a worm of guilt squirm in her stomach. "But she betrayed me, and she betrayed my sister. Hell, inside, you said she betrayed *you*! That doesn't mean I wanted anything bad to happen to her. I . . . didn't know it would."

People had begun to gather around the scene of the fire—neighbors watching the blaze from a distance with phones pressed to their ears. However, Nadia could tell they were intentionally keeping their distance from this little group congregated across from the Kaminski Mansion. Grace and Kaleena's raised voices probably broadcasted that this wasn't a battle anyone else should join.

"You can't trust a word that comes out of her mouth, Nadia." Grace flashed a glare at Kaleena. "Don't you leave with her. You'll regret it."

Unease weighed heavily in her stomach, but Nadia couldn't see what other choice she had if she ever wanted to be truly free again. "I'm sorry, Mom. I have to."

"I imagine she enjoyed spilling the beans about the car accident, knowing she'd get you exactly where she wanted you." Grace's voice hardened, a sneer distorting her face. "But I bet she kept quiet about what happened to Nick *because* of her, didn't she?"

Nadia's world went sideways, the solid ground turning swampy under her feet. Miles caught her by the arm before she could stumble, and though she wanted to launch a barrage of questions at her mom, all she could manage was a quiet "What?"

"I doubt she even knows that I know," Grace went on, casting a dirty glance at Kaleena before turning back to Nadia. "I didn't want you to go after her and get yourself killed. I wanted you to heal and move on. But since your sister doesn't seem to mind tearing open old wounds, maybe I shouldn't either."

"Another trick, little sister," Kaleena said, but there was something unusual about her tone. It sounded tighter than normal, her body language completely rigid.

Grace put her hand on Nadia's shoulder. "Listen to me. Nick came to me for a wish over a year ago, but I couldn't give one to him because of the debt. I never mentioned it because he asked me not to." Her voice hitched. "I swear, honey, I'd have done my damnedest to break the rules, no matter the cost, if I'd known he would go to Kaleena instead."

"Is *that* what this is about?" Kaleena smiled stiffly. "Sure, Nick asked me for a wish. But I never made that deal with him. Mixing family and business has never ended well."

"What wish did he want to make?" Nadia growled, clinging on to Miles to keep herself upright.

Kaleena shrugged. "How should I know?"

"You always ask people to do something for you in exchange for their wish," Grace shot back. "It was Nick working for you, to pay off *his* debt, that got him killed."

Kaleena wagged her finger. "Again, not true. Nick wasn't working for me. He must've gone to someone else after I said no, if he really wanted a wish that badly. I don't know why anyone wanted him dead, but it didn't have anything to do with me."

Nadia's head spun, her mouth dry with smoke and anguish, her chest heaving with latent fumes and the enormity of what they were saying. Bile rose in her throat. All this time, she'd been kept in the dark about her husband's last hours, days, weeks leading up to his death. She'd tortured herself, night after night, day after day, wondering if there was something she could've done, or said, or seen that might've saved him. Now, she was hearing that both her mom and her sister had known more, and neither had breathed a word.

"You were in so much pain after he died, Nadia," Grace said softly. "I didn't want to make it worse by telling you about the wish. You wouldn't have been able to cope with it, and when you got better, I didn't want you spiraling back into that pit or having your memory of him tainted."

Nadia glanced at Miles, as if for answers. "I . . . don't understand what's happening."

He gave her arm a squeeze, his expression nervous but his voice steady. "You just keep breathing, yeah? In and out, in and out . . ."

Kaleena took a step forward. "Surely, it's obvious. What further proof do you need about who's responsible? Our dear mother"—she spat the words—"never wanted you to bring Nick back to life, all so that she could hold you to ransom twice over: for the debt that wasn't yours and because you had nowhere else to go. Me—I've got no problem with it. I've got nothing to hide. If Nick were here, he'd tell you I had nothing to do with his death."

Grace looked like she might slap Kaleena again. "The Wishmaster is only *allowing* you to go after that goal because she thinks it's impossible." She turned to Nadia, her eyes ablaze with righteous fury. "Kaleena says she has nothing to hide, but she does. She's great at hiding things. After all, she wished to 'kill those who would do harm unto others, with impunity.' A clever little workaround to avoid getting blocked by the Wishing Tree. So now you know, Nadia—just like some of her other so-called 'loyal' servants. That's right, Kaleena, one of these days, one of them is going to take it from you."

Nadia gulped down air, trying to make sense of all this.

"That's why you wanted the box, isn't it?" she blurted out, facing Kaleena. "That's the wish Basha pressured you to make, so she knew the wording, and you don't want anyone to have it in case they burn the paper and take your wish. And you don't want anybody to know that you . . ."

Nadia could hardly breathe. If Basha made Kaleena wish to kill those who would do harm unto others, that explained Adrian. But Kaleena having something to do with Nick's death didn't make any sense. He hadn't hurt anyone. Maybe Grace had gotten it wrong. Maybe she was lying. Maybe this was one big misunderstanding. Maybe . . .

"*Basha* made me make that wish!" Kaleena snarled back at Grace. "I wouldn't have chosen something so vulgar, but it's still *my* wish! How dare you reveal it!"

"Vulgar?" Grace sneered. "Vulgar? You don't have a problem with its vulgarity when you *use* it, do you?"

Nadia stared at her sister. With a wish like that, Kaleena could kill anyone without a single shred of evidence ever pointing toward her. What if Grace was right about Kaleena getting Nick killed? What if Kaleena had *murdered* Nick? The thought alone made her sick to her stomach. Her own sister killing her husband. But why? What would drive Kaleena to do something so unspeakably horrible?

Kaleena scoffed. "Stop looking at me like that, little sister. Grace is wrong, no matter how loudly she screams otherwise. Nick's death had nothing to do with me."

"I want to know the—" Nadia began.

"It's simple. Do you want Nick back or not? I'm offering you the wishes to do it, as promised. Grace can't—or rather, *wouldn't*." She paused. "Do I think resurrection is impossible? Sure. Will I help you? I already said I would. Don't be fooled by Grace. She's just like Basha."

"That's not true!" Grace protested. "Everything I've done, I've done for the two of you. I didn't deny Nadia a wish because I don't want her to get Nick back. I denied her because . . . Well, I didn't want to see her hurt again."

"Bullshit." Kaleena shook her head vehemently. "You've never done anything for either of us unless it benefited you. You had every opportunity to stop all this, to stop Basha from screwing me and Nadia over, to be a good mother. But you failed. At any moment, you could've stood up and said no, but you didn't. That's what makes you just as guilty as Basha. That's what makes you a failure."

Grace let out a strangled whimper, her face crumpling. "I . . . tried."

"It wasn't good enough." Kaleena glanced back at the street, where the faint halo of blues and reds could be seen flashing in the evening's dim light. "You've got a different punishment coming for you, Grace— bigger than the guilt you're going to be feeling. After all, there's a man's body in the backyard with your fingerprints all over it."

Nadia's stomach dropped. It had to be Dominic. Maybe part of the reason Kaleena could "kill with impunity" was because someone else got framed for her crimes. The best way to find out was to stay close to the Wishmaster. And now that Nadia knew the wording of Kaleena's wish, she could steal it just like Kaleena had done to Dominic, if she ever got her hands on some wishery paper. She would let it burn into the ether rather than take such a nasty power for herself, since that was the best way to ensure Kaleena could no longer use it. That understanding set uneasily on her mind alongside the knowledge that Kaleena *knew* she knew.

Without warning, Grace lunged forward. "Tag. See if anybody can catch me!"

"What are you—" Kaleena's eyes widened to the whites as she dodged Grace's charge. Spinning around, the Wishmaster waved forcefully at a pair of her goons positioned along the sidewalk, beckoning for them to catch Grace before she reached her car.

What the hell was her mom thinking? But then Nadia figured out the obvious: Grace had turned her escape into a game. If she hadn't been reeling from everything she'd heard, Nadia would've laughed at the absurdity of the situation. Only her mom would come up with that type of ridiculous workaround.

One of the goons caught up to Grace by her Range Rover, but she ducked out of his grasp. The other tried to tackle her into the back of the SUV, but she bent back almost double, sailing right underneath his outstretched arm and sending him crashing hard against the rear bumper instead.

Nadia watched, dumbfounded, as her mom evaded Val with a juke that would make an NFL running back envious, then reached the front door of the Range Rover. Before her pursuers could stop her, Grace had locked the doors, and the engine roared to life. As she pulled away, the Wishmaster's thugs had no choice but to dive out of the way to avoid getting run over.

Keep driving, Mom. Nadia's chest grew heavier as the car raced down the street and vanished down a left turn. She had no way of knowing if she'd ever see her mom again, though she supposed she could always pay a secret mental visit to find out how she was doing, wherever she ended up.

Apparently Kaleena had the same thought. "Grace touched you. Go into her head, now!"

"It doesn't work like that," Nadia half lied. "I have to be the one to touch them, and Mom was pretty hostile about me being back, so I couldn't get close to her. If you'd given this wish to Miles, you'd have a direct line, no problem. But I'll try." She closed her eyes, pretending to get into Grace's head. "No, nothing. There's no link there."

Kaleena clicked her tongue. "It goes to show that our dear mother is the same as always, not even bothering to hug you in case Basha lost her temper."

She did *hug me.* Nadia glanced at Miles, who was staring at the ever-rising flames.

"I'll figure out another way to find her," Kaleena said, seemingly more to herself than Nadia. "Too bad you didn't use your wishes on something useful, Miles."

Miles turned. "I am what I am. If it's not short-run gratification, I don't want it." He smiled wryly.

"Get in the car," Kaleena ordered, walking away from the gates. Miles and Nadia obeyed, if only to escape the sweltering heat that came off the house in stinging waves.

Once inside, however, Kaleena twisted around in the driver's seat. "Nadia, go into Basha's mind. I want to check if the old hag is dead yet or not. Those fire engines are almost here, and I'd hate for her to get a last-minute reprieve after I've driven off."

Nadia nodded, then concentrated on her grandmother, trembling with the possibility that there would be no mind to find, that Basha was gone, and that she'd been Kaleena's tool to do it. The familiar vortex sucked her away from her body. As her vision cleared, displaying Basha's age-blurred view of a weed-strewn passage between two houses a few streets away, she released a small mental sigh of relief. Basha had escaped somehow, though where she was headed was anyone's guess.

Retreating from Basha's mind, Nadia returned to the back seat of the Tesla, putting on a show of being freaked out. "It's just black. I couldn't feel anything or see anything at all."

"Good," Kaleena said as she started the car.

Nadia's mind raced. Both Grace and Basha were on the run now, and she had a feeling she knew what Basha would do while lying low. Her grandmother had made it clear she wanted to knock Kaleena off her perch, and when Basha set her mind to something, nothing on Earth could stop her from succeeding—no matter who she had to step on to get it done.

If Kaleena ever found out Basha was alive, she'd know Nadia had lied—and then Nadia would truly be seeing nothing but darkness. Plus, Kaleena would surely be keeping a closer eye on her little sister from now on, knowing that Nadia was aware of the phrasing of her first wish. But at least Nadia now knew for certain that being the "perfect spy" didn't mean she had to always tell Kaleena the truth.

As the Tesla pulled away from the curb, Nadia stared out the window at the flames devouring the remains of her home. She'd grown up within those walls, had her first steps, her first heartbreaks, her first everything there. A shudder climbed through her—whatever Kaminski family bonds had existed had burned to cinders when Kaleena set the mansion on fire. Well, that wasn't exactly true. As Nadia had learned tonight, the foundations of the home might've seemed sturdy, but it had collapsed long before the fire consumed it.

It's not all doom and gloom, she reminded herself. At least now she had a hope of reviving Nick. Regardless of what Grace or Kaleena thought, it wasn't impossible. Basha was living proof of that, and Nadia had the journal down the back of her jeans that would hopefully show the way. If—no, *when*—she brought him back, she'd get her answers at last. She'd ask him who killed him and why, filling in all the blanks that had tortured her for a year.

And I'll ask you what you wished for. That was a fresh blank she'd have to deal with, but once Nick was back where he belonged, beside her, there wouldn't be any more unanswered questions.

Chapter Thirty

The drowsy halogens of the wishing cellar added ten tons to Nadia's already heavy lids. She tried to focus on the two smooth wooden jars on the circular table that acted as mediators between her and her sister, but every couple of seconds, the wish traps blurred into amorphous blobs.

Thanks to the smoke inhalation—plus all the towering emotional peaks and gutting troughs in the last twenty-four hours—Nadia felt close to collapsing. If it hadn't been for the rushing fizz of gaining two potent wishes from Kaleena, she'd have passed out already.

"I don't see why we had to do this now." Nadia's jaw clicked through a painful yawn.

Kaleena tutted at her. "We're almost done, so strap on your big-girl boots."

Nadia didn't even have the energy to respond to the condescension. "I'm exhausted, Ka—Wishmaster."

After returning from the house, Kaleena had marched Nadia straight here to start the process of give-and-take. This was how the Wishmaster rolled. When a bargain was struck, she gave the indebted the number of wishes they didn't have, then took them back with a respective secret, before keeping those wishes as collateral until their end of the deal was fulfilled. Nadia tried not to think about what might happen to people who refused. If Kaleena could kill anyone "who would do harm unto others" without getting caught, it was probably easy enough for her to twist the parameters to suit her needs. All she'd have to do was believe that the other party intended to do harm, the way Grace simply had to make something into a game in order to win it, and Kaleena could whip out her license to kill.

Kaleena remained unbothered, flipping open the lid of the first wish trap. "You don't leave this room until I have those wishes back, so start spilling secrets. Just two, unless you feel like confessing more for the hell of it."

Nadia clasped her hands together and wedged them between her clamped thighs, feeling completely exposed. It had to be a good secret —a heart secret—or the wishes wouldn't wing their way back into the wish trap. But, considering her fragile mental state, she wasn't too far off a total breakdown, and the last thing she wanted to do was reveal something that might endanger her or her mom or her babcia or Miles—

Miles. I'd feel better if Miles was here. The thought surprised her, but then again, he seemed to be the only person she could rely on. Maybe that was why Kaleena had him hauled off elsewhere when they'd arrived back at HQ.

"I'm waiting." Kaleena drummed her fingernails on the table.

Nadia nodded. "Right, a secret." She swallowed the frog in her throat. "Well, I suppose . . ." The words struggled to come out. "About two and a half years ago . . . No, two years, three months, and one week ago, I had a miscarriage. Afterward, the doctor said I was about eleven weeks along, but I hadn't been sick, and I had my implant so there weren't any missed periods to let me know. I found out I was pregnant and that I'd lost the baby in the same day. Depressing, really, to have that kind of news delivered in such a brutal way." Her breath hitched, her eyes stinging with tired tears. "I never told anyone, not even Nick. There didn't seem to be a point."

Nadia put a hand to her chest as the dual wish rush fizzled down to a singular tingle. One down, one more to go. She lifted her gaze to see if anything she'd said had reached her sister, but Kaleena's face remained impassive as she touched the wish trap, apparently satisfied: a blank, cold sea, with no ripples or hidden currents of emotion beneath.

"That's one," Kaleena prompted, opening the lid of the second jar.

Nadia wanted to scream, but she bit her tongue. "My second secret . . ." She waited for inspiration. "When we were kids, I suppose I always felt sorry for you having to scrape Mom off the floor after Dad left. But I was secretly glad it wasn't me having to fill those big shoes when he was gone."

Kaleena wrapped her hands around the wishing jar and sighed. "Not strong enough, little sister. Dig deeper. You've been in this game long enough to know what constitutes a heart secret."

Of course, Nadia had a bunch of secrets, but not many she could share with the Wishmaster. "Basha is alive" would get her skewered. "I can see where our mom is" would end the same way. "Your spying wish has some major flaws" was one she wanted to throw in Kaleena's face, but it needed to stay hidden for as long as humanly possible.

After a minute of nervous hesitation, she found something in her well of shared memories that she hoped would cut it as a heart secret. "It was my fault Roscoe died when we were kids. I let him out of the rabbit hutch after you told me not to, and the neighbor's cat got him. He didn't nibble his way out; I sawed that hole myself afterward."

Kaleena clapped her hands together. "I knew it!" She looked down in confusion for a moment, as if unsettled by her own outburst. Slowly, she sat back down and touched the wish trap. She smiled and closed the lid.

"All done. See, that wasn't so bad, was it?" Kaleena sat back in her chair. "You can sleep now, and we'll start on the second task in the morning when you're bright-eyed and bushy-tailed."

Desperate as Nadia was to hit the hay, a creeping worry held her in her chair. "Just tell me what the task is now. Otherwise, I'll never be able to sleep."

"I have other things to attend to, and you look like crap. It can wait." Kaleena gathered the wish traps into her arms and called out, "Calypso!" Her lackey entered, flashing those dead shark eyes. "Escort Nadia to her room. And make sure she gets a change of clothes and a shower—she smells like old fireplace logs. Come back here afterward. I've got another job that needs your skills, if you're up for it."

"Will do. You know me—all work, all play. Gotta keep my aim sharp." Calypso took out her knife and spun it on her palm, then turned her blade to Nadia, flicking it up to tell her to stand. "And don't try touching me, or I'll show you that my aim isn't all I keep sharp."

Evidently, news of what Nadia could do had spread to Kaleena's inner circle. She glanced at her sister, but Kaleena had turned away—and she was humming to herself, as nonchalant as ever. Why wasn't the Wishmaster more worried after Grace's warning? Had her ego really inflated to such bulbous proportions that she believed no one would even consider crossing her? Or did she know something Nadia and Grace didn't?

After traipsing through another muddled labyrinth of corridors and hallways, Nadia found herself being marched along the upper floor of the building.

"This is yours." Calypso gestured to a sturdy-looking metal door. She opened it wide for Nadia to enter, but movement two doors down made her pause. Croak had just emerged from another room, a familiar face behind him.

"Miles!" Nadia broke away from Calypso, knowing the shark-eyed woman wouldn't dare to grab her, in case it left her open to being spied on.

He cracked a grin as she ran up to the door. "You still up? I thought you'd have conked out ages ago, since you fell asleep twice on the way back."

"I thought *you* were down in the vaults!" Nadia said, her chest swelling with relief. "I just came from a meeting with the Wishmaster. She's got something big planned for the morning."

"I got the same invite, so I guess we'll find out together. Maybe she thinks we make a good team. Either way, I'm looking forward to wiping out this debt ASAP. Already told my manager I'm extending my *relaxing* stay in Savannah."

"Enough chitchat," Calypso growled. "The rules are for you to stay in your rooms. So get in there."

"I've got some meditation to do anyway," Miles said. "I have to be in my zone at 11:11, to really channel those chakras." He gave Nadia a meaningful look. "If I miss it, I'm not myself."

Nadia understood, or at least she thought she did. Come 11:11, she'd have some channeling to do.

~

For a moment, Nadia stood in the small annex, observing the bedroom beyond. She'd expected stark walls and sparse furnishings, to remind her she wasn't free here. Instead, she found a room that looked like it belonged in a boutique hotel. Just how big *was* this place?

She kicked off her shoes and socks and let the plush, plum-toned carpet envelop her bare feet as she shuffled over to the regal four-poster bed that took up most of the room. An obnoxiously large TV hung on the wall opposite the bed, while a solid oak writing desk took pride of place before an expansive window with a view of the street below. A thin plastic film that coated the pane made it impossible for Nadia to see much beyond vague light and shadow outside, and she was sure the same was true for anyone looking in.

She found a closet with freshly laundered jeans, T-shirts, and sweaters in her size, plus some more formal attire—a blazer, a striped shirt, and cigarette pants—that resembled Kaleena's fashion choices.

The bathroom was sleek and well apportioned: a rainforest shower, a bunch of hotel-sized samples, and even a freaking bidet. This was a cage, but a well-gilded one.

"Don't fall asleep, don't fall asleep, don't fall asleep," she told herself as she sprawled out on the bed, sinking into the deep, cozy mattress and burying her face in one of the marshmallow pillows.

Lifting her head wearily, she checked the LED clock on the bedside table. It read 11:09. Two more minutes and she could zip away to Miles's mind. What her autopilot body would do while she was gone was anyone's guess, but at least it wouldn't be able to get out of the room. Small mercies.

When the clock changed to 11:11, she closed her eyes and concentrated on Miles. The sucking vortex had become familiar enough that she barely felt it anymore, so it came as a bit of a surprise when she found herself staring at Miles's face. For a terrifying moment, she worried she'd somehow zapped outside of his body and was just floating there—a bodiless entity with nowhere to go.

He leaned closer, his eyes comically wide. "You in there, Nadia?"

Still panicking, she realized she could feel his hands braced against a hard surface, along with the flutter of nerves in his stomach. The soothing, familiar smell of hotel shower gel drifted into his nostrils.

Holy crap. It's just a mirror. Oh, thank God. It's just a mirror. She breathed a sigh of relief inside his head.

"Guess you can't talk back, huh?" Miles smiled anxiously. "If you're not in there, I'm just a weirdo talking to myself in a mirror. So, you better be. Unless my message wasn't clear? I tried to be clever, but maybe it was too vague. Ugh, I guess I'll have to ask you in the morning and feel like an idiot then."

I'm here. She knew he couldn't hear or sense her, but she felt she owed him a conversation instead of a monologue.

He tapped his temple. "You know, the Wishmaster wanted to send me out solo on that 'errand' to your house. But I asked her to let you come with me because, well, I figured you'd want the chance to talk to your family again. Though I'm real sorry it turned out how it did."

Me too. A sudden swell of admiration hit her, even in astral form. He had pressured Kaleena not out of self-interest but to ensure that *Nadia* could have some sense of closure.

"This might sound stupid, but I feel like I've known you forever now," Miles continued. "It's like being in a band, you know? Your bassist might've done some dumb shit—chucked a TV out a hotel window or something—but you have their back because . . . well, because you've stuck together, so you might as well keep sticking together. Does that make sense? Nah, probably not.

"Anyway, as messed up as the past couple days have been, it's almost been *good* for me." He paused, thinking. "Working with you has been a way to prove to myself that I'm more than just a rich, famous, good-looking, talented musician, with an ass you could bounce a quarter off." He grinned cheekily. Nadia would've grinned back, if she'd had the lips.

He busted out laughing, clutching his abdomen. "Did I just say that? Now I'm hoping you ain't up in there. You won't let me live that down." He calmed to a soft chuckle. "I'm hoping you can't read my thoughts either, but I got the feeling that ain't part of the body-hopping deal."

She couldn't, but she could feel the nervous energy bubbling inside him, like champagne fizzing in a flute. If she'd been in the room with him, she'd have reminded him that his charisma and his good humor probably had a lot to do with his success. He deserved an ego stroke after going out on so many limbs for her recently.

"Damn, this psychoanalysis stuff ain't easy." He rubbed a hand across his buzzed head. "I see why folks pay you the big bucks to do it for them. Yakking in a mirror is probably a one-way ticket to crazy town, right? Hey, that's an album name if there ever was one, maybe for like a—"

You're rambling . . .

"I'm rambling, aren't I?" he said, as if he could hear her thoughts. "Anyway, look, I'm just glad we're still alive. And seeing your situation, it . . . I don't know, made me *get* you more. I mean, you've got a lot of baggage trailing you. You're tough, you know, but you're also . . . softer. Softer than I'd be, if I'd gone through what you have—and I mean that in a good way!

"When my mom died, I couldn't get out of bed for a week," he went on, his eyes glazing over. "I leaned on some crutches that wouldn't have made her proud at all. It took a while for me to wake up and smell the stale smoke, and I realized I had two choices: drown everything out in the white noise of being drunk or high, or turn myself around and try to pour all that grief *into* something. A terrible album with the reviewers, sure, but it was my therapy. And mock my baths all you like, but that's part of my daily decision to be a better version of myself. Seems like I still fail most of the time, but hey—live and learn."

Nadia spoke back to him in her mind. *What if that better version of me is gone? What if I had it, and it died when Nick did? I've tried to get myself together, I've tried to move forward, but going back to the way things were is the only way I can heal. I know it is.* It embarrassed her to admit, but she wasn't sure who she was without Nick. Maybe that revealed a lack of character, but it was the truth, nonetheless.

"What I'm trying to say is, I can't imagine what it was like for you to lose your husband." He dipped his chin to his chest, lowering his eyes. "And I just want you to know that, now that we've gone through all this shit together, we're . . . stuck together. Welcome to the band, I guess. Or maybe I'm joining yours. Whichever." He yawned, his speech slowing.

Moving away from the mirror, he padded through to the bedroom and flopped back on the bed. "I've got your back, Nads—that's the last time I'll call you that, I swear—and I know you've got mine." He laughed to himself, and she sensed he might say more. But as the silence stretched on, his eyes closed slowly, and his breaths grew softer. In his loose, relaxed body, Nadia could feel that he'd fallen asleep.

Leaving him to his well-earned rest, Nadia returned to her body to find it standing in a robe in front of the bathroom mirror, brushing her teeth, her hair wet. She burst out laughing, confused by how her body seemed to have a mind of its own while her actual mind was elsewhere. Who was running this puppet? Whoever it was, she was grateful it'd had the sense to shower. It wasn't all fun and games, though—if her body did what it wanted while she was gone, she'd have to be careful about that in the future.

After swilling the toothpaste from her mouth, Nadia stared at herself in the mirror, echoing him. "You're a good person, Miles. And I'm lucky to get to see a side of you that no one else gets to see."

She headed out of the bathroom and crawled into bed. Tired as she was, she still couldn't sleep. Her body was begging for rest, but her mind wasn't playing ball, no matter how many times she flipped and flopped under the covers.

Exasperated, she got up and searched her pile of clothes for the journal.

She untied the black ribbon that held the book closed and opened it to the first page, which read: *This journal is the property of Julita Kaminski.*

Sitting cross-legged, she began to read the delicate, expressive handwriting of her own great-grandmother. The same one whose image hung above her bed. Or used to. Having been driven straight here, with no opportunity to watch the news, she didn't know how much of the Kaminski Mansion remained, if any.

I should've saved that picture, but at least I've got a piece of you here. She hadn't allowed herself to think about the house too much, knowing it would only break her exhausted heart. There'd be time to grieve it later, along with all the family heirlooms that'd been lost to the ashes.

Her eyes flitted across every filled page, stumbling now and again over faded writing or Polish words that called for her to rack her memory of Basha's language instruction. She was pleasantly surprised that some of it was written in English. Reading the journal softened her sharper feelings toward her grandmother, though Nadia still had a long way to go before she could think of Basha fondly.

She was so absorbed in the journal, drinking in every passage, searching for the part that might help her, that she barely realized it had started to rain. It pattered against the window, like a lover trying to catch her attention.

"I'm getting closer to you, Nick," she whispered, smoothing her fingertips over the old pages.

She watched droplets slide down the mirrored windowpane like the tears upon her cheeks, and imagined those speckled splashes were the shooting stars of wishes yet to be made.

Chapter Thirty-One

The following morning, way too early for Nadia's liking, she was back in the wishing cellar, sitting at a round table in a mostly empty room that she hadn't seen during her previous visits. Its only real defining feature was a grandfather clock that ticked away in the corner. Miles sat opposite her, going to town on a vast selection of pastries, which he washed down with freshly pressed orange juice. Nadia, on the other hand, couldn't handle a single bite, her stomach sloshing with anxiety.

As the clock chimed out seven strikes, Kaleena strode in, dressed in a floaty blouse with an anchor brooch, and cream pants with a navy pinstripe. A slight darkness colored the underside of her eyes. That one detail made Kaleena look utterly human for a moment, filled with fears and regrets buried under layers of emotional barricades.

The Wishmaster didn't bother with pleasantries. "Now, let's talk about your assignment."

Miles put on a saccharine smile. "We're all ears."

Kaleena walked to the grandfather clock. She pressed her palm against a concealed panel on its side. After she scanned her fingertips, followed by her retinas, she typed in a lengthy code. Several holes twisted open in the stone floor. From their subterranean hiding spots, five pedestals rose, bearing glass display cases as if they were in some super-modern, gimmicky museum.

The display cases revealed a variety of wish traps: a ring box covered in white and black pearls, one reminiscent of Nadia's broken wishing box, and a rounded one shaped like an old-fashioned hat box, the wood so thin and malleable that it looked like painted cardboard. On another pedestal stood a pale wooden sphere, with faint markings etched along the smooth surface. The third pedestal presented a wooden book, likely a cleverly concealed wish trap.

But by far the most interesting items to Nadia were the single strip of gnarled bark; the tiny, oily-black acorn with an almost white cap; and the dried, gray leaves. These were the flesh and fruit of the Wishing Tree itself—Nadia would have staked her life on it.

Nadia pointed to an unoccupied pedestal. "That one's empty."

Kaleena shot her a withering look. "Ten points for observation." She walked up to the case bearing the bark and acorn and caressed the glass. "These are the most potent wishes in my possession. I'm saving them for a rainy day, or maybe I'll just keep hold of them forever. Call me judgmental, but I've yet to meet someone who deserves their power."

Miles gave a low whistle. "What's that collection worth? Millions? Tens of millions?"

Kaleena smirked. "Priceless, actually."

"Where did they come from?" Nadia asked.

Her sister delivered an appreciative stroke to each filled case. "Where all wishes come from," she purred. "But these have such special stories: an army medic who dragged an entire battalion, one by one, to safety; a woman who hugged a suicide bomber to stop him from triggering the device; a teacher who saved a bus full of children after it veered off an icy road; a novice pilot who took control of a plummeting airliner after both its pilots passed out. These wishes are real, genuine power in a world full of fake dreams and manufactured hope."

"And let me guess," Miles said with a sigh, "you want another big one for that empty spot?"

Nadia's heart sank. She could guess where this was going.

Kaleena turned and smiled. "Do you know Ethan Lovell?"

"The actor?" Miles nodded. "Sure. I met him once, when I played Burning Man a couple years back." He paused. "But I don't really *know* *him* know him, you know?"

Kaleena pressed her palm to the panel, and the pedestals sank back into the ground. "Well, get ready to. He has something I want—he just doesn't know it."

Dim memories of Hollywood gossip that Grace had blathered about a week ago struggled to the forefront of Nadia's mind. "Wait, Ethan Lovell is the guy who stopped an accident on set, isn't he?"

Miles whistled. "Ooooh, shit, yeah. I remember now. Filming on a railroad, and Ethan was way up the line, set for some motorbike stunt where he'd ride along the tracks, wasn't it?"

"That's it," Kaleena said. "An eighty-car freight train passed their site, even though the tracks were supposed to be clear, and Ethan realized the crew was on the tracks just a few miles down. So he hopped on his motorcycle and rode ahead of the train, across a railroad bridge —at full speed. He got there just in time to warn the crew to get off the tracks, right before the train obliterated the entire film rig and set trailer, then derailed. Cost the studio four and a half million dollars and counting, according to the tabloids." Kaleena smiled, the smile of a shark presented a school of fish. "Also saved the lives of seventeen of the production crew."

Nadia remembered Black Hat telling her about a big client the Wishmaster wanted to target. With a wish like that in Ethan's tank, it had to be him.

"He's scheduled to film in Savannah for a week, starting next Tuesday," Kaleena said. "I want that wish before somebody else steals it. The LA and Atlanta wish hunters are probably all trying to work an angle already, plus there are other Adrian wannabes out there. Fortunately for us, Ethan is a famous actor and notoriously private." She looked pointedly at Miles. "This is where you and Nadia come in."

Nadia sat up straighter. "So, you *do* want this to be a team effort?"

"Unless you'd rather work alone?" Kaleena raised an eyebrow.

Nadia shook her head. "No, no, a problem shared and all that. Will you give me back my car at least, or did Val drive it into the river out of spite?"

"Your precious orange Chevy is in the garage, safe and sound," Kaleena said. "I'll have someone get it for you later. I know how attached you are to it, ugly as it is."

Nadia was so relieved, she almost said a sincere "thank you." But she wasn't about to do more ass-kissing. "We'll need it for the mission, although we can't exactly just drive onto a film set."

Kaleena waved a hand. "It's *usually* difficult to get close enough to the rich and famous to steal wishes without outright kidnapping them. Not that the ultra-rich save very many lives in the first place. They tend to be *consumers* of wishes, not generators of them." She gave Miles a pointed look, and his lips pressed into a thin line. "You won't be as lucky as you were with Miles, little sister. However, I figured Miles is the perfect in. All the better that they've already met."

Nadia frowned. "Then where do I fit in? Am I supposed to pretend to be Miles's assistant or something?"

"Whatever you need to do," Kaleena replied with a shrug. "If I have to figure it out for you, I don't have a use for you."

Nadia tried not to let her face betray her emotions. She had no desire to find out what happened to people Kaleena no longer "had a use for," and she had no more illusions that being family would protect her.

"There's not some 'hey, I'm famous' club, you know," Miles said. "Even for me, it's not as easy as just—"

"Figure. It. Out," Kaleena snapped, then turned to Nadia. "Once we finish up here, you will cancel all your appointments for the month. Working for me is a full-time job, and I don't want any distractions."

Nadia dug her fingernails into her palms to keep quiet. Counseling was her job, not wish hunting, and her clients were important to her. But she said nothing, thinking of the endgame: two wishes to use.

Kaleena nodded. "I trust that won't be an issue." It wasn't a question.

"No," Nadia lied.

However, there *was* a pressing issue. Kaleena wanted her to clear her schedule for an entire month. According to their great-grandmother's journal—which Nadia had stayed up all night devouring page by page—she had only 128 days left to bring Nick back. After he'd been in the ground for that mathematically perfect number of 496 days, all would be lost. And if Julita's experience with Basha was any indication, the resurrection process promised to be time-consuming, and it required two wishes.

But at least Julita had given her the exact wording of the first wish she needed to make.

Nadia clenched her jaw. She and Miles would just have to move quickly. She didn't care. Even if it took her stealing a thousand wishes from a thousand movie stars, she was going to see Nick again, to hold his hands in hers, to give him all the love and want and need she'd bottled up inside her since he'd died. She would get him back, no matter what obstacles Basha or the Wishing Tree or the Wishmaster put in her way.

She was going to live again.

Acknowledgments

We wish to give our deepest thanks to all of the talented and supportive people who have made this book possible. From our family and friends to our invaluable critique partners, we have appreciated your enthusiasm in seeing this passion project come to life.

As a collaborative novel, *Wish Hunter* was designed in tandem through the minds of Diane Callahan, Hero Bowen, and Jordan Riley Swan. You'll see pieces of each of us in these pages. Angela Traficante of Lambda Editing took the book to another level with her developmental feedback. We're also immeasurably grateful to our beta readers: Alyssa Wejebe's insightful world-building questions helped us look at the story with fresh eyes, and Nicholas Fuhrmann's attention to characterization and realism paved a clear path for revisions.

Special thanks goes out to Juno E. Baker, whose insights into the characters and diction helped create a more inclusive work. In addition, we were excited to have Kayla Black, the Museum Director of the American Prohibition Museum in Savannah, as our fact-checker for the book's setting. We're also lucky to have Crystal Shelley of Rabbit with a Red Pen as our incomparable copy editor. The custom *Wish Hunter* candles you might see on our social media pages were made by the esteemed Kate Glass of BriarWick on Etsy, who specializes in book-themed scents.

Diane in particular would like to say *tusind tak* to Jeanette Nielsen for her continual support and brainwaves. Laura Sukalac also deserves a warm hug for her cheerleading sessions during sleepless nights of editing. And Diane awards her biggest thank you of all to her husband Steven for being the devoted photographer of all *Wish Hunter* promo pictures, as well as for inspiring the "Polish-family-in-Georgia" basis of the Kaminski family.

Hero would like to thank her sister, Kate, for inspiration, the best childhood anecdotes, and being her Savannah tour guide. In addition, she'd like to thank the usual suspects. Hopefully, you know who you are.

Jordan takes his bow for Erin Spencer and Lisa Flanagan, the producer and narrator, respectively, of the incredible audiobook production. And he supposes that he owes Story Garden's marketing manager Laurie Cooper a "thank you" for putting up with him.

And to you, dear reader, we bestow our best wishes.